First published 2000 by Diva Books, an imprint of Millivres Ltd, part of the Millivres Prowler Group, Worldwide House, 116-134 Bayham Street, London NW1 0BA.

Distributed in Europe by Central Books, 99 Wallis Rd, London E9 5LN
Tel: 020 8986 4854 Fax: 020 8533 5821
Distributed in North America by Consortium Book Sales and Distribution, Inc. 145 West Gate Drive, Saint Paul, MN 55114-1065, USA Tel: 651 221 9035 / 800 283 3572
Distributed in Australia by Bulldog Books, PO Box 700, Beaconsfield, NSW 2014
Printed and bound in the EU by WS Bookwell, Juva, Finland

THE DIVA BOOK OF SHORT STORIES

EDITED BY HELEN SANDLER

Contents

Acknowledgements

I would like to thank everyone who has helped with this book, especially those who sent in their stories, whether or not they were included in the final selection, and those who spread the word.

The following people have been particularly generous with their support, advice, contacts or all three: the Diva Books publisher, Gillian Rodgerson; Rose Collis, Emma Donoghue, Frances Gapper, P-P Hartnett, Alison Hennegan, Queenie aka Valerie Mason-John, and my partner, Jane Hoy.

Many other people at the Millivres Prowler Group (the parent company) were involved in making this book happen – in particular, Andrew Biscomb, Kim Watson and Debra Doherty.

Introduction

I didn't want to be insular. But when I planned a Britdyke anthology, I did want to see what I'd get if I limited my scope to writers who are based in the UK, wherever they come from. The aesthetic is different, the language is different, the culture is different. And by that I mean, of course, that it's different from the United States.

There are quite a few debuts here, and many more names which should be better known. Among them are writers I've admired for years and others who were recommended to me. I appealed in *Diva* magazine (this imprint's mothership) as well as asking writers, editors and workshop leaders to spread the word. The response was tremendous, with close to three hundred stories landing on my desk from all over the country. I also hand-picked a few of the best from the magazine, which has consistently been a home for new fiction under the editorship of Gillian Rodgerson.

The writers had to be lesbian or bi women, but the work just had to grab me. If I made noises while reading, then the story was in with a chance. There were arguments with myself and a few emails to authors inquiring whether they thought there was any special lesbian sensibility to their story about, say, cooking and eating one's own limbs. But mostly there was just a shiny moment of welcoming another tale to the 'yes' file.

There were several short-cuts to one of my shiny moments. Anything that named any street in Manchester, where I grew up, had an instant advantage. But more importantly, anything written in the style that I am coming to call Modern Lesbian.

It's a style that has burrowed its way into me over the last year, since I became commissioning editor of Diva Books. It's a way of weaving a story without sticking to a single thread, of letting the thoughts wander into wordplay or a witty aside without losing the plot. It's a use of the vernacular which looks casual but isn't. And it reflects the life of the lesbian or bisexual writer as an observer not just of dyke life but of the mainstream society that never feels quite like home. So nothing is taken for granted.

You only need to read the first piece in the book to see what I'm talking about. 'Ella' is by seventeen-year-old Ella Kaye, who plays with the fine line between fiction and autobiography. A young shop assistant is nervous as a brief connection with an older woman steers close to flirtation, but she doesn't lose her cool...

This very short story introduces one of the running themes of this anthology: the importance of what is unsaid or cannot be said between women; the use of code to find out who's a dyke. In the next story, 'Black Eye' by Sue Vickerman, it is a poem which serves as the connector between pupil and teacher and as a metaphor for the sensitivity that the girl hopes they share.

But teenage girls are not only intense, they can also be vulnerable. The unsaid grows horribly sinister in 'The Theme is Power' by Ali Smith, while the girl in 'Eureka' by Cathy Bolton suddenly sinks out of her depth in the adult world.

These opening stories remind us that, however much 'community' we've developed in les/bi Britain, there are plenty of young women struggling to find their place and their identity.

Community is fragile, in any case – it can be destroyed by a diagram on a sheet of paper, as Hannah Richards shows us when the fun spirals out of control in 'The Shag Tree', or by someone's hand in the collective's till, in 'Whatever You Want' (Helen Smith). And are those the same jugglers causing mayhem in Hannah's story and in 'Kissing on the Way Up' by Julia Collar?

The latter focuses on the power of love to overcome external and internal pressures, and we see how far that goes in Stella Duffy's story, 'Ten Times Proud'. Strangely, just three years after it was commissioned for *Diva* magazine, this piece has gathered an extra layer of sad nostalgia: for a time when everyone went to Pride and called it Pride.

We move from mourning to jealousy in the dark territory of Jeanie O'Hare's 'The Guinea Pig', where small animals and small people are somewhat unsafe in a dysfunctional lesbian family. More pets and pettiness follow in 'The Cost of Things' by Emma Donoghue, when a trip to the vet signifies the end of romance.

Lesbians have our own language, and sometimes our words are stolen from the mainstream, as Frances Bingham illustrates in 'Double

Tongue'. And sometimes straight people can be very stubborn about misunderstanding us – like the mother in Robyn Vinten's 'Shopping with Mother'. Ma has a more damaging role in 'The Root of It' by Linda Innes, and the damage can't be undone by any amount of love. The cynic at the centre of this story contrasts with the romantic in 'The Perfect Ceremony of Love's Rite' by Cherry Smyth, proposing marriage to her less romantic sweetheart.

Relationships. They may go weird in the end but they often start so sweetly. Just look at the horseplay from Jenny Roberts ('Making the Horse Laugh') or the illicit bed-christening in Shelley Silas's 'The Suit with the Purple Lining'. And you don't get much sweeter, or much more sour, than the revenge of 'Hi, Sugar' (Susanna Steele). At least there's good reason for that revenge. I won't give away the ending of 'You'll Do' by Rosie Lugosi, but don't read it in bed. Then again, my own story, 'Modern Interiors', might well have you turning all the lights on to check for little visitors, if you're not already being kept awake by the girl next door.

The difficulties between neighbours continue in Frances Gapper's bouncy story of that name, while there's perhaps more neighbourly interaction than we might wish in Julia Bell's 'Outskirts'. Her dark tone is picked up in 'Still Precious' by VG Lee, in which a woman takes to her bed after the death of her mother and recalls the relationship thus: "Mother's attitude to her only child: I had little visible use." At least she had the benefit of knowing her mother, unlike the woman in 'Big Milk' by Jackie Kay, whose jealousy of her lover's bond with her baby sends her on an urgent personal quest.

Even where there is a fairly straightforward connection with our families, we may be kept apart from them by the anti-gay authorities, as Kathleen Bryson explores in 'The Day I Ate My Passport'. As with so many of the stories in this book, humour only sharpens the attack. Jo Somerset's 'Passion Prioritised' has us laughing at a different kind of pomposity; then the pace slows for 'Tuesday's Child', Manda Scott's Highland tale of art as closure.

When it came to the order of the stories in this book, some groupings forced themselves on me, others were more random. Everyone will make their own connections but some just leapt off the page. For instance, a younger woman makes a cameo appearance at the end of 'Altitude Sickness' by Edana Minghella. Her attempt at seduction in the great outdoors is rebuffed. But could it be that she goes on to star in her own satire – the search for love that is 'Single Again' by Clare Summerskill? Either way, watch out girls, as hiking can be dangerous...

It's been an honour to put this book together. I've felt like the temporary hub of the wheel of lesbian fiction, and even if that's nothing more than a sleep-deprived delusion, I'm very pleased with the results. Pleased that so many of our best-known writers gladly sent me their work, and pleased that so many less-known or brand new voices are brought together here. Overall, the results are dark and funny, scary and striking. I hope you like them as much as I do.

Helen Sandler, September 2000

ELLA KAYE
Ella

I work at Hobbs. I love it. I took the job there because I like the atmosphere. Ella Fitzgerald occupies at least a third of the play list. Jazz. I'll never tire of it. And I like the people. I like the other staff and I like the customers. They're mostly businesswomen, 25-45. They can afford to look good. My boss says the cream trousers appeal to people who have Hobbs taste/no taste. Most of the stuff's all right though, elegant. Especially the suits. Sophia jacket and 50s flap pocket trousers, silk linen, light khaki, priced... not worth thinking about.

Sometimes we get customers who stick in my mind for months. There was the Irish woman who kept telling me I was a 'good girl'. The accent sounds Welsh when I do it. And the World's Easiest Customer, who spent £700 in two minutes (two cashmere blend coats, if you're interested). And the woman who would have been the World's Worst Customer if she hadn't been so beautiful. I can understand why somebody might need to try on trousers in two sizes, but three! And in both regular and long. How could she possibly have thought she needed long? She was about five foot two. She made a point about this when trying on a pair of flat shoes.

"Do I look small in these?"

Of course you look small, you're five foot two.

"Small, but perfectly formed." I didn't actually say that. I wish I had.

And then there was the woman who was a better-looking version of Andie MacDowell. ("Not possible," said my dad.) I wouldn't say I'm a fan of Andie MacDowell, but this woman was sublime. I went to talk to her; to give her 'the personal shopping experience'. She picked out a short bias dress, soft linen, navy, priced... and went to try it on. A few moments later she came out of the changing room, twirled and leant against the doorframe.

"Well, what do you think?"

"I think you are the most beautiful woman I've ever seen, and that dress, well, words escape me."

I didn't actually say that. What I really said was, "Yes." Of everything I could have said, I chose yes. It wasn't even an answer to her question.

"All right, I'll take it." She knew she looked good.

At that moment Ella Fitzgerald came on singing 'I Get a Kick Out of You'. You may see that as significant, but since approximately 100% of the songs she sings are on that kind of theme, I refuse to note it as interesting.

"Ah, Ella Fitzgerald," she said. "The best."

"I couldn't agree more. I was named after her."

"You're an Ella?"

"Yes."

"I'm an Ella as well."

"No."

"Yes."

"No."

"Yes."

"Really?"

"Yes."

"It's a gorgeous name. I've never met another Ella. I've heard of a couple of younger Ellas, but never an older one, except Ella Fitzgerald, of course. I'm a huge fan. That's why I wanted to work here, they play a disproportionate amount of her music."

"I've noticed. I was named after her as well."

We had a bond.

"No."

"Yes."

"No."

"Yes."

"Really?"

"Yes. So tell me, Ella," she paused and savoured the strange sensation of calling somebody else by her own name, "Do you enjoy working here?"

"When I get customers who are as beautiful as you, I do. What are you doing at six o'clock today?" is what I didn't say, settling once again for, "Yes." She nodded and that was the end of our conversation. She motioned me towards the till.

As she was about to leave I told her, "A recent survey showed that 80% of the women who shop in Hobbs return. Will you?"

"Yes," she said. And then she left.

SUE VICKERMAN
Black Eye

Stella snogging my neck, Stella's warm breasts against my arm. Soft nipples brushing. Her legs clamping me playfully before she tumbles over me and out of her bed.

I'm awake. Delicious. That musky smell when linen has softened up. New bed; new room – sunlight splashing through the crack between folds of opaque velvet. Shades of blue like at dawn, misty. Drape of white muslin.

Stella, naked, stumbles over my DMs – "I'll get coffee. Stay right there." I focus on our blue jeans entwined on the floor, our clubbing gear strewn everywhere. I'm in love with this blue, peaceful, morning place. A haze, a slight pall of smoke, seems to hang in the centre of the room from last night's cigarettes. Last night's sweat. Last night.

I slide deeper under the quilt, turning; scan the ceiling like a new sky in a foreign country; stretch, then curl. On the end of my nose, out of focus, a blur of faces. Stella's life in photographs. I'm a purring cat, breathing into the pillow, drowsy, looking at a small team of girls in white judo robes. Stella distinct among them, a boyish kid, grinning with a trophy. Red tracksuit of their coach standing alongside.

Suddenly I'm focused. Tanned skin, freckles, that half-smile. Weight on one foot; the angle of her hip. She wore a lot of red. That's how she stood as she wrote on the board, still talking to us over her shoulder.

I'm weird, shy, ugly, all those schoolgirl feelings again. And it's that day again when I'm feeling too funny to finish my Shreddies. I'm putting them in the dog bowl, feeling sick. Now I'm having butterflies during geography, during maths, because it's the day of Mrs Taylor's break duty.

There goes the bell!

And there's me, needing the loo, and finding those year eleven slags smoking in the end cubicle again. I know I'll be absolutely *dying* for a wee before the end of French if I don't go now, and Mr Dollis *never* gives permission to go out... But there's no way I can use the loo when *they're* in there.

Have to cross my legs.

And it's that morning when Kevin Goodman's got a little white box bulging in the breast pocket of his shirt. His mate is shouting out to the entire school, "Do you know what these are?" (Prod prod at Kevin's chest). Kevin's swaggering about like God's gift to women and they're all laughing these dirty laughs, then just as I'm going through the common-room door someone shouts out, "She wouldn't know, would she?"

Do they mean me? I'm going bright puce anyway. Horrible dirty-old-man snigger erupting behind my back.

"She ain't even got tits so what would she know?" Yes, they mean me.

Now that I'm in, I'm messing about with my flask of coffee, occupying myself while waiting for Mrs Taylor. Only pretending to drink though, that day, so that I won't need the loo more.

I've got this thing for Mrs Taylor. I feel like it's burning a hole in my bag.

There was that other day, when I went into the toilets and a year eleven smoker, wearing mascara, jumped up at my door while I was on the loo. I never used to sit down, as I thought I might catch something from the slaggy types. There I was, my skirt all bunched up, terrified of anyone seeing anything.

The mascara girl had just been shrieking about when her boyfriend had come round to watch telly and had put his hand *right there* even when her dad was in the room behind his newspaper. Meanwhile there I was, trying to pull off a piece of that crisp, hard toilet paper quietly, but the metal holder went clank and someone shouted, "Who's that slag in there?"

"It's a year eight slag. Look at her granny shoes. My nan wears those." I couldn't use the bog paper. I just had to pull everything up without tucking in properly and get out of there.

So here I am on this day when it all happens, not even able to go to the toilet.

In the common room, the girls who aren't slaggy are sitting quietly round the edges, or are setting off in twos to pester a teacher about some fussy detail. Meanwhile the boys are piling into a scrum, or else barging about screaming at the tops of their half-broken voices. I often breathe the word 'morons'. Never audibly, though.

But Goodman and his two mates are exceptions. Tall. Spiked hair. Grubby-looking chins. Very faint moustaches. Somehow *oily*. And every girl secretly wants to go out with one of them, though it's only the slaggy girls who manage it. Goodman's territory is the corner with the foam seats. Certain girls always rush in to get those foam seats because they know the boys will come and sit there. That day, like every day, I'm hating it. Watching the flirting, and hating.

And Lisa's doing her usual, where Goodman goes "All right?" and she goes "No, I'm half left," and now she's pulling her school sweatshirt off so we can all see her bra straps under her blouse, and I feel desolate, knowing Lisa and three other girls in our year have already *done it*; gone all the way. Even though Kevin Goodman and that lot are total freaks.

There was that day when Goodman put his hand right in a girl's blouse. She went bright red but she just sat there and the whole common room was riveted and my heart was racing.

I'm remembering myself, sitting in my usual corner with the bolted-down orange chairs like in Burger King. I've chosen my spot carefully for Mrs Taylor being on break duty. She'll be wandering about with her cup of tea, and when she first comes in I'll be hidden, so I'll have time to think. In case she turns round and speaks to me, or something.

"Goodman's got rubbers in his pocket!" There's that tiny boy, Oliver, yapping like a terrier.

I'm remembering the week before: the lesson on condoms. The lads twanging them about the classroom, asking Miss Spinks if she's got any ribbed ones. Lisa Dobson and Shelley putting up their hands – what does wanking mean, Miss? – and tittering. There I was, taking it all very seriously because of AIDS and everything. Storing information for the future like I was supposed to. The future: working in an office, getting engaged, hen nights, bridesmaids, buying a sofa on h.p.

I wanted condoms to be for men and women, not us. The future, not now. Not like those slags.

Mrs Taylor standing in the common room. Me – snatching up my coffee cup so if she turns round I'm busy doing something. My heart thudding crazily. I'm staring, trying to sip coffee in a nonchalant way. Mrs Taylor's asking what the racket is on the foam seats, her back turned.

One hand is on the hip of her slacks and the other is holding a china teacup. So... elegant. Like an advert.

It's a typical breaktime racket. Squeaky-voiced Oliver is jumping up and down on a seat, thinking he's It now he's been chosen for the main part in the school show. Next to him, Kevin Goodman is nearly on top of Shelley having a good snog. Goodman's two sidekicks are nearly beside themselves, watching. Baboons, I'm thinking. The other slaggy girls are staring Mrs Taylor in the face and nudging each other.

There I am, transfixed by her tanned neck between the streaked blonde-grey hair and silky shirt. She told us once, in English, about her trip to the Sahara Desert. I'm tingling, imagining her all-over tan. I'm seeing her stretched out on a sunbed, what everyone has to do before they go on holidays like that. Sultry sand dunes. Taking her clothes off. I suppose her husband was there too. He's rubbing oil all over the even, brown skin of her slim arms, her long legs. Mrs Taylor, silhouetted against one of those giant, red fireball suns that hang low on the horizon in the Bounty adverts. Mrs Taylor. A Taste of Paradise.

There's me, thirteen, feeling weird, not knowing anything. Storing up my feelings for later, for in bed at night after my sister's asleep so I can feel it all again in safety. Feeling this stuff for a woman older than my mother, seeing her beauty, explaining to myself that, to a man, Mrs Taylor would look sexy.

In my dreams, Mrs Taylor and I stroll up the spinney in golden evening light. All the kids who usually play there are at home, or dead, or something. We're alone. We have long, meaningful silences because she's read all my poems and knows how deep I am and there's no need for words, she just *understands* me. I glide along at her side, swooning on the waft of her lemony smoky scent. Arms round each other's waists. Close.

And when I meet her in school after all this, after I've had full-length conversations with her in bed, I go tongue-tied, get desperate. Collecting my English book from the front, I stand right in her scent, staring at her slim, veined wrist over her shoulder, looking down on her hair, breathing her in. She looks round, doesn't see me. Ticks her papers, murmurs. I'm desperate for recognition. She must know how I feel. It's electric.

*

There was that time, coming in from the annexe. I'm being barged by year sevens and my bag gets jammed in the outside door. They won't let me in; they're obsessed with escaping. Thing is, it's freezing out there where I'm trapped. So I'm shoving, being rough. Everyone screaming swear-words; everyone punching, pushing. Me, squashing through that bottleneck of snotty kids. Here I am, like a cork popping out. Here in the corridor at last, looking like I've been through a mangle.

And suddenly there's Mrs Taylor, standing right there, really calm, behind the rabble that's bursting out through the door to the annexe. My hair's all over the place but the worst is, one popsock's down round my ankle. I'm nearly dying on the spot because I know I look like a kid. She's got these faint, large freckles in the soft, deep pads hanging beneath her eyes, her gorgeous eyes, looking straight into mine so she doesn't even see my popsock and anyway it wouldn't matter to her. I'm melting. I even think I'm having a real heart attack, as my chest is pounding so hard it's making me gulp.

"Hi," she goes. I'm thinking, hopefully: bet she says that to her real friends. There's me trying to say "Hi" back but this "Haagh" comes out because it gets mixed up with a gulp. I'm wishing – oh god – I'm wishing I didn't look like a silly year eight girl. *I'm really not like that inside. Look at me!* Come up the field with me, away from all these pupils, this school. Let's go through the back hedge where we do cross-country. I can take you to a nice spot where we can sit on the grass. We can talk there. Do what we want.

"Hi," she says. "I've been looking for you. We need some poets for an inter-schools competition and of course I immediately thought 'Ruth in 8A'."

That intense week, writing that poem.

And now I'm in the common room waiting for her to turn round and see me because here it is, all finished in my bag. It had to be a love poem. I think it's great – a soldier going off to the Gulf the day after his wedding and she waits faithfully for him but he comes home in a bodybag so she overdoses on Panadol. So here I am, acting unconcerned, pretending to sip my coffee out of my Mickey Mouse flask with my legs crossed (squeezingly) and my skirt pulled down over my knees trying to look normal although there's that weirdness in my chest again; that pounding heart.

Oliver's just looking at Mrs Taylor's face and for once his gob's shut and he's sitting on the foam chair. Kevin Goodman is lolling back giving Shelley a rest, displaying his bulging breast pocket, skinny-ribbed as a whippet. Everyone suddenly behaving, just because she's there. Everyone eyeing her. Everyone gone quiet. At last. And now she's turning to leave.

"And here's Linda! Have you got something for me?"

The shock, on that desolately ordinary school morning. One of her beautiful eyes is a purple mulch like the elderberry pulp of my dad's wine-making. There is no eye to be seen. It's slicked closed like a line of dark stitching, oozing something glisteny. Tears thickened into jelly. That lovely freckly pad that was beneath her left eye is a lumpy black half-moon with outer rings of yellow and green, shading into each other like marble.

I'm thinking – she's not going to say anything. Not here, not with everyone's ears flapping. She'll explain it all tonight after my sister's asleep.

I'm fingering the poem in my bag, like I have been all day. I'm pulling it out but it's childish crap. I can't speak. I see she can't speak either. Of course she can't speak to me here, in front of all these. I know she would if she could.

Mrs Taylor saying "Great!" Mrs Taylor smiling with her mouth, but her other eye giving it away. Mrs Taylor taking my poem and leaving me without saying anything else. Mrs Taylor disappearing out of the door, and everyone hearing that her teacup is wobbling.

One of Kevin Goodman's mates is telling the slags something, as though he was their teacher.

"My Aunty Anne got one of those from my Uncle Bruce," he's going, "because she was having it off with someone while he was at work."

Lump in my throat, making me feel sick. Strong, masculine hands oiling Mrs Taylor's arms and legs and back and breasts in the Sahara Desert under a sizzling red sun. Strong hands, clenched, hard; a punch – I feel it – right into the same thing they touched with tenderness.

The bell ringing for assembly. An announcement, that day: all year eight girls to go to the hall for a special talk. There's me, still bursting for the loo, but unable to go. It's the pastoral year-head so everyone starts saying it's about sanitary towels down the toilets again. But it isn't. It's big news: Shelley Hobbs is pregnant and she's having it, too. Can we all 'be supportive'.

And I'm thinking – that's what comes of flirting. That's where it starts.

All I wanted in the world by then was to go home, have a wee, and be private.

Coffee. Groan of heavy curtains being yanked aside. Pink light flooding behind my eyelids. Stella nuzzling my neck, Stella pulling the quilt back:

"Open your eyes." Stella looking down on me. I reach out a lazy hand, touch the pinboard by the bed.

"This woman in the tracksuit. Who is she? Was she your judo coach or what?"

Stella laughs in recognition: "Self-defence teacher," and rolls over me to scrutinise the photo for a second: "Look at the smile on my face!" She comes back, rubs her face in my hair.

"Mm, yeah. Kim Taylor!" Stella croons the name in my ear. "I was fourteen and she was my lover."

I snap awake, see the glitter of chrome by the bed, black coffee steaming in a Bodum. I want to sweep the Bodum aside, watch the black river scald out the past like molten lava. I want to piss out all my adolescent frustration, the bottled-up energy that bloated me, made me ill. I want to punch them all in the eye, all those people who gave me grief.

Stella moves to pour the coffee, but I grab her hands, thighs, lips with mine; pull myself into the present.

ALI SMITH
The Theme Is Power

The thing is, I really need you with me in this story. But you're not home. You won't be home for hours yet.

I stand about in the kitchen for a while, not knowing what to do about it, because the story is right at the front of my head, and I decide to do something, I decide to do the dishes. They need done anyway (three days' worth) and what's more, with my back to the table standing at the sink I can imagine you, sitting up on it with your legs swinging, eating an apple. So. Listen to this. This is what happened.

It starts with Jackie and I standing at a bus stop in Trafalgar Square. (So it happened quite long ago? you say behind me.) We had taken our rucksacks off; she was sitting on hers and I was leaning on mine, and we were tired and happy, nearly home from a little travelling, still excited by being in such a famous square in such a big city even if we were only there for the half hour it would take to catch a bus.

A woman came over. She was wearing a headscarf tied tightly round her head. This was strange because it wasn't raining, it was mild and clear though it was dark, an evening in late September just after nine o'clock.

Her mouth was a straight set line in her face. Hello girls, she said.

Hello, we said.

Have you just arrived in London? she said.

We told her we'd just got back from Paris, we'd gone there on a Magic Bus special fare of only £7.00 return and now we were catching the nine-thirty bus on our way to stay with my sister who lived with her four sons and her husband near Reading before we went up home tomorrow to Scotland. That was where we were from, Scotland, and not just Scotland but right up in the north of Scotland. We told her all this, detail after detail, without being asked. When one of us had told her one detail, the other would come in with something else. We were charming. We'd have told her anything. I think we must have felt privileged that a stranger had chosen us to speak to out of all the millions of people in London. But more: she'd looked unhappy, and that was a shame.

It's very late to be travelling, she said. You must be tired, coming all that way. Wouldn't you rather stay here in London for the night? I have a flat you could stay in, just for tonight. It's free, you wouldn't have to pay, since it's only for one night. You look like nice girls. My flat is right above Miss Selfridge. That's right in the middle of Oxford Street.

I nodded. I knew where Miss Selfridge was, because I had been to London before on a weekend break with my parents and our hotel had been just off Oxford Street, a moment round the corner from the Miss Selfridge shop.

You see, the woman said, interrupting me. You could go shopping in Oxford Street tomorrow morning if you want, and then you could catch the bus to your sister's. It's a very nice flat. There's plenty of room, it's very roomy, and I live there by myself.

We both said what a good place that must be to have a flat.

Yes, she said. I've got a stereo, and hundreds of records. Lots of the latest ones, practically everything that's in the charts. I could give you a lift. My car's just over there.

We thanked her very much and I said that my sister was expecting us and would already have made us something to eat.

Are you sure? she said. My car's just round the corner. Or maybe I could give you a lift to your sister's house. Sometimes the buses don't stop at this stop, you know. Sometimes they miss it out on their way round London, and I'm not busy tonight. You're in luck. I could give you a lift.

Some more people came to wait at the stop. The woman stepped back. We thought she must be very shy. We said goodbye and thanks, and watched her cross the road.

That was kind of her, I said to Jackie.

Yes it was, Jackie said. It was nice of her to offer.

I tell you. We stood there, seeing and hearing nothing, myself and Jackie, my best friend, my first true love, below a rumbling rockfall, an avalanche that would have buried us, swallowed us stonily up. We must have looked about fourteen or fifteen to that woman, small and adolescent thin. We must have looked like we'd run away from somewhere. Naive, bedraggled, in unwashed clothes after a week in the cheap hotels of Paris with their toilet floors all cracked linoleum and scuttling beetles, the woman at the reception desk grinning so we couldn't not stare at the gap where her front teeth had been and telling us, yes I know, I know, one bed is better for you girls, also it does not cost so much and that is also a good thing, yes? We had looked young enough to get in for nothing at the Louvre and to pay only half price on the tube when we got back to London, even though in reality we were nearer twenty. In guilt-stricken love with each other for just over a year by then, a year of pure fumbling and ecstasy; I don't use the word lightly, we knew all about purity. We were high and pure as Michael Jackson's child self singing *I'll Be There*, and we knew about things like loneliness and longing, and how to hide them, how to hide our sadnesses and kindnesses. We believed in the superiority of feeling, and we believed there had to be some superiority in everything we felt since we felt it so strongly in the face of such taken-for-granted shame. I can still see our heads together, our eyes and our mouths, intent and pretty and serious as stoats, as we thought things as innocent and perilous as, for instance, that suicide must be a good thing, at the very least a truly romantic thing, something all truly romantic people would do, since people so clearly felt so much when they did it.

You know what I think? Jackie said as we watched the woman in the headscarf cross the square away from us. I think that poor woman is a very lonely person.

I didn't want to be outdone on the superior understanding of feeling. Yes, I said, yes, and a very sad person too.

We nodded sagely. The bus drew up. We loaded our rucksacks on, and the bus circled Nelson's Column, and we saw from the bus window the same woman with the headscarf leaning out of the window of her car, and behind her in the car there was a man with a thick black beard. This man was so huge, so looming he took up nearly all the back seat. She glared up at us out of the window, and as the bus pulled away we saw the man getting out of the back of the car and running round to the driver's seat.

They were there behind the bus all the way through the city and then all the way along the motorway. We watched them out of the back window; we saw their faces below us every few yards, distorted under light and glass when we passed under the streetlamps. After three quarters of an hour we couldn't be sure if they were still coming; they weren't directly behind the bus any more. When the bus stopped to let us off in the dark outskirts of the village where my sister lived, Jackie stood at the wheel and, near breathless with fear, told the bus driver about the people following us.

So? the driver said. He shrugged his shoulders. The bus door hissed shut and left us on the verge.

We abandoned the rucksacks, left them lying. We stumbled three hundred yards along a main road so unlit that I remember the grass of the verge as black. We found the passageway to my sister's street, and when we got to her house we hammered on the door and stammered it all out on the doorstep about the woman and the man. My sister's husband phoned the police while we drank tea and ate toast and sat dazed and safe in front of their television watching *What The Papers Say*, but I could tell from the tone of his voice, embarrassed and explanatory in the hall, that he thought we were overreacting, or maybe even making it up.

So that's the first part of the story. I put my hand into the water below the foam and feel for the cutlery, try not to lift out sharp knives by their blades, and even now it makes me shake my head a little, like I would if I woke up and opened my eyes and found I couldn't focus properly; even now after all this time it terrifies me, what might have happened to us if we'd been good enough or docile or hopeless enough to have gone with that woman, when she asked, to her nice flat above Miss Selfridge.

You see, this is what I mean. I believed, and somewhere in my head I still believe, that this flat existed. Of course there wasn't a flat there at all, or if there was, it certainly wasn't hers. But all the horrors, all the things I don't want to imagine, still take place in that muffled flat, above the lit-up window displays and the darkened shop floor, the rows and rows of clothes, the silent accessories of the year 1979 and the late-evening traffic roaring past at random on the street outside.

The other thing is, my father is here visiting. I forgot to tell you. He's why I began thinking about all this. Here, he said to me earlier when we were having our lunch at the art gallery, do you remember that time you and your other friend, what's her name, were at that bus stop and that woman tried to get you into her car?

He's asleep through the front. He just turned up. I don't know how long he's staying this time. This morning I was reading a book and he arrived at the front door. Never mind that, he said. Come on. Let's go out. I'll take you out for your lunch. Where's your friend? Out? Never mind. Let's go.

You wouldn't have caught him dead in an art gallery when I was a child. Then after we'd been a few times I realised that he wants to go there specifically so he can say things like: What's that then? what's it called? *A Woman's Face*? well it doesn't look like a woman's face to me, it looks like a dog's dinner, unless she's really ugly in which case she should get surgery, you know, plastic surgery, *A Woman's Face*, is that her nose? is it? God help her, I could do better than that and I can't even paint, she'd have been better off with me painting her. And what's that? what's the point of that? *Boulder In Room*. A boulder in a room? a picture of a boulder in a room? eh? that painter's got his sizes all wrong, his perspective, how would that size of boulder have got into that room? that boulder would never have, it's too big, the room's too small, he'd never get it through the door, you'd have had to build the bloody house round the boulder to get a boulder that big into the room. I used to explain, laboriously and painedly, about cubism and surrealism and modernism and seeing things from different perspectives. Then I realised I was being patronising and irrelevant, and that he wasn't listening anyway. It's much better now when we go. This morning we had a really nice time. We walked round all the rooms so he could say the things and I could nod and listen, and after that we went to the art gallery cafeteria.

I don't know if I've ever told you this story about my father before. When I was about nine, one summer evening I was out playing by myself, kicking around in the cinders behind the garages, and I saw a man. He was sitting in the empty square of space and rubble where a garage had been, and holding his hand down low he said, can you see? Yes, I can see, I said. I thought the man must be stupid. I wasn't blind. Then I saw that what he was holding, what he wanted me to look at, was his penis. I looked at it for a while like I was supposed to, then I waved my hand at him to say goodbye and strolled back to our garden with my hands in my pockets, rather pleased with myself, a little cocky you might say, about what I'd seen. My father was cleaning our car outside our garage. I told him about the man. Dad, guess what? I said.

I had never seen him be so lithe, move so fast. He threw down the sponge; it splashed into the bucket and sent the water slopping out over the ground. A moment later, with me falling further behind him in the mob of children drawn by the noise of something happening, there he was, my father, several strides ahead of the group of other fathers he'd gathered from the houses, and all of them racing across the field after a man who was right at the other side of it. When they reached him my father was the first there and the first to punch him down. I wasn't sure if it was the same man, but it didn't matter; all the fathers stood in a ring round him until the police came to take him back to the mental hospital, which was only half a mile away across the canal and was where he was an inpatient, the man they'd beaten. My father was a local hero for weeks after that, for months. People from the street where we lived then would probably still remember the night; it had an air of celebration, like Bonfire Night, or like the night when John Munro's father took his lawnmower and in a stroke of genius mowed a football-pitch-sized square for the first time into the long grass of that field.

I pile the bowls and cups up on each other, a bit unsafe. (Don't you feel bad about that man who got beaten up? you say behind me. Quiet, I say, I'm thinking.) These days my father can fall asleep just about anywhere with the blank ease of, say, a kitten or a puppy; I look around and he's gone again, his head down, his chin on his chest and his breathing heavy and regular. He's fallen asleep through there with the television up quite loud, and I can still hear him sighing out a rhythm over a relentlessly sincere speech of Clinton's. When I went through to collect his cup he was sleeping through footage of dead Iraqi people, a mother and a child lying poisoned where they fell in their village street, their faces bloated. I switched it off. He opened his eyes. Put it back on, he said, I'm watching the news. I switched it back on. There was a graph on the screen showing Clinton's soaring popularity, and a shot of a film star saying, we don't care how much tail he chases so long as he does his job, and my father sighed, closed his eyes and went back to sleep.

(But is it connected? I'm a bit lost, are they connected, the story about your father and the story about the woman with the headscarf? you say behind me. You throw your applecore at the bin with perfect aim; in it goes. Yes, but wait, in a minute, I say. Bear with me.) I'm thinking how my father fell asleep at the art gallery too, after lunch, sitting on a cushioned stool. For a while I stood on the other side of the room and watched him sleeping. Lately he's grown a beard, for what I think is the first time in his life. He looks like a different man, like a salty old seadog, like Sean Connery. He told me proudly earlier about a woman flirting with him in the supermarket. I'm not surprised; he looks better now – is better-looking, is in better shape – than he was ten years ago when his business was folding. He looks a lot better than he did when he was in his mid-fifties even, that much younger than he is now, the age he would have been when Jackie and I arrived back from London full of our story, and full of lies about how we'd slept, how we'd only had one room but there'd been two beds, or how there'd only been one bed so one of us had slept on the floor. But my father and mother were distraught, hardly listened to us; so strained-looking that for the first time in my life I realised they would break; and this was all because someone had sent an unpleasant, unsigned letter to the local tax office about how my father's business was far too booming.

(Aha, you say.) But now I'm thinking of my father's shop, which sold lightbulbs made to look like candles, with pretend plastic wax dripping down their sides and bulbs whose elements flickered like flames. There were dusty stacks of batteries and plugs, and cables of all widths rolled in great reels on steel poles on the wall; there were kettles and irons and mini-fans and hairdryers, there were drawers of parts and drawers of fuses, drawers filled with anonymous bits of plastic and rubber that could make things work. Behind the counter there were two loose wires, live, for testing lightbulbs; he used to tease me, here, touch these, go on, and sometimes I would, just to get the queasy feeling all over again and to see if it really felt as horrible as I remembered. Propped on the back wall behind and above him was an old piece of cardboard from the nineteen fifties when the shop first opened. On it a dapper-suited man was demonstrating a lamp to an ecstatic woman with the words The Theme Is Power radiating like a rainbow over their heads, and over the head of my serving father, in a lit-up exclamatory arc.

His shop was next door to the Joke Shop, which had blackface soap, electric buzzers for shaking hands, fake dog's dirt and bluebottles and nails-through-the-finger, brandy glasses with the brandy sealed inside the glass so the drinker would be fooled, and special bird-call whistles which my father, whose laugh rang down the streets and round the shops from a great distance away, showed me how to use; how to tuck metal and leather into the roof of your mouth, moisten properly with your tongue, and then you could imitate any bird you heard. It sold x-ray specs, which my mother confiscated from me when she saw the sharp nail-points holding them together next to where the open eye would be.

You see, I tell you. My mother was still alive, and pretty well, when Jackie and I got back with our bus-stop story; but it was the beginning of her worrying herself awake every night wondering which acquaintance, which friend, which familiar face had sent the letter; maybe someone who'd been round for a cup of tea and had sat smiling at her in that very armchair, had complimented her on her kitchen full of shiny electrical things and their house it had taken them nearly forty years to own. It was a terrible time. A man who worked in the tax office, a neighbour, an old friend, came round; he sat on the couch and hung his head. His aftershave was apologetic. He said, usually we get these crank notes, and usually they go straight in the bucket, I'm so sorry, I didn't see it otherwise it would've. My mother patted his hand. My father gave him a whisky, patted him on the back.

(Then what happened? you ask.)

She wasted, became ill. He aged twenty years in one month. He worked with the inspector who came to take his business apart; she was young, a woman in her late twenties, and she found an accountant's old mistake in his books, charged him for that, and when she was finished she shook his hand and said she'd enjoyed her time with him and that enjoyment was a rare thing in her job. Then that was it, over. But my mother sat on a low stool in her kitchen, drinking tea on her own and staring at the food mixer, at nothing, knowing for a fact that someone had wanted to hurt her.

I turn round. You're not there. I knew that. There's no one here, just me, and my father breathing next door.

So I wipe down the table. I wipe the crumbs on to the floor instead of into my hand like I should, and my mother laughs down at me. Now that she's safe in heaven dead she tends to laugh at all the slatternly things I do, all the things that would have enraged her when she was alive. I leave a sheet on the line for two days and two nights, regardless of rain and the judgements of neighbours, and she laughs delightedly. I blow my nose on my clothes and she laughs and laughs, claps her hands. I try sewing anything, anything at all, and she roars with laughter in my ear like it's the funniest thing she's ever seen.

My mother, all her illness gone; holding the soles of her feet and rocking with laughter up there above us. When I was about thirteen, back when I felt scared and guilty all the time, I asked her once if there wasn't anything she'd done in her life that she still felt bad about. She was getting ready to go out to work. Her hand paused by her mouth holding the lipstick, and her face went thoughtful. Yes, she said suddenly, lots of things, and she laughed, then her face fell, she looked crushed, she sat down on the side of the bed. Yes, there was the time someone stole my new shoes and it was my fault, and my mother, your granny, I'd never seen her so angry. We were poor. I've told you before, though you can't imagine what that means. We were poor but your granny always made sure we had shoes, it was a thing of decency for her. So there was one year we got our new shoes for going back to school, but my best friend was barefoot and I wanted to be too. I didn't want to be any different. So I took my new shoes off and I hid them in the grass outside the school, and I was barefoot all day. But when I came out they were gone, someone had taken them. It was terrible. It was the end of the world. I had to go home to my mother with no shoes.

She sat on the bed with the wardrobe door open opposite her, and she waved her hand over all the shoes, hundreds of shoes hardly scuffed, piled several-thick inside each other and on top of each other on the wardrobe floor. Look at that now, she said. Then she lifted the hairspray tin and shook it. This'll chase you, she said. Off you go you monkey, I'm going to be late because of you, or if you're staying, cover your eyes and take a deep breath, I'm going to spray.

(I still don't really get the connection, you say.) Well, no. OK. Actually you don't say anything, you're not home yet. But you'll be home soon, so I imagine your key in the door, you kicking off your shoes and hanging your jacket in the hall, and coming through, stealing up behind me and kissing the back of my neck. Your face will be cold, and when I turn to kiss you back, your nose will be cold and you'll taste of outside. You'll say, you're doing the dishes, what's happened, has the world changed? is someone here? is your father here? your father must be here. You'll point to the drying crockery. You'll stand back to admire its pile-up, like people admiring art. Brilliant, you'll say. Pure sculpture.

You always say something like that.

And then it's later, it's late, it's nearly midnight now, and you're home. You came home half an hour after I finished the dishes. Now my father is in bed in the spare room. I can hear him snoring all the way through two walls. It's disturbing, as usual. It's too familiar.

I'm lying in bed. You're tired; you're not saying much. You didn't say much at supper. I think you might be in a bad mood. You undress, folding your clothes as you take them off.

I'm a little worried for my father. It can be cold in the spare room; I should have given him a hot water bottle. I think of his shop, dark and gone. The last time I passed it, it had become a clan heraldry shop, its windows full of little shields; a bored-looking man sat behind the counter and there were no customers. I think of the art gallery today, and the picture we saw with the massive rock in the room and the door blocked behind it. My head full of dark thoughts, I think of Jackie again, of how finally we betrayed each other, fell out of love, in love with others; we couldn't not.

I stop thinking about it all. It's too sore.

Outside someone goes past, a drunk angry man, and it sounds like he's hitting the cars parked along the road with a stick or his fist. He's shouting. I'm doing your fucking cars, he shouts. You better come out and get me. None of yous will. You're all fucking cowards. I'm going to do all your fucking cars.

His voice fades as he moves down the road. You get into bed. You switch the bedside light out, and we're in the dark. You sigh.

Listen, I say, and I want to tell you the whole story, but it rolls around dangerously in my head. So I say,

What if there was a great big boulder in the room, and you've no idea how it got in, it's so much bigger than the door.

What? you say. You turn beside me, speaking into my back.

A boulder. It's nearly as big as the room, I say. And it's slowly coming towards you –

Towards me? you say.

Towards us, I say, and it's crushing all the things in the room.

It'd better not, you say. We haven't paid this bed off yet, I'm not having it destroyed by a stupid, what is it, boulder?

But listen. What if there was a great big stone in the room, I say, big enough to almost be up to the ceiling, and as wide as from there to there.

A stone, you say sleepily. As big as the room. Coming towards us. Where's my chisel? get me a chisel, find something we can use as a hammer. You'd pay a fortune for that much rock at a stonemason's.

Under the covers you take my hand and turn it around, put your fingers through mine, interlocked, and you fall asleep like that, holding my hand.

That's all it takes. One glance, one sidelong blow from you, and a rock as big as a room explodes into little bits of gravel. I pick around in the shards of it, remember someone I saw today in the art gallery, a stranger, a man who sat down next to my sleeping father with such care, trying not to wake him. I remember my father like he was way back then, showing me the inside of a plug and which colour went where; and I think of my father now, flirting with a woman in a supermarket, playfully circling each other in the checkout queue. I make the woman very good-looking, to please him, and a little like my mother, to please us both. I remember the man I saw all those years ago in the space where the garage had been, cradling his genitals like he was holding a creature, something new-born, furless; and the fathers, stupid with protection, hurling themselves along the backs of the houses; and my mother telling me to shield my eyes so the hairspray chemicals wouldn't get in them. And then I think back to Jackie and me in London waiting at that bus stop, two teenage girls in a random city, good enough to believe the lies that a stranger told, even caring in the first place that a stranger might be sad.

You're next to me asleep with my hand still in yours, my father is snoring along the hall, and I'm not long from sleep myself. I lie in our unpaid bed and trust you, carelessly, precariously, with my whole heart. That's the story finished, that's all there is to it. One last time though, before I lock the door on it for the night, turn the sign from Open to Closed, I picture Jackie, wherever she is, wherever she might be in the world.

I imagine she's holding such a hand. I imagine her safe and sound.

CATHY BOLTON
Eureka

I was only there to show my face. Jen wanted to show off her new friend, Ellie – works in marketing. My Mum must have had someone from every department in the Town Hall. Ellie's younger than usual, bit of posh too. You can tell she's freaked by the idea of a teenage step-daughter – can't work out how to talk to me. I've had them all over the years: second mother, fond uncle, big sister. They've all tried to buy my affection. Ellie's no different. She's got a contact at Old Trafford, can maybe get hold of a season ticket.

The same old crowd started to fill our back room. Teachers and social workers, dressed in their latest Gap combats and Shelly's trainers. It's sad the way lesbians won't admit to being middle-aged.

Jen had put me in charge of 'music'. I knew the routine – bunged on one of her famous compilation tapes – 80s nostalgia with the odd indie and house track to get people dancing. Later in the night it would be boy band covers of the 70s.

Miss Barrington, my old social science teacher, made a lurch in my direction. I quickly raised the volume to *It's Raining Men*, nodded vaguely as she mouthed something about mocks. Silly cow wouldn't take a hint – just stood there grinning at me, like I was some guru about to tell her the meaning of life.

"There's no use sucking up to me, the whole fucking school knows you're shaggin' the deputy head," I wanted to shout. I made a big deal of looking at my watch. Jesus, time was dragging.

I was about to sneak upstairs to watch *Eurotrash* when I noticed some woman giving me the look. I didn't recognise her at all: frizzy brown hair down to her shoulders, girlie silk blouse showing lots of cleavage. You wouldn't think 'dyke' if you saw her in the street. It was the hands that gave her away. Strong, tanned, long fingers buckled with chunks of silver. There was an easy confidence in the way she cradled her bottle of beer. She glided past my defences, smooth as a Beckham free kick.

"Couldn't lend us a smoke?" Her voice was slow, grating; American – I couldn't say which state.

I reached for the packet from my breast pocket, flicked it open. I hoped Jen wasn't watching. I'd promised to give up if she bought me a leather jacket. I was wearing her side of the bargain.

"Aw, but it's your last one," she whined, her hand hovering perilously close to mine.

"Take it. I was just on my way to the garage to buy some more." I needed a quick getaway.

"Got a light to go with it?" She leaned into me as I struck a match, her face shone neon in its small glow. She took a deep drag, her eyes slipping down my body. "I'll come with you." She turned and gestured to the frowning woman she'd abandoned by the dips and chips table.

We had to pass Jen in the hall. "You off somewhere?"

"My friend here's just taking me out for supplies." My new friend linked her arm through mine and tossed my Mum a knowing wink.

Soon as we were out the door, she did a spitting mimic of Jen's expression. Something between bewilderment and horror. "Guess I'll be strung up for cradle snatching if I dare return."

I sniggered nervously, stuffed my hands in my jeans pockets before she had a chance to chain me up again.

"Hope you don't mind me dragging you out of there. Only you looked like you needed rescuing."

"I do now," I thought. It was raining, a thin drizzle but enough to make the silk stick to her skin. The pattern of her black lacy bra shone through her shirt like a brass rubbing.

"How far is this gas station then?"

"Not too far." We headed for the all-nighter on Wilbraham Road.

"So you like older women?"

"Uh? No, not especially."

"Well they seem to like you." She gave me another of her top-shelf smirks. "I bet a young thing like you knows where to find a good time in this town."

"There's lots of bars in the Village." Jen had dragged me round enough of them last Mardi Gras. All those half-naked men in dog collars and bald girls in flowery pinafores and ridiculously clumpy boots choking up the streets – fashion over-statements.

"How about we take a cab into town and you show me the sights."

"I dunno. I... I haven't got much cash."

"No worries, I'm loaded." She pulled down the waist-band of her slacks to reveal a discreet money bag. "Look here's one now." She flagged down the black cab turning into the main road.

Everyone was queuing up to get into the throbbing bars. I didn't know which one to pick. Where I'd be safe from loose tongues. Boys at school were always bragging about their perv baiting trips to queer street. Claimed they could earn a ton from wanking off a few sad bastards down the canal.

"Now this is more like it," Toni beamed. I'd gotten most of her life history on the five mile drive into town. She was over for a conference at the University – something to do with Internet communities. Was staying with an old friend she'd met at Greenham. "Glory days," she confided with a giggle.

We joined the queue for Velvet. I wanted to check out the shopping channel in the toilets. My mate Trish had been raving about them. She thinks it's cool having a lesbian mum. That's because she's a dyke herself – it's obvious to everyone but Trish.

"Hey this is quaint." Toni pointed to the goldfish swimming under the perspex bottom step. I tried to hide my own curiosity – like I'd seen it all before.

"You want a beer?" I nodded. Hung about trying not to look conspicuous while she joined the scrum at the bar.

"This is great." She came back with two bottles of Bud. "So where you taking me next?"

I shrugged, made out like I was mulling over possibilities.

"I feel like dancin'. Take me dancin'." She put her arm round my waist, suddenly lunged forward, her mouth on mine. Her tongue expertly needled its way in, prising my lips open. It was surprisingly sexy. Nothing like those tonsil stripping snogs I'd endured at Trish's parties.

"Mmm. I've been wanting to do that all night." She took a swig of beer. "What about this Paradise. I've heard that's a pretty fun place."

Not according to Trish. Any place you're likely to bump into a teacher automatically goes on the sad list.

"I guess I should be getting home," I feigned a yawn.

"Home! You're joking. It's barely midnight. You're not going to turn into a pumpkin are you?"

I gave a faint smile.

"C'mon let's have a bit of fun. There's no girlfriend waiting at home for you is there?"

"No, there's no girlfriend."

"Then what's the problem?"

"No problem." With any luck the party wouldn't have fizzled out by the time I rolled back home. Jen'd be wearing her concerned mother face but she wouldn't start a scene in front of her guests.

We joined another queue outside Paradise. Toni was starting to shiver. I gave her my jacket.

"So butch," she teased, pinching my bare arms.

I was enjoying playing the gigolo. I'd never been treated like a sex object before. Jen and her friends are always so careful not to influence my choice of sexuality they treat me like a eunuch. If they refer to my sex life at all it's to ask if I've met any nice boys recently. As if.

The bouncer at the door asked if I had any ID. "She's got me," Toni answered on my behalf, pulling me in through the door before he could pursue his interrogation. Once we were safe in the huddle of sweating bodies she asked, "So, how old are you?"

"Old enough," I lied.

"And not a day over. C'mon let's dance." She dragged me into a sea of jerking limbs. The strobe lighting made everyone look like they were in the throes of apoplexy. Toni must have been the oldest person there but she didn't seem to care. I caught a couple of girls sniggering in our direction – probably wondering what I was doing out with my mother. She'd already given me my jacket back. When she suddenly pulled off her blouse a small cheer went up from the boys next to us. I shook my head when one of them offered a bottle of poppers but Toni was game for anything. Luckily they slowed her down. A few minutes later we were out on the street so she could get some air.

"Guess I'm getting too old to party. Sorry I'm spoiling your night."

"No, it's OK. I'd had enough, anyway."

"How about you take me back to your place?"

"No, I can't," I answered too assertively.

"So there is someone waiting at home for you. You've been holding out on me."

"No. It's just my landlady. She's a bit funny..."

"Say no more. I'd invite you back to my pad only I don't think my hostess will be talking to me right now. I guess it's a hotel then. Where do you recommend?"

"I... I don't know." Now I was the one shivering. I could hear Jen's nagging voice in my head. "Don't be afraid to say no. Say it loud and clear – men are slow to comprehend." But what about women? She'd never mentioned them. I needed to walk. Walking helped me think. It's how I revise – pacing round the house like a caged animal cramming facts into my brain.

We were following the line of railway arches, the UMIST tower looming off-side. There was something comforting in the distant rumble of trains. I stopped to look at a statue of a naked man rising from a tub with a constipated shriek.

"Eureka!" Toni screeched in my ear. "This is no short cut right?"

"Huh?"

She had me trapped against the damp curve of red brick, her stale nicotine breath warming my skin. One hand squeezed my tits while the other struggled with the buckle of my belt. Soon her ice cold fingers were jumping inside me. I tried to enjoy it but I was worried we might not be alone: drunks looking for a place to piss, dirty old men in search of a wank.

Then she knelt on the glass-littered concrete, wrestled my jeans down to my knees. I tried to pull her back up.

"Stop, please!"

But she wouldn't budge, just looked up at me with a milky stare, "You smell delicious: red apples and baled corn."

More like sweat and stale urine. I felt sick. There was no way I was going to suck her rotten fruit. How had I let this happen? I wanted to be home in my room, surrounded by posters of Gigsy and Becks. Safe and sexless again.

"Angie, that you?" A familiar voice bleated from the dark.

"You OK? I saw you in Paradise." It was Steph, one of Jen's exes. "Your Mum know where you are?"

Fuck, how old did she think I was, twelve? I'm stood there with my knickers round my ankles, a prize turkey about to be stuffed and she asks about my Mum!

"Did she say Mom?" Toni stared up at me with the look of a startled sleepwalker. I wish someone could have slapped me awake too, but no, the nightmare had just begun. I had the whole fucking child protection team waiting at home for me.

HANNAH RICHARDS
The Shag Tree

Years ago, when Chris and I had only just met, and were still getting to know each other's histories, we created a legend. It started out innocently enough, with two cups of steaming coffee, lounging on sofas in a comfy coffee-house in Oakley-on-Sea. I was relatively new to the scene, and thrilled to be finally meeting all the women I'd been secretly watching for years, but there were so many women around, back then, that I was having difficulty keeping them straight – so to speak.

"Chris," I mumbled through a flapjack, "was Emma sleeping with Anna while she was still seeing Maria? Is that why there's a bad atmosphere when Anna and Maria get together?"

"No. Maria and Anna have never got along. Teri, Anna's ex, had an affair with Maria before they split up."

I let my head fall against the back of the sofa.

"And didn't you used to see Emma? Or was that a different one?"

"No, that was the same Emma. Except she was going out with Laurie at the time. They had an open relationship."

"Chris," I moaned, "I'm never going to get all this. I keep thinking that I'll put my foot in it really badly one day."

"OK!" Chris jumped to her feet, and reached over to the notice board. She selected a red flyer (for aromatherapy massage, I think), and plonked it, blank side up, on the table.

"Look, this is how it works." She grabbed the pen from our completed crossword, and wrote her own name on the paper. Then she drew an arrow to my name. Then she wrote Emma's name, and linked herself to Emma... Chris went on adding names and drawing arrows until I could see at a glance who had slept with whom.

There were arrows bristling around Chris's name, and only one from mine. I felt oddly substandard, and told Chris so. She laughed.

"You're an idiot, Beth. That's my old life, and it's history now. As long as I have you, I really don't need anyone else. I'm glad you don't have arrows like me. There's no politics with you, and that's refreshing."

People say that Chris and I look alike, but I can't really see it. We've both got short, dark hair, and we're roughly the same size, but that's it. Perhaps the fact that we wear each other's clothes has something to do with it, and now, years on, we probably have similar habits, but we didn't back then.

I picked up the flyer, and folded it carefully.

"I'm going to revise from this!" I joked, but back at home I stuck it up in the kitchen, and noticed it daily. It was small then, with a handful of women connected by scribbled biro lines, but it was to grow into a monster.

Over the next few months, our shag tree developed almost as fast as our relationship. Two months after we met, Chris moved her things into the flat, doubling our wardrobe and CD collection. We began to make new friends as a couple; women neither of us had met before, and as our social circle began to widen, the shag tree became increasingly complicated and interlinked. Our names still kept their original arrows, but our friends all seemed to be sleeping with each other.

One night, at the regular women's club night in town, we were introduced to a group of women who were in Oakley for the weekend. One of the group, Sam, had recently finished a fling with a friend of ours, and was now sleeping with a blonde-haired woman, Elise. We knew that Sam was already on the shag tree, and we also knew that Elise had only recently moved away from Oakley. Had she slept with anyone else that we knew? I'd had a few drinks by this point, and it became increasingly important to discover whether I could link her in with other shag tree members.

"Elise!" I yelled into her ear. The music was pumping out. "Were you seeing anyone in Oakley before you left?"

Elise gave me a strange look. I knew I was being a bit presumptuous, when I'd only known the woman an hour or so, but that's alcohol – and shag trees – for you.

"Why d'you want to know?" she yelled back. We were standing slightly apart from the rest of the group; Chris was at the bar, over the other side of a sea of sweaty women.

"I know you're seeing Sam now..." I didn't think she could hear me over the music, so I leant closer to her. That's when she put her arm around me and pulled me against her. That's also when Chris chose to make her appearance with the drinks. Fortunately, Chris isn't the jealous type, and she arrived in time to see me slip out of Elise's embrace without causing any lasting emotional damage.

But neither Chris nor I have ever been one to shirk a duty, and we eventually got the sordid facts from Sam: and they were worth the wait! We added ten new names to the tree that night, including three illicit affairs... always the best names to have, because they often created circular patterns, and even, sometimes, arrows between every woman in the circle, to every other woman in the circle. Who says only gay boys are promiscuous? If we did realise one thing, though, it was that we were creating a dangerous record of lesbian sex. We decided that we would keep it just between ourselves, and resist the temptation to produce sought-after copies for our friends. However, it was outgrowing the page I'd faithfully copied it onto, from our original flyer, and one evening, in front of *Ellen*, I transcribed the whole thing again. It became an A3 masterpiece.

Concealed as it was on the inside of a kitchen cupboard door, we often forgot it was around. Chris's name was still almost obliterated by multiple arrows, mine still had its solitary connection to Chris. It eventually became so familiar – we saw it every day – that we began to forget what an outsider would make of it. At about this time, Chris's mother paid us a visit. Now, Chris's mother is a great woman; Chris and I are 'out'n'proud' to her, but we still thought it prudent to remove one or two more offensive items from the house. The tasteful black and white prints of us making love were taken down and hidden under the bed. But we didn't even consider the shag tree, though we must have opened the cupboard at least a hundred times before Clare's visit.

It all passed rather smoothly at first. Chris and I sat with our arms around each other, we called each other darling, we were even caught snogging in the bathroom, but Clare liked me, and was simply pleased that Chris was happy. Chris had never concealed her lesbianism from her mother, but the only thing Clare didn't know was just how popular her little angel had been with the ladies. Of course she soon found out.

We were eating pasta and salad for dinner on Clare's second evening with us. Clare went into the kitchen to fetch a bread knife, and we heard her opening drawers. We carried on chatting.

Chris called, "Mum! Can you bring me a wine glass? Second cupboard along." And then to me, "This is going really well. I only ever let her meet Jude and Kate before, and she didn't really like either of them."

Clare was taking ages. It was silent in the kitchen.

"Mum!" Chris laughed. "What are you doing in there? The food's getting cold!"

Chris and I smiled at each other. Things were great for us. That's when Clare came back into the lounge – holding the shag tree. I actually saw Chris's face go white.

"This is an interesting read." Clare put the paper down on the table, next to the salad. We all stared at it. I saw, as if for the first time, Chris's cluster of arrows. For a second I wondered whether Clare knew what it was, but only for a second.

"What the hell's been going on in your life, Chris?" Clare was visibly upset.

I could see Chris searching for an answer. I was thinking hard too. Clare was looking at Chris as if she didn't recognise her. I felt terrible.

"I think I might cut this short, girls. I have a meeting at the end of the week, which I should really prepare for." We were all aware of just how poor the excuse sounded.

"Mum, we should discuss this. It's not quite as bad as you think. Also, I'm with Beth now, things are different..." Chris was close to tears.

"Well, Chris. I hope you manage to stay with Beth. All this..." she swept her hand over the shag tree "...makes me think it's not in your nature."

I should skip over the next few hours, the days of long phonecalls, and just mention that Chris and her mother managed to salvage their friendship... just. Chris wanted to destroy the tree, but I persuaded her to fold it up and hide it away instead.

We were shag treeless for about three months. I made mental notes during those months, intending to add names when Chris felt comfortable with the tree being put up again. Eventually, our closest friend, Lucy (already on the tree), slept with a woman who was new to the scene. It was gossip-sex, by which I mean it was such a bizarre match that everyone had heard about it, and had an opinion on the subject.

"Please, Chris!" I begged. "We have to join up Lu and Charlie. It's just too funny not to!"

Which was how the shag tree was restored to our kitchen, and the beginning of the end began.

Back up, the tree began to take on a rather eerie growth-spurt. Friends in the pub, who thought the tree was a harmless piece of fun, would suddenly launch into their university exploits, and even created mini shag trees on the backs of beer mats, for us to add at home. Chris and I knew a lot of women, and Chris was also working part-time in the pub we all drank in; she saw and heard almost every infidelity. Whenever anyone wanted to check a sexual history, they asked us. But we'd learnt a lot since Clare's eventful visit, and we were (reasonably) discreet. We did, however, add the names of women from all over the country. All the dykes we knew had lived elsewhere: all of them had ex-partners whom they would discuss when drunk. We were amazed to discover that we could link women together from opposite sides of the country. Honestly, the lesbian scene is a lot smaller than people think... and a lot more incestuous. Our tree grew saplings: smaller, linked trees that spanned almost every city. Soon the whole cupboard door was covered, and we had to rehouse it in our hoover-plastic-bag-ironing-board cupboard. It covered the whole of the inside of the door.

Two weeks after the tree had been settled into its new home, I was lying in Chris's lap at London Pride (as it was then). The sun was out, and we were enjoying Boy George camping it up on stage, when a shadow blocked out the sunlight. We both looked up in surprise. A woman was looking down at us. She sat down on the grass.

"Hi. I'm Carol. I was just chatting to a friend of yours over there." She glanced over her shoulder. "The thing is, she told me that you guys have a, um shag tree, I think she said."

"Yes" I said, guardedly. I wasnt certain that discussing the tree with a stranger was a great idea.

"Well, I wonder if you'd give me a copy. I'm doing research on lesbian sexuality for my thesis. It would be great to have some factual information, like, How loose are lesbians, really?" Carol laughed.

I felt a bit prudish, but I explained that it had grown out of proportion, and that there was too much classified info to give a copy to anyone, particularly someone we didn't know.

Chris agreed: "We'd have to leave town if anyone else saw the thing now. It's ridiculous."

Carol appeared to understand, we chatted for a while, and she left us to meet some friends. Chris and I couldn't believe that our scribbled notes had turned into an infamous piece of lesbian interest. We discussed it, and decided that the best thing to do would be to take the tree down – quit while we were still ahead, if you like – and store it away in the loft.

But we forgot everything when, the next day, Chris was offered the job of her dreams. It meant that we had to leave Oakley, but we were thrilled at the prospect of buying our own place at last. We planned a huge leaving party, and spent a lot of time on motorways, driving between our old and new towns, searching for houses. Change was certainly in the air, and it felt good. We were rarely at home, and we had to rush to shop and clean the house on the afternoon of our leaving party. Chris took the shag tree down, folded it carefully, and hid it under the potatoes in the kitchen. We were sure that, no matter how wild the party became, no one would be in need of potatoes. We were almost right.

We were in the middle of a heatwave that year, so Chris and I threw open every window in the house, but we were still glistening with sweat when the first guests began to turn up. The music got louder, and more women arrived, bringing wine, beer and food. People began to sit on the stairs, and to spill out onto the front patio, laughing and clutching wine glasses. Our neighbours stopped by, with small gifts for our new house. We felt good, and seized a moment in the kitchen to hold each other.

"I love you, Chris. I'm glad we're doing this, it feels right to be planning a future with you."

"I love you too, Beth. I'm sure things will really work out well for us... and you can go back to uni, with the money I'll be earning." We could hear the sounds of laughter coming from outside, and Lu stumbled into the kitchen.

"Guess who's here!" She lurched past us to the fridge. "Anna! Remember she was seeing Marcie just before she moved away? Well, she's back, and apparently, she's seeing Emma!"

The three of us started laughing.

"I thought Anna said she'd be celibate for life, after the mess with Maria," Chris observed. "Let's go and speak to them."

We made our way outside, where it was slightly cooler. I slid my arm around Chris's bare shoulders, tanned and smooth, and felt incredibly lucky. I still feel like that, even now.

The party was going rather well. We set up an impromptu barbecue in the garden, and raided the freezer for sausages. Someone made an enormous bowl of sangria, and both mine and Chris's – straight – work colleagues arrived, looking rather bemused. I caught my boss, later, sitting on the stairs, sharing a joint with the butchest woman I know. Apparently, they've now been together for almost three years!

Perhaps, looking back now, I can see that things were going so well that they were bound to end in catastrophe. They do say that all the best parties have someone crying in the kitchen...

I was starting to feel the effects of the sangria, when someone announced there was to be a talent show in the garden. Sam was already standing on the table, reciting her own bawdy poetry, to the delight of the drunk women on the grass. Someone else had run home to fetch her guitar, and a woman I didn't know very well, Ella, wanted to juggle.

I'm not sure where I was when it happened. I think I was out the front of the house talking to Lu: Chris was definitely upstairs fetching her own guitar from the bedroom, but I heard a shout, and a woman's voice scream, "You fucking bitch! I knew it, I've always known it, and you always denied it!"

A sick feeling began in my stomach. I hoped it was just a drunk row going on, and that it had nothing to do with me, Chris, or anything we might have hidden in the house... But of course I was wrong. Chris appeared at the front door, holding her guitar.

"Beth. This is really bad. Come into the garden." We walked through the house. Almost all of the women were in the garden by now, and they had formed a group around the table. I didn't really need to see what they were looking at, and when I saw our potential juggler, Ella, holding our potatoes, I knew. Just about every woman in the garden was on that bloody piece of paper. They were jostling to get a better view.

"Oh fuck," I whispered to Chris. "This is going to cause such a mess. Why the hell didn't we get rid of the bloody thing when we could?" But we both knew the answer: we had been creating it for such a long time that we treasured it, we hadn't wanted to put an end to it.

Some of the women were laughing. Most were studying it in silence. I saw Maria walk away in tears, and sit down by herself. Then Niamh, who had obviously just discovered that her partner Emily had slept with Sam, walked over to Sam and punched her in the face. After that, it went downhill rapidly. Four relationships ended that night, and I'm sure many more only just survived. We eventually had to call the police when a fight broke out between five of our friends, and Anna was arrested.

Chris and I watched in horror as the women we'd known and loved – some of them literally, for Chris – broke up their relationships and friendships, and trashed the house. Almost everyone left without saying a word to us, but my boss was impressed.

"What a fabulous party!" She was draped over our butch friend. "Make sure you invite me to your housewarming!" They giggled as they got into a cab.

It was about five in the morning before everyone had left. We sat in the wreckage of our lounge, and I began to cry. Chris put her arm around me, and pulled me close. We didn't speak, and we eventually crawled into bed. The sun was just rising.

*

By the end of the week, we had cleaned, packed, and were on our way up North, with a new life awaiting us both. None of our friends had contacted us before we left, and we almost felt relieved to be leaving. We had spent three years together, and gained a great group of friends, and now we only had each other, and a van full of possessions to show for it. I know that we were both hoping it would be enough. We never saw the shag tree again: it had vanished by the time we went to look the next day.

And that, as far as it went, was that. But last week, three years after that party, we found ourselves back in Oakley. It was festival time, and Chris and I thought that enough time had probably elapsed; people would have forgotten all about it, wouldn't they? We had come back for a conference that I needed to attend, and we had booked ourselves into a bed-and-breakfast for one night. We were slightly apprehensive about revisiting our old haunts – we weren't sure what sort of welcome we would receive, so when our landlady mentioned that a new dyke bar had recently opened, we thought we could be fairly inconspicuous there.

It was rather stylish, actually. All glass and chrome, with good music and even better beer. It wasn't very busy, that early in the evening, and we were relieved to find that we didn't recognise anyone. We took a couple of beers to a corner sofa, and sat down.

I must have looked nervous, because Chris said, "Beth, we'll be fine. Oakley's such a transient place. Everyone will have moved on by now."

"Yes, and we probably caused them to." I still had occasional nightmares about that hot evening, three years before.

The bar began to fill up with women. Still, we didn't recognise anyone. I did see a colleague, who was there for the same conference, and we exchanged small talk for a while.

When she left, Chris leaned over to me with a cheeky smile, and slid her arm around my waist. "Beth, I know you're tense. They have a back room here... Shall we take our drinks in there?"

We grinned at each other. It seemed like a great idea – some stress relief was just what I needed. We rose, and made our way through the crowd to the door marked, Private space: enter at your own risk! It was slightly darker inside, and slightly less busy. We started to cross to the bar, when we both stopped dead, at exactly the same time. Opposite us, covering the entire wall... was our shag tree.

Not only was every name still in its correct position, but many, many more had been added. There must have been at least three hundred women's names on that wall. We stood and stared: it was as if someone that we knew to be dead and buried had suddenly appeared in front of us.

"Let's get out of here, Chris. I can't believe this has happened!" I tugged at her arm. But Chris was astounded.

"Just look at it! I can't believe we started that!"

It was then that we heard a voice calling our names. Too late, Chris and I tried to make a speedy exit, but someone was blocking the door. It was Anna. The last time we had seen Anna, she was leaving our house in a police car.

"Anna!" I cried. Then, pathetically, "How are you?"

"I'll tell you how I am!" she began, angrily, then she laughed. "Fucking rich! This is my bar, I opened it about six months ago. I'm so pleased to see you guys... After that party, I could have killed you both, and the police! Jesus! What a night..." Anna looked vacant as if remembering, then said, "But I took the bloody shag tree – I felt it was only fair... and when I was looking for an original idea for this place, I suddenly remembered it, and thought what a good concept it would be. Of course it causes arguments, but it also generates interest – and money!" Anna laughed. Chris and I looked at each other in amazement, then we laughed too.

The three of us spent the evening under the giant that had once been a scribbled diagram, discussing old friends and Anna's new lover. We left Oakley the next day, with a slightly better conscience about the whole thing. I had been worried when we lost it, and I was happy to discover where it had ended up, but as far as I was concerned, it was now Anna's problem. Good luck, Anna, you'll probably need it!

JULIA COLLAR
Kissing On The Way Up

"Duck!" Mariam yelled and she and the passer-by both covered their heads and jumped instinctively backwards. Mariam grinned and winked at the stranger who then decided that lingering to watch any further attempts at juggling was far too perilous and, in fear of his perm and wet-look gel, plodded away towards the bandstand.

Hefting the clubs from one hand to another, she watched him go before swinging down to retrieve the errant fifth club which had kissed with the fourth on the upswing and been sent spinning wildly into the afternoon sunshine.

"You overthrow," said a voice somewhere behind her in that insolent and hard tone only a teenager can manage.

"Excuse me?" Mariam turned. The girl was indeed young and viciously dressed for ultimate parental shock-value.

"The reason you keep dropping one is because you overthrow." She spelled it out for Mariam in world-weary sarcasm.

"Well, if you're so good at detecting my faults then maybe you should show me – there's another set of clubs in my bag." Mariam nodded towards her rucksack and tried to suppress a smile as the girl eagerly scrambled to accept the offer. She was good though, hardly breaking rhythm even when a club threatened to move beyond arm's reach, and Mariam watched her, relishing the sunny afternoon laziness that trotted through the park like a stray dog who has all the time in the world to sniff and ponder.

"Now, it's your turn 'cos I need to sit down," the girl said, catching the clubs to a stop and flopping down on the grass. Mariam began her cascade, this time with only three clubs, and even managed a few tricks along the way. The girl was watching her but not for her juggling skills and Mariam gradually became more and more uncomfortable.

"Are you a lesbian?" the girl eventually spilled out.

"That's what the T-shirt says. Why? Are you?" Mariam teased, throwing a shimmy into her juggling stance so that her 'Girls who do Girls' slogan rippled as her breasts shook. The girl mumbled something and Mariam wasn't about to let this opportunity pass so she asked loudly, "What did you say?"

"Too young to know." The girl repeated crossly.

"Who told you that?" Mariam snorted.

"Doesn't matter." There was silence for a few minutes. "Where did you learn to juggle, then?"

"There was a circus-skills workshop as part of a self-development thing run by the women's group at Uni, I've kept it up because it's a great stress buster... but, to be honest, I really like the attention. One guy earlier gave me a couple of quid and this family picnicking gave me a tuna sandwich so, all in all, it's a pretty cool thing to do of a Sunday afternoon. What about you?"

"I got this book out of the library, *Juggling as a Metaphor for Modern Life*, it told me to start out with fruit."

Mariam considered the idea of starting out with fruit. She pictured a neat and tidy mother and father instructing their daughter in the art of responsibility. It was the daughter's seventeenth birthday and, instead of giving her a television, stereo, or car, they placed sternly into each of her hands ripe, round, and lustrous fruit, telling her that once she had learned to look after these and could show the strength and integrity not to eat them, she might then gain access to a rusted banger or a third-hand 1970s black and white television set whose knobs and dials had been replaced by lumps of plasticine. Mariam saw the daughter later in bed, crying softly with the fruit still cradled in her palms.

"Juggling as a metaphor?" Mariam asked as her vision of the girl and her fruit faded away and rolled under the bed with the peelings.

"Yep, life is all about juggling: keeping career, mortgage, family, and relationships all up in the air and moving without dropping any of them," the girl parroted in her best quotation style.

"Do you believe that?"

"Nah, not really – I just liked throwing fruit about and pretending that it was something really deep and meaningful. My parents seemed to think that it showed I was growing out of a 'phase' so it was useful to keep them off my back for a while." She rubbed her nose and looked up into Mariam's face.

"What 'phase' would that be?" Mariam challenged again.

"Oh, you know..." There was a glowing blush in her cheeks and a sparkle in her eyes as she trailed off.

"Yes, I think I do." They both grinned. Mariam nodded at the clubs on the ground, "You can keep them if you like."

The girl smiled so broadly then that she seemed to regress into childhood. Mariam packed up her remaining set of juggling irons and went off to meet the figure that was waving to her from the car park. She turned back once and the girl was still juggling; in her vision the daughter's hands and lips were wet with juice and she was smiling to herself and anticipating with quiet malevolence the row which would ensue when the skin and pips of her gifts were discovered underneath her valance.

"Who was that?" Angela asked, kissing Mariam's cheek and taking her bag from her.

"Just some kid. Anyway, how did it go?" Mariam slid into the car and glanced into the back seat, expecting to see shopping bags.

"I couldn't find anything I liked," Angela muttered, putting on her sunglasses.

"So what are you going to wear then? It's tomorrow afternoon – I suppose we could go shopping again if we get up early or something. What about that black dress – did you ever get that dry-cleaned?" Mariam suddenly wondered why the car hadn't moved and then realised that Angela was bent over the steering wheel crying. "Ange? Love? What's the matter?"

Angela rammed the key into the ignition, put the car in gear and screamed the vehicle backward over the gravel and out onto the streets. She was silent and angry, the frustration rippled off her like heat waves. To get home from the municipal park generally took twenty minutes, Angela made it in ten by jumping lights and breaking the speed limit and cutting up every other female driver she came across. They travelled in a volley of horns and curses shouted through open windows, sunroofs and convertible soft-tops. Angela replied with screeches of "You bloody tart!" and "Have you heard of food, you emaciated Kate Moss wannabe?" Mariam kept quiet and clung to her seat as they lurched round corners. She kept her eyes on her trainers because if she looked out at the busy roads she would be even more terrified.

Once they were safely in the house, Mariam launched herself at her lover, throwing her arms around her tightly. The momentum knocked them onto the sofa where Mariam managed to wrap her legs round Angela as well, so she was truly enfolded, unable to move and, more importantly, unable to tear at the flesh of her wrists. Angela really started crying then. To begin with it was the rage continuing to pour out and then it became quieter and more sporadic as the pain and hurt settled in. A few times Angela tried to bite at herself or slip a hand out from Mariam's grasp to shred at her wrist with her nails but Mariam grabbed her back, squeezed her tighter, gave her discomfort from being hugged too tight rather than from scarring herself. When Mariam knew that Angela could hear again, she whispered her mantra into her ear over and over and over, "I've got you, it's OK, I've got you, it's OK..." until Angela went slack and still, occasionally coughing or sniffing.

Mariam released her grip a little and attentively stroked the chestnut hair away from Angela's flushed and damp face. More time passed and Angela regained her ability to speak but it was into that strange, coy and acidic monologue that she fell, the stage in which she seemed to converse only with herself.

"I'm bad," Angela began.

"Hush, love." Mariam replied softly, knowing that Angela would ignore her but would still expect her to say something.

"I'm ugly."

"Love, you're beautiful and I love you."

"I'm..." The exchange continued for a time until the next stage was reached in which Angela's negative comments turned more into questions, and afterwards would come the breakthrough when Angela would begin to ask ridiculous and funny things, she would laugh and it would still hurt but at least she had come back and they could talk about it properly.

"I've got fat bits?" Angela tried.

"Where, love?" Mariam held out Angela's arm and looked at it thoughtfully, she ran her fingers over the body she still held, she trailed a finger down one thigh and then the other and sighed, "Nope, I can't find a single fat bit – just beautiful and sexy, your bits, and they're even more wonderful than I remembered." This made Angela smile and she squirmed a little so that Mariam's hands would feel compelled to stroke and massage her body some more.

"I'm all cellulitey and stretch-marky?"

"Love, stop it. You're beautiful. I love you."

Eventually Mariam managed to persuade Angela to have a bath. The hot water helped her relax and the small neatness of the bathroom felt comforting and secure. They had come a long way really, Mariam thought as she turned off the taps and swilled the bubblebath around. These episodes used to last for weeks at a time, then days and now just a few short hours and sometimes (and these were glimmering and fleeting times) Angela would be upset for only a few minutes, need only some chocolate and a cup of tea before the smile crept back across her face.

Angela padded in wearing a bathrobe and then hesitated. She was still reeling from her self-hatred and Mariam, rather than pull her lover against her, untie the belt and nuzzle her flesh as was their normal bathtime custom, made a big deal out of having to turn round and get some tissue to blow her nose. When she turned back Angela was happily settled into the foam, gently undulating her body so she could feel the water moving over her, so she could feel she was moving, so she could feel that she was real again.

"So, what happened?" Mariam asked, kneeling beside the bath and slipping a hand under the bubbles to caress Angela's hip.

"I hate those bloody changing-room mirrors. Everything I tried on just looked awful, my skin is horrendous and my hair is worse. Don't even get me started on the size of my arse!" Angela pouted and then smiled shyly.

"So, did you see anything you liked?" Angela loved clothes and always knew exactly what she wanted and how she should look. More often than not, a depressive episode after shopping would be caused by not being able to match a mental picture against reality. Then Angela would turn in against herself. They both knew it was silly, but it was still important.

"No, but I did see a couple of things you'd look great in. I wish I had your figure." Angela replied with a heavy sigh.

"What, and be all short and bony, with nothing much in the way of a cleavage, shapeless legs…"

"Oh, who's down on herself now?" Angela teased. "Mariam, you're so lucky to be small – all the things I want to wear just don't look good on the tall and robust like me."

"I just consider myself lucky that *I* look so good on you."

Angela let out a mighty fart in the bath and they both dissolved into endless giggles.

She is beautiful though. My Angela. My Angel. I watch her getting dressed and it's all that I can do just to stay still and not rush to her, to catch her up in my arms for a different kind of embrace – not one of reassurance but one of devotion and wonder. She is extremely sexy too. She knows I'm watching her because she spends too long hunting through the drawers for underwear and she stretches just that little bit too elegantly as she dots moisturiser onto the backs of her shoulders. Yes. She is tall and yes, she is well built but there is no shapeless flab upon her. She is like a series of curves thrown together by some cunning art, a pebble washed smooth by the beach. Her limbs are powerful, her hands are elegant and her eyes just go on forever. Sometimes cat-like and vampishly seductive, sometimes mannish, but always mine; she is the club that always kisses on the upswing and the one I always try so hard to catch. Today, she is caught and I am relieved and inspired.

The mobile rang as they were in the changing rooms. The curtain of the cubicle swished as Angela rooted about for the phone and thrust it out for Mariam to take. It was The Parents. Mariam was very cheerful with them though she winced a little when they asked her to drop round on the way home. The curtain was suddenly whisked back and there stood Angela looking devastating, a vision in blues and green, sleek and elegant and it was no longer an emotional wince that rushed through Mariam but one that was sheer and physical, warm and melting. She stuttered and fell into silence.

"Mariam? Mariam?" her father shouted through the earpiece.

"Sorry, I dropped something," she replied, winking at Angela and then nodding approvingly as her lover slowly turned round to give her the full benefit of the outfit and the cut-out feature at the back which revealed rather a lot of tanned and soft shoulder.

"You are so careless. Now, can we expect you to be bringing that girl with you?" His thick accent betrayed distaste.

"Yes."

"Are you joined at the hip? You never go anywhere without her," her father chided.

"That's because we are lovers. You don't go many places without Mum," Mariam replied with patience.

"I'm sorry, I didn't hear that – there was a crackle on the line, maybe the reception is breaking up?"

"It's fine at my end, Dad, but you just go on hearing what you want to hear."

"I beg your pardon?" He snapped back.

"I said, we'll give you a ring when we're getting near." Mariam checked herself and then rang off. Angela emerged in her jeans, smiling and looking pleased with herself. That cheered Mariam up and they went to the counter to pay.

"I tried that one on yesterday. About three times. I can't think why it didn't look right then," Angela said, slipping her credit card back into her wallet.

"You were probably just tired, love, sorry I wasn't with you. You do look delicious though. I'm not sure how I'm going to get through this wedding knowing your shoulders are on view – you might even upstage the bride!" Mariam slipped her arm around Angela and tried to kiss her.

"You've had words with your Dad again haven't you?" Angela moved away from her reach and raised an eyebrow.

"No, not really. Same old, same old." Mariam shrugged, feeling caught.

My Mariam. My Mary. She's my love and my rock but she has a battle of her own to fight. It's not that her parents are very religious or anything, it's more a question of not believing in something, our miracle, which is right under their noses. Faith is a strange thing. Mariam is very determined to be out, that's why she wears those T-shirts, that's why she wears those earrings, that's why whenever she has the opportunity she will talk and hound people to express their own sexuality to her. If you're gay then you should be out in her world of creamy brown and white where the Asian gay scene is still gathering momentum and her parents refuse to look at her for more than a few seconds put together. Whenever there is an exchange of words between parents and daughter it makes my love try even harder to be out, makes her more outrageous and determined. It eats her. It devours her. Inside. Outside. I'm on side to protect her, to comfort her but how can I become involved in this personal, family struggle where I'm constantly reminded of how fine my own parents are and how well adjusted and welcoming they are to us both? I can't help but love her parents. They are really sweet and generous people and clearly love her and, though stilted, manage to extend a warmth to me but it's as if they refuse to notice that she has two legs, or two arms, or that we are two. They choose not to see us as lovers. They choose not to see us at all sometimes and weeks go by without them ringing or answering our calls. Other times we may see them several days in a row, spend time eating and laughing and reminiscing together so it almost feels like we're getting somewhere and have accepted each other. It was me they called to come round and see his mother when she was ill, it was me who left that room a few minutes after I'd arrived to tell them that she had slipped away. It was me who signed the death certificate. It was me who bought them the first bunch of sympathy flowers and it was me who drove them home from the temple after mourning prayers. Still they hold me distant. Still I love them. Mariam though, she loves them deep down, deeply in that bottomless loving of hers, the place that crackles and is full of life and thrives on smiling but up here, where we speak not our truest thoughts but our unconsidered hurts, she says she hates them. That's a truth of sorts, I believe that she does hate them but because they never shout at her but resort instead to sniping or that blindness I spoke of before. If they would just open their mouths and throats, crack open that reserved and guarded place that knows but will not say and just scream into her face. She doesn't really know what they think of her, sometimes what they say seems playful and affectionately mocking of her and at other times it's vitriolic; they are inconsistent and it burns her through and through. When they cut her, my Mariam, she turns to me like she's become possessed by a spirit of lust and desire, she has to have me, put hands on me, kiss me, take me, whether in public or private she comes to me and it is sex and aggressive affection she seeks because she has to prove to herself that she is still gay, is still desirable, is still Mariam, in case she loses a grasp

*on herself and becomes the quiet, normal, career girl her parents designed for
her in her cradle. We've never so much as sat next to each other in her
parents' company, with them or without them they always sit between us.*

"I'll wait in the car," Angela said, rummaging for a magazine.

"I don't think so," Mariam snapped back, grabbing the supplement
from Angela's hand and tossing it over her shoulder. "You've got to
come in with me and change anyway or else we'll be late for the
church."

"You're right, I'm sorry." Thankfully Mariam missed the rolling of
the eyes or else she would have exploded.

They walked up to the door and were soundly hugged and kissed
by both mother and father, it was obviously a good day. The house
smelled of warm cake and coffee making their bellies growl and they
were soon ensconced on the three-piece suite with a cup and a plate.
There was a brightly wrapped parcel on the table under the window;
the paper was covered in horseshoes.

"Is that for Mike and Lisa?" asked Mariam.

"Yes," said her mother, "We got them a toaster – one of those old-
fashioned looking chrome ones."

"That's really kind of you both, I'm sure they'll love it." Mariam
smiled. It was extremely sweet of them to buy a wedding present for
her university housemates from two years ago.

"Will you be going to the wedding, Angela?" asked the mother in
all honesty. Angela opened her mouth but someone else was talking.

"Of course she is, Mum. She's my partner," Mariam said loudly.

"What was that you said, Angela?" The mother cocked her head to
hear better.

"I was on placement with Mike for a year," Angela said, glaring at
Mariam.

"Yeah, we used to go out on double dates together," Mariam shot
back.

"He's such a clever and handsome boy, isn't he? I bet he had some
good looking friends, eh?" The father chimed in.

"You might say that," Angela managed, trying not to notice how
furiously Mariam's leg was joggling.

"We're also going to see if we can get some ideas for when we have our commitment ceremony, you know, flowers, caterers and so on." Mariam was not going to let it lie this time. "I'll write the date on the calendar for you, shall I? Just in case you forget. You'll receive a proper invitation, though, nearer the time and of course we'll announce it in the papers – we might even get the ceremony videoed so the family back home can see it too!"

Father and Mother sipped their coffee as if all that had happened was a natural break in the conversation. Angela narrowed her eyes at Mariam and mouthed something rude at her. Mariam had flopped back into her chair in defeat, picking at her cake, tears welling up in her eyes. Angela put her own cup and plate down and realised she was feeling quite angry herself. There was no commitment ceremony. They had never even talked of such a thing. Ever. But she liked to think that should they one day decide to make some kind of public declaration, and it had legal standing, that it would be at a time when Mariam's parents would feel able to join with them to celebrate. Angela rubbed her eye, there was an eyelash in it and it prickled something awful.

"Mariam, have you got any eyewash stuff with you? I've got an eyelash somewhere and it won't come out."

"I could get you some saltwater," Mariam's mother said, perching on the edge of her seat.

"Let me take a look." Mariam got up and Angela stood in the light and tried not to blink as they tenderly tried to remove the offending hair from the corner of her eye. The parents were watching with curiosity and amazement, they had never seen the two of them touch before. The eyelash gone, Angela looked at Mariam and then at her parents, who were still looking at them with surprise, and then Angela leaned into her lover and they kissed. Not a deep kiss but just a sweet, affectionate, thankyou peck before returning to their seats. The father looked quite amused and the mother pressed her hands with contentment into her lap. It was a curious moment, none of them spoke of it but suddenly the room seemed full of relief as if the moment Mariam's parents had feared had passed and wasn't as bad as they had thought it would be.

They left with promises to visit for dinner the next day and, as the car pulled away en route for the wedding, the rear-view mirror showed Mariam's parents framed in the doorway, side by side, one arm around each other and waving fondly with the other.

"We should have done that sooner," Mariam said with a fake tutting noise.

"Yeah, I wonder what they'll do when I throw you over the kitchen counter and spank you with the fish slice."

"Maybe they'll get us a toaster."

Later that evening Mariam and Angela were strolling through the park on the way to the wedding reception in the hotel that overlooked its lake. A little way off Mariam noticed the juggling girl from the previous day. She was laughing and holding, hand over hand, the arms of another girl of about the same age, trying to teach her to juggle with three clubs. It looked like a lot of fun.

"I wish you'd teach me like that," Angela said wistfully.

"You look really beautiful tonight," Mariam whispered, caught up in her own thoughts.

"I know. But you're avoiding the subject! Do you have a monopoly on circus skills or something?"

"I didn't know you wanted to learn," Mariam replied, grinning as the two girls overbalanced trying to retrieve an overthrown club and ended up sprawled on the grass.

"Will you, though?" Angela prodded her lover in the ribs.

"What?"

"Teach me?"

"Of course. But you ought to start out with fruit." Angela looked confused but Mariam just laughed and took her hand and they continued walking as the girls righted themselves and started another upswing.

HELEN SMITH
Whatever You Want

"I'm going to be rich by Christmas," said Jess.

Could this be my best friend speaking? The one who gets her clothes at Dr Barnardo's, laughs when interest rates go up on mortgages, and affords her nicotine habit by smoking my cigs?

"Happy Carrot Kate lent me these tapes. You listen to them and then you can get whatever you want. Get happy, get rich, get anything."

"Beats signing on then," I said.

She nodded. "All you have to do is believe." She paused to light a cigarette.

This was not my sceptical best friend speaking.

"In yourself," she concluded.

Maybe it would work then. Jess does have self-confidence.

"Sixteen of the tapes are instructions on achieving your goals in life, the other four are subliminal messages for the unconscious."

I could imagine the subliminal messages. "Buy more tapes. Buy more tapes."

"The problem is," said Jess, "the tapes tell you how to get in the right frame of mind to get rich, but not exactly how to do it. What sort of business would suit me, do you think?"

"Dope dealing? The rag and bone trade? Turn supergrass?"

Jess looked interested. "It says on Tape 6 that Jealous Friends may try to undermine your confidence."

I couldn't think of an answer to that.

"Anyway," she said, "I'm planning to go in with Laurie Lawson. There's lots of money in slot machines."

I refrained from saying that you need a key to get it out. And I restrained myself from adding that people who play slot machines, which is what Laurie Lawson does for a living, get skint quick. Nor did I say that Laurie Lawson's theories for winning are extremely boring.

And two days later I was quite glad that I hadn't said it. Jess won. I was astonished at the news, and yet she looked quite glum.

"Laurie's not speaking to me," she said. "I thought we could really work together."

"Tell me about winning the money," I said impatiently.

"Well," she said, "I didn't win on my first coin. I was so

disappointed I nearly went home then, but I could hear the voice on the tape saying 'Don't Allow Failure to Frighten You', so I put another one in. All I remember was all the fruits spinning round and Laurie yelling in my ear and suddenly all this stuff was spilling out the bottom."

"Money, you mean?"

"Yes. Tons of it. I had a plastic bag to stick it in because the Visualisation Tape had said to Imagine Success. I told Laurie I was off to the Crown and Cushion, and she started getting all agitated, said it was against all the rules not to put another coin in. So I said to her 'Quit While You're Ahead' and she went bananas, started kicking the machines. The manager threw her out in the end, but she wouldn't come down the pub with me."

"Oh," I said helpfully. "Was that another quote from your tapes, Quit While You're Ahead?"

"No," she said. "I made it up. But I don't need a tape to tell me Don't Act Daft."

"So if you're celebrating," I said, "how about a smoke?"

She gave me another of her interested looks.

"Perhaps if you kept a clear mind," she said, and waved her hand at my collection of half-finished pictures. Sometimes she goes too far.

The next day, when I popped into the Happy Carrot for my week's supply of tamari-coated peanuts, the place was in an uproar. Jess was hanging out by the ecological toilet rolls.

"What's up?" I asked her.

"It's Kate," she said. "I popped in to give her the tapes back, but she's gone. Disappeared. Went off with Saturday's takings. Apparently she's had her hand in the till for months."

"Another of life's winners," I said, but I got no reply off Jess. She was clutching the tapes to her chest, miles away.

The day after that when I went past the Happy Carrot on my way to the laundrette there were two new notices in the window. One was about the collective who'd stepped in to keep the shop open. A 'Dedicated, Unpaid Collective' it said, in a pale, modest ink that looked as if it had been squeezed out of lentils. The other notice was an unmissable Dayglo.

I Got Rich With Magic Tapes!!! it said. I was Programmed to Fail, and Afraid to Achieve, but with these tapes my Life Became a *Success Story*. Don't *You* Deserve to have Your Dreams Come True? Knock Down Price!!! Contact... and there was Jess's phone number.

I suppose, with Kate gone, Jess had inherited the tapes. I was glad she was getting rid of them and packing up the Get Rich business. I just hoped the whole miserable flop wouldn't depress her too much.

She turned up at my place with a smile that split her face.

"What do you think of wholefood collectives?" she asked.

"They'll swallow anything," I said.

"Then get this," she said. "You saw my ad? Well, the Happy Carrot Collective has decided they want to make a go of the shop. They're going to buy the tapes off me so they can work out how to be as rich as me."

"No," I said.

"Believe me," she said. "And buy in a few pounds of those revolting nuts you eat. Prices will be going up, have to, to cover the cost of the tapes."

"How much did you get for them?" I asked.

"Well," Jess paused, but she couldn't resist. "If I mentioned the sum of two hundred pounds all told, would you believe me?"

My mouth did that thing you read about in books, and fell open.

"Mind," she went on, "that includes my fruit machine money, and I did the Happy Carrot a one-day workshop. Mostly on the importance of Keeping a Clear Mind. At the end I suggested they rid themselves of temptation. Look at this."

She went into her pocket and pulled out a hugely promising, bulging, plastic coin bag. She reached for a record sleeve and began putting Rizla papers together in that special way of hers that I love so well.

"Strikes me," she said, "that if you get too carried away by success, you can lose touch with the Important Things in Life."

She sat back, with a great fat spliff lit up in her hand. She played her fingers on it like Groucho Marx on his cigar. "It's nice to be rich," she said, "but is it everything?"

STELLA DUFFY
Ten Times Proud

It is the end of midsummer June, my love. Our time is here again. Like unorthodox Easter or a moon-bound Jewish holiday, our anniversary is a moveable feast.

When Alice and Martha met, there were almost fifty thousand people to witness the event. That was the police estimate, the television and radio reports. From inside we saw a full circle rainbow of at least two million.

On Pride morning I wake you with a slow kiss before the magpies begin their ritual dance on our roof and in our sun-swept bedroom we make an early gentle love that turns as quickly as you turn in me to wanton craving. We do not take our time over this one, there is much to do. Hot and spent you fall asleep in the sweated vessel of our lust. Half an hour later I bring you raspberry jam toast, milky tea and the news that your bath is run. It's time to get up. Good morning.

Martha met Alice at Pride. Ten years ago today their eyes locked over a rolling sea of sweaty bodies and they fell through the dancers and the singers and the drinkers and the sunbathers, past the really out ones (even louder and prouder than usual) and the nearly out ones (who've told the world but not mum and dad) and the completely straight ones (just visiting for the day). Each met the new hail of kindred spirit and they fell into each others' eyes, arms, lives. They are still falling. Alice loves Martha like vertigo. Each year they celebrate their anniversary with a surge of complete strangers and one or two invited guests.

Five years ago it was your aunt, sixty-two and counting. With us for a week from Birmingham and so excited to be going out for the day. Her first march in over fifteen years. She walked between us and told the story of her first husband. She told it quiet and sad. He was her first love, but she was not his. He was her last love, but she was not his. They married in the fifties and even then she was brave and defiant and married a man beyond her social circle. She did not know at the time she had married a man beyond her sexual circle. Gay and not out and no way then of knowing how to be out, he wore a divine mask of suburban endurance. They had their babies and their semi-detached cul-de-sac idyll and a kitchen where he put up shelves and a nursery where she bathed their son and a bedroom where he took his lover. Sometimes he even travelled there with her too. But not so often after a while. And then came the sixties and he was one of the first, the early brave. He was a gay liberationist and she was an early feminist and from husband and wife they graduated to friends and despite their fears, the children were not bullied but envied because their parents were so cool. Your aunt told us this part of the story, the part your family tolerance myth has eclipsed, with no bitterness. Just a tiny, half voiced melancholy, because in spite of all the marches organised from her sitting room and the banners painted in her kitchen and the passion of that swelling political wave, he was still her first love and, after all, it was the fifties.

Alice watched Martha at the Gay Olympics, her girl running down the track from crouching baby to ready set go all woman. Long fast legs taking giant strides to the grandmothers' footsteps crawling beside her. Alice screamed approval, face burning with joy as Martha's lungs burned in exertion. Martha won two medals that day. One in competition placed publicly around her neck and the other which Alice herself kissed into place, low slung around her lover's belly and heavy with wanting. The first medal sits polished on their mantelpiece, the second sits quiet in Martha.

We have worn matching dresses to Pride. Yours blue, mine brown. Short in thin cotton and silly flowers, better with your legs than mine. Yes it was stupid and of course we were freezing half the time, the sun was only occasionally out that day in Kennington Park, but I loved it. Loved the obviousness of our coupling. I have never wanted to be anywhere other than with you. Even before we met, I knew my place was with you. I believe in destiny, but not fate. The dresses were your idea and you do not usually like things like that. Matching me matching you. You are more cool than I know how to be. I am not cool with you. I am hot with you. Warm in warmer places and even your cold white wine turns to heat on my lips.

*

Martha was alone at Pride that first day. She saw Alice dancing on the grass with mutual friends. Saw Alice though a field of tall dancers rippled between them. And she made her way across the park with the deliberation of a visionary. From first sight to first date to first sex took all of ten hours, immutable physical laws contracting space and expanding time to contain their explosive two body collision. Martha is a research physicist, applauded for her knowledge, but even she has no equation for this lust.

We walk through a London changed for the day. Policemen smile and Japanese tourists wave at us from open-topped buses. Corner shops welcome the chocolate crazed walkers and, as old Americans crowd to windows in shock and envy, young Australians and New Zealanders congratulate themselves on so successfully following the route of their mothers and fathers, now made doubly welcome by summer and the discovery of good coffee in central London. This bliss is not without awareness. We know that people will be careful leaving the park. That men will be advised to depart in groups rather than alone. But we are women and the fear of dark places and lone streets follows us anyway, follows us every day. Today is not an exception for the potential for violence, it is an exception in attitude.

Martha and Alice carry an easy light with them and brighten dark corners as they go. There is safety in numbers and they are not two halves of the same whole but ten thousand in one, striding strong and boundless in their pleasure.

Last year we marched with my mother. At this rate we'll pride all the old ladies in the land. Too easily tired to walk very far, ears all drummed out after seventy-six years and over-sensitive to the screamed elation all around, her shapely legs still stirred in misplaced answer to the whistle calls of a thousand men. It's not her fault. They are only limbs, how could they know better. And she smiled at the girls, told again the story of her two "friends in the army", then squealed in delight at the dancing queens. She has always been a dancing queen my mother, and I have inherited her desire for sequins and taffeta and lace, but we sighed in united genetic envy as the beautiful ladies strolled by. Even in our stiletto-stilt heels, my mother and I will never stretch beyond five foot four.

It was a surprise to discover that perfection can be burnt out. Six years ago Pride arrived on its due date, though Alice and Martha were not speaking. Two nights of unsettled and vicious fighting, coarse words like hair pulling and bitter recriminations standing in for bite marks and scratches, they walked exhausted from each other and drained by the hate. Martha and Alice marched three feet apart in silence and fear. The following week when the full moon passed and the aftermath of jealous rage was a soft bruised quiet, they walked again. Together alone, they pride-paraded wet summer London, penance rain walk for the week before.

We have stolen uncertain kisses in Prague and Athens and Barcelona and Sydney and New York and Paris, poached them a little more certain in Amsterdam and pickpocketed them so obviously in Old Compton Street. But in the street on Pride day your arm is around mine and stays there, afternoon sun burning your imprint on to my skin. You have three inches more height than I, which gives you greater purchase to hold me tight and we walk together and when I feel like it, which is very often, I turn up my face and kiss you. All day. Like the couples in the tube and the couples at the airport and the couples at their weddings. And usually we wouldn't want to be those couples anyway. We are more private with our passion, almost enjoy the need to save it up, the exquisite tension of sexual waiting. Besides, you think it's rude to slobber over your lover on the Northern line, I just think it's dull. Too teenage to be worth the sore lips. But on that special collection of afternoon hours the summerlight softness of your lips sends a lightning rod from my mouth to my cunt and I am easily sixteen.

Martha and Alice expect Pride to remain theirs forever. Not just London Pride either. Theirs is an international hubris. They have planned trips away, Mardi Gras and Hero and Europride and Manchester and New York and San Francisco. Weekday trips as innocuous girl partners to galleries and quiet cottages and evenings of theatre and recommended local cuisine and then a fiery weekend of the abandoned obvious.

This is what happens to us every year. This is what we do.

And then – this is what we did.

Alice and Martha will not walk Pride together again. In ten years they have used up far more than a lifetime's love.

And so to today. I walk with you now, holding you close through streets of colour and life and vision. From the corner of my eye I catch the pitying glances, the concern of our friends and family, but assure them they do not need to worry about me. Not today. Tomorrow may belong to my grief, as did yesterday, as will all the days to come, but today is ours. In the midnight calm of a hot London night, a parade of dancing lovers crosses the river and I set you free on the Thames. I breathe deep and slow, hold the sigh long enough to feel you breathing in me. There is understanding and there is knowledge. I understand that I kissed the grey lips. I understand I will sleep alone tonight. But this is not what I know. I know you are not gone. You are not cold. I am not alone. I know that I will hold you forever living warm in me. Happy Anniversary my darling.

Don't cry. Alice and Martha had a perfect love. So really, no one died and nothing bad ever happened and they both lived happily ever after.

Of course they did.

I miss you.

JEANIE O'HARE
The Guinea Pig

The hailstones hit the window like God was out to get someone. Marianne loitered around the kitchen then shuffled along to the study to look through the crack in the door. Sarah was staring at her screen and tapping rapidly at the keys. Marianne made a scratching noise on the door.

"Play?"

Without looking up Sarah threw a stapler at the door. It shut. As Marianne walked away she shouted back to the study that she was 'going gardening' and went outside in her slippers.

It was icy underfoot. The bread she had thrown around earlier was now fixed to the ground. A few hailstones lay scattered. She crunched away from the house and away from the study window and stood at the bottom of the garden drinking her coffee, looking back at the house. They had bought it together, breathlessly, four years ago, as somewhere to be naked. At least that was how it seemed to Marianne at the time. Sarah didn't care too much for nakedness these days.

Sarah was draining the last drops from the cafetiere as Marianne wiped her feet by the back door. She stirred in half a sugar. Marianne spoke first.

"Why don't we go for a walk after lunch?"

"Hmmm."

She sipped her coffee, glanced at the day's headlines, then used the yes which means no. She said she would see how her work was going. Just before the study door clicked shut she added that Robin would be coming back from his Dad's after tea. Marianne sat down with the paper and wrote 'FUCK' in all the four-letter spaces on the crossword then went out to the newsagents to buy another copy.

Sarah didn't come out of the study until Robin arrived at six. She gave him broccoli, fish fingers, a bath and a bedtime story. She spent all evening on the phone.

Marianne was making pastry in the kitchen. She caught a small moth under the rolling pin. She cut a perfect square all around it and lifted it out of the sheet of pastry. She washed the rolling pin and closed up the postage stamp hole with short quick movements from all sides. When she had finished trimming the piecrust she picked up the insect to look at it. One antenna quivered. She placed the square of pastry on the centre of the pie and put the pie in the oven. She watched through the glass door as the moth curled and blackened in the heat.

Sarah was on the phone to someone Marianne assumed was Robin's Dad. She was giggling. Marianne took two glasses of wine through to the living room and listened for the change in tone. Sarah talked seriously about swimming lessons and weekend access.

"Dinner will be ready soon."

Sarah hung up.

"Robin's coming to stay over half-term. Do you mind?"

Marianne took a mouthful of wine.

"No, not at all. It'll be fun."

Half-term was soon with them. Robin brought with him the guinea pig that was a present from his Dad. It was black, shiny and ran in straight lines along the edge of the carpet. Robin called his pet Captain Black.

"Is he indestructible Captain Black?" Marianne inquired.

"No silly. That's indestructible Captain Scarlet."

Marianne took the animal and turned it over in the palm of her hand. She stroked its soft belly and, with her thumb and forefinger, squeezed the area between the hind legs. Something tiny and pink appeared.

"Look Robin, it's a boy!"

Robin took his pet back and held it on his shoulder.

"The man in the shop already told me that."

Monday afternoon was quiet. Marianne sat on one side of the kitchen table and Robin sat on the other. He gripped his wax crayon tightly and drew loose approximations of Captain Black. As he finished each drawing he climbed off his seat, went into the study and returned with a fresh sheet of paper. Marianne turned over the last of the sports pages.

"What's Mummy doing?"

Robin continued drawing as he spoke. "Working!"

"Robin darling, look at me when you talk to me." Robin looked at Marianne. Marianne stared back, then smiled.

"OK, go back to your drawing... and keep your crayons tidy."

Marianne made herself some fresh coffee and wandered around the kitchen circling the table. She blew on her coffee without drinking, sighing with every step. Robin concentrated on his colouring-in: this was a blue guinea pig with orange ears. Marianne poured her coffee down her leg.

"Ow! Fuck!"

Robin looked up as Marianne was plucking steaming fabric away from her scalding skin.

"Quick! Go tell Mummy I'm hurt."

Sarah came running, Robin bobbing along after her. She stopped when she saw the scene in front of her. The two women locked eyes. Sarah said nothing. She let her shoulders drop.

"Well done Robin." She turned and kissed him on the forehead then returned to her work.

After lunch Marianne suggested to Robin that they play with Captain Black.

"Robin, you must learn how to look after him."

"I do look after him."

"Do you know that humans and guinea pigs don't produce their own vitamin C?"

"No."

She taught Robin to say 'vitamin C' and rattled for his attention the child-proof plastic container she found in the kitchen. She wanted him to know exactly what he was doing. While humming the tune of *Animal Hospital* she showed Robin how to drop pellets of the vitamin through the bars of the cage.

"Do you know what you are doing Robin?"

"Yeah I am giving Captain Black his vitamin C."

Marianne rolled the pellets with her fingers. She made about thirty from the wad of cotton wool she found stoppering the plastic jar of orange tablets. Robin dropped them through the bars of the cage and Captain Black gobbled them up.

At about 9.46pm Robin ran from his bedroom to the television room with Captain Black sliding around the bottom of an old Nike shoe box. Marianne, Sarah and Robin stared into the box. Captain Black was struggling for breath. Every few seconds he made a small squeak.

"Weet... weet." The sound became softer and weaker.

There were about ten seconds before anyone noticed that the moment had come and gone. Robin dropped the box to the floor and threw his arms around his mum.

Marianne picked up the animal from where it bounced and asked Robin if he wanted to stroke him, "While he is still warm." Robin stopped crying. He was tempted. Sarah pulled him away. Marianne sat in the armchair stroking the animal belly up listening to Robin asking why Captain Black had stopped breathing.

"Was it because I gave him too much vitamin C?"

"No, of course not darling. You did your best. Some guinea pigs are born weak and no matter what you do, they find it hard to survive."

By half ten everyone was in bed.

Breakfast was earlier than usual the next day because Sarah was off to London. Robin sat in the kitchen eating while Marianne put Captain Black into his coffin. She sealed the cereal box with strips of sellotape pulled loudly off the roll. Robin stared at the black ribbon she tied neatly around the package and spoke quietly.

"Is there any vitamin C in my Rice Krispies?"

"No. But there is calcium in the milk."

He was subdued during the short ceremony under the tree. Robin waved goodbye to Captain Black as Sarah pushed some earth back into the hole. Rain was falling in big drops from the branches. Sarah gave him a hug.

"It's time for me to go. I'll be back late, I'll come in and see you."

Marianne stepped aside to let Sarah pass.

"Will you be late?"

Sarah looked stranded for a moment then kissed Marianne. "No... no. See you later."

"Don't worry. I'll cheer him up. We'll have a nice day. Wave, Robin." Robin waved to his Mother.

When Sarah had gone Marianne took out her penknife and showed Robin how to carve the Captain's initials into the tree trunk. His hands were too cold for the task. He let the knife drop.

"You're not going to cry again are you? You have to finish his initials or he won't go to pet heaven."

"Did he die because he was weak?"

"Maybe."

"Am I weak?"

"Yes."

Robin picked up the knife and started sticking it into the ground. Marianne realised that if he did it any harder he would stab Captain Black. She took the knife and carved two neat, deep initials.

Marianne and Robin got on with their Tuesday together. Marianne cooked lunch while Robin tidied the tins in the cupboard. He was quiet and kept looking at his reflection in the concentric circles of the soup tin lids. She extended the game after lunch and persuaded Robin to tidy all his toys into the garage. He played quietly in there for the rest of the day.

That afternoon Marianne got a call. Sarah would have to stay in London overnight, meetings were running late and there was no way she could make the last train. She would be home in the morning. Sarah asked how Robin was.

"D'you want me to send him back to his dad's for the night?"

"No," snapped Sarah. Then more tenderly, "You can see to him tonight can't you?"

"I see more of him than I do of you these days. We really must..." Sarah's money ran out.

*

Marianne cooked pork chops for tea. She watched the rind blister and spit under the grill. She left her portion to cook a little longer while she served Robin.

"I can do it myself."

"I'm just being nice."

She cut the meat into big pinkish squares. The meat was tender and juicy. He forked the first square into his mouth.

"Do you know about protein Robin?"

He stared at her while chewing a quantity of pork he could barely move around his mouth. He was still chewing five minutes later when Marianne put her meal on a tray.

"I'm going to watch the news. You stay here until you've finished."

She ate while flicking through the channels then dozed through the weather forecast. Something woke her up. She turned the telly up. "...INCREASED CHANCE OF HEAVY SHOWERS THROUGH THE NIGHT." The sound continued. Marianne realised it was the sound of choking. She picked up her tray and went into the kitchen.

"Are you OK?"

He nodded. There were tears in his eyes and his cheeks were flushed with panic. He had only eaten three pieces of meat. The rest were cold. Two were half chewed on the side of his plate including the most recently regurgitated. Marianne picked him up and hugged him.

"There, there. Are you sure it's all gone?"

"Yes." She looked at him.

"Your Mum would hate anything to happen to you." She hugged him tightly.

"Good job I was here. It could have been terrible... just think... I'd suffer from post-traumatic stress disorder, your Mum would have to comfort me, we'd get to spend some time together, maybe go to grief counselling together... d'you have any idea what I'm talking about Robin?" He shook his head.

Marianne gave him some Angel Delight and put him to bed in fresh pyjamas. She sat with him for a while and hummed a slowed down version of the *Top Gear* theme.

"I'm not sleepy."

"Goodnight."

At eight o'clock Marianne wandered into the kitchen for some more wine. She found Robin there whimpering in his pyjamas. He had fallen off the counter by the noticeboard and lay on the kitchen floor in a heap.

"What were you doing up there?"

"I wanted the number."

Robin's Dad's number was written on a scrap of paper pinned to the noticeboard. Marianne took it and handed it to him.

"Here."

Robin moved to the chair by the phone but was still too crumpled to do anything useful. Marianne noticed he had started to cry.

"What's wrong?"

"I want to go home."

"That's fine by me."

She took the number from him and went to the phone in the living room. She dialled the number. Sarah answered. Marianne couldn't speak.

"Hello who is it?"

Marianne hung up and looked straight at Robin. She thought for a moment.

"Your Dad's not at home Robin. You'll have to stay with me."

Robin leant on the door frame, not knowing whether to leave the room or stay. He stared at the carpet then moved wearily back to the kitchen. He picked up his Action Man and settled on the bottom stair in the hallway.

The phone rang. It was Sarah.

"Where are you?"

"I'm at Peter's. You know I am. You just rang."

"What are you doing there?"

"Talking... about Robin."

"You said you couldn't come home tonight. Peter only lives ten miles away. Get him to drive you."

"He's had a drink... we've had a drink."

"Get a cab." There was no response.

"Are you coming home tonight or what?"

"We've got a lot to talk about. It's Robin."

"ROBIN!" Marianne shrieked, Robin came running. "Robin is here with me. Are you coming home?"

The line went quiet for several minutes. Marianne pressed the receiver hard to her ear, desperate to hear what they were saying. Sarah came back on the line.

"I'm getting a cab. I'll be there in twenty five minutes," she paused, "Marianne... this isn't how it looks."

Marianne put the phone back in its cradle. The receiver had left a deep red impression on the side of her face. Robin had gone back to sitting on the bottom step staring at the front door. She walked over to him. He jumped. She studied herself in the hall mirror. She turned to look at him. He spoke without looking up.

"What?"

"Get your shoes on we're going for a drive."

It was wet on the roads and the car was cold. Marianne had not picked up her coat and Robin had just his anorak over his pyjamas. He was shivering. She drove towards the ring road. Robin clicked and clicked and clicked his seat belt.

"This isn't the way to my house."

"LEAVE your seatbelt alone."

They drove for an hour along the bypass onto the motorway past the airport. Robin stayed quiet. He seemed mesmerised by the orange lights overhead. He was briefly excited by the sight of a white bellied 747. Then he remembered.

"This isn't the WAY to my house."

Marianne slowed down and parked on the hard shoulder. She switched off the windscreen wipers and looked at Robin who was now pulling the eyebrows off his Action Man.

"Don't do that Robin."

He stopped. They waited. The car rocked as a lorry passed by. Spray covered the car. Robin started kicking the back of Marianne's seat. She spun around to tell him off, but thought better of it.

"What is it?" he asked, "What?"

She turned away and watched the traffic. She bounced her head gently off the top of the steering wheel. She checked her reflection in the rear view mirror. The red mark left by the telephone had faded. There were tears in her eyes.

Without warning she pulled the keys out of the ignition and got out of the car. The rain chilled her in seconds. Her hair darkened. She stood on the hard shoulder looking back into the car. She was soaked, rain in her eyes, rain in her ears. She circled the car. She waved to Robin. He seemed to be waving her back into the car, out of the rain. Another lorry splashed by. She backed away onto the grass. She let the keys drop from her hand onto the water-logged embankment. Robin stood up between the seats, watching her. She knew it was her move. She walked backwards out of the light until she knew he couldn't see her anymore, then clambered up the muddy slope and ran.

EMMA DONOGHUE
The Cost Of Things

Cleopatra was exactly the same age as their relationship. They found this very funny and always told the story at dinner parties. Liz would mention the coincidence a little awkwardly, then Sophie, laughing as she scraped back her curls in her hands, would persuade her to spit out the details. Or sometimes it would be the other way round. They prided themselves on not being stuck in patterns. They each had things the other hadn't – Liz's triceps, say, and Sophie's antique rings – but so what? Friends would probably have said that Sophie was the great romantic, who'd do anything for love, whereas Liz was the quiet dependable type, loyal to the end. But then what did friends know, what could friends imagine of the life that went on in a house after the guests had gone home? Liz and Sophie knew that roles could be shed as easily as clothes; they were sure that none of their differences mattered.

They had met a few months before Cleopatra, but it was like a room before the light is switched on. After the party where they were introduced, Sophie decided Liz looked a bit like a younger Diane Keaton, and Liz knew Sophie reminded her of one of those French actresses but could never remember which. At first, their conversations were like anybody else's.

Then on one of her days off from the gardening centre Liz had come round to Sophie's place to help her put up some shelves in the spare bedroom. Sophie insisted she'd pay, of course she would, and Liz said she wouldn't take a dollar, though they both knew she could do with the money. When the drill died down they thought they heard something. Such a faint sound, Liz thought it was someone using a chainsaw, several houses down, but then Sophie pointed out that it was a bit like a baby crying. Anyway, she held the second shelf against the wall for Liz to mark the holes. They were standing so close that Liz could see the different colours in each of Sophie's rings, and Sophie could feel the heat coming off Liz's bare shoulder. Then that sound came again, sharper.

They found the kitten under the porch, after they'd tried everywhere else. Its mother must have left it behind. Black and white, eyes still squeezed shut, it was half the size of Sophie's cupped hand. Now, Liz would probably have made a quick call to the Animal Shelter and left it at that. She didn't know then how quickly and completely Sophie could fall in love.

It knew it was onto a good thing, this kitten; it clung to Sophie's fingers like a cactus. They said it for the first few days, not knowing much about feline anatomy. It was hard to give a kitten away, they found, once the vet told you she was a she, and especially once you knew her name. They hadn't meant to name her, but it was a long hour and a half in the queue at the vet's and it started out as a joke, what a little Cleopatra she was, said Liz, because the walnut-sized face in the corner of the shoebox was so imperious.

Sophie was clearly staggered by the bill of $200 for the various shots, but soon she was joking that it was less than she spent on shoes, most months. Liz was a little shocked to hear that, but then, Sophie did wear very nice shoes. Sophie plucked out her Visa card and asked the receptionist for a pen, it having been her porch the kitten was left under. Liz, watching her sign with one long flowing stroke, decided the woman was magnificent. Her hand moved to her own wallet and she spent ten minutes forcing a hundred-dollar bill into Sophie's breast pocket, arguing that they had, after all, found the kitten together.

Cleopatra now belonged to both of them, Sophie joked as Liz carried the box to the car, or rather, both of them belonged to her. It was, what was the word, serendipitous.

That first evening they left the kitten beside the stove in her shoebox with a saucer of milk, hoping she wouldn't drown in it, and went upstairs to unbutton each other's clothes. So, give or take a day or two, they and Cleopatra began at the same time.

These days she was a stout, voluptuous five-year-old, her glossy black and white hairs drifting through every room of the ground-floor apartment where Liz now paid half the rent, never having meant to move in exactly but having got in the habit of coming over to see how the kitten was doing so often that before she knew it, this was home. On summer evenings, when Sophie took out the clippers to give Liz a No. 3 cut on the porch, Cleopatra would abuse the fallen tufts as if they were mice. There was a velvet armchair in the lounge no one else was allowed sit on, and in the mornings if they delayed bringing her breakfast, the cat would lift the sheet and bite the nearest toe, not hard but as a warning.

They had a fabulous dinner party to celebrate their anniversary, five years being, as Liz announced, approximately ten times as long as she had ever been with anybody else. Three of their guests had brought champagne, which was just as well, considering how hard Liz and Sophie were finding it to keep their heads above water these days. Sophie's hair salon had finally gone out of business, and Liz's health plan didn't stretch to same-sex partners.

Over coffee and liqueurs they were prevailed upon to tell the old story of finding the kitten the very day they got together, and then Sophie showed their guests the marks Cleopatra had left on her hands over the years. Sophie had bought an appallingly expensive steel claw clippers at a pet shop downtown, but the cat would never let anyone touch her feet. Her Highness was picky that way, said Liz, scratching her under her milk-white chin.

They knew shouldn't have let her lick the plates after the smoked salmon linguini, but she looked so wonderfully decadent, tonguing up traces of pink cream. That night when they had gone to bed to celebrate the best way they knew how, the cat threw up on the Iranian carpet Liz's mother had lent them. It was Sophie who cleaned it up the next morning, before she brought Liz her coffee. Cleopatra wasn't touching her food bowl, she reported. She must be still stuffed with salmon, the beast, said Liz, clicking her tongue to invite Cleopatra in the bedroom door.

The next day she still wasn't eating more than a mouthful. Liz said it was just as well, really, Cleopatra could do with losing a few pounds, but Sophie picked up the cat and said that wasn't funny.

They'd been planning to take her to the new Cat Clinic down the road to have her claws clipped at some point anyway. It took a while to get her into the wicker travel basket; Liz had to pull her paws off the rim one by one while Sophie pressed down the lid an inch at a time, nervous of trapping her tail. The cat turned her mutinous face from the window so all they could see was a square of ruffled black fur.

The Clinic was a much more swish place than the other vet's, and Liz thought maybe they should have asked for a list of prices in advance, but the receptionist left them alone in the examining room before she thought of it. Cleopatra could obviously smell the ghost aromas of a thousand other cats. She sank down and tucked everything under her except her thumping tail. The place was too much like a dentist's waiting room, but Liz, who knew that Sophie relied on her to be calm, read the posters aloud and pretended to find them funny. 'Why Your Furry Friend Loves You,' said one poster on the wall. 'In Sickness and In Health,' began another. The two of them whispered to each other and gave the cat little tickles, as if this sterile shelf was some kind of playground.

Dr McGraw came in then, spoke to the cat as if he was her best friend but stroked her in the wrong place, above her tail, which flapped like an enemy flag. When he took hold of her face, her paw came round so fast that she left a red line down the inside of his wrist. Liz and Sophie apologised over and over, like the parents of a delinquent child. Dr McGraw, dabbing himself with disinfectant, told them to think nothing of it. Then he called in Rosalita to wrap the cat in a towel.

Swaddled in flannel, Cleopatra stared at the doctor's face as if memorising it for the purposes of revenge. He put a sort of gun in her ear to take her temperature, and bared her gums in an artificial smile to see if they were dehydrated. He squeezed her stomach and kidneys and bladder, and she made a sound they'd never heard before, in a high voice like a five-year-old girl's, but it was hard to tell if she was tender in the areas he was pressing, or just enraged.

Liz had to make out the cheque for $50 as Sophie was already up to her Visa limit. They carried the basket to the car, Cleopatra's weight lurching from side to side. They laughed on the way home, and called her Killer Kat; the vet wouldn't try calling her Sweetums next time.

That night on the couch Sophie yawned as she put down her book, let her head drop into Liz's lap, and asked in a lazy murmur, what was she thinking? In fact, Liz had been fretting over her overdraft, and wondering whether they could cancel cable as they hardly ever watched it anyway, but she knew that was not what Sophie wanted to hear, so she grinned down at her and said, guess. Which wasn't a lie. Sophie smiled back and pulled Liz down until her shirt covered Sophie's face, then they didn't need to say anything.

Cleopatra still wasn't eating much the next day, but she seemed bright-eyed. Sophie said the Clinic had rung, and wasn't that thoughtful?

The following evening when Liz came home the cat wasn't stirring from her chair. Liz began to let herself worry. Don't worry, she told Sophie as she dropped her work clothes in the laundry basket, cats can live off their fat for a good while.

The two of them were tangled up in the bath, rubbing lavender oil into each other's feet, when the phone rang. It was Rosalita from the Clinic. Liz felt guilty for the cheerful way she'd answered the phone, and made her voice sadder at once.

Rosalita was concerned about little Cleo, how was she doing?

Liz didn't like people who nicknamed without permission; she'd never let anyone call her Lizzy, except Sophie, sometimes. Not bad, she supposed, she told Rosalita, hard to tell, about the same really.

By the time she could put the phone down her nipples were stiff with cold. She'd left lavender-scented footprints all the way down the stairs. When she got back to the bathroom Sophie had let all the water out and was painting her nails purple. What did she mean, the cat was not bad, Sophie wanted to know? The cat was obviously not well.

Liz said she knew. But they could hardly take her for daily checkups at $50 a go, and surely they could find a cheaper vet in the Yellow Pages.

No way, said Sophie, because Cleopatra had already begun a course of treatment with the Clinic and they were being wonderful.

Liz thought it was all a bit suspect, these follow-up calls. The Clinic stood to make a lot of money from exaggerating every little symptom, didn't they?

Sophie said one of the things she'd never found remotely attractive about Liz was her cynicism. She went down to make herself a cup of camomile and didn't even offer to put on the milk for Liz's hot chocolate. When Liz came down Sophie was curled up on the sofa with the cat on her lap, the two of them doing their telepathy thing.

Liz thought Sophie was probably premenstrual but didn't like to say so, knowing what an irritating thing it was to be told, especially if you were.

She knew she was right about that the next day when Sophie came in from a pointless interview at a salon downtown and started vacuuming at once. In five years Liz had learned to leave Sophie to it, but she was only halfway down the front page of the paper when she heard her name being called, so loudly that she thought there must be an emergency.

Sophie, her foot on the vacuum's off switch, had dragged the velvet armchair out from the wall and was pointing. What did Liz call that, she wanted to know?

Vomit, I guess, said Liz.

Why hadn't she said something?

Because she didn't know about it, said Liz, feeling absurdly like a suspect. Yes, she'd been home all day, but she hadn't heard anything. A cat being sick was not that loud. Yes, she cared, of course she cared, what did Sophie mean didn't she care?

That night Sophie didn't come to bed at all. Liz sat up reading a home improvement magazine, and fell asleep with the light on.

The next day Rosalita called at eight in the morning when Liz was opening a fresh batch of bills, before she'd had her coffee. Nerves jangling, Liz was very tempted to tell Rosalita to get lost. She wondered whether the Clinic was planning to charge her for phone consultations. Hang on, she said, I'll be right back. She went into the kitchen to look at Cleopatra, who was lying on her side by the fridge like a beached whale and hadn't touched her water, even. Sophie was kneeling beside her on the cold tiles. Liz wanted to touch Sophie but instead she stroked the cat, just how she usually liked it, one long combing from skull to hips, but there was no response.

Sophie went next door to the phone and asked Rosalita for an appointment. Please, Liz heard her say, her voice getting rather high, and then, after a minute, thanks, thank you, thanks a lot.

Liz took the afternoon off work and brought the car home by two, as promised.

That afternoon the two of them stood in the examining room at the Clinic, staring at the neatly printed estimate. Rosalita had left them alone for a few minutes, to talk it all over, as she said with a sympathetic smile. The disinfected walls of the little white room seemed to close in around them. Cleopatra crouched between Sophie's arms. Liz was reading the list for the third time as if it was a difficult poem.

After a minute she said, "I still don't really get it."

Sophie, staring into the green ovals of Cleopatra's eyes, said nothing.

"I know she's sick. But surely she can't be as sick as all that," Liz went on. "Like, she still purrs."

Sophie scratched behind the cat's right ear. Cleopatra shook her head vehemently, then subsided again.

"It's not that I'm not worried." Liz's voice sounded stiff and theatrical in the tiny room. She went on, a little lower. "But eleven hundred dollars?" It sounded even worse out loud.

"That's an extraordinary amount of money," said Liz, "and number one we haven't got it –"

At last Sophie's head turned. "I can't believe we're even having this discussion," she said in a whisper.

"We're not having it," said Liz heavily. "It's not a discussion till you say something."

"Look at her," pleaded Sophie. "Look at her eyes." There was a tiny crust of mucus at the corner of each. "They've never been dull before, like the light's been switched off."

"I know, sweetheart," said Liz. She stared at the crisp print to remember her arguments. "But eleven hundred dollars –"

"She's our cat," Sophie cut in. "This is Cleopatra we're talking about."

"But we don't even know for sure if there's anything serious wrong with her."

"Exactly," said Sophie. "We don't know. We haven't a clue. That's why I can't sleep at night. That's why we're going to pay them to test her for kidney stones, and leukaemia, and FOP disease, and anything else it could possibly be."

"FIP," Liz read off the page. "FIP disease. And it's a vaccine, not a test."

"Whatever," growled Sophie. "Don't pretend to be an expert; all you're looking at is the figures."

"Hang on, hang on," said Liz, louder than she meant to. "Let's look at it item by item. Hospitalisation, intravenous catheter insertion... Jesus, $60 to put a tube up her ass, that can't be more than thirty seconds work. IV fluids, OK, fair enough. X-rays... why does she need three X-rays? She's less than two foot long."

Sophie was chewing her lipstick off. "I can't believe you're mean enough to haggle at a time like this."

"How can you call me mean?" protested Liz. "I just get the feeling we're being ripped off. This is emotional blackmail, they think we can't say no."

There was a dull silence. She listened out for other voices from other rooms, and wondered if Rosalita was standing outside the door, listening.

"Look," she went on more calmly, "if we left out these optional blood tests we could trim off maybe three hundred dollars. What the hell is feline AIDS anyway? Cleopatra's a virgin."

"I don't know what it is, but what if she has it?" asked Sophie. "What if two months down the road she's dying of it and you were too damn callous to pay for a test?"

"It's probably just crystals in her bladder," said Liz weakly, "the doctor said so, didn't he?"

Sophie curled over Cleopatra, whose eyes were half-shut as if she was dreaming. Liz stared around her at the cartoon cats on the walls, with their pert ears and manic grins.

After a few minutes' silence, she thought they'd probably got past the worst point of the row. Now if she could only think of something soothing to say, they'd be onto the home stretch.

But Sophie stood up straight and folded her arms. "So what is she worth then?"

"Sorry?"

"A hundred dollars? Two hundred?"

Liz sighed. "You know I'm mad about her."

"Yeah?"

"I can't put a figure to it."

"Really?" spat Sophie. "But it's definitely under eleven hundred, though, we know that much."

"We don't have eleven hundred dollars," said Liz, word by word.

"We could get it."

She was finding it hard to breathe in here. "You know I can't take out another loan, not so soon after the car."

"Then I'll sell my grandmother's fucking rings," said Sophie, slamming her hand on the counter with a metallic crack. "Or would it make your life simpler if we just had her put down here and now?"

"Give me the damn form," said Liz, pulling the estimate towards her and digging in her pocket for her pen.

Sophie watched without a word as Liz signed, her hands shaking.

Dr McGraw carried Cleopatra away to the cages. The cat watched them over his shoulder, unforgivingly.

Out in the car, Sophie sat with the empty basket on her lap. Liz couldn't tell if she was crying without looking at her directly, but she had a feeling she was, like in their early days when they went to the cinema a lot and Liz always knew just when Sophie needed her to reach over and take her hand.

She drove home, taking corners carefully.

"I'm just curious," said Sophie at a traffic light. "What would you pay for me?"

"What?" Liz's voice came out like a squeal of brakes.

"If I was rushed into A&E and a doctor handed you an estimate. What would I be worth to you?"

Liz told her to shut the fuck up.

Rosalita rang the same evening, her voice bright. Crystals in the bladder, that's all it was. Little Cleo was doing fine, had taken well to the new diet, and they could pick her up the next morning. That would be just $98, they could pay by cheque.

So the cat came home, and for a while everything seemed like it ever was.

And when six months later Sophie left Liz for a beautician she met at the Cosmetic Academy, and moved into the beautician's condo in a building with a strict no-pets policy, Liz used to hold onto Cleopatra at night, hold her so tight that the cat squirmed, and think about the cost of things.

FRANCES BINGHAM
Double Tongue

Yes, it's true. I have got one. Although, of course, it has its advantages in life, I usually keep my double tongue hidden. Sometimes it shows accidentally, the flicker of lightning in my ordinary talk. Sometimes I can tell that people have guessed there's something strange, some secret, by the odd looks they give me. Most often, everyone is so sure that you can only have one tongue, that it's how everyone is, that it doesn't occur to them there might be another filling my mouth. (Forked or cloven things aren't natural.) If my second tongue slips out, sometimes I try and cover it up, sometimes I try and explain. Let me explain.

Most words mean two different things to me. They have two disparate meanings, depending on which tongue I'm using. I'm not talking about shades of emphasis, the inevitable variations in perception of language's exact sense which keep communication approximate, like white noise interfering with perfect reception. No, I mean lots of everyday, working words have a double life, can quick-change into alternative selves, costumed or undisguised depending on your viewpoint. I don't find it confusing in my own speech; I know what I mean. But sometimes I find that I'm reading my own sense into texts which are untranslatable, by intention. That can cause problems of interpretation, especially since my private language is unofficial, the dialect which is not accepted usage.

Take the word 'boy', for instance, a commonplace little word. Boy is not an attractive concept to me. It speaks of loud, callow males, intrusive and irrelevant. Little boys are nasty, big boys are nasty; that was what I thought when I was younger, the last time I considered boys. Boys are not a subject of interest. It is not a word freighted with significance. But then, the same word in the mirror, the other vocabulary which sounds the same but carries its cargo of sense heavy below the water-line. 'Boy' as in beautiful lesbian boy, the boyish dyke of the small ads, boy as shorthand for handsome strong woman. That is a different story. Oh, boy, now you're talking.

All boys together, smooth-faced and crop-headed, big-booted, lounge-suited, we swagger and tease. We're all heroes and handsome, we boydykes, well-muscled seventh sons of seventh sons, always ready to stride off in our seven-league boots, or ride away into the sunset (providing the fairytale woman comes too). We're all great lovers, of course, as you can tell by something about the eyes. Fancy yourselves as God's gift to women? Well yes we do, actually. We boys with breasts think women were made for each other. There are boys in their leathers still straddling invisible Harleys, butch icons doing a James Dean lean on the bar, and slick gigolo boys, brilliantined matinée idols wearing braces and mascara. There are boys who cross-dress and go to work in a skirt, hiding their tattoos under an office blouse, and boys who would rather starve. There are boys who smile and boys who scowl; the one thing they have in common is that they don't want boys of the other sort. In my curious dialect, it's never the girls and the men, it's always the boys and the women, and they're both female.

Maybe this seems an obvious case of a subculture appropriating mainstream vocabulary for use as a code. Of course there's some truth in that; I do know dykespeak quite well. And nearly everyone has a private language of sorts; slang, jargon, foreign adoptions, even if they're not fluent. But my second tongue is a bit more obscure than that; it co-exists so closely sometimes that it's hard for me to remember that my version may not be authorised. Holy, let's say, is a word I use quite often, but I mean it. I don't mean holy: churchy, pious, sanctimonious, hypocritical. There is a meaning there to make me shudder. I think of a congregation of cardigans, vying for tea with the vicar, staring with hard curiosity which soon turns to malice. I think of a claustrophobic world where images of torture are presented for worship, of mourning women whose only life is in reproducing their men, of the bloody cross embedded in old cotton-wool. Holy jumble sales. Smelly relics in hot churches. A muddle of different associations, all bad.

What I hold sacred is holy to me, however; and my holy is different. My lover is the high priestess of our obscure religion, she is dedicated to it, and she knows its power. She can cast out my demons, exorcise them and hold them at bay with her calm gaze, level unblinking eyes compelling them to feel their incongruity, and depart. Always where she goes there is the aura of the holy place, the calm of the bright sanctuary, the leaf-susurrus of the sacred grove. Under her protection I am safe, favoured, my dreams auspicious and the omens lucky. There are offerings we make to this deity, not to propitiate but in gratitude, gifts it is necessary to give. We tend the flame, keep the spring welling up clear, feed the temple doves on honeycakes. And the shrine is the place we are in, the altar the bed we lie on, the rites those of love.

Nor is it that my holy is pagan, and the alien holy christian; there is room in my holy for that iconography too. My lover is holy to me as a wild angel with great fierce wings, who swoops down to enfold me in ecstasy. She changes my water to wine on a daily basis. As my good bread, my strong wine, salt-of-the-earth, milk and honey, she spreads a feast for us which is a communion of sweet delights and solid nourishment, a eucharist I should taste daily for the good of my soul. And, though she's no saint in many respects, I've undoubtedly put her on a pedestal; a beautiful image which works miracles. She brings me to my knees. To me, our love is holy, holy, holy.

So now do I need to translate into my own tongue and say that by 'lover' I don't mean my shadow, echo, twin or doppelganger? And nor am I hers. She may be a mirror to me (as I am to her), but there is no narcissism in our gazing at each other. When I look at her, I see the difference between our so-called similarities; we measure our hands against each other's and they are not alike. Yet when I see myself reflected as she sees me, it's the perfect looking-glass for me to go through, not distorting, not magnifying, just a little rose-tinted. I see myself as her lover; the gypsy who could charm her down from her tower to dance in the snow and ride off in my coloured caravan, the poet who would wait all night beneath her window, the sailor returning to the warm house by the hill, the handsome stranger who kissed her under the apple tree. I like these selves.

So what is she? How does she see herself reflected in my eyes?

My lover is the beloved to me, of course, my muse, my madonna, made for love. She's also the lonely genius, the hermit artist who creates out of her white hot passion, who's a priestly magician by virtue of her powers. I'm fuel to her fire. But there's more to her picture in me – how can I put it?

Say, she's a mermaid, peacock-scaled tail entwining my waist as I pick her up from the sand-expanse, and all her colours seashore-washed; eyes summer saltwater blue, hair beach-blonde and sun-touched, flesh toned in amber, dune-pale, coral, sandgold flecked and pebble-freckled. Not the kind who combs her hair or makes shell-necklaces to ensnare, but who calls, certainly, across from one element to another. Like the seal-woman who chooses a mortal lover as her consort, and comes up out of the waves to have a land-life by choice, she's summoned me to the sea's edge to find her, and taken me, allowed me to carry her off. Or, she's a necromancer who knows the magic word of transformation, who can unroll a magic carpet and set out on it a banquet or a bed. She can conjure up this place wherever we are, and it is home.

(Home. There's the ultimately doubled-up word. Some people use it to name where their parents live, even when they don't live there themselves. Curious. But even if I'm enough of an outlaw to know very clearly that home is where the heart is, it still has that little quiver of nostalgia about it. The romance of exile, perhaps. If I press the key labelled Home, the cursor goes back to the start of the line, returns to its blank beginnings. There is that place we can never return, more imagined than remembered, the other home. What I mean by it, in my own heart's meaning, is the place where we are together, the landscape of our love.)

My lover reads me like a book, not judged by its cover – though maybe picked up for it in the first place. She speaks the same language, there's no need to translate, no parallel text. She understands even the most difficult chapters, takes the time to think about it. Her eyes confirm my meaning; she affirms that the words I'm made up of are real, a valid usage. Her tongue shapes my name. Her hands hold my entirety. I've trusted her with the unexpurgated version, uncut; she's got the whole story. I don't expect anyone else to know it; I don't expect them to think that they do after one glance at the title.

'Lover' is the word I could meditate on, translating and re-translating in a search for the perfect synonym, until mine comes and says to me that it's late, I shouldn't still be working, I should come to bed. Boy, holy, home, lover – just a basic vocabulary to demonstrate my bilingual talents. I won't comment on the choice of words; call it chance. The one that's obviously missing – one of my personal favourites – is woman. That's a word that always makes me feel happy somehow. (Maybe I could string those words together into the perfect sentence?)

Woman. I've forgotten what it means exactly, in that other foreign speech which I usually master as fluently as my secret tongue. Something slightly derogatory, isn't it? I've lost my powers of back and forth translation, suddenly there only seems to be one possible way of saying the word, only one known meaning; one way of being understood. (In the beginning was this word, it is now and ever shall be, world without end.) It's impossible for me to produce my alternative thesaurus-list of possible ways of saying woman. Then it comes to me, the inspiration from my muse, who encompasses everything; boy woman, holy woman, home woman, lover woman. She who makes my tongue whole.

ROBYN VINTEN
Shopping With Mother

They were coming to London, my mother and father. It was a once a year thing. Father had a business meeting, stockholders get-together or something, he never really said what, and I didn't ask. Anyway, he left Mother with me, it was my job to keep her out of trouble.

I had thought about changing my phone number, or moving and not telling them, like they did once when I was away at school. But for one day a year it seemed a little drastic.

Mother had said on the phone that she wanted to go shopping. So over coffee at Paddington Station after Father had deposited her with me, I asked where she wanted to go.

"Shopping?" She looked at me blankly. "I have everything I need, why would I want to go shopping?"

"OK." I said, trying not to panic. "Let's go sight-seeing instead."

I took her to Selfridges – it is after all a famous London landmark.

"It's too noisy," she complained. "Why do they have to play that terrible music?" The Spice Girls in the lift. "And so loud."

I had to agree. 'I Wanna' seemed all wrong for Selfridges.

We moved on to Covent Garden: my mother might have had everything she needed, I certainly didn't. There was a jacket in Paul Smith that I particularly needed.

"It's a man's jacket," she said, gingerly fingering the sleeve.

"No," I said, doing up the zip, wondering if silver wasn't a bit much in a puffa jacket and maybe the black would be more flattering. "It's unisex."

She looked at me dubiously.

"For men and women," I explained, in case she thought I meant something rude.

She muttered something about 'in her day'.

"They're very practical," I said, looking at myself sideways in the mirror. "It will be useful on my bike." That was a lie, it was purely a fashion thing, but words like 'useful' and 'practical' usually won her over.

She still looked doubtful, but fished her Mastercard out of her handbag. "If that's what you want," she said as though she couldn't quite believe it.

I put up a token resistance to her paying, a ritual protest for the sake of my self-respect and as an assertion of my independence.

"Oh... OK then, if you insist."

The camp young man behind the counter winked at me.

A hundred pounds for a day with Mother, I thought that seemed reasonable. But that was before lunch.

We ended up at BHS. There are hundreds of nice places to eat around Covent Garden, but no, Mother wanted to eat at BHS.

"They do lovely ham sandwiches."

I was a vegetarian since seeing the film *Babe*; I had told Mother this.

"And little meringue things with chocolate on top."

There were no little meringue things, and the ham sandwiches were curling up at the edges, apparently with embarrassment at their mean fillings. It was neither of these things that upset my mother, though. It was the fact that the decor had changed. It was now all white with bold diagonal yellow stripes. I hated it, and therefore thought she would have liked it.

"They had little floral curtains and matching lampshades."

I found a jacket potato, dry as an old sponge, with bold diagonal stripes of leathery cheese.

"Nice comfy chairs too, none of this modern nonsense." She eased herself on to the vinyl-covered bench, bolted to the floor.

I nodded and ate my potato. Being around Mother made me hungry, probably because I knew how much it annoyed her to see me eat a lot.

There was silence while we both ate. Then, "Oh, I can't eat another mouthful of this, I'm so full." She looked at me rather pointedly. I carried on eating, even though the potato was turning to ash in my mouth.

She put down her fork and sighed. "Did you notice I've lost some weight?" She sat up straighter in her chair.

I shovelled in the last of my food and shook my head.

"*You* haven't lost any."

"No?" It came out as more of a question than I intended. I was perfectly happy as I was, or I was until I was around my mother.

"You know, you could make something of yourself if you tried."

I had visions of *Blue Peter* and masses of sticky-back plastic.

"A good haircut, nice clothes. A bit of make-up, some high-heeled shoes..."

I took a good look at her for the first time that day. She was small and still slim, in a nice grey skirt, pink twinset, though no pearls, a brooch instead. A light blue raincoat, permed hair sitting in obedient curls around her face. A touch of lipstick, pearly pink, and blue eye shadow. Understated elegance, I would have thought if she was anyone but my mother.

She had lapsed into silence, staring off into space. I felt suddenly hungry again, and went and bought a large Danish pastry.

"Skirts," she said when I sat down, as if there had been no break in the conversation. "It wouldn't hurt you to wear a skirt now and then."

I had put on clean chinos that morning, ironed, and a silk shirt. I had made an effort, and now I resented it.

"I hate skirts," I said with a mouth full of Danish.

"Or plastic surgery," she said as if it was the logical step after skirts. I nearly choked on my Danish.

"We'd pay, of course."

I noticed some people at the next table looking at us, a nice elderly couple in matching anoraks.

"Mother," I said when I had recovered. She was pushing the curled-up crusts of her sandwich around her plate with a fork, not looking at me. "I'm quite happy with the way I look, thank you."

"A nose job, a few tucks, it's amazing what they can do. So many people are having it done, you'd be surprised."

She still wasn't looking at me. I began to suspect this was her way of trying to tell me something. I looked carefully at her face, it didn't look any different.

"Mother, you haven't...?"

She looked at me sharply. "Don't be ridiculous, I'm far too old for that sort of nonsense. But if you wanted to..."

"Well I don't," I said, hoping to end the conversation, and wondering if I could squeeze a Mars Bar in.

"Or an operation."

"An operation?" She had lost me again. "What sort of operation?"

She leant across the table and whispered. "The operation, you know." She pointed a manicured finger down at her plate.

"A ham sandwich operation?"

"No!" She started to blush. "Oh, don't be so dense." She folded her napkin onto her plate and looked around to see if anyone was listening. The matching anorak couple were suddenly taking a great interest in the ketchup bottle label.

"A sex-change operation." She mouthed the words rather than saying them.

"A sex-change operation!" I said it louder that I meant to, everyone in the cafe must have heard.

"Shh." She waved one hand at me.

"Why on earth...?" I started and then stopped. There was something missing here, some vital link had passed me by. I took a deep breath, we could be in for a long haul.

"Why do you think I would want a sex-change operation?" I said it slowly and carefully.

"Don't you?"

"No."

"Well, that's all right then." She didn't sound very relieved.

"But why did you think I would?"

"No reason." She was suddenly very interested in her napkin, folding it and re-folding it on the plate. "Can't we just drop the subject?" She looked up at me sheepishly.

"No we can't." Sheepish didn't work on me any more, I wondered if crying would. "Why did you think...?"

"Keep your voice down."

"Then answer me."

The couple at the next table had moved on to reading the sugar sachets. At least they seemed to be enjoying our conversation.

"Well, I thought..." She paused to think about what it was that she thought. I could see it was quite an effort, then an idea seemed to come to her. "It's because you aren't married."

"Not married." That was too ridiculous, even for my mother. Then it occurred to me that this was something to do with me being a lesbian. I had told her years ago, in the middle of an argument about something else. She had completely ignored it at the time, and for all the years since. Maybe she had taken it in after all. Still, it was too ludicrous an answer to be let go.

"Cousin Brian isn't married, do you think he wants a sex change?" I hoped she didn't know he was living with his girlfriend.

"He's engaged."

"Aunt Bridget." My father's sister who was a nun. "She's not married, do you think she wants a sex change?"

"Well…" She paused, clearly undecided.

This was interesting, I'd heard rumours about Aunt Bridget.

"She just might." She started to collect her things. The couple at the next table looked disappointed, but I wasn't finished yet.

"So, you think all unmarried people want sex changes?"

"Don't you go putting words into my mouth."

"It's just me then."

"Well, you do dress like a man."

"I wear trousers, lots of women do. You even do."

"Not all the time."

"I'm very happy being a woman."

"Good. Now can we go?"

I could feel the point slipping away from me, I needed to change tactics. "The Pope's not married, and he wears frocks. Do you think he wants a sex change?"

As soon as I said it, I knew it wouldn't work.

"You're just being stupid now." She stood up. "I'm going downstairs to the lighting department."

"I thought you had everything you needed?" I stood up too. I'd lost like always, some things never change. I don't know why I bothered – Mother had been the under-sixteen county tennis champion, she hated to lose anything. It was just habit, I guess.

"You can never have too many lamps."

I followed her down on the escalator.

"How's that nice Jane?"

"Jane?" She never asked after any of my friends, and I didn't have any close friends called Jane.

"Your flatmate."

"Jude." My lover. "I thought you didn't like her."

"She seems a very nice girl."

She had said to me, "You'll never find a man if you keep hanging round with that girl." Maybe she wasn't as stupid as she made out, my mother.

"She's fine."

"Good, that's good."

We were in the lighting department now; she headed straight for the chintz lampshades. "Would you like one of these for your flat?"

"No thanks." I had chucked out my chintz long before Ikea launched their ad champaign.

"Does Jane want...?" She wandered into the ceiling light section.

"Want what?" I had a pretty good idea of what she was getting at, but I was still bitter about losing the argument.

"Well, she's not married either. Or is she?" She looked at me, suddenly hopeful.

"No she isn't."

"Oh."

"Does Jude want what?"

"What we were talking about before." She picked up a paper lampshade, like the ones I had in my flat.

"A sex-change operation?" I said it deliberately loudly.

"Keep your voice down."

"No she doesn't, she's very happy being a woman too. We both are, both of us together are happy being women, together."

"Oh." She looked at the shade in her hand. "Horrible thing, I bet it's a fire hazard."

"Mother." I took the lampshade off her. "I think you're confusing gender and sexuality here."

She looked at me as though I was speaking a foreign language, and to her I probably was.

"I don't know what you mean." She sounded aggrieved.

"I don't want to be a man, I'm a lesbian. They're two totally different things."

"Shhh." She looked around to see if anyone was listening. I spotted the anorak couple lingering by the outdoor lighting display.

"You're just saying that to upset me."

"I'm saying it because it's true."

"You never told me."

"I did."

"When?"

"Years ago."

"Then how am I supposed to remember, if it was years ago?"

And I couldn't really argue with that.

"Mother..."

"Please, don't. I'm too upset." She couldn't seem to rustle up any tears, but she sniffed delicately. "I think I want to go home."

I looked at my watch, it was three. We weren't due to meet Father until four-thirty. If we walked very slowly...

As it happened, it was nearly four-fifteen by the time we got back to Paddington. Between buying a pair of chintz lampshades and a person under the train at Edgware Road station, it took over an hour to get to Paddington.

We didn't say much to each other. She was, of course, charming to the young man who finally served her in BHS. And I waved goodbye to the couple who joined the queue behind us, with their oversized security light. I hope they needed it, because we didn't provide them with any further entertainment.

Mother struck up a conversation with a woman and her young daughter when we were stuck in a tunnel between Baker Street and Marylebone.

"Oh, isn't she a doll." Mother said of the daughter. "Enjoy her while she's young, they grow up soon enough." She threw a dirty look my way.

I was reading the *Time Out* I'd brought along for just such occasions. The gay section had an article about how important it is to be out in every aspect of your life.

"Don't mention a word of this to your father" were her last words to me as we sat down in the station cafe to wait for him.

I had another Danish pastry and was rewarded with a tut and a roll of her eyes, then I slipped off to the loo for a fag. It was one thing telling her I was a lesbian, but there was no way I was going to risk telling her I smoked.

When I got back, sucking a mint, Father was there. He smiled at me as I sat down.

"Good meeting?" I asked.

"Oh yes." He puffed up with self-importance.

"What exactly...?" I started to ask, but Mother cut across me.

"Come on, George, we'd better go."

"But it's only..." Father wasn't allowed to finish either.

"I want to get a good seat." She was putting her coat on. Father sighed and stood up to help her.

"Well it was nice..." Father managed before following Mother to the door.

"Yes." I waved him off.

"Maybe Christmas?" he called from the door.

"Maybe," I said and started planning a trip to Siberia.

"Oh well." I sighed and finished my mother's coffee. At least I got the jacket out of it. The most expensive jacket I had ever owned, in more ways than one. I felt under the table for it. It wasn't there. I could see Mother and Father walking down the platform, and there between her BHS bags was my Paul Smith. I put my head down on the table. Game, set and match to Mother then.

LINDA INNES
The Root Of It

No milk had been spilt. Just thickened in the bottle, from slow cream, through sickly curds, to thin green. Mum and me, together, almost like it used to be when I was a kid. But entirely different.

Folds of skin at her neck ruched into feathery tree bark. She was working something around in her soft mouth, thoughtlessly.

"No milk yet," I said, "Can you wait for your tea?" She wouldn't have heard.

From this house, I had waded out from the limits of the living room, then swum beyond even her reach.

A moan. I plunged back towards her.

"Just a song at twilight..." quivering... *"When the lights are low..."*

I crouched down beside her and held her hand. It was safe now.

"And the evening shadows... Softly come and go..."

She crackled into laughter, her mouth hollow, her shiny gums and tongue like newborn birds.

"Mum!" I tested.

She focused and crooked her finger towards me, "Listen! Here!"

I smelt cheese; old dogs. "Where's me teeth?"

I looked on the table, where a stocking lay twisted over the yellow butter dish. No teeth. Draining board. Windowsill. No teeth. Fridge. Teeth. The faded bubble-gum palate was speckled with something yoghurty, so I rinsed them. She bundled them back into her mouth and snapped them into a smile.

"Now then. Come here. I'm not going to bite you," she clacked her teeth together and chuckled deeply. Then stopped. She bent her finger to her mouth, and whispered, "Listen to me. Listen to this."

I stopped my breath to catch the wind of her words. I knelt closer.

"Never trust a wolf in women's clothing." She sat back. Nodded. Arms folded. Fell asleep.

I looked out for the milk. Across the patch of front garden, long grasses swayed with the weight of seedy plaits. My hiding place. One of them. I remember playing in the back garden. Our next-door neighbour, Mrs Shimmin, was a white shock, a dandelion clock. Through freckles of privet and ribbons of blossom, she shook and couldn't stop. There was no end to it.

"I can dance the Dying Swan," I'd told her. "Look!" I pirouetted till

I was dizzy and slid down the side of the shed.

"Lovely," she'd said, and shivered into a round of applause.

Mild and buttery, now, when my *mother* dissolved, what would I have left of her? Her bite mark smiling from my shoulder; the small scar she gave me, when I was eight, like a splash of milk on my cheek; the knot at my wrist where the bones hadn't knitted together; the nights I'd still wake, mewing. And the time it took my lover to settle me, to skim me with her cool hands, to separate me.

I can't remember being a child.

"Your childhood was stolen," Mary said.

"Report it on *Crimewatch*, then," I said.

Mary took her hand away from my cheek, and got up. Good. Now we wouldn't speak for a couple of hours, and I would wait for her to apologise to me. Then we would drink wine and make love. And she would not hold me too tight, so that I knew that I could always escape.

And in the silver light through muslin curtains, I would wake and see the slope of her hip, her milky skin, the gentle valley of her breasts, her sleepy nipples, and I would nuzzle and suckle there, till her nipple came hard and alive and Mary stirred and clasped me to her and opened her legs to my plunging fingers and fist.

Mary, sweet and tender, all her gestures tinged with understanding, and I would choke on the gall rising in my throat, and I would fight against the urge to hurt her. And mostly I would hurt her.

I hurt her where the bruises would not show. Not where my mother hurt me, physically, when I was supposed to be a child, but in the secret places of the heart. I hurt her so that no one but us would know, until she left me for another lover. Then it would all show, and Mary would know how it was, and how it would be.

It is a matter of fact.

She traces her soft fingers over my scars. At first, that made me wince. Not from pain, I don't know what. Mary could give it a name, no doubt. She has lots of words for all occasions, all apt and evocative. She should be telling this story, not me. She would make it moving and beautiful, and there would be a moral in it somewhere.

Mary knows best, and what she doesn't know will hurt her.

My mother still lives, and I am learning tenderness with her. We are both of us bad teachers, and worse students. Let Mary alone with us, years ago, and we would have cruelly dealt with her. But in age, my mother is the child she never had, and I am learning to be mother. Mary is most fortunate to know us now.

Mary, for all her gentleness, is a brick shithouse of a girl. Robust, ruddy, all fat and six feet tall. In bed she is all soft roundness, like a fertility goddess, large breasted and juicy. I like to drink from her, like a baby, like a lover. I do not like her to touch me.

She smells of the countryside and of the sea. Places I know exist in a kind of mythology.

But enough of this, for I am a jolly, light-hearted character, and don't like to go out of my depth. Let us be shallow, where it's safe.

I am a loud woman. I am the loudest librarian there is. I hoot with laughter if I am amused. If I want someone, I will shout. You can't be too sacrosanct about libraries. Or in them. Anyway, it hasn't held me back at all: I'm a branch librarian in a town we'll call Middlesbrough, because that's its name.

Mary came into the library one lunchtime. We hadn't known one another very long, but she was in love, eager to see me, to surprise me with smiles, and a rose. I shouted. I told you I liked to shout – I shouted, as furiously as I could, "GET OUT!" and she did. Too shocked to do otherwise. She brought up the matter in bed in the early hours of the morning. She never brought it up again.

Oh, Mary, soft as melting butter. And me – butter wouldn't melt.

At infant school, I used to play with Debbie, who had skin falling off her face and cracks in her hands that bled. I played school and when she was the teacher, she had to cane me really hard.

"I don't want to," she sobbed. But I told her if she didn't take a stick to me and beat me with all her might, I'd shake her so hard her face would drop off.

"On the mountain stands a lady, who she is I do not know...
All she wants is gold and silver, all she wants is a nice young MAN"
And then you jump in and join the skipping.
I didn't.

Back at home, mum would have her head in the gas oven again at 4.10pm. After all, high time I was home from school.

I panicked – screeched – the first time – screamed and ran, clawing her out, tore one of my fingernails inside out, blood-blistered, ripping her dress. I never did that again.

The gas was sometimes on, sometimes not. That was the pain of it. The thrill of it.

If I push Mary to the point that she can't stand it, then she should go. She won't. I must be quite an interesting case. She must get a lot out of it, as I hold her tightly, and whisper endearments, like "Doormat". She says she needs me. I say she's too needy.

When I was two years old, I packed a bag and left home. I toddled up the street, my auntie said, heading for my grandmother's. They smile indulgently. But what does a two-year-old pack when she runs away from home? I am afraid to ask. I am afraid it was a knife, a box of matches, some rope.

Mary was unpacking the shopping. Lamb chops.

"Mary had a little lamb," I observed, "Its fleece was white as snoo-ow."

I shot up. Mary flinched, but I was marching across the kitchen at her.

"And – ev'ry-where – that – Ma-ry – went..." I grabbed her waist. She froze.

"That lamb was sure to go-oo," I pushed my hand down the waistband of her jeans and bit her neck, gently. She relaxed a little, so I turned her head towards me and stared her straight in the eyes.

"What are you thinking?" I asked.

"That I love you," she said.

She only *thinks* she loves me. So I pulled away.

I rarely visit my mother. She is hanging onto life and lucidity, and the community cares for her. I don't. Recently, her existence has become more problematic to me, and I am forced to have her in my mind and in my life: I communicate with social workers, nurses, doctor. I don't communicate with her. Mary likes to press, to urge me to visit, to build a relationship before it's too late. It is. If Mary were to know everything, she would be frightened, so I tell her little, but enough. "Shutting her out", she says. So I shut her out. If she can't accept me as I am, then I don't see the point in telling my past. Mary likes to build up stories, to know the details; she is hungry for the scraps of past that make up my history, my identity. I am endlessly fascinating. I leave her to her imagination. She wants to understand me. I don't want her to be understanding.

When I was seventeen, I had a boyfriend. Many girls do, before they realise that they are lesbian; or to contradict the fact that they are lesbian. When I was seventeen, I had sex with this boy. Many girls do. And who can say what pheromones or vibes I gave off or what aura I had, who can say what womanly confidence I displayed, or what a show-off I'd been, but for some reason my mother must have known. Soon afterwards, I came home from school to find my mother having sex with this boy – my first lover. I'll leave it there. If you're anything like Mary, you can make up the rest of the details, and accordingly, believe what you like.

Mary is warm in bed. Mary is warm out of bed. I am cold. Mary feeds me warm milk at night and tucks the sheet around my shoulders and strokes my hair until I fall asleep or fuck her.

3.45am. A ringing sound rudely awakens me. I am annoyed, but Mary passes me the telephone, whispering "The hospital".

And I am driving, two hundred miles, through the night, alone, despite Mary's hysterical complaints. I don't want her. I am driving, two hundred miles, alone, without stopping. You think it's the last chance, the once in a lifetime, the deathbed reconciliation, the dying words. It's the end of a story you've been on the edge of your seat to finish. The one you couldn't put down.

I am driving through the night, sick with expectation. Visualise the scene.

I burst into the side room. My shrunken mother on a thin bed. She turns watery eyes towards me. I don't know what my face says. She uses all of her strength to wrench the oxygen mask from her face, to cry, "FUCK OFF!"

The nurse whispers, "Don't worry – she's not in her right mind – she doesn't recognise you."

By now, Mary is tidying up the patch of front garden outside the house. She crouches close to the earth. Her back is broad, a creamy ellipse of skin stretching between her jeans and her tee-shirt. There is a fine vertical line of golden downy hair glistening there. Her fingers are unaccountably slender and strong, brushing earth delicately from the petals of flowers she has just planted. The flowers are brightly coloured, almost cheerful. She has removed the rough patch of grass that I left to grow long and seedy, laid down some fresh green turf, and dug out flower beds. Now she is settling bedding plants. She says she wants to make it lovely for us.

She can't.

CHERRY SMYTH
The Perfect Ceremony Of Love's Rite

My wife does not believe in marriage. I worked hard to persuade her of its perversity. It was the summer my younger brother announced his wedding date. The family went into overdrive, ruffling up its feathers like a contented fat hen, strutting from relative to relative, their news bursting out in well-crowned smiles. Silver-embossed invitations followed, needlessly. I'd never heard of wedding lists till I saw Gary and Siobhan's. They faxed me a list of presents in which household items were allocated to prospective buyers to avoid duplication and guarantee a fully equipped kitchen. Even model numbers and colours were advised. A Santa letter for grown-ups. "What happened to the notion of a unique surprise?" I asked Androula. But the list got under my skin and swelled like a juicy tick.

Androula is a practical woman. She remembers to file her nails before they break, run ragged or cause damage. Nonetheless, we have a toaster which burns one side, leaving the other pale and clammy. She rescued it from a junk shop in Bethnal Green and remains attached to the price she paid, its Bakelite handles and its fabric-covered flex. It was the first line in my offensive for gift equality. Gary and Siobhan wanted a Philips glass toaster and so did I. But Androula was steadfast.

"You'd swop your principles for a blender," she said.

"A Robochef, yes." I almost said Braun to be sure.

"But dearest," she said sweetly, "you don't cook."

"But I will. Given the gadgets."

I promised to relocate the book she'd given me two years before – Elizabeth David's *French Country Cooking*. I had been put off by the chapter which began, "To show what can be done with a cabbage..." Then I had looked at the pictures. There's a beauty called 'Thin Lunch' by Alexandre-François Desportes, which shows a plate of murky oysters, five crusty loaves, a basket of dim figs and a huge triangle of rough cheese. Or Walter Sickert's 'Roquefort'. The wooden table, the knife, the bottle of wine, the wineglass and the shadows themselves all have the pocked inconstancy of damp roquefort. The book made me want to paint more than cook. Could a wedding list begin with an easel and a set of oil paints?

I made some filter coffee and visualised a Krups cappuccino machine, its self-important little steam chimney hissing into a stainless steel jug of whole organic milk. I had begun to want in departments where my greed had never roamed before. I just needed to convince my girl.

"It's an institution of ownership and control." Androula was beheading withered geraniums on the windowsill.

"Lighten up! It's the chance for a mega party. Star Trek theme."

"You want me to get married in a prosthesis?"

"OK, you choose the theme."

"Dated."

I tutted and refused to smile. "It wouldn't mean monogamy, or anything."

"You want to be non-monogamous now? To get married to legitimise having an affair?"

"No, no –" I waved my hands around in graceless frustration. "I don't."

It was true. I'd never been more faithful. The only time I was adulterous was when I went shopping. Androula ran an online book company and sneaking into a bookshop was tantamount to a blistering and secret liaison.

Androula looked at me. I could see she was asking herself why I was so wound up.

I went to my room. Or what was my room in the early days and is now our study and junk room, with a futon for guests. It's also the Row Room. The room for the expelled. One night on six bounceless layers of stale cotton and you're ready for conjugal reconciliation. I switched on the PC. The Internet would rescue me. The cursor beat like a slow, fading heart. I clicked my way to Californian web-sites on queer ceremony, rites for radical faeries, a case for dyke bigamy. Your Special Day complete with a selection of rainbow-friendly verses from the Torah, the Koran, the Song of Solomon and Kahil Gibran. Commitment rings. It's a thriving light industry. It made me feel quite ill and oddly excluded.

I told myself I didn't need a matrimonial splurge, that I would be romantic in an everyday kind of way. I tried to remember lines from a Shakespeare sonnet. "As an unperfect actor on the stage, Who with his fear is..." is what? "Who with his fear..." It wasn't about romance, I realised as I exited the www. There was something rigid in the way Androula planned her future that made me feel dispensable. It could happen without me. She'd have savings, a comfy, paid-off home no matter what. I felt like a lodger in her life.

I returned to the kitchen. Androula was sweeping the floor and I swung chairs out of her way in a moody tango. Where capitalist materialism had failed, I tried petulance and goading.

"You're not really committed, Androula."

"How does a piece of paper with no legal status grant us commitment?"

"It's been six years. A wedding's a marker. A prize."

"Haven't we been through all this before?" Her voice hit a whine curve. "I thought we agreed that all marriage laws should be abolished and we'd invent new structures of kinship. Remember?"

I watched her fists grip the broom which angled into every corner. The brusque movements of her flat narrow wrists reminded me of her mother, her heels clacking round the stone floor of her Cypriot kitchen. Androula's manic phase could only signal one thing. And I'd used the last tampon. I should have kept out of her way.

"We should talk about drawing up our wills," she went on. "That's more important in the long run." Androula was wiping down the cereal cupboard door, something which would never have occurred to me to do. Things that were once complementary between us were edging towards the incompatible. It made me panic.

"I'd rather exchange rings."

"We do that already. Remember that thick silver ring I loved?" She was staring at me, hand on hip. "You lost it."

I thought for one awful moment that she was going to point.

"It's about having witnesses. People who will rally round in times of doubt and convince us to give it another go."

"So we stay together for other people? I never understood that. Like my sister. She should have left her husband years ago. Why have one man declare you can stay together and another a couple of years later to say you no longer have to? Ministers and judges."

"We'd... I mean... we'd have a woman and compose our own ceremony." I sounded like an exile from Women's Land. I was making myself cringe.

"You'll be suggesting headed stationery next. I can see the typesetter's face. McLoughlin-Kostopoulos. Or would you prefer Kostopoulos-McLoughlin?"

"That's the whole point. Taking this straight supremo ritual and reclaiming it. It forces them to see how much we matter to each other."

"I'm sorry, love," she shrugged. "To me, it's like a mouse for a dog."

Androula was no cat lesbian, even in her metaphors.

"Yeah, I know," I said.

"This is probably all about Gary."

"Gary?"

"Yes. Your brother Gary. Whatever Gary gets you have to get."

"That's ridiculous."

Afraid that she'd see she was right, I took my coffee cup into the bathroom, and spurred by a wave of household guilt, got down on my knees and squirted Jif round the bath. I shone the mixer taps. Somewhere at the back of my mind was a small bright dream, almost as old as I was, which betrayed all I stood for. In the dream there are rows of people I love in their best gear, looking ahead, waiting under a tall vaulted roof. I walk between them on my father's arm. Our strides are measured and even, our feet in step. From the other side, the woman I love, Androula, walks towards us, all her crowd behind her on either side, her arm clutched by her mother. Her mother is in slippers, her feet silent. We meet in the middle and promise to be loving, loyal and kind. No faithful, no obey. We kiss. Everyone cheers and starts to slow-clap and sing 'We Are Family' by Sister Sledge, with full harmonies. We leave in a silver car with tin cans trailing behind and 'Just Married' sprayed in shaving foam across the back window. We go somewhere guiltless and bearably hot and make love in a large white bed in a large white room. After that, we live in nuptial wonder – no rows, no walk-outs, no insults, no bitter sobbing. No boredom. No regret.

Androula appeared at the bathroom door.

"What's this? A chore to implore?" She laughed. I laughed. How could I compete? She was sharp as a lawyer, a politician, a poet, a tack.

We were not to be married.

"It's OK, I've dropped it."

"If it ain't broke, why fix it? I want you. That's what counts."

I stood up and rinsed my hands. I was so virtuous with cleaning and capitulation turned me on. I pulled her into my arms. She smelt of geranium. I licked the delicate coral of her ear. She likes that. She made a pre-sex sound, all sweet acquiescence. I touched her breasts. She kissed at my cheeks, my jawbone, my mouth. We slid down to the floor, like in the old days, full of a desire to fuck all day and all night, anywhere. My right hand headed for home.

"Call me names," she whispered.

I took my voice down an octave. "Come here, you little slut, I'll sort you out."

She made no sound. No murmur.

"You're such a bad little tart."

Her breathing didn't quicken.

"Totty. Whore. Jezebel. Bitch," I said slowly. It wasn't working. The boy in the boat wasn't rocking anymore.

"Beloved –"

"Yes," she said.

"My sweet bride –" She hardened.

"Yes."

"Be mine, my spouse, my one and only wife, mother of my children…"

Bingo!

Androula came, ejaculating all over the thigh of my jeans.

Since then I call Androula my wife, but we'll have no truck with marriage.

JENNY ROBERTS
Making The Horse Laugh

I just couldn't believe I was doing this. Until last week I'd been resigned to my single, well-ordered, undemanding urban life. I would be thirty in five weeks; I felt I'd earned the right to avoid difficult social situations.

Yet, here I was, driving along a country lane, going to see a woman I didn't know, to give her my expert view on something I knew nothing about.

I blame it all on Stella. This was all her idea. I'd been over to see my friend for the day and had mentioned casually that I'd bumped into this fabulous woman in the supermarket in town. It would have ended there if Stella hadn't been low on petrol and called in at her village filling station.

The woman was there again, leaning against her beat up old Land Rover, gazing around and looking sad, whilst George pumped in the diesel and attempted his version of conversation. Her short blond bob was being blown around by the wind and every so often she had to push the hair back away from her face. Stella saw me staring as she waited in the car for her turn – self-service hadn't reached Tenterton yet – and passed her hand in front of my eyes. "Sandra, it's rude to stare."

"That's her." I said, surprised but pleased at the coincidence.

"Really?" said Stella. "She doesn't look a bit like you described her."

But she had the same effect on me as the first time. She was my age but a few inches shorter than me: around 5'2" with a neat oval face, and a small full mouth. She wore no make-up but she had a strong natural colour as if much of her life was spent outdoors. Her denim, blazer-style jacket hung casually from her shoulders over a white shirt and dark blue denim jeans.

George ambled off to the office with her money and she followed him, kicking at pebbles as she went, looking disconsolate and a bit lost. For all my determination to stay single, she made me feel involved, she made me feel like I wanted to gather her up in my arms. It was just the same the last time I'd seen her – in the supermarket, buying mushrooms. I was in a hurry and caught the side of her trolley as I passed, which bumped into her. She dropped the bag, spilling the contents all over the floor, swearing loudly and obscenely.

"Oh sorry about my language," she said, self-consciously, when I bent down to help her gather them up.

"No, it's my fault, I shouldn't have been so clumsy."

As I said it, I had been drawn right into her sad, deep-blue eyes and my whole body had gone AWOL.

Now she came back to her vehicle and looked across at us, the way people do when they sense they're being watched. I turned away casually, as if I had just been idly looking around. But Stella carried on staring. "You really do fancy her, don't you?" she said, grinning her wicked grin. "Go on, quick: chat her up, say hello again." She poked me in the ribs. "Go on, whilst you have the chance!"

I scowled at her. This was vintage Stella – single for the last five years but ever-ready to push me into something at the drop of a hat. "Don't be daft, I can't do that, I don't know her!"

By then it was too late anyway, she was in her Land Rover and gone. I was left gazing after her, wishing that I had more courage. I hadn't had a relationship since Anna, nearly three years ago now. And, somehow, after loving one person through most of my twenties, I'd lost the knack of chatting up. I mentally shrugged, I'd had quite enough hurt for this lifetime; it was safer this way.

Maybe it was. But Stella, being Stella, didn't see it like that: I could hear her talking to George as he filled the car up.

Tenterton is only a small village – a few hundred houses, no more – and gossip gets around fast. The gruff old bugger who runs the garage isn't known for his discretion. If you want to know anything about anybody – ask George. If you want to spread a malicious rumour – tell George.

His eyes lit up when Stella asked about her but his face remained set in the same miserable expression that he'd spent the last fifty years cultivating. "Aye, she's just moved in round 'ere." He said matter of factly in his flat North Yorkshire accent. He looked at her dolefully (Go on, ask me some more).

Stella pushed the money for the petrol under his nose. "Whereabouts, George? Somewhere in the village?" I felt like a small child again, waiting for a treat, waiting whilst Auntie Stella asked the nice man if it was still available. And feeling embarrassed, wishing she wasn't making it so obvious.

"Oh aye, she's moved in down on Carr Lane – just over t'hill – y'know, the old Hawksby place." I missed the rest of the conversation, but with my attraction to the woman, and Stella's persistence, I might have known it wouldn't end there.

Stella had visited her within the week – as a sort of neighbourly, villagey thing, she said. The sort of thing country people do all the time, she said. She broke the news to me when we met in town the following Friday and part of me wanted to crawl into the usual hole. But, this time, there was another part that wanted to know more, to know everything there was to know. I let the two of them fight it out as I listened.

"She's called Debbie... and she's S-I-N-G-L-E!" Stella gushed excitedly. "Moved here two months ago from up north, after her lover ran off with another woman."

I remembered her eyes. She was someone who needed loving, someone who liked to have someone else around. Then I remembered how much I preferred being on my own and the whole thing began to feel distinctly dodgy. "So she's straight is she?" I said, hoping that this would be the end of the matter.

Stella shook her head, still glowing from every pore. "Didn't say, love – I tried to worm it out of her, of course, but she avoided all the pronouns – just referring to her lover, her partner." She grinned at me meaningfully. "She must be a dyke, a straight woman wouldn't do that."

"Fine." I said, feebly hoping that this was the end of the matter. "So now we know."

"Yes," said Stella, her enthusiasm unbounded, "and Sandra..."

"Yes Stella."

"...She's got a horse that's depressed."

I looked at her hoping for some sort of rational explanation. She grinned at me dramatically and made a sort of trumpeting sound whilst waving her hands about.

"Don't you see?" she said, speaking very slowly, metaphorically underlining every word as if I were thick. "Her: *attractive single woman with depressed horse.* You: *drowning in your own secretions every time you see her."*

Maybe I was thick, but all this was still beyond me. "Stella?"

"Yes, Sandra."

"Just what the fuck are you rabbiting on about?"

She sighed impatiently. "It's obvious, isn't it, Dumbo? You know about animals, you fancy her... so..." She paused for effect, overwhelmed with her own cleverness. "I told her you used to be an animal counsellor, and that you would be pleased to sort the horse out."

"Stella..." I said, trying to ignore the sinking feeling in my gut, "I worked as a vet's assistant for six weeks, three years ago."

She waved her hand dismissively. "Oh, you! You're so pedantic."

I followed the narrow country road until I saw the sign for Garth Cottage on my right at the top of a rough-looking lane. The cottage was tucked in about 25 yards down. It wasn't the 'roses-and-clematis-round-the-door' kind you find in stories, more the 'this-is-a-rather-boring-(and-very-small)-brick-built-house-that-we've-called-a-cottage-because-there-is-no-other-way-to-make-it-interesting' sort of place you find in real life.

I parked the car on the grass verge and pushed open the rusty iron gate, wondering if I was really doing this and only half convinced that I was. The door was open, so I shouted out a half-hearted 'hello'. My stomach muscles were cramping up now with fear and I could feel the adrenalin priming my body for a fast escape across the cornfields all around me.

Hold on Sandra. Fucking hold on.

No answer. Ah well. I tried Stella, I tried.

I was retreating gratefully back to the safety of my car, when I heard her voice from the garden to my right.

She was only feet away, dressed in shorts and T-shirt, her hair spilling out from beneath a floppy khaki hat, her knees and legs all scratched and grubby and a bunch of weeds in her hand. But her eyes were the same – deep blue and sexy and still a little sad. Eyes that could swallow you whole. She smiled when I turned – the sort of smile that sent everything around it into soft focus. Including me.

I think I probably stood there for hours, my legs wobbled and then disappeared completely, the rest of my body followed. All I had left was a brain that was a vortex of fear and longing. And a big wet ache where my bits should have been.

She put her head on one side and looked concerned. "Are you all right?"

"Er... yes... sorry, it's just the heat and too many late nights." I lied. "Bit of a dizzy spell. I'm OK now though." My head felt like it was on hinges and I had to get a grip to stop myself from nodding like one of those dogs you see in the back of cars. "Erm... I'm Sandra, I think you know my friend Stella?"

"Oh yes!" she exclaimed brightly. "She said she'd get you to come round. It was about my horse, wasn't it?" Now she was fidgeting. Good, she was nervous as well, that evened things up a bit.

"You're... er... an animal psychiatrist aren't you?"

I swallowed hard and tried to bring some saliva back into a mouth that was as dry as the Gobi Desert. "Well, more of a behavioural therapist, really," I croaked, self-consciously, my face getting hotter and hotter. Just you wait Stella.

"I think you'd better sit down for a while," she said. "I'll get you a cold drink of lemonade, I made some fresh this morning – it's just in the fridge."

I did as I was told and sat on an old bench, my heart pounding like it was going to take off very soon. She touched my shoulder as she left and it went into a spasm.

She was a nice woman. And vulnerable. The more I saw of her, the more I liked her and the less I liked myself. This just wasn't fair. I felt like I was taking advantage. Whatever Stella would say, I had to leave. I couldn't do it.

She returned and held out a glass. "Here you are, Sandra, drink this. It'll cool you down."

I drank the whole glass of cold sharp liquid in one go and felt calmer. I smiled at her nervously. She smiled back weakly. The freckles around her eyes seemed to be jumping around. I blinked hard.

"Look, I haven't done this sort of work for years...."

"But you will try and help, won't you?"

She was looking down at me with those sad eyes.

"Well, I was never very good. Stella exaggerates..."

"Please, you're my only hope now..."

Oh fuck.

"All right, I'll try." It didn't sound like my voice.

She nodded quickly, and more of her hair spilled out from under the hat. "It's my mare, Flo... Oh, er... She's called Flora really." She smiled apologetically. "But I changed it when I bought her. Uh, I didn't think she looked anything like a tub of margarine... but she's acting like one at the moment."

I laughed weakly and she looked embarrassed.

"The vet says there's nothing physical, that it's probably some kind of equine depression. But I've changed her feed, I exercise her regularly, I groom her every day – sometimes twice – and I've given her all the supplements she suggested..." She dropped her arms to her side and sighed with frustration. "And she's still fed up"

"OK," I said, surrendering, unable to do anything else. "Maybe we should take a look." Maybe I did know a little bit about animals. Maybe I should at least try.

We walked across the garden to the fence behind the house, where there was a small green paddock, spotted with of piles of dung. The mare was mooching by the fence and looked up briefly as we approached.

"There she is, Sandra. Isn't she lovely?"

She was a big chestnut, and though she was obviously mature, she can't have been as old as she looked just then, her head down, her ears back, sagging everywhere a horse could sag. This was one really pissed-off equine.

We climbed over the fence and she held her whilst I stood and watched.

"Well?" she asked.

I looked at her. "What?"

"Well aren't you going to examine her?"

"Oh, yes of course..." I stuttered, trying to stay calm. "I was just making an initial assessment. You hold her, whilst I have a look." I tried to think of what a behavioural therapist would do, and tried to look as if I was doing it.

I stood back and studied the horse. Then I walked slowly round it, keeping well clear of the rear, grunting knowledgably all the time. Flo turned her head, following me every inch of the way, her great big, beady brown eyes staring pointedly at me, deriding me: Uh! Behavioural therapist? Bullshit!

I returned to Debbie, nodding seriously, frowning slightly.

"Is she going to be all right?" she asked, turning those eyes on me again.

I looked at her, then I looked at the mare. Are we really going to let this woman feel that there is no hope? Flo looked back, her eyes overflowing with boredom. Uh, said the horse, who cares.

"When did all this start?" I said, regaining my composure and discovering that I had put a protective arm around her shoulders as I led her back to the garden.

"About five months ago, back in March. My partner and I had just split up – we'd been together for nearly five years. We'd done all right, well financially anyway. House in the country near Carlisle, a horse each, a pleasant lifestyle..." She shrugged, disconsolately. "But we weren't happy. Then another woman appeared on the scene... And that was that."

"I'm sorry," I said.

"That's life," she said.

"So *she* left you?" I said. I had to know. Use a pronoun, woman, tell me.

She looked at me briefly and continued. "Well, anyway, I went to stay with my mum, whilst we got everything sorted, and put Flo in stables. She was all right at first, then after a few weeks she started to go downhill. She went off her food, lost all her energy and..." she pointed to the mare "...started to look like this."

"Then you came here?"

She nodded. "Yeah. I thought she would improve as soon as she was put out to fresh spring grass." She shrugged. "But she didn't. Now I don't know what to do..."

She paused, looking at me, waiting. Hoping I had the answer.

I had, of course. Stella and I worked it out days before. Before I met

Debbie properly, before I saw how attached she was to the horse, before I met Flo.

Maybe what I was doing wasn't so bad after all. The woman needed some kind of hope, after all. Maybe I was just being kind. And, bloody hell, she was nice.

We sat down next to each other on the bench. It was a small one and we were sitting close. I could feel the heat from her body and smell the warmth of her skin. She was still looking at me. Her eyes wide open and damp, her mouth turned down slightly at the edges, her hands fidgeting again.

"Well," I said, trying to sound objective and professional, "it looks like a case of bereavement adjustment to me. I think that Flo is simply missing your ex... What did you say her name was?"

She looked a little taken aback. "Er Kate..." she said guardedly, "how could you tell it was a woman?"

I shrugged, matter-of-factly, getting into my stride at last. "Oh, you know, behavioural therapist and all that."

She looked impressed. "And you're... er...?"

"A dyke? Yeah." I said, as off-handedly as I could, though the joy and relief of her answer was still reverberating around my body. "Yeah," I continued knowledgably, "I would expect Flo to find it hard. Some horses are more sensitive than others. And, with them, it can be just like children. In a separation, you expect kids to feel a degree of trauma. It's no different for horses like Flo."

She looked at me, a light crossing her face and then fading again. "But what can I do about it?" she said. "I'd never take Kate back. Is that mean? Should I try and make up for the sake of the horse?" She shook her head. "I just couldn't."

I took her hands in mine, to reassure her, to enjoy her touch. The skin was smooth, her fingers long and sinewy. I wanted them.

"It's OK, Debbie." I said squeezing her hand. "You don't have to get back together. Horses like Flo get used to a relationship between their owner and another. It's the existence of a relationship that counts, not who it's with."

She looked at me with that lost look, and my heart started bouncing around in my chest again.

"I can see that, Sandra. But there's no way I can just go out and get another girlfriend. I've just moved here, I don't know anyone. I haven't even got any friends."

I paused. This was going better than I'd ever dared hope. Stay cool Sandra, for Christ's sake stay cool.

"Well... I suppose I could help." I said, as reluctantly as I could. "I'm pretty free, work-wise, at the moment."

She looked puzzled.

"Look, you don't actually have to have another relationship, you've just got to make Flo believe that you have."

"And how do I do that?"

"Well... if you want... I could come around here for the next few days and we could do the sort of things that you and Kate used to do – sort of make Flo feel more secure again."

She looked at me gratefully. "Would you really do that for me?"

I coloured up in spite of myself. "Yeah. I'd be pleased to help." I said. "But it will be a few days before I can be sure of the prognosis – we need to see what progress is made."

Debbie breathed out with relief and, for the first time since I'd met her, she looked satisfied and happy.

I looked over the fence at Flo. She'd turned her back to us now and she lifted up her tail and farted.

Stella was beside herself with curiosity when I saw her that night. But she was temporarily thrown when I asked to borrow her mare for a few days.

"But you haven't ridden for years, Sandra."

"Oh yeah, I know. But it's like riding a bike, you don't forget, do you. I'll be fine."

I could see she was torn. It was wonderful to behold. In order to get me fixed up, she was going have to do the unthinkable and lend me her mare. I knew Stella well enough to know that there was no contest.

She was like a mother hen when she helped me tack up the following morning and watched, concerned, as I left and rode awkwardly through the village astride Beth, a big grey mare of character, rather odd to look at, but sturdy. I didn't exactly cut a dash but it was the best I could do at short notice.

We trundled down the lane to the cottage, Beth picking her way through the potholes and stumbling occasionally over a small stone. My legs ached already, my bum was sore and the brief feeling of confidence I had from yesterday had evaporated. I wondered again why I was doing this. Then, when I saw Debbie, I knew. She was tacked up and waiting. A black riding hat on her head, her blond hair dropping underneath neatly encased in a net. My eyes ran down over her body across the tweedy hacking jacket down to her stomach, along her jodhpured legs to her shiny brown riding boots. I felt upstaged and overawed.

She smiled as I approached. "You look smart," I said, feeling like a scruff in my baggy jumper and jeans.

She didn't seem to mind. "You look great," she purred. "Being on horseback suits you."

Flo's ears had pricked up at the sight of another horse and Beth too lifted her head and tiptoed around excitedly. I gripped my knees and hung on.

We had a good ride. We kept to a slow pace, thank goodness; Flo wasn't up to cantering in her present state and I didn't know if Beth could have managed it if she'd tried. But I couldn't take my eyes off Debbie as we trotted, her back straight, her breasts thrusting forward rhythmically, her body rising and falling, the tight material between her legs brushing the saddle.

When we got back we leant against the fence and watched the two mares in the paddock. They were nudging each other, half-heartedly trying to decide who was boss. Maybe Beth didn't have the energy for confrontation and Flo lacked the motivation. But they looked good together and, for the first time, I saw Flo's ears pick up. Within minutes, and quite incredibly, they were cantering round the field like two young fillies. Then they stopped near us, by the fence, and both of them looked over.

"Sandra," I said, my confidence and my passion rising. "Did you and Kate... er... ever show... you know... affection in front of Flo?"

"Oh all the time." She nodded, smiling a little.

"Well," I said, as seriously as I could. "I really think we should do the same."

She turned to me straight away and put her face near mine, resting a hand on my arm.

"It's got to look convincing if it's going to work, Debbie," I said, behavioural therapist to the end.

She nodded seriously, putting her hands around my neck and her lips on mine.

We held each other close and kissed. Finding each other's lips, searching for the right angles, exchanging techniques. After a few minutes we were both starting to get the hang of it and awkwardness faded as pleasure took over.

Then we both forgot about the two mares completely, as we explored each other's mouths and bodies, lost in a passionate embrace right there in the middle of the Yorkshire countryside.

But the guilt was still nibbling away at the edges of my consciousness. I was a fraud. I was on the make – and this lovely, vulnerable woman had played right into my hands. I had to stop, I had to say something. I pulled away, suddenly feeling bad.

"Debbie, I have a confession to make."

She looked at me expectantly, her beautiful weather-tanned face looking up into mine.

"You won't like it," I said.

"Try me," she replied.

"Well... I don't know how to say this..." I hesitated, scared that I would lose her. "Debbie... I'm not an animal behavioural expert." I stepped back, waiting for the rejection, feeling miserable. "In fact, I don't know anything about psychology. I just fancied you like mad and it seemed a good way to get to know you."

She looked at me, amazement in her eyes, and giggled. "Oh, I'm sorry Sandra, I haven't been very fair with you. You didn't really think I believed all this behavioural therapy stuff, did you?" Her face broke into a big smile. "I've grown up with horses – I've known all along what's the matter with Flo."

Now it was my turn to look perplexed.

"She's lonely, Sandra – just like me.

"When Stella came to visit me, I soon realised that her friend, the 'animal therapist', was the woman I'd seen her with at the filling station." She stroked my head gently. "And, more to the point, the woman who I'd met in the supermarket." She laughed gently and kissed me briefly on the lips. "I didn't care what you were. I played along with her. Uh, I played along with you. Stella told me you were difficult about meeting people. I knew you were a dyke, I knew you liked horses... And I liked you."

"You mean, you knew I was fibbing all along?" I felt slightly offended but enormously relieved.

She moved in close again and put her arm around my neck, rubbing my nose with hers.

"Yeah, we both were. I just wanted to get to know you. Uh, what I didn't expect was this."

I turned and looked out into the field, trying to take it all in. The two mares were standing, head to tail, licking each other's parts and leaning together. Flo glanced at us momentarily, her ears up, her eyes bright. And I could swear I saw her smile.

Debbie saw them too and snuggled into me again.

"Lesbian horses," she breathed. "Do you want to do that?"

"What? Lick a horse?" I said.

Debbie rolled her eyes, took my hand and led me inside.

SHELLEY SILAS
The Suit With The Purple Silk Lining

Annie hadn't planned on buying anything exceptional today, just a pint of milk, skimmed and organic, wholemeal bread and bananas. But the suit caught her attention, standing out among the other, run of the mill items, displayed in no apparent order in the shop window. Other people's clothes always fascinated Annie. And the suit was no exception.

She found it in a second-hand designer shop: a little black number for special occasions. She stared at it for a long five minutes. There were two pieces, a skirt and a jacket with a purple silk lining. It was the lining, the colour of a foil wrapper from a box of Quality Street, that caught her eye. There was no price tag, which meant one of two things: unaffordable or they hadn't yet got around to pricing it.

She was forced to enquire, to see if it would fit. She didn't need a fairy godmother and two white mice to play Disney with her thoughts. She eased her way to a dressing room, makeshift corner of the shop with stainless-steel shower rail and bright yellow material to keep prying eyes away. She knew she shouldn't have been doing this. But she did it anyway. Skirt first. Pulled up and over, wetsuit perfection against her hips.

The jacket fell off the hanger onto the floor. When she bent to pick it up she noticed the scent, someone's perfume still on the collar. She wondered idly whether the suit had been cleaned or not, as she warmed to the smell, someone else's smell. Someone she didn't know. And then she slipped the jacket over her shoulders, tunnelled her arms in and out at the other end. The cool purple against hot morning skin brought a tingle to her flesh. She was enjoying it too much.

Then she took it off, jacket first. Suddenly her torso felt lifeless. The skirt didn't want to leave her body, so she unzipped it quickly and jumped out of it before it had time to miraculously zip itself up again. She wanted but didn't need. Wanted to need but couldn't justify paying £80 for a second-hand designer suit. Her inability to make a decision challenged her for all of ten minutes.

Gradually, Annie eased her eyes off the two-piece, convincing herself that, no, she didn't need more clothes. Her cupboard was full of new, almost new and never been worn. She had made a pact with Lucy only a month ago, no more clothes until her birthday. And that wasn't for another six months.

After a week of no shopping, Annie had treated herself to some underwear. And soon her one-hour lunch breaks stretched into extended shopping hours, and became too common for bank balance comfort. She'd return to her desk at the BBC, British Bed Company, designer and chain-store bags fighting for prime position in her hands, only to be thrown under her desk, beside the dustbin and her shoes, which would remain there until it was time to go home. And at home, Lucy would complain that Annie was taking up more of her side of the wardrobe with clothes that would soon be relegated to unwanted, unworn and worst of all, unloved. Unloved clothes were as bad as unloved pets. All they needed was attention, love and cleaning when necessary.

"There is nothing worse than having an item of clothing that sits in a drawer or cupboard, never to be worn, never to be loved, never to be shown off." These were Lucy's words, used often enough against Annie and her inability to say no to more bargains, to the temptation of designer, chain-store, special edition bits of material that she would buy on impulse, because she thought that one day, she might just need them. But 'might just' was not good enough for Lucy.

When the phone call came, Annie was unwrapping the suit from its bag. The cool purple pressed against her skin. Seeing it again now, draped half in, half out of the transparent plastic container, confirmed her need for this special purchase. She'd wear it for Lucy tonight. Standing in her new suit, naked under the cool lining, so Lucy could eye her up and down and Annie could slowly unzip and unbutton and let drop with the merest swish of material sliding gracefully from flesh to floor.

The phone rang four times. Annie pulled the receiver to her face, out of breath from post-shopping excitement.

"Hello," she said, hot breath against cold plastic mouthpiece. She listened to the voice on the other end. She'd been expecting the call, perhaps not so soon, but now it was here she had to deal with it.

"Where?" Annie asked. "All right," she said, "I'll be there," and hung up, hand scribbling furiously on a piece of paper. Annie didn't believe in lengthy phone conversations. She preferred to exchange words with someone face to face, and not indulge in high-tech talk.

By the time Lucy came home, dinner was on the table, candles lit, although it was too June bright for naked flames and would be until the sun went down some time after the nine o'clock news. But Annie didn't care. Candles made her feel sexy. And she wanted to feel sexy.

Lucy chatted all the way to the kitchen, where Annie stood, apron wrapped around her size ten frame, soon to be accompanied by Lucy's arms. Lucy didn't leave much space for Annie to speak, so Annie listened, the ever patient girlfriend, and even though she had other things on her mind, she looked interested, nodded and muttered upward inflection expletives in all the right places.

Dinner was a silent affair, Delia's seared salmon, two veg, and fruit for dessert, candles burning bright between them. Annie showed Lucy the note, scribbled during her phone conversation. And Lucy shrugged and walked into the other room, trailing her feelings behind her. She hadn't been invited. Hadn't not been invited, but hadn't even been mentioned, let alone asked. And she wouldn't gatecrash such an affair. Couldn't.

Lucy had chocolate in her bag, took it out and bit deep into the milk and nut bar. She held it out to Annie, a sweet-tooth peace offering. Annie declined with a gracious nod of her head. So Lucy ate it all, in the hope that the sweet would cut through the bitter, but even Lucy could not be pacified by the taste of such honeyed things.

Annie hadn't seen her girlfriend – her ex-girlfriend, her first girlfriend, her first girl love – for a while. That was Helen's choice. Before her decision to keep herself away from the eyes of ex-lovers, they used to meet every few months for a coffee and chat. No more. And never with their partners. Annie had left Helen for Lucy. Lucy was the bad girl and Annie her accomplice. Annie had dumped Helen for a younger model, fell in lust with another so she discarded the first because she could. Like a piece of clothing. And now she felt guilty. Then Helen met Frances and one became two and all four lived happily ever after. But there are never any truly happy endings.

"What time will it be tomorrow?" Lucy asked, really not wanting to know, private-school politeness hot on her heels.

"Midday," Annie said.

Lucy didn't ask any more questions after that, contented herself with bittersweet chocolate and the occasional smile from Annie. Also bittersweet.

Lucy saw the suit in the bag, was about to comment on Annie's broken promise, thought better, bit her tongue instead. Bit into more chocolate. Later, before they went to sleep, Annie took the suit out, hung it up, creases unfolding, one, two, three. This would be her special occasion suit, and seeing Helen was going to be a special occasion.

Lucy watched, tried to read Annie's thoughts.

"Will you wear that tomorrow?" she asked.

Annie's head flicked up and down quickly, like a flame in a stream of wind.

"It's a lovely suit," Lucy said.

"Yes," Annie said, climbed into bed, detached from Lucy now.

Lucy sleeps soundly. Annie does not. Her mind races back to seven years ago, when she met Helen in a Barcelona bar. They were both trying to get the attention of the dyed blonde with the deep suntan and a voice that sounded like gravel at the bottom of the Pacific. Arms outstretched with foreign money, Annie was served first and bought Helen a drink as compensation. They slept together that night in a hot hotel bed, with bottles of beer and water, balcony windows open, late night people on the streets, singing and talking, holiday fever reaching its zenith as they reached theirs.

Lucy is sound asleep.

Annie's thoughts are with Helen again, the first night in their flat. Three months into the relationship and estate agents had never been kept so busy. They settled for the basement flat in a huge Victorian house, with a garden all their own. It was a small space with a kitchen the size of a photo booth and a bathroom that had a huge sash window, allowing the early morning light to drift in, slow summer mist on an eighty degree beach. The first night they moved in, Annie came home to find a candlelit dinner for two, picnic-style on a rug in the lounge. Greek bread, hummus, olives, dolmades, chicken and rice. They had dessert in the bedroom. No crumbs to clear up. They were not messy eaters. And midwinter, indoor picnics are always fun.

They had one sofa, no table, no chairs. Helen had run a bath for Annie, bathed her in three inches of tepid water. Water-heater timer hell. Have to be careful how much we use, we'll have to buy one of those plastic shower attachments, Helen had said. But she never did. Shallow water is better than none.

Lucy snores gently.

Annie thinks about the day Lucy came along and the night she told Helen she was leaving. Leaving their home, their perfect-happiness-nothing-can-get-in-our-way state of being. Nothing and no one could get in their way. Ever. They were joined, they were one. But even atoms split in two.

Lucy came along with her long blonde hair, her brilliant blue eyes and a smile that made Annie feel that first love lust deep down tingle. That first lust tingle she had felt with Helen and swore she would never ever feel again. Could never feel again for anyone who was not called Helen.

Annie met Lucy at work. Lucy had come in to buy a bed, hand-made to order. Annie had seen her outside, observed the leggy blonde as she gazed through the window and waited until she walked through the door of the West Hampstead shop, before their eyes met for a moment longer than either of them had anticipated. Gay girl blue brown eye to eye gaze. And don't it make your brown eyes blue.

Lucy bought a bed and Annie delivered it. The personal touch was always well received. But not as personal as this one had been. The bed in place, Lucy produced a bottle of champagne and they drank a toast and made love until the bubbles were flat and the bed christened. It was a multiple christening.

Lucy turns and groans and sleeps once more.

Two months after Annie and Lucy had moved on from new bed sex, to kitchen sex and living room sex, Annie told Helen the news. Broke her heart while she broke the news, said, I'm leaving. I've met someone else. Sorry. Annie didn't believe in dragging things out. Say what you mean and mean what you say. And she did. Then she went to Lucy's, took all her things the following day, left Helen to clear up the crumbs.

Lucy dreams and speaks in her sleep, names and places that only her mind knows about. Annie gets up and lights a candle, for Helen.

She died yesterday, and her funeral will be tomorrow. And as if by divine intervention, Annie now has the perfect suit, not too sombre, with a flash of colour to lift her mood and anyone else's, if they care to study the purple silk.

Annie lights the candle and sits in the lounge and cries so deep and hard she thinks the entire house will wake. But Lucy sleeps through anything. And Annie stays awake until dawn comes and her heart is sore.

Lucy makes breakfast, toast and thick-cut orange marmalade, strong coffee and a Granny Smith. Annie gets dressed. Alone. There are no words this morning, just the clinking of cups and cutlery, the splash of water and the vibrating thump thump from the speakers upstairs. Outside of Annie's thoughts, life continues as usual. People go to work, traffic jams are in full force and the weather is unusually warm and sunny. For June. In London.

Slowly Annie puts on the skirt, lifting up past her knees to her waist. The button slots into the hole with the greatest of ease. Like it was made to fit. A second skein skin. Then the jacket. No need for a shirt. No tights, her legs are tanned enough thanks to Lancôme, and shoes, just plain black with a low heel. All the better to walk in.

Then there are words.

"Sure you don't want me to come?" Lucy asks.

Annie shakes her head.

"Don't suppose she'd want me there," Lucy mumbles through breakfast teeth, the emphasis of 'she' making Annie frown.

When Annie leaves, she kisses Lucy gently. There is little feeling between the two this morning. Annie's mood is for Helen only. This is Helen's day.

The cemetery is in North London. Men in skull caps and weeping women huddle together, creating a ghetto. Annie has never been to a Jewish funeral before. There's a first for everything, she thinks, trying to divert her tears. But even she cannot hold them back long enough and soon her face is wet and salty.

She thinks she sees Frances, has only met her once before and that was by accident. She stands outside the hall, between Helen's parents. It was not always this comfortable. Their denial of Annie, then Frances, suddenly changed. From years of not wanting to know, refusing to listen, shutting out the truth, their mood changed and they could at last play at happy families.

Not so happy now.

Frances stares at Annie, then gives her an unexpected, old friend hug and bursts into uncontrollable tears. Their shared history is dead. She whispers to Annie how much she loved Helen, how she will miss her and her life will never again be the same. And while she is whispering, Annie's nostrils are caught up with a familiar scent, strong against Frances's skin. Frances says her hurt feels so deep, this is a wound that will never heal. She thinks it will never heal. Annie nods and pats Frances, hoping to calm her. She shakes Helen's parents' hands, firm and old. When she walks away she sees them look at her and ask Frances who she is. A friend, Frances says. Now is not the time for the past to catch up with the present. Now is not the time for Annie to meet her ex-girlfriend's parents.

They walk through to the hall. Men to one side, women to the other. Frances sits with Helen's mother, with Helen's sister-in-law and two nieces, squashed on a bench. Helen's father, beside his son, their black caps for special occasions only.

In the middle of the silence, the coffin is wheeled in, on a rickety device that needs oil. The crowd turn as Helen is brought down, mid-room, while all eyes try and imagine the body beneath the wooden box.

There are prayers and tears, Frances's body trembles. Someone says some agreeable things about Helen, her father speaks of the daughter he loved, of his pride and joy and great, great loss. They walk outside in perfect midsummer sunlight. Blue sky, the colour of faded cornflowers, reminds Annie of Lucy's eyes. And she thanks God her sweetheart is safe at home.

Annie follows the crowd to the hole in the ground, where a digger stands by to pack it with soil.

They say prayers for the dead. Helen's mother wants to put a stone on her daughter's grave. Not yet.

Bare box lowers gently to the ground, groaning fathers and wailing mothers watch the thirty-something woman as she is laid down in a bed of cold dirt.

One at a time the men cover the box, passing the shovel from hand to hand. Frances takes her time, Annie drops just a bit, bites her tongue, once again the tears come of their own free will and her salt flows down into the hole.

Suddenly it feels cold. Purple silk brushes against Annie's nipples and she feels sexy in the midst of all this sadness.

Back in the room, the family tear their clothes, a sign of mourning. Annie is tempted to do the same, but will not ruin her funeral suit. Her special occasion suit. Her second-hand suit.

They go back to the house for tea and cakes. For almonds and raisins and thoughts that will make them sad. The men pray while the women eat and chat and in between words the tears come and go. And in between words the people come and go.

Frances is calm now. She talks about Helen non-stop, as though talking about her keeps her alive. The phone rings constantly. Annie thinks it's time to go.

She waits for the right moment, until Frances is on her own.

"I am really sorry," Annie says. "Really sorry. Lucy is too."

Frances shrugs, catches a glimpse of the purple silk under the black.

"Nice suit," she says, "Helen had one just like it. She gave it to some second-hand designer shop." Frances throws back her head and laughs at a happy memory. One she keeps to herself.

"She had good taste," Annie says.

Frances nods. "She has," she says. She's not ready to slip into the past tense just yet. "Thank you for coming," she says.

"Thank you for asking me," Annie says.

"She would have wanted you here."

Annie nods, turns to go, turns back to Frances.

"Nice perfume," she says.

Frances's eyes grow red and watery. "Thanks," she says. "It's Helen's."

Annie walks slowly out of the house, purple silk cold on her body, swishing against her legs. Inside she shivers. And the familiar smell of a dead woman's perfume won't go away.

In the morning Annie folds the jacket in half, feels the lining as the material closes in upon itself. She folds the skirt, puts them in a bag. Lucy sees the bulges through the plastic of the orange Sainsbury's logo.

"What are you doing with that?" she asks.

Annie shrugs. "Nothing. Taking it to a second-hand shop."

Lucy's silence is followed by a swift nod of her head. Annie is unsure whether this means Lucy is agreeing with or simply acknowledging her words.

Annie sighs. "I felt like I needed a clear out."

Lucy smiles. The last time Annie had a clear out she came home from work with double the amount of clothes she had got rid of.

"Besides, it's served its purpose. I don't think I could wear it again. I mean, how many clothes can a girl wear?"

Lucy thinks about it, pours the coffee.

"As many as she has," she volunteers.

"Is the right answer," Annie says.

Annie drops the dead woman's suit in a dustbin, somewhere along a crowded London road. And as she walks away she swears she can see the suit float up and out of the bag and piece itself together, arms waving, skirt hugging tight. And the silk purple lining glistens in brilliant morning sun. And all day, the faintest smell of perfume lingers above her head.

SUSANNA STEELE
Hi, Sugar!

It's funny how you can live with someone for years and not know some things about them. I knew a lot about Hannah but I didn't know she didn't like broad beans until three months before I left her. In fact, I only found out when she turned down a forkful of succotash in a restaurant. No thanks, she said, I'm not keen on broad beans. We had gone out for a quiet and, hopefully, romantic dinner together as part of our plan to rekindle our relationship. Looking back, it was more ashes than embers by that time but we were doing our best and I tried hard to forget that she still had a lover she saw on Tuesdays and Thursdays and every other weekend. And I believed her when she told me that Pope Joan wouldn't threaten the special place in her heart that was reserved for me only. Personally, I would have preferred a more substantial relationship with her anatomy, physical rather than metaphysical, but somehow she made it seem as if I was getting the best deal. It was a pleasant enough evening. No voices were raised and neither of us ended up sobbing into our napkins.

Then I developed a craving for broad beans. In all the five years we had been together I realised that we had never eaten them in any way, shape or form and suddenly I missed not having them. I remembered that there's a particular pleasure to be had in prising fresh broad beans out of their cosy pods. And I was no longer willing to forgo it. But that thrill was nothing to the undeniable delight I found in watching Hannah sift through a casserole or a salad with her fork and seeing her leave them by the side of her plate, a cairn of green pebbles, without saying anything.

Sometimes I spent hours on my own browsing through cookery books looking for recipes when I felt like doing some serious cooking. But more often than not I just threw a handful into whatever resourceful concoction I was stewing up with whatever was in the fridge. I usually made a dish that included broad beans on a Wednesday before Hannah went out or sometimes on a Friday. And when I cooked lunch for us, every other Sunday, I took to making a quick dip by whizzing up broad beans with yogurt and garlic and a few fresh herbs. That way you couldn't really taste them so I could watch Hannah scoop up the pale green purée with a finger or two of hot pitta bread or a handful of tortilla chips as she sat drinking a glass of wine and reading the lifestyle sections of the Sundays. She seemed to enjoy it. So did I.

By then there were few things that we did together that gave us both pleasure. "I love Sundays at home just pottering around with you," she said one lunchtime, "it's so nice having time to myself and getting things sorted out for the week." I said nothing. We'd agreed not to say anything that would start one of those never-ending wrangles that would spoil the time we had together. After all, we had spent a fortune on couple therapy and, believe me, we really worked hard when we in that room: crying over the personal baggage what we had each brought into the relationship, showing our anger at each other in a safe environment, talking about the nature of desire in a long term relationship and how there's an ebb and flow to these things that could be worked through if we were willing to take the risk. I even got Pope Joan into perspective.

We went every Monday for months and we didn't actually decide to stop going. It was more that life got in the way. I had to work late on Mondays. Tuesdays and Thursdays were out. Hannah babysat for her sister on most Wednesdays. Weekends were difficult. And our therapist didn't work Fridays. So that was that.

But we got a lot out of it when we did go. Every time we left that room everything felt possible and we'd glow for the rest of the evening. But when I was on my own on Tuesdays, well, I admit that I did sometimes wonder what it was all for. Nonetheless, I still tried my hardest to keep my end of the bargains we agreed to. So when she said that stuff about getting sorted out for the week and it was on the tip of my tongue to say, "You mean for the fortnight," I just carried on cooking. I did not want to be the one who started it. But as I was stuffing the wrapper from the bag of frozen broad beans into the bin, making sure it was well hidden under the potato peeling and the coffee grinds, I couldn't help thinking that there should be more to a relationship, that there used to be more to our relationship, than a clean bathroom and a companionable silence interrupted only by the rustle of newspaper that had become our every other Sunday ritual, doing the housework, having lunch and reading the papers. Hannah had even started working her way through the sports section. All of a sudden she was interested in cricket.

Soon after that things began to get really petty. I don't know who started it. What I do know is that it was Hannah who stopped taking out the rubbish. So I let the bin fill to overflowing. She stopped hanging up my washing. I stopped clearing hers off the drying rack. She didn't clean the sink. I didn't hoover the hall. When I went shopping I didn't buy eggs. When she went shopping she didn't buy butter. But there wasn't a cross word spoken between us. In fact, there were very few words at all when we were in together and the Sunday silences became just that: two people reading the papers on their own and sometime not even in the same room.

By that time I think we had forgotten how to have a good time of any sort. Of course, it hadn't always been like that. Our first three years, no, our first two years together were wonderful. We had Christmas in Morocco, summers in Greece, weekends in Amsterdam and sex everywhere then. We had such good times. But I'll always remember Corfu best of all.

It was June, our last holiday before we moved in together, and we hired a villa. It had a courtyard with bougainvillea and jasmine, all in blossom. The first night we were there we bought a bottle of Metaxa and a bag of little squidgy cakes at the supermarket and sat outside: drinking, watching the stars come out and the moon rise over the walls of the house. It flooded the courtyard with silver and we dipped the cakes in our glasses and fed each other sweet brandy soaked morsels. We made love there in the moonlight with the air still warm and full of the scent of jasmine. Oh, it was a sweet, sweet evening.

However, in the morning I was woken by this terrible noise. I knew Hannah was already up because I'd felt her slip out of my arms but I was really dozy so it took me a couple of minutes to work out what was happening. Hannah was screaming. I was up and outside as fast as I could and there she was, flat against the courtyard wall, screaming and shaking. My first thought was that she had been bitten by a scorpion or something and I started shouting, "Hannah! Hannah! What's happened? What's wrong?" She stopped screaming but she didn't speak. She just whimpered and pointed at the table, tears streaming down her face.

When we'd gone in the night before we'd left the last cake on the table and now it was covered with ants, a seething mass of them crawling all over what was left of the sponge cake and a line of them marching off, head to tail, each with a tiny crumb in its pincers. Another line was moving in to grab what they could. They stretched across the table, up the wall and over to a crack in the cement at the roots of the jasmine about fifteen feet away. A seamless, living, black line. A two lane highway of ants. "Get rid of them! Get rid of them!" Hannah was sobbing and whimpering and clinging to the wall. I went over and put my arm around her and took her inside. She was shaking, trembling all over and sobbing over and over again, 'Just get rid of them. Get rid of them, Viv, please!' I helped her onto the sofa and went and put on a pot of water, nothing clears ants like boiling water, and went to have a closer look. I'd never seen anything like it. There must have been thousands of them, all desperate to get at the last crumbs of what had been a fair-sized piece of cake.

I splashed the hot water all over them and rinsed away the mess on the table. Then I went inside and sat with Hannah and held her close. "What if I hadn't noticed, Viv? What if I'd sat down at the table and they began to crawl over me? They'd have been all over me, Viv." She was rubbing at her hands and her arms as if she was wiping away marauding ants and as I held her in my arms I could feel her shuddering. So I held her and stroked her until she was calm. Almost singing to her like you would to a frightened child: "All gone, Hannah, all gone now, sweetheart, no more ants, Hannah, no more nasty ants. It's OK. You're safe now. They're all gone." I never knew anyone could be that scared, not of ants.

Not long after that we moved into a flat together. It was fun at first. We shopped and decorated and gardened and, well, nested, I suppose you'd call it. It had a sort of forever feel about it for the first nine months. It's not even that things started going wrong after that, it just got cosy. That's all. We never actually had matching slippers but we might as well have had. As soon as we realised what was happening of course we did something about it. Basically, we started doing more things on our own. I took up Tai Chi for a while and she went windsurfing two nights a week on a gravel pit somewhere outside London. That's when Pope Joan turned up. At first it was only in conversation, but as far as I could make out Joan knew everything about everything. It was "Joan says" and "Joan knows" and "Joan thinks" and "I must ask Joan". Then it was the occasional windsurfing weekend away that I found out later took place in Peckham, at Pope Joan's palace. Maybe it was the effect of two nights a week doing slow motion exercise because by the time I caught on to what was happening Hannah was already staying away every other weekend, windsurfing with the Pope.

But she said she still loved me. Me. And I really wanted to believe her. I really thought we would come through it and still be together. I really did.

I finally left the day I found the Visa bill. I shouldn't have opened her mail and when I did I should never have read it. I should have just put it back in the envelope as soon as I saw it wasn't mine. I didn't. But it was a genuine mistake. The two bills arrived in the same post one Wednesday morning just before I went to work. I was just on my way out when I met the postman on the doorstep and he gave me the letters. I could see they were Visa bills straight off, one for each of us. I can't resist opening my mail as soon as I get it even if it is only a bill, so I left hers, or so I thought, on the doormat and went back inside to the kitchen with mine, pushed my thumb into the back of the envelope and ripped it open. I don't remember if I checked the name on the front of the envelope or not, I can't have done. I just thought I was opening mine.

As soon as I unfolded the bill and saw Hannah's name on it I should have just folded it up again and put it back in the envelope. Hannah would have understood. Anyone can make a mistake like that. But she doesn't use her card very often and there was only one purchase listed and the name of the shop just jumped out at me. Dilight £62.45. More than sixty quid at a sex shop? That's serious shopping. And none of it, not even the two pounds and forty-five pence, had seen the light of day or night in our flat. In fact, we were so busy working on a meaningful relationship that it had been six months, and I know it had been at least six months because I sat in the kitchen counting it up on my fingers, six whole months since we'd blown the dust off the stuff we had stowed in the bottom of the wardrobe. More than sixty quid at Dilight? Whatever she'd bought, it had nothing to do with me or with windsurfing.

I shoved the bill back in the envelope and just sat there. What did I expect? After all, isn't that what having a lover is all about? Sex. Whole-hearted delight in another person. Discovering new things about her, about yourself, and taking pleasure in the limited time spent in each other's company. What else did I think had been happening over the past nine months? OK, so maybe that's not all there is to it. But there's no bathroom to clean and no washing to sort out. No chores. By the time I rang in sick at eleven o'clock my heart was hurting. I still wanted her. I wanted that sweet, hot urgency we had had between us back again. I wanted it back the way it was when we'd set up home together.

I didn't wait for Hannah to come back from work. I packed up all the things I needed and rang Julie to see if I could stay at her place. Before I left I just took out the Visa bill and left it open on the table. That's all. No need for a note.

I didn't go back to the flat until two months later. Of course I saw her. We had hours of hysterical phonecalls and we met in restaurants and down by the river, public places, where we hoped we would be able to talk and not get too angry or upset with each other. When we met one Sunday in the park she said that she still loved me and that maybe we could get back together after she had finished with Pope Joan. Loved me? I just looked at her.

"What sort of love's that, Hannah? I want joy, desire, lust, intimacy. The sort of relationship where it's a pleasure to work to keep the heat alive. Not where I sit reading the papers on a Sunday in a silence that's turned distinctly frosty, dreaming up more freaky dinners. That's not my idea of love, you wanting to sod off to Pope Joan's three times a week until that burns itself out and coming home to potter around doing cosy domestics. There's cold comfort in that, Hannah," I said to myself in the car on the way back to Julie's. The whole way home I was shouting and crying and raging at her as if she was sitting right there next to me in the passenger seat, taking it all in. There was a scalding, raw feeling around my heart that made me drive like I was the only car on the road and no one and nothing was going to get in my way, not even red lights.

But at the time, sitting on the bench by the pond, I just looked at her and thought of that honey skin of hers and all the sweetness that we used to have together. All of it, every tender feeling, gone.

It was three weeks before I had the nerve to go and collect the rest of my things. I took an afternoon off work just to be sure I wouldn't bump into her. As I crept in through the front door I felt like an intruder, but nothing much had changed. The photographs of us that used to hang in the hall had gone. Hardly surprising. And there was a sweater hanging on the back of a chair that I didn't recognise. A very fancy number in soft black wool. Expensive. I picked it up and held it against me to see if I would have borrowed it if we were still together. I wasn't prepared for the feeling, the hot tight feeling, that I got in my chest, when I didn't recognise the smell on the collar. I dropped it back onto the chair but it slid to the floor so I left it there and went and washed my hands. I was tempted to dry them on the sweater and leave it like a wet rag by the sink. But I didn't.

When I began to take my books from the shelf my hands were shaking but I carried on stacking into boxes all the paperbacks I never intended to read again, but that were mine. By the time I stared sorting through the recipe books I'd calmed down, even congratulating myself that when I caught sight of Hannah's handwriting inside the ones that were hers it didn't result in any feelings at all. Not a flicker of a response. I collected together all the plates and dishes that I knew were mine and left all the ones that we had bought together carefully on the shelves. Everything was under control again and I was breathing easily.

The garden was overgrown, weeds everywhere, and convolvulus was strangling the shrubs. I wasn't surprised as I was the one who had looked after it all, spending weekend after weekend digging and planting and snipping bits of twig off with secateurs when she was off windsurfing. But the hibiscus cuttings that I had taken in the spring had survived. I scraped the earth off the bottom of the pots before I took them inside.

I was just setting them down on the table when the phone rang. I must admit I went to answer it, in fact, I was already standing next to it, just about to pick up the receiver, before I remembered I didn't live there any more. I stood and looked at the phone as it rang and then the answering machine clicked on. I expected the mute button to be on. It always used to be. We never actually monitored calls. We just played the messages back when we were ready. So the phone would ring and then the answering machine would take over and all you would hear was a click, silence as the caller left a message and then the whir of the tape as it rewound. But as I stood there Hannah's voice came out of the machine. It was like she was in the room, talking to me again with that smile on her face that always came when she was relaxed and easy. I found myself smiling back at her. Then there was a throaty sort of laugh as the caller started, "Hi, Sugar! Welcome home…" then that laugh again. I punched the mute button before I heard any more.

The tears started in the garden. I didn't want them to, they just came. I brushed them away with my sleeve and carried on lifting pots and cleaning the mess off the bottom of them, but the tears still came. Sugar, she called her Sugar. That summed it all up, didn't it. Summed up exactly what had happened. Sugar. She's been my Sugar, my honey-skinned sweetness, my sweet cake. I didn't need to hear Pope Joan call her Sugar. And that laugh. I didn't need to hear that sexy, giggly laugh. I stabbed at the pots with my trowel, sending the woodlice scurrying into the grass, the tears rolling down my face and my heart scalding in my chest.

I squashed the first ants I saw with the back of my trowel when I disturbed their hiding place under the tub of lavender. Force of habit I suppose. But more and more of them just kept coming. As I sat there watching them running around frantically looking for a safe place to go, I stopped crying.

Finishing getting my things together didn't take long. I stowed all the boxes in the car and went back into the flat. There was just one more thing to be done, one last goodbye.

We never bought sugar. Neither of us took it in tea or coffee and I could see that things hadn't changed when I opened the cupboard.

Obviously Hannah was sweet enough for Pope Joan. But the jar of little packets that we pocketed at cafes and service stations was still there behind the Grape Nuts. I tore each of them open, emptied the sugar into a bowl and stuffed the papers in the bin under the coffee grounds and empty tins. Just like old times! Then I took the bowl into the garden and laid a trail of fine white sugar from the ants' nest towards the kitchen door. It was almost invisible to the human eye but to an ant it must have seemed like they'd won the lottery. They were on it immediately. Hundreds of tiny black ants were picking up the crystals and heading back home to tell their friends and relations to get on out and get some. I was careful not to put too much in the garden, just enough to tempt them inside. By the time I'd sprinkled a trail across the kitchen floor I was like the Pied Piper. As soon as I dropped the sugar there were ants all over it, crawling in through the side of the door frame. I tested them out, leaving gaps in the trail that I wasn't sure they could cope with, but they did. They just kept on coming. As soon as each ant picked up its load, it was off back to the garden and by the time I reached the bedroom door there was a two-lane highway of ants seething its way back and forwards from the bedroom, down the corridor, through the kitchen and back outside.

I opened the top drawer of Hannah's chest of drawers and scattered the remains of the sugar in amongst her pants, closed it again and crossed my fingers. Yes! The ants were really going for it. A whole line of them paraded their way up the front of the furniture and disappeared through the edge of the drawer. I sat and watched them go in. It can't have been easy for an ant to get hold of the sugar in there amongst the creases and folds of the fabric and they must have had trouble finding their way out of the maze of silk and lace because more were going in than were coming out. But they kept on coming.

When I left, there was still a trail of them heading towards the bedroom. I closed the front door behind me, locked it and slipped my keys through the letterbox. Welcome home, Sugar!

ROSIE LUGOSI
You'll Do

I'm driving with my girlfriend through town after fuckwit town. Just to get away, but that's another story. We've left all that behind us now. She's driving, I'm riding. She doesn't mind, which is good, because I don't drive. Can't drive. Just never got to learn. I'm the only person I know who doesn't drive, apart from my old girlfriend Janet, and she was weird in other ways too. Lives in Maine now. There you go. Weird. We couldn't hold it together. Both of us stationary. Lack of transportation got the better of us, I guess. That was a long time ago, before all of this.

I look over at Nancy. She doesn't complain. She's driving in that detached way that feels comfortable to me now. I know she's not blanking off from me; she's just a little drawn into the road out in front. It's like a meditation, a restful state for her. And I don't disturb it. Drink it in myself. I've found her calmness increasingly calming, now I've gotten over resisting it. She was patient with me in those early days, more than I deserved, I used to say. She'd say right back that just showed I had low self-esteem and we'd laugh.

The light catches the silky hair on her forearm, resting on the wheel. Blond, fine like baby hair, but long. Sometimes when we're lying down I search her arm and find these hairs two, maybe three inches long on her arm, like mutants. She laughs, won't let me pull them out. She doesn't complain. She knows it's not criticism. I just love to explore her body. I love the difference in all women's bodies. From the start I've always been drawn to bodies like mine, yet so unlike when you get down to it. Yeah, you've worked it out, we're two girls together. You can say it: dykes. That's OK. I've been called as bad and survived worse. I sleep with women. Fuck them too. And if you're a man reading this, I guess there's a four in five chance you go for girls as well. So hey, that makes for some common ground, right? Anyway, it's not important for this story. This isn't some heart-rending tale of unrequited lesbian love in a car across one of the more tedious of this great nation's states. No pussy scenes, guys. You can check out here if that's all that got you this far.

So we're driving.

The land is flat and nearly featureless. Far away to my right there's a line of grey hills running parallel to the road; pale rock, no vegetation. More miles away than I care to imagine, probably. One of those tricks of the light. Because they're damn near the only thing to look at they seem closer than they are. I think about how long it would take to walk to them and my head goes into movie mode; what Nancy calls my fertile imagination. I see myself trudging over the pebbly ground, staggering a little maybe, looking up at the sun which burns down out of a big silver sky, raise my circular canteen to my lips, but it's empty, so I throw it away, just like in those old black-and-white movies I'd watch on a Saturday afternoon as a kid. I never understood why the guy threw away the canteen. What if he found some water? What would he put it in? It happened in every movie and I thought it was real stupid every time.

I pop open a soda for Nancy and one for me. Who says there's no such thing as association? Nancy gives me a real nice smile.

"Watching movies?" she says.

"Yeah." I smile back. "Those hills made me think of *Treasure of The Sierra Madre*, and all those ones I can't even remember their names: used to watch them on TV."

"Yeah. And the hero always threw away his canteen, didn't he?"

There's a twinkle in her eye, like she knows what I was thinking all along. These days I'm not surprised, more sheepish that I could forget how well she knows me. She reaches over with her free hand and runs her fingers through my hair where it flops over my forehead. The car doesn't swerve. She keeps us on course. After a while she puts her hand back on the wheel.

"I want to stop soon and get some rest," she says. "Sleep rest."

The first motel we come to is just before we enter the town. It's advertising bar-be-q special midweek for $9.95. It looks like a dump.

"Yeah, well, I'm not that tired," says Nancy, barely slowing the car. "Let's see what's in town."

Town is one of those descriptives you realise fast is an overstatement. It's a mile-long stretch of ugly tarmac, with two intersections where traffic lights sway over damn-near deserted roads. We pass one diner fronted by a parking lot with a handful of trucks and cars scattered across it. It looks like it's going to be our only choice for food later on. Oh great.

"Not what you'd call crowded," I moan.

"At least it has a few customers, so it can't be poisoning folks."

"Unless it's killing them off with the tuna special and selling their cars as a sideline."

"Where did that come from?"

"Just my great sense of humour, honey." I give Nancy a cheesy grin.

By now we've passed through and are out the far side of town. The buildings dwindle to a trickle, then nothing. There's one large, low building on the left and we slide up to it. It's a motel, and looks even less exciting than the first. We pull up.

"Christ, this one doesn't even have bar-be-q for ten bucks. Let's go back to the other one. Or do you want to drive on, honey?" I look over at Nancy. She suddenly looks real tired, lets out a long breath, crumples a little before my eyes. I realise just how long she's been driving, remember just how much we've driven away from. She scratches the back of her hand with a nervous gesture I've not seen for so long I'd almost forgotten it. I reach over and cup my hand round her cheek.

"Hey sweetheart." I smile at her and she looks at me. "We don't have to stay here, but you're exhausted. So we stop here if you want. As long as it's got a shower and a bed, that's fine. I'll go and fetch us some food."

She leans into my hand. "I had no idea I was this tired until we stopped," she sighs. "I guess it's not a surprise. But yeah, the other place looks better than this. I'll drive us back. I'd rather."

She shifts the car into reverse and backs into the driveway to turn, and the car cuts out. She turns the key. Nothing. Cars are a mystery to me. They start, they don't start. One is as mysterious as the other to my way of thinking. And this one is refusing to start. Mystery or not, it's a pain in the ass.

Nancy is starting to get frustrated. She jiggles the key around a few more times without success, heaves out a long breath, turns to me and says *sorry*, head bowed. This surprises me more than the car dying on us. I can't remember when was the last time I heard Nancy apologise for something that wasn't her fault. She's fair. If she's out of line she says so. But not this.

"Hey, it's OK, it's a machine. You don't need to say sorry for a heap of metal."

"Yeah, you're right." She lifts her head. "I'm tired, I guess. Well, it looks like we might be staying here after all." She pauses. "They can tell us where the nearest car mechanic is. I cannot be bothered getting under that hood, however simple the problem."

She's back to her decisive self again. Good.

We get out the car and walk across the empty lot towards the office. It's part of a large, one-storey building with a flat roof. The motel cabins are over the other side of the parking lot. Low, flat roofed again. At least they look clean. But the place is so empty. I go into movie mode and imagine tumbleweeds rolling around, the squeak of the motel sign as it sways in the wind, the whine of Ennio Morricone music playing in the background. But there's no air moving here.

I expect the door of the office to creak as I push it open, but it's noiseless on oiled hinges. There are some deep horizontal scratches in the plastic woodgrain like something heavy's been dragged past. But neatly painted over. Well, they're houseproud, which I hope is a good sign. I think back to some of the places I've stayed with Nancy, and not just in the good ol' U. S. of A. Some people don't like two women staying either because they figure we'll be hauling back carloads of guys and beer and having an orgy, or they figure we're dykes and just hate us anyway.

The office is dim and cool after the direct sun outside. I look for a bell on the counter, but a door in the wall behind it opens and a small woman steps through. I get a glimpse of a kitchen area behind. Her features look as if they were arranged in a hurry by someone whose work wasn't checked carefully enough. She pushes her lips together in what I guess is a smile, but is more nondescript. She stands there and blinks at us.

"We'd like a room," says Nancy.

"A room! Right, ladies." It's like someone's switched her on. She broadens what is passing for a smile into what she must think is a grin and reaches under the counter, dragging out a large book.

"If you'll just sign in here." Her voice has a sing-song quality, as if she's learnt this spiel by rote and says the same thing to all comers, substituting *gentlemen* where appropriate. And I guess that is exactly what she and countless other motel owners do across the country. Tiring quickly of finding new things to say to the faceless people who pass through.

Nancy's finished scratching in the book, so I take my turn. The woman takes it back off me and contemplates our scribblings for a moment, squinting up her eyes. I prepare to say we're sisters, but she's not interested and slides the register back where it came from. She looks back at us and moves those features around into what I'd swear is meant to be sincere apology.

"I'm afraid I'll have to ask you ladies to pay in advance..." She lets her words hang in the air.

"That's no problem," smiles Nancy, showing her how a genuine smile really can be done. "We'd really appreciate it if you could tell us where the nearest garage is. Our car cut out in the driveway back there."

Nancy tilts her head back in the direction of the car and the woman follows the movement with large glassy eyes as if she can see it, which of course she can't as there's a wall in the way.

"Well, I'm sorry to hear that." Her face has switched into concern now. I could watch it for hours. "My brother's an auto mechanic. He'll be back in a half hour."

Nancy isn't the kind to demur, and certainly not as exhausted as she is right now.

"Just see it as part of the service we offer. And of course, I don't expect you to pay in advance without seeing your room. There are the cabins over the far side of the parking lot," she says, "and we also have a new development of more luxurious hotel-style rooms in this area." She really does sound like a glossy brochure now. "We're rather proud of them. Each room has ensuite luxury bathroom with bath. Direct from Europe."

She just said the magic word. A bath. What wouldn't I give just to stretch out in a tub. Fuck the expense. I want to dance around and shout, *Yes we'll take it!* Then run on in, turn on both taps full, tear my clothes off and jump in. Instead I restrict myself to a small smile.

"That sounds just great," I say.

The proprietor smiles back. Hey, she's getting better at it too. Maybe she just needed the practice.

"If you'll follow me, ladies."

She swings up half the counter top and comes through, walking over to a door in the wall I hadn't noticed when we came in. She's wearing neatly pressed chinos which surprises me a little. I had her down as a skirt type. Closer to, her face look less haphazard. Maybe it's the kind that grows on you. Her jaw seems firmer. In fact, it dawns on me that she looks rather dykey. And she did mention a brother rather than a husband. Well, well. Baths from Europe and now a lesbian motel owner. I try to catch Nancy's eye to see if she's guessed too, and fail. We step through the door and I realise I'm beginning to enjoy myself.

We're in a corridor that's pleasantly cool and has four, five doors off it, each spaced a long way from the other. The rooms must be pretty big. Maybe they need to be to fit that bath in. I see myself lounging, surrounded by bubbles in a tub the size of Nevada. We troop in the first door on the right and are steered straight for the holy of holies.

"So, the bathroom!"

Our guide clasps her hands over her breasts, breathing excitedly. They really have gone to town on it. The tub is massive; gold taps, fancy tiling, mirrors that look foreign and expensive. And the carpet, I swear I could sleep in it, it's so deep and soft. I'm in heaven, grinning like a kid. The owner looks at me and smiles right back. She seems much more, well, real now. Like she just needed to warm up some.

"It's fantastic," I hear myself saying.

Out of the corner of my eye I see Nancy's head flick in my direction, so I turn to her. Usually she's good at veiling her face in the presence of others, but I catch a powerful if unspoken shot of *what the hell are you on about?* She's looking at the room like there's roaches crawling on the bathmat. I question her with my eyes and she fixes me with a look that could fell a horse. I'm thrown. Two minutes ago she was all sweetness and smiles.

The motel owner places her palms together in something that's halfway between prayer and subservience. She's too much.

"I'll leave you two ladies alone to decide. I'll be right outside." She slides out of the room.

I whisper, "What's up Nancy?" but she shrugs me off like I'm poison. She's shaking. It dawns on me she's angry, which throws me even more. Then I'm angry too, out of nowhere. This is more than tiredness.

"Look at me, will you?" I hiss. "We get here, the rooms are great, the motel's clean, the owner looks like a dyke and her brother's going to fix the car for chrissakes. What the hell more do you want?"

Nancy swings her head around and fixes me with her eyes. "What I want..." she says, her voice trembling with something that's nearly tears, "is for you to stop the fuck making eyes at this fucking woman. She looks like *Jackie*, for god's sake."

"What?" The breath goes out of me. Jackie? A name, maybe *the* name out of all the names we're driving to leave behind. I know Nancy's got to be worn down after these past few days, weeks, we've been through, but what *is* this? The proprietor may look like a lesbian, but there's no way on god's earth she looks anything like Jackie. The edge of my delight has gone. Nancy and I are brewing for a huge fight, which I know is going to erupt the minute we're left alone. And I have no goddam idea where it's coming from at all.

All this happens in seconds. Then the woman in question is standing in the door frame. She looks at Nancy, then me, then back at Nancy again, with that fixed half-smile of hers. C'mon lady, I think. If you're a lesbian, you've seen this a million times. But her smile is blank, non-judgemental. She raises her arm and gestures us out of the room. She really does not look like Jackie. And I am not, repeat not, making eyes at her.

"So?"

"It's fine. We'll take it," I say flatly. I know all the enthusiasm I felt a few minutes back has drained from my voice and I feel a twinge of guilt. The bathroom is clearly this woman's pride and joy and here I am, sounding like I've been offered a can of past-the-sell-by-date beans. What the hell. It's not my problem.

"Well, if we go back to the office we can settle up."

If she's noticed my lack of spirit, she doesn't indicate it. I feel absurdly grateful. We trudge down the corridor. She pauses and glances at us again. For a moment, I feel like an ant in a jar.

"Let's cut through the kitchen." She sounds almost conspiratorial. "It's quicker to the office and I'd like to show you our refit. I can tell you ladies appreciated the bathroom."

What the hell planet does this woman come from? She wants us to look at her new kitchen? OK, the bathroom was nice, but I don't want a house tour. I want to be alone with Nancy. I open my mouth and close it again. It feels like far, far too much effort to argue. Nancy's not saying a word. I look over at her but her head's tilted away from me so I can't see her expression. She looks like her stuffing's leaked out. I want to put my arms around her, say *sorry, let's just work this out, honey.* But I don't. Instead I follow our hostess up the passageway.

She opens the kitchen door, strides in and swings round to face us. Her eyes are shining and there's a pink flush rising from her neck. I half-expect her to raise her arms and shout, "Ta-daa!" like a ringmaster announcing the big act, she's so worked up. Hell, if she is a dyke, she can't have much of a sex life to get so excited about a goddam kitchen. She can barely contain herself.

"It's real nice." I feel I have to say something. It is big, I'll give her that. Must take up the whole of one side of the building. The walls are lined with cabinets and appliances. Everything gleams. I turn round to check on Nancy and she's just behind me, looking over to the far side of the room. I follow her gaze to where there's a kid sitting, dwarfed by a huge table.

Though he's perched on a high chair, his shoulders barely clear the top of it. There's an empty plate in front of him and I can't tell whether he's just cleared it or is waiting for it to be filled. He's very still and is surveying us intently. The motel owner has also followed our eyes and sweeps over the shining floor to the boy.

"And this is Dean," she beams. The flush is creeping over her cheeks now. "My brother's boy. My brother just loves kids. Say hello now, Dean."

Dean declines the invitation and continues to stare at us. He has the same sort of blank, faraway look as his aunt. Must be some kind of family trait. Or maybe it's just living out here. How many people do they actually get staying? Presumably enough to finance this fancy refit. Or maybe this rather dowdy dyke is a cocaine dealer for some

Colombian cartel. Oh, yeah, right. More likely her brother's loaded. Christ, listen to me. Why am I bothering to waste my time thinking about this shit? I'm so tired I could cry. I've no idea what the hell is wrong with Nancy. It's making me frantic. And here I am wondering where they get their fucking money from. Jesus.

Dean decides to concentrate his attention on me. His aunt's gazing at him like she's besotted. Then she follows his line of vision and rests her eyes on me.

"So, you'll stay?"

For a second I think she means just me. As in, "you" in the singular. I push the idea away.

"Yes," I say.

"No," Nancy splutters simultaneously. I turn around.

"Nancy?"

She looks like she's fighting to hold down a tornado of rage, and gradually losing her grip. Her mouth is twitching. I've never seen her this mad. I've never seen *anyone* this mad, period. She doesn't trust herself to answer me. Suddenly I want to scream, *what in christ's name is up with you? We have no car, this is embarrassing, stop it, let's get a room and sort this out.* But I squeeze out, "Nancy, honey?" and pray she gets the message.

"I am not staying here," she says very slowly, picking each word carefully.

I guess, more than any other moment, that's when everything changes. I turn away from her and back to the motel owner.

"So, you'll stay?"

It's like she hasn't heard, or is ignoring Nancy. Then I realise that she is talking to me, just me. And I know that, yes, I am going to stay. So I say simply, "yes".

She holds me with eyes which are now warm and animated. I feel something like relief wash through me. There's this voice somewhere in my head saying, *you're home, you know.*

"Unless, of course, you want to go with your girlfriend."

There's the tiniest edge of sarcasm in the last word.

I turn back to Nancy, who is swaying slightly in front of me. Must be my eyes. I don't really know why I'm doing this.

"No," I say.

Nancy gives me a look of pure unadulterated hate, which kind of swims over me now.

"You lousy fuck." It's like all the contempt she's ever felt is concentrated into those words. But I don't cry. I don't feel much of anything. I'm floating above all of this. The little voice is still there, saying, *hey, Nancy's lost it. She's nuts. You're seeing what she's really like, deep down. You don't need her. Let her go.* I'm finding it so easy to listen to that voice.

Nancy walks away. Or maybe I move a few steps closer to the motel owner, I don't know. What I do know, as I look at her, is that I am going to stay. More than just the night. Something's happening here. I know with a certainty that if she asks, I'm going to follow this woman for the rest of my life. And I have no idea why.

She raises her arms lazily and holds them out to me. Now, I think, she will touch me and I will understand. I wait, my eyes half-closed. Her fingers reach my shoulders and I wait for her to pull me to her, but she doesn't.

"You'll do," she says quietly.

Her hands slide up quickly and fix lightly round my throat. Instinct makes my eyes spring open and my own hands fly up to my neck. She's not letting go. She's still smiling at me as she starts to swell. Her face is now scarlet to the roots of her hair, which is growing as I watch, fanning out around her like it's charged with static.

She's filling up, expanding. Her hands grow larger round my neck, and though they seem to be just resting there, I can't loosen them. I claw at them furiously. I feel one of my hands grow slick, and look at it. I've ripped off two of my nails and my hand's covered in blood. My blood. I'm not leaving a scratch on her. I flail at her face frantically, but can't reach her now. Her head's like a red balloon, features stretched out, distended. And that blank smile is stretched right across her face like some obscene cartoon. The rest of her body is growing too, and I feel my feet lift off the ground as she expands up towards the ceiling. I kick desperately, trying to keep my toes in contact with the floor.

I cast around wildly, searching for Nancy, but all I can see is the child Dean, sitting silently behind his empty plate. He's picked up his knife and fork, and is watching me die with detachment. As my eyesight starts to fade it occurs to me he's a lot older than he looks. Older than me. Older than all of us. It makes me want to laugh. A rattle rises from my constricted throat and I feel water run out of my eyes. I'm laughing, I'm crying. My face is wet with snot.

Then I feel another pair of hands on me. I twist my head round as far as I can and see Nancy. She's shrieking at whatever's got hold of me to let go, scratching, hitting, screaming, and like me not leaving a mark. We lock eyes for an instant and in that second I want her to know that I understand now how we've been set up. Right from when the car cut out. Most of all I want to say sorry. Then it's over. Nancy catapults away from me as Dean grabs the hair on top of her head and drags her back. He has grown too, is now the size of a man, but still with the proportions of a child. He wraps his arms around her and hugs her to him, like he's keeping a favourite toy to himself. He looks down at her with curiosity while she's struggling, then reaches out to the table, picks up his empty plate and slowly begins to push it into Nancy's mouth. Her screaming becomes a high-pitched squeal coming from the back of her throat. The plate's too wide to fit, but he keeps pushing. Her whine gets higher, crazier, as the sides of her mouth start to split open under the pressure. He keeps forcing the plate in. Blank-eyed. He's not even focused on her. She isn't going to get away.

The last thing I see is my killer's face. Her distended head is brushing the ceiling and she's hauling me up towards her face. Her mouth is pursing into a kiss, one that can swallow me whole. Somewhere below and behind me I hear a retching sound and a wet slap as Nancy vomits onto the floor. Those clean, clean tiles. Oh, Nancy.

I think of the last time we were ever alone, in the car back out there in the driveway. How tired she looked, how I cupped my hand round her cheek. How much I was in love with her. How much I do love her. I want to hold onto that.

Things are ebbing away. My arms have fallen to my sides. They're starting to twitch and I can't stop them. My bowels loosen and I sense liquid seeping down my legs. All that's left of me is retreating into my head. I try to hold onto Nancy in there. I want Nancy to be the last thing on my mind. But I'm losing her. Pushing her aside are questions: how many people stop here, how many ever get to use that bath, what these people, if that's what they are, will use to bait the next trap. Most of all, I wonder what this is all for. I never get any answers. Finally, what fills my head is the memory of those scratches I saw on the door of the office when we came in. The long horizontal marks as if something heavy had been dragged past. Deep, animal scratches.

Then it all goes black.

HELEN SANDLER
Modern Interiors

I didn't start off hating her. I had been warned but I was feeling kind of mad myself and it's all relative, isn't it?

I had come back to take a second look at the room, worried about the marks around the lock, thinking that someone had broken in recently – or tried to. I wound my way up through the house, knocking on doors to find a neighbour. At the top was a single door marked 'Penthouse'.

The girl who answered was younger than me, with a stronger version of my accent. She asked me in and told me that no one had been burgled but that people sometimes kicked in their own doors if they were locked out.

"The landlord's lost the spares," she said, as if that explained that. "He's a bit crap really but the heating's included. What's he charging you?" And we got on to rents in London and the impossibility of buying, and my anxiety started to lift. She gestured around her own bright kitchen and told me: "He lets you decorate, anyway, you can do what you like to your flat – saves him having to bother."

Then she added, "I should tell you this, though. I bet he never said anything? The thing is, Helen, the girl next door to you is mad."

"What like?"

"I'll just say this, right. Ignore her."

"Why?"

"Oh, she's not taking her tablets and if you give her any attention, anything at all, right, like saying good morning to her and looking at her, then it can set her off."

"What like, though?"

"Just daft talk and insults. Just don't speak to her."

"OK. Thanks."

"Don't speak to her?" I thought, as I ran back down the stairs, surprised to find it was only three floors down and not four or five. "We share a bathroom, for god's sake."

I let myself back into the room. Advertised as a studio flat, it was in fact a large bedsit, which someone had divided in two by positioning all the cupboards and bookcases down the middle so that one narrow half was the bedroom, which had the benefit of windows, and the other was a dim kitchenette with a little table. But it had potential.

Even I could see that.

My experience of decor was limited to the past year's sub-editing on *Modern Interiors* magazine. I got into it through my sister. It didn't matter that I didn't know a pelmet from a finial and had to ask what MDF stood for. You could pick it up. And sure enough, I picked it up so quickly that I was able to answer "Main reasons for hanging voile at a window?" in the fun quiz at a company barbecue within weeks of starting the job. (Maintain privacy while letting in light.)

Being exposed to hundreds of pictures of attractive modern interiors, and writing advertorials for accessories that would look smart and stylish in any home, had activated a previously dormant bit of my brain – the bit that wants to liven up a dull room by painting a bright square of colour on one wall. (Create your own modern art for the price of a tester pot.)

It was a year since the breakup with Pascale had forced me into an unsuitable flatshare. Now felt like the right time to try living alone.

The girl from the 'penthouse' upstairs and her boyfriend helped me shift all the storage units to one wall, where it became clear they'd been made to measure. Suddenly the room opened up to light and possibility.

You can paint white melamine units in bright modern colours after sanding and priming – and I did. It was while I was taking up the carpet that my next-door neighbour made herself known. She had been staying with her boyfriend for a few days, she explained, as she hovered in my doorway, trying to look into the room.

"Come in," I said encouragingly – I already felt as if I was lying just from the effort of not saying, "I hear you're a total nutter." She didn't quite believe the invitation was for real, and dithered before entering.

"What you payin' for this?" she asked in an *EastEnders* accent that had taken me by surprise. The house is in a part of London that doesn't have a distinct accent, just a generalised Estuary English.

"Ninety," I replied.

"Ninety? You're being done, intya? Bloody cheek." Then, with a sudden childlike horror and delight: "What you doing to the carpet?"

"I'm taking it up. I'm going to paint the floorboards."

"You're never! Paint the floorboards? Why?"

"It will look nice. Like this." I fumbled through a pile of back issues to show her the full-page pic of a spacious loft apartment with its sunny yellow floor which dazzles visitors. (I remembered having to ask the art room to flip the pic so that the Purves & Purves wall clock was the right way round.)

Already I could feel the dilemma closing in on me. She was not acting normally but then neither was I. I was a nervous wreck, in fact. Her speech seemed strangely exaggerated but that might be my own patronising response to hearing a Cockney accent – where I come from, you put on that accent to mimic the banter in the Queen Vic. And people down here, of course, do the same for the Rover's Return.

I gave her a cup of tea and she told me all about her boyfriend. "Really he's like a fiancé," she said, and her small sharp face jerked a tiny jerk that would later become my special alert to an untruth. "We're so in love, Helen." (This was the second neighbour to overuse my name and I wondered if they were all desperate for a sense of community, testing it out, or just reminding themselves of the name of the new girl so as to avoid future embarrassment.) "We'll get married, probably. That's all I want. Get married, have children. We'll have our own flat." Her face was glowing, her eyes big and blue and eager.

"Everyone wants that, don't they? We're all only living here till we get married, get our own homes."

"I'm not," I said, feeling brave and honest and true. "This is my home." It did not sound brave and honest and true. It sounded false and pathetic.

"Oh right. You not got a boyfriend, then?"

"No."

"What are you anyway, eh?" I was about to say I was a lesbian when she added: "Are you an actress?"

"No. I did a bit of acting at college. Why did you think that?"

"Think what?" Fear gripped her face.

"That I'm an actor – actress, whatever?"

"Oh that." She relaxed and laughed a high-pitched staccato. "*Actress*. It's actress for a woman, isn't it? You couldn't be an actor, could you?" She laughed again and I felt we were spiralling together into one of those plays I never actually read at college – Pinter or something. And bizarrely, at that moment she was on her feet and pulling a Pinter text off the lime-green bookcase. I flinched.

"You've got all these plays, so I thought you was an actress. I was going to be an actress but then I got all my plays, you know, and I threw then on the floor, I took them off the bookcase and threw them on the floor and I took them to the cancer shop – they won't let me in there now and I tell you what, they've had enough stuff off me – and I thought, there now, that's the end of that."

"Oh."

"Yeah."

"So what are you going to be now? I mean, have you got a job?"

"No. Not now, no. But I'm going to work in production. On television. But Helen, it's so hard to get a job. You don't know anyone in television, do you?"

By the time she'd gone, I was only fit to lie on the bed, go over every line of dialogue and ask myself if it proved her madness and if it mattered.

But I felt shaken. My boundaries – as a psychotherapist, a homeopath, a polarity therapist and an osteopath had told me in the last year – were fucked. They didn't all put it like that, but that's what they meant. I was supposed to feel myself as a channel of energy between the earth and the sky, gently close up the petals of any chakras that opened too wide, keep off caffeine and dope, exercise daily, meditate daily, sit up straight and eat fruit. I had started going to yoga but even there I noticed that other people's stuff was affecting me. If they lay down too close to me and my mat, their vibes started zapping me as soon as the teacher told us to fill the space around us with our energy.

New age spirituality and home decoration – I might have thought as I dragged myself from the bed and pulled it out from the wall to get at the carpet – twin voices of our age. Strip back to the bare boards and sit on them. As you chant, remember the tree that made this floor.

*

I hadn't known her long when it became clear that, without my having said anything obvious, she had twigged I was a dyke. Of course, she may have seen my books when she was looking at the plays on my shelf that day, or she may simply have guessed.

But her response was the same as for many straight people – she wanted to introduce me to the one other lesbian she knew. In this case, however, not only did she barely know me but she barely knew the other party.

"Have you seen that girl?" she asked one day when she'd knocked on my door for no good reason.

"Which girl?"

"I see her all the time. In the park. You should say hello to her. You'd like her. She's very nice, very friendly. And nice looking. Bit like you. D'you know what I mean?"

It wasn't a figure of speech – she was checking I'd understood her code. I nodded.

"Go and talk to her. She's there most days."

"What time?" I asked, trying to find a loophole in the plan.

"All the time. She works there! Near the bird home. She's called Jennifer – it says so on her badge. She's lovely."

I had a doctor's appointment later that week at 11, so instead of my usual rush to work I went to the park for a coffee. Then I remembered about Jennifer and asked for her at the sanctuary – a set of giant cages full of dying birds. I was told she didn't work there, she worked for the council and I might find her in the rangers' building.

By now I felt I was on an adventure. I was strangely elated and particularly pleased not only to be avoiding the office of *Modern Interiors* but to be looking down on it from the great height of the park – I could see the company's ugly grey tower sticking up next to the river, miles below me.

So I went and found Jennifer. She was wearing a green ranger's uniform and the badge, putting a collection of dead bats in order. "We had a bat walk last night," she explained. I wondered if this was the spoils or if she walked these same dead specimens around the park every full moon. "What can I do for you?"

I was not convinced she was a lesbian, with her long dark curls and that bluff friendly tone that outdoorswomen often use to everyone. We hadn't immediately made a special lesbian connection.

I told her that my neighbour had suggested I come and say hello. It sounded odd. Then I added, "I'm a bit worried about her actually and I thought you might have a better idea what's wrong with her."

This was perfect. It was a bit of a lie but it was bound to work with this kind of caring professional, even if she cared for trees and bats instead of people.

I saw her eyes flicker as she focused on me properly and took in my cropped, greying hair and baggy menswear. I held her gaze for a second and it was done – we both knew. But I didn't know what clue my neighbour had seen in Jennifer unless it was just the masculine cut of that green uniform.

Well, you can see where this is going. We had a good talk about Madam and agreed she was barking and needed help; Jennifer said she bothered her every day, nearly; I said she hassled me every evening. Then I had to go off to the doctor's so we arranged to meet in a pub near the park after work.

And when Jennifer came back to the flat after the pub, I fucked her on the floor with my hand over her mouth to stop her shouting or laughing or moaning and attracting the neighbour's attention.

It sounds unfeeling when I retell it: her madness, Jennifer's fanciability, it's like I was unaffected. But in fact I was affected very deeply, just not in the right way. Perhaps having her next door was getting in the way of everything. And she was getting worse.

First she had the boyfriend over – or *a* boyfriend. Instead of a romantic evening planning a family or a wedding, they fought so loudly that I began by wishing I'd encouraged Jennifer to scream the house down on our first date, and ended by realising in cold-blooded horror that he was knocking her all round the room.

I was just reaching for the phone to call the police, my heart beating uncomfortably fast, when the noise turned to something like consensual sex.

Next day was a Saturday. I like a lie-in at the weekend but I was woken early by them shouting. She turned him out of the house as an effing bastard, shouted down the street at him to never come back, and then cleaned the room noisily for most of the day. The climax was some kind of demolition job. After watching children's TV for an hour while the bangs and exclamations continued, I realised she was taking the bed to pieces without a screwdriver.

That night she knocked on my door after 12 and asked what I thought I was playing at. As I was at my most harmless and passive (lying in bed listening to Simon and Garfunkel in Central Park, half-stunned by spliff, making plans for Jennifer and me to go and live in Skala Erossos where she would track dolphins and I would produce a sapphic magazine in two languages), I wasn't sure what I was playing at.

"What?" I asked.

"Are you trying to drive me mad? Don't pretend you don't know. First him and now you, playing your music so loud, don't you know there's other people living here?"

The look she gave me was frightening. I said I'd turn it down, though I could already barely hear 'The Sound of Silence'.

Seven hours later, she woke me by knocking once again and telling me how sorry she was that she'd been 'rude' but all her plans were ruined, her man a bastard, she had loved him so much and my music was just the last straw.

Jennifer had seldom stayed the night. Partly I was avoiding intimacy but mainly I feared that my coping mechanisms around the neighbour would be put under too much strain.

If I heard my neighbour going to our shared bathroom, for instance, I stayed in my room until I heard her come back. I didn't want her to stop me in the hall and tell me all about a boyfriend who might or might not be the same one – how strange that he never called, what did I think had gone wrong? And I certainly didn't want her appearing to me naked as I was going downstairs, by opening the bathroom door just as I was passing and letting out a piercing scream. This had already happened twice to me and I was not the only one.

Then there was the whole thing about noise – at first I just didn't want my neighbour to know I'd got off with Jennifer but later I became obsessed with keeping quiet all the time so she had no excuse to knock on my door. When she did knock, my blood pressure rocketed, my mind spun behind my eyes, I forced myself to the door for the next frightening encounter, all the time trying to seem normal so she didn't ask what was wrong with me.

"What's the matter with you?" she might demand, spitefully. "You're all white!"

Her disturbances, which were probably fairly mild on the scale of personality disorders, created or encouraged disturbances in me that could not have been much more forceful if a known lesbo-killer was at the door. But I had to deal with it alone. Jennifer joking about hiding in the wardrobe, Jennifer running a bath for two as if the bathroom was a safe and peaceful zone, well, it didn't help. It just underlined the fact that Jennifer was normal, grounded, sane, and I was not.

She suggested I stop answering the door. "If you can't deal with her," she smiled, tucking her hair behind her ear like Carol off *ER*, "don't answer the door. Don't engage. She can always come and bother me at work tomorrow if she needs a friendly ear."

I kissed her friendly ear. "You just don't get it," I whispered, resigned to a lifetime of sane girlfriends.

"Well, what's the worst that can happen?" she asked as she drew the curtains (in the same blue as the bedspread and the floor, to create a feeling of unity).

"The worst? I'll tell you the worst. Because it's fucking happened, actually. The worst is that I don't go to the door because I'm too fucked – because, say, I'm crying myself to sleep because I feel so lonely and desperate..."

Jennifer looked lovingly shocked and I almost melted.

"And then she starts to shout at me through the door about what a nasty selfish cow I am and how I shouldn't expect anyone to help *me* when I need it. And I can't shout back because I'm not supposed to engage."

Well, Jennifer had plenty more tips but I just thanked her and sent her on her way. She lived nearby with a jealous ex but that was her problem. Until the mice came. Then, I lost the plot.

*

I saw the first one almost as soon as the weather changed for the worse. I heard a scratching that I'd heard before. Stoned and paranoid from some grass that the guy in the penthouse had promised was wicked, I froze in my bed. It was 3am and I'd been dozing through dreams where the magazine came back from the printer full of serious errors that were clearly my fault; captions that read, "Helen to fill here blah de blah de bollox Helen to fill."

Now I got up and crossed the few feet to the kitchenette. Two glinting eyes shone in the beam of my torch. I shouted, "Fuck! Fuck off!" It scuttled along the skirting board. I threw a shoe. Minutes passed. Then a scream from next door and a man (what man?) apparently chasing it on to the landing while my neighbour cried, "On the bed! Bleeding hell, no! On the bed!"

This chilled me. I had to watch TV all night, including American football, but I also had to wear earplugs so I wouldn't hear the mouse if it came back.

At dawn I called Jennifer. I was still shaking and my brain felt like it had shattered into fragments which were whirling and re-forming beneath my skull.

She, as usual, sounded breezy. She was preparing autumn leaf worksheets for visiting schoolchildren, as she brightly informed me. She laughed when I told her about the mouse and offered to bring round a humane trap.

I got home that night to find Jennifer cooking dinner and playing Radio 4 so loud I could distinguish every word.

"It's too loud!" I said. Then, "Hello. Can you turn it down?" I turned it down myself. "Don't you know voices carry louder than music?"

"It's all right," she said as she took the five spice from the cupboard above her head. "I told her I'm here to catch the mouse and she told me to make myself at home."

"You spoke to her? Jennifer! She's not supposed to ever know you're here."

"But I'm here professionally."

"Professionally? You're not a ratcatcher."

"Yes I am, actually. Ratcatcher, mouse trapper, squirrel tracker, bird ringer. You should come on one of our wildlife walks."

"Can't we just kill it?" I asked weakly.

"No." She dug in the pocket of the green trousers, which still seemed indecently defeminising on her. "Here." She thrust a photocopied sheet into my hand and smiled.

It was headed, 'The mammals who share our homes.' It was a survey of householders, to gather data about the eating, nesting and breeding habits of mice.

Four illustrations showing the same furry funster in varying poses were labelled common mouse, field mouse, brown mouse and house mouse – or something like that, I didn't dwell over it.

"There's no need to kill them," she said as she shook droppings from a plate into the sink.

"Fuck!" I said, wide-eyed. "Droppings!"

"Didn't you see how Hugh Fearnley-Wotsits dealt with it?" she asked. "He had them spirited away to the shed by a kind of exorcist."

"So I heard. I've been hearing about how to get rid of mice all fucking day from my helpful colleagues. But if we're going to exorcise anything in this house, I can think of higher priorities than a mouse."

"Oh, I thought it was vital to get rid of it?"

"It was, but it's also vital to keep it secret about you and me, and you've fucked that right up. I don't want to attract her attention!"

"Well, don't shout then."

There was a knock at the door. I shot a look at Jennifer and answered it.

"Sorry to bother you, Helen," she said as if respectfully petitioning at Number 10, "but I wonder whether Jennifer, the ranger, you know, whether she caught the mouse?"

"Not yet," Jennifer called sweetly. "They usually enter the traps at night."

My neighbour stared past me at Jennifer, who was now right behind me with her hand on my shoulder.

"Come in," said Jennifer. "There's plenty food."

*

Of course she behaved normally over dinner, while I couldn't eat, couldn't speak and deliberately kicked Jennifer twice just for an outlet.

But then she surprised us both by saying she felt ill. "Do you think I've been poisoned?" she asked, twitching in panic.

For a second I thought of mice and poison but then I remembered the humane trap. There was no way to reassure her, I realised – saying no just made us seem like lying poisoners and even Jennifer saw that we had to get her out of the flat before she came up with anything worse.

"Stop being nice to her," I begged Jennifer when my neighbour had been rerouted to the safety of her own room.

"I thought you wanted to help her? I don't understand what's happened to change that. When I first met you, you said you were worried about her. Or was that just to get my knickers off?" Even this language was not in her nature and she flushed with confusion and embarrassment.

"I was worried about her, I *am* worried about her, but my therapist says I have to cut off from her because I don't seem to have the resources to help her. She suggested I refer her to her, actually."

"What? Who?"

"The neighbour. The neighbour to the therapist."

"And have you?"

"No! What will that do to my fucking boundaries? I spent the rest of the session asking what she was thinking of and she finally admitted she'd just said the wrong thing by accident."

"Well, isn't she seeing anyone?"

"She's meant to see some shrink at the Whittington according to everyone else."

"Who's everyone else?"

"Oh, the greengrocer, the woman in the bookshop. And the landlord. I'm surprised you don't know, when everyone else in the village does. Funny how small London gets when you've got a nutter to share."

"I haven't asked her about treatment. It seemed tactless."

"Well, I asked her why she didn't get a better counsellor or something and she laughed and said why didn't I give her some cash and she'd go and see Susie bleeding Orbach. I was surprised she'd heard of her."

"Why?"

"Because I'm a patronising middle-class git. Take off your uniform, I need to relieve my bourgeois stress on your tanned and muscled gamekeeper's body."

We were woken at three by the trap snapping shut. Jennifer thought it was exciting. She whooped. She picked it up and told me with delight that she could feel the little mouse trying to move about inside the box. She wanted me to hold it but I told her to fuck off, with more sincerity than I'd used since June, when a man waiting for the nightbus asked to pinch my nose.

She made me get in the car with her and she unlocked the park gates and drove to the other end. Apparently mice will return home within a certain distance. Then she released the little fucker. Then she attempted to seduce me with bats flying overhead. She failed.

After that, Jennifer thought her work was done. She went to Lanzarote on an exchange visit. Something to do with a volcano.

Unfortunately it was not the only mouse. When I heard scarpering on the Wednesday night, I would rather have died than have to deal with it. Jennifer had left the trap so of course the mouse went in it and then I was left with the problem. I was whimpering as I carried it outside. I was swearing in a kind of mantra as I walked down the street with it to the park, in my pyjamas. I was crying as I desperately tried to shake the fucker out of its trap and through the railings in the moonlight.

I thought I'd done it and pulled the trap back towards me when I saw the tail flick out. I screamed and threw the trap, kicked it under the gate. But I couldn't leave it there. I knew I would feel worse without the trap in the room as a terrible defence. Tentatively, I reached through the railings and shook the trap from the closed end. There was still something in there. I banged the box against the railings till the damned thing fell out, brain damaged or dead from fear. Then I ran.

Back at the flat, though, I was less safe. It might come back and there were bound to be more. Already the kitchen area smelt faintly of mouse piss. I washed out the trap. I had not anticipated either the stench of frightened critter or the quantity of squishy droppings. With all the lights on (to reduce fear), I saw more than I wanted to see.

The mammals who shared my home were taking over.

I rang the council but the exterminator had flu, there was a waiting list and the best thing for me to do was to bait a few sprung traps with chocolate digestives and call back in the new year.

It is not an exaggeration to say I lived in terror. The days at work were not so bad. Mostly I pretended to be OK but sometimes went out at lunchtime to cry in a secret corridor, down the side of the Oxo Tower. But the evenings, when even if I went out after work to see a friend or a therapist, I would have to come home to the possibility of my neighbour's visits; and the nights, when the mice ran freely round the flat because I could no longer bear to set and empty the trap... Things were not good.

I tried to block the holes under the sink and behind the fridge, the places where the mice could run between her room and mine or just emerge from under the floor into the wall cavity. I dunked pieces of an old sock and balls of newspaper into a pot of Polyfilla and stuffed them in the holes, only to wake to the sounds of mice building nests out of newspaper.

I could not lay killer traps with chocolate digestives because I knew I could not deal with their little corpses. Jennifer phoned once but she seemed more interested in some prehistoric homes she'd seen in underground lava bubbles than my problems.

It didn't take four therapists to tell me that the mice and the neighbour were combining in a supreme test of my boundaries, but that didn't stop them all from charging me for this wisdom.

Then she took to locking me out of the bathroom. The first time, I developed a paranoid fantasy that she was dead in the bath and I spun it out all night. But I soon realised that she was just taking the key from the bathroom and locking it from the outside so I couldn't get in.

I knocked on her door on the third occasion.

"Who is it?"

"Helen."

"What do you want?"

"The key to the bathroom."

Her face appeared, screwed up and ready for a row. "Don't use that tone! Don't you speak to me like that! Who do you think you are?"

"I just want the key to the bathroom."

"It's not your bathroom, you know."

"Yes it is."

"It's my bathroom too. You think it's just yours to use whenever you like."

"Well yes. When I need the toilet. Please don't lock it. I can't tell if you're in there. I can't get in."

"So what? Why should you get in whenever you want? You don't own it. I lived here before you. Coming here, looking for a fight – you need help."

I snapped. "Oh fuck off, you stupid cow!"

I went back in my room. For the rest of the evening, I stayed in bed. Intermittently she came into the hall to shout outside my door. I knew I shouldn't have spoken to her like that but it was an enormous relief. I felt purged of all bad feelings.

Eventually of course the mice came out to run freely round the room, under the bed and in and out of the cupboards.

I left the room without turning on the light, got on my bike and rode off to the heath for a slash.

She never hit me but she did hit the girl from the penthouse over a misunderstanding – Madam thought 'penthouse' was a serious claim to a superior home rather than a joke about a small flat on the top floor. The word appeared on a letter for upstairs and she pounced on the girl in the hallway and it ended in minor violence.

Then it came out that she had been bound over to keep the peace since an incident in the cancer shop.

*

I was sat on the kitchen sink when she knocked just before Christmas. I'd taken to weeing there to avoid the problems surrounding the bathroom.

By the time I got to the door, there was no one there. But the door to her room was swinging about in the icy draught from the hall.

I called hello and a weak voice answered: "Who is it?" Her perpetual response.

"It's Helen. Did you knock?"

"Come in."

It was the first time I had gone inside. I'd caught glimpses in the past, nothing surprising, nothing to prepare me for this. She was lying on a mattress on the floor, with a cheap 80s patterned curtain as a bedspread. The duvet cover hung at the window: too small, it was pulled taut and pegged to the curtain rail. The floor was uncarpeted and painted thinly with what appeared to be a single coat of white emulsion.

Her pale face was thinner than ever, pointy and pained. The place resembled a Romanian orphanage but the ammoniacal smell was not piss but bleach.

"Oh!" I gasped. "Are you ill?"

A bony arm, draped in a thin white nightdress, flapped above the covers. "I'm not well. I have to take pills but I don't like them. They make me worse."

"What are they?"

"They gave me them at the hospital. Bloody buggers. I told them I was sick..."

"Are you taking them?"

"They make me sick. Can you help me, Helen?"

"I don't think so. You should be in hospital."

"Bloody buggers."

"What exactly is the matter?"

"I can't take them pills."

Empowerment. She needed some kind of empowerment – or so I thought, in an effort to shift the responsibility away from me.

"There's not much I can do," I said. "I'm going away for Christmas. You need to phone the hospital."

"Phone's been cut off," she replied.

*

Things changed in the year 2000. The landlord told me that for more than three years she hadn't paid the full rent. The housing benefit only covered part of it and she never made up the difference. He felt sorry for her at first, then afraid, eventually so exasperated – and so pressed by the other tenants – that he took her to court.

We had a house party the day she was evicted. All the neighbours running in and out of each other's flats doing high fives and laughing, music blaring out. Someone turned their TV up as loud as it would go and left it like that for half an hour, just because they could, because it was funny, because we were free of her and her lack of irony. Perhaps that was her illness – lack of irony.

Jennifer took her room and now we sleep in my room and use hers as a living-room-cum-study. (I enjoy writing that because at work we're not allowed to use the word 'cum'. Apparently it looks obscene. We have to use a slash, which doesn't sound much better when you read it out loud.)

My gamekeeper has stuck a handwritten card on the wall reading Mice is Murder, as a memorial to the rodents, which the council eventually terminated for me with slow-acting poison. Otherwise there's little conflict.

We're testing my boundaries. One day she hopes to be offered the lodge building in the park, where I could be the ranger's wife or husband or something.

My neighbours came down from the penthouse last night for a drink and a chat. They said they saw her last week. We still say 'she' and 'her' as if it's dangerous to invoke her name. Or as if we're so bound together by the experience that there can only be one 'she'.

They saw her walking down the road with some guy. They ducked into a shop.

"What did she look like? Did she look all right?" asked Jennifer.

"D'you know what?" said the girl, suddenly fiery and intense. "I don't fucking care! I didn't look twice. I just got out the fucking way. She can drop dead in the street, far as I'm concerned, and I won't cross the road to check her skinny pulse."

Silence. Then her boyfriend said, "It is good, in't it, this floor? We're thinking we might take the carpet up in ours, paint it red. What paint did you use? Take long to dry?"

I went next door to find the paintpot we'd used in Jennifer's, and when they'd had a read of the label, we realised it was late-night shopping and we all got in their car and went down to Homebase. I bought some special Polyfilla for large holes. I want to have another go at the wall under the sink.

FRANCES GAPPER
Neighbours

The day I discovered that Olive next door had stolen my trampoline – and had been bouncing on it! – was the same day that Margery from up the road invited me to a Christian meeting.

This neighbourhood is not very neighbourly, or else I'm not. When I saw an elderly woman with a familiar face coming towards me along a narrow bit of pavement between the fence and the unruly Nature Strip, I waved awkwardly and dodged out of the way behind a nice big holly bush. She had never seemed particularly friendly and we'd never talked. To my surprise, however, she skipped around the other side of the holly bush and we met in the road.

"Hello, I'm Margery. I've seen you going up and down – tell me, do you live round here? Did I meet you at Ruth's get-together?" she enquired.

"Er, no. I live at number 81."

"And have you been here very long?"

"Not very. Six years," I said apologetically, knowing six years to be a mere nothing in the eyes of Stainmore Park Drive. Three or four decades seems to be the average. "What about you?"

"Oh, I'm not one of the *real* old guard," Margery said. "I moved here in 1964. When we were first married, my husband and I lived in Hackney. I brought up my children in two rooms in Stoke Newington. I had to save hard to get a bigger place..."

This sounded interesting and I hoped she would continue telling me her life story, but she then changed tack. "I don't want to load Christianity on you, but let me tell you about these meetings we have at the local church..."

All at once my mind cleared of confusion, as I perceived her motive for buttonholing me. Not betraying disappointment – hardly even feeling it – I focused on keeping an alert expression pinned to my face.

"It's mainly for young people trying to find their way in the world..."

I wondered if she thought *I* was young. Margery's face is deeply wrinkled, the once soft cushions of her cheeks and chin collapsed to fleshy bags. I could feel the skin stretching back from my own eyes and the lines scored across my forehead and etched either side of my mouth. Though I might be a quarter century behind Margery, I'm not young.

Meanwhile she was telling me about the home-cooked food provided at these Alpha meetings and how the atmosphere was friendly and non-pressurising. An opportunity for getting to know our neighbours. She would put a leaflet through my door, she said, and so we parted. I went home to find a message on my answerphone from one of my brothers, expressing interest in how I was getting on and asking if by any chance I could babysit that evening, as their arrangements had fallen through at the last moment.

Is this what modern life consists of? I wondered bitterly. The sting in the tail of the apparent friendliness – that people always want something, are not really interested in you at all. Or is it human nature? I rang my brother and sister-in-law back and left an effusive but regretful message on their answerphone.

Then I sat on the sofa and stared at the dusty artificial coal fireplace, thinking how life was full of petty irritations. For instance, why hadn't my trampoline arrived yet? Maybe I should ring the crazy sales agent. She was also evangelical, only about trampolines. Within five minutes of our first telephone conversation – I got her number from a newspaper article – she had talked me up a model. She even tried to persuade me to buy two, one for home use and the other for work! She quoted statistics at me: 80% of people hardly ever use their exercise bikes, etc. A trampoline in contrast, she pointed out, requires no complicated assembly, is always ready to be bounced on, can double as a coffee table.

I began to worry about my phone bill, as when last year I spent so long on the phone to Enfield Council that BT suggested nominating them as my Best Friend.

Three days later she rang me. Had my trampoline arrived yet? No it hadn't.

"We've just had the results of our customer satisfaction survey, which you might be interested to know about..."

I looked at my watch. It was after 10pm. "I'm sorry but I'm just on my way to bed."

"Oh. All right then," she said, in a slightly hostile way.

That was five days ago and the trampoline had still not turned up, so I took a deep breath and rang her. "Oh yes," she said, still with a trace of resentment in her voice. "You're the lady who wanted an early night. Well, I'll check with our delivery firm."

She rang back. "They have delivered it. Your neighbour at 79 took it in."

Just then, I heard again a peculiar noise, which I had previously been unable to account for, coming through the party wall. A rhythmic squeaking. It was coming from Olive's sitting room.

At once I realised the truth, but my mind rejected it as being incredible. Certainly beyond the bounds of acceptable behaviour.

My trampoline! Being used by Olive!

Energetically, it sounded like.

I charged out around the front, pressed my neighbour's bell hard and rattled her letterbox.

After a long pause she opened the door. Her face was flushed and she was wearing – or had just pulled around her for modesty's sake – a pink quilted dressing-gown.

"Have you got my trampoline?"

"What trampoline?" she asked, looking guilty.

"The one they tried to deliver the other day. Addressed to me. That you took in."

"Oh, that one!"

It's hard to feel angry with somebody in her 60s and quite plump, who when in her curlers – as she was – resembles Mrs Tiggywinkle.

"You've had it all the time! Why didn't you let me know, so I could come and collect it?"

"Oh, I thought they'd put a note through your door," Olive explained, lying blatantly. "I waited, but you never came round. So I thought you didn't want it. Well, you can have it now."

I followed her down the hallway, into her neat sitting-room, crammed with china ornaments and photographs of grandchildren. There it was, standing on the pale green carpet, between the television and the French windows. Its springs must have only just stopped vibrating.

We both inspected it, standing side by side. "A bit shop-soiled..." Olive mused.

"Yes, because you've been bouncing on it."

"What me? At my age? Linda, can you seriously accuse me?"

"Well, *someone* has," I said sternly. "Who do you suggest, if not you?"

Olive's eyes slid towards the cat – a rotund tabby, snoozing on the sofa. This animal, Flossie, gets prawns every day and a saucerful of cream.

I made an impatient noise and Olive gave up trying to deceive me. "Do you want the packing it came in?" she asked, in a small defeated voice.

"Yes, please."

"It's upstairs, waiting to go in the attic. My son-in-law kindly volunteered... My arthritis has been troubling me and I thought it might help," she said, plaintively reverting to the trampoline. "I only had one little go on it. Was that such a terrible crime?"

Climbing the stairs, she heaved a sigh. "I'll think carefully next time, before putting myself out to help one of my neighbours..."

So in the end my trampoline reached its proper destination, according to all legal rules and principles of natural justice – my sitting-room, not Olive's. But my righteous indignation soon ebbed away, leaving me feeling a bit lost.

I thought I would go to the Alpha meeting, after all. No harm in taking a look; peering out from behind the net curtains of my mistrustful, settled life. Of course I ran the risk of being possessed by the spirit of Christian lunacy, but this was unlikely to happen. I had striven for so long, over so many dreary years, to achieve the appearance of being sane and normal. And had succeeded. Bearing my powerful shield of appearance, I could go anywhere now and be invulnerable.

No, my heart would not be filled with the Lord. I was too middle-aged for that game. And too bogged down by material concerns.

A woman of pure and generous heart would simply have shelled out for another trampoline, I thought – thus pleasing both Olive and the sales agent. A Christian woman with a large bank balance.

I gazed sadly at the trampoline. Remembering the energetic squeaking sound – a happy sound – I'd heard through the wall. Thinking how Olive was to be admired, in a way. She lived her life to the full, with zest. I couldn't work up that amount of enthusiasm for anything, certainly not trampolining. In fact I'd completely gone off the whole idea. Was I still within the 15-day approval period, I wondered? Would I be eligible for a refund?

The letterbox clicked. My Alpha leaflet lay on the doormat.

An opportunity to explore the meaning of life, it said. The Alpha Course – starting soon at a church near you.

Alpha is a short, practical, no frills, introduction to the Christian faith.

What is the point of life? What happens when we die? Is forgiveness possible? What relevance does Jesus have for our lives today?

For some reason my eyes had filled with tears, so the words swam together and I read Olive by mistake for our lives.

What relevance does Jesus have for Olive today?

Good question.

What fragile threads stretch between us? Would Olive be interested in accompanying me to an evening of learning and laughter, including a delicious meal of home-cooked food? The leaflet said we might be asked for a contribution to the meal. I would pay Olive's contribution, if we could let bygones be bygones and she felt like coming along.

JULIA BELL
Outskirts

I watch through the nets as the car pulls into the space right in front of the window. You have to park it with the nose to the windowledge to get it right off the road. It's a shame, taking up all the space like that, if Carol got a motorbike or something we could put some plants out, a couple of chairs, sit outside and have tea and watch the world go by.

She comes in kicking the plastic door open because it's started sticking. She's stocky and neat with spiky blond hair and sexy muscles. She's much older than me, old enough to be my mother.

"Did you have a good day? Did you miss me?" She sinks into the sofa, kicking off her brogues. She's still got her nurse's uniform on. Sometimes she keeps it on for sex. "Make us a cuppa, there's a love," she says.

I've only been here a few weeks, it still doesn't quite feel real. I still feel like I'm on holiday. This is the first time I've ever lived with anybody, a girlfriend, I mean. I used to live in a house closer to the city, full of foreign students but Carol didn't like visiting me there, she said it was shabby and studenty and that I was worth more than that.

"What've you been doing with yourself all day then?"

I shrug. "Not much."

"Students," she tuts. "D'you make me dinner then?"

"No. I made you a cup of tea."

"I suppose it's something," she says.

Carol's house is brand new. They're still finishing the ones down the road. Carol said she bought it because it was a good investment. Old Catton, right on the outskirts of Norwich. "Good people out here," she said, "nice area. Close to the countryside." She reckons the people in Norwich are all fakes, trying to be something they're not. "Too bloody middle class," she says with a sneer. "They're all morris dancers with mobile phones."

We get a takeaway. Balance it on our knees in front of the telly with the volume on low. I can hear kids playing in the road outside, the scratch of Carol's spoon against her tinfoil tub.

"Pass us the TV guide," she says, reaching out her hand to me without looking round.

Carol has nineteen holes in each ear. She can't wear more than one pair of earrings for work, but when I met her she had all her studs in, it looked like someone had drawn round her ears with metallic pen. She bought me a drink and brushed her hands against me, casually at first.

"You're pretty you are. You got a girlfriend?"

I liked the way she moved, confidently, deliberately, like a man. I blushed when she spoke to me.

"No."

"Wanna beer?" She handed me a can of Stella and looked me straight in the eye.

My stomach lurched. I could imagine us kissing, her hands on my face, my breasts, it made me so frightened that I trembled.

Back at hers, in the double bed, she stroked my hair and told me I was beautiful. No one had ever said that to me before. We fell asleep holding hands. In the night her hand slipped between my legs. Started running fingertips over my thighs. In the morning, she said she didn't know she was doing it, that she thought she was doing it to herself, as if we both had the same body.

I dream that we are standing on a beach in a howling gale. She is shouting something at me, but the wind catches her words and blows them to rags. I don't know if it's hello or goodbye. But I know that I don't want her to go. Every time I move forwards she steps back, just out of reach. I wake up suddenly with a gasp. She flinches and turns towards me.

"Don't leave me," I say, kissing her before she is properly awake.

"I won't," she says, sleepily.

I look at her face, gently tracing the lines around her eyes with my fingers. I like the fact that she's so old. That she's lived all those years more than me.

She tells me bits and pieces about her life, random things, that I try to fit into place in my head like a jigsaw. I know that before me there was someone called Christine, but she was a fling, and before that a woman called Marcia who she lived with in Australia.

I run a fingertip over her forehead. She opens one eye and looks at me. "Stop tickling me, child," she says. "I want to sleep."

*

The phone wakes me from a thick, headachy lie-in. It's boiling in these houses in the summer. They're like overgrown Lego and hot as incubation tanks with everything double-glazed and rubber-sealed. The air gets unbreathable after a while.

"Carol please." The voice is sharp and Scottish and female.

"Uh, she's not here."

Whoever it is puts the phone down. There is no number recorded.

I open the curtains, the sky is a deep dark blue and already I can see the tarmac shimmering. There's kids out on bikes, zipping up and down the close squealing at each other. The people round here are all right, what I've seen of them. Couples mostly, a few with kids. Ordinary, like us.

I walk down the road to Gateway. Old Catton: it's supposed to be the country but it's too close to the airport to be peaceful. There's fields round, granted, but only mushy, scrubby ones that have overgrown with horsetails and a yellow spongy moss. Right by our new estate there's a little square of shops in the middle of this block of 1970s maisonettes. Carol says it reminds her of where she grew up. She says the people round here have got hearts of gold.

Outside the supermarket, leaning on the railings overlooking the car park, are a gang of boys. All in tracksuits, all with skinheads, all smoking. Everything about them twitches: they are whistling and pointing. As I start to walk up the steps towards them I wait for the jeers. But as I pass them I realise they're not even looking at me. One boy sees me, then his eyes glaze over, like he's looking through me into space. They're shouting at someone behind me.

She's beautiful. Long blond locks, belly-button showing a sparkly piercing, lots of lipgloss. The boys are singing 'Mr Loverman' and whooping. She's smiling and pretending to ignore them, swinging her hips as she walks past.

She nearly bumps into me at the top of the steps.

"Sorry," she says, sidestepping to move past me. The boys cheer as she gets closer. "Boys," she says, raising her eyebrows into acute angles, trying to catch my eye.

"I wouldn't know," I say, turning away from her.

Girls like her make me sick.

*

I cook Carol a lasagne. It gets so hot I have to open all the doors to get a breeze going. The phone goes again but I don't answer it. It goes on and on, really insistently like someone knows I'm ignoring it.

"Someone phoned for you," I say to her when she gets in.

"Oh, who?"

"Dunno, they never left a number. Sounded Scottish."

She makes a face. "Don't know anyone Scottish. You made me some tea?" She puts her arms around my back, holds my breasts in her hands as if she's weighing them. I can feel the hairs on my neck prickling. "You smell of sweat."

"It's hot." I wriggle against her.

"No no, I like it. You, sweating over my dinner." She tweaks my nipples. "It's sexy."

"You're weird," I say, breaking away from her, blushing.

We lie together on the sofa later, watching a Stallone film. Carol likes his muscles. She says that most of the time she'd rather be a man.

"Wouldn't it be good to have muscles like that?" she says pointing at him as he bares his pecs.

I snuggle into her breasts. "No, I love you because you've got tits."

"But just imagine having a chest that tight. None of this bloody padding."

"I thought you liked my tits."

"I do, I just don't like mine."

We watch the rest of the film in silence. Carol's seen it loads of times. She knows the dialogue off by heart. I can hear her muttering it to herself under her breath. When it finishes she kisses me on the top of my head. "See? Told you you'd like it."

"Let's do something," I say.

"We are doing something."

"No, I mean, go out and do something."

"Go where? I'm not going into town. I hate the clubs in town, they're crap."

"Oh come on, we haven't been out for ages."

"Sweetheart, I only go out to pull." She sits up. "And when I've pulled I stay at home till they bugger off and then I go out and get another one." She laughs.

"Oh..." I don't know what to say. "Oh."

"How old are you?"

"Twenty."

"Exactly. I'm old enough to be your mother."

"Oh come on, Carol, please, just for a drink, a coffee, anything. We haven't been out together for ages."

"You're whining."

"No I'm not."

"Yes you are, you're whining." She tickles me, making me squirm. "We'll go to the pub round the corner tomorrow but only if you stop whining."

I spend the morning doing laundry. Carol's vests and boxer shorts and thick cotton Y-fronts. She never wears knickers, she says they make her feel like she's in some crappy hetero porn film.

I sit out the back with my sunglasses on, trying to read. It's cool round this side of the house in the mornings, until the sun creeps over the roof and the building starts to creak as it absorbs the heat. Over the fields I can hear the roar of planes from the airport and the rush of traffic on the main road out of town. It's kind of peaceful once you get used to it.

But then the bloke next door starts doing his lawn. I glare at him, or at least at his receding hairline over the fence. It sounds like the mower my dad used to use. Every fucking Sunday at half past nine. Even when it was drizzling. The grass manicured into perfect stripes that we weren't allowed to tread on. Ever.

He must be cutting the grass to shit, he's been at it nearly twenty minutes. I stand up and peek over the fence. He catches my eye and the mower phut phuts to a stop.

"Sorry, love, didn't see you there."

He's got his top off, and his chest is glistening with sweat. I can feel myself blushing. I don't know why. He's not even very attractive.

"Bloody hot." He wipes an arm across his forehead, I can see the fuzz of his armpits and a dark birthmark on his shoulder. He's getting fat, his gut spills over his trousers, in a pink, babyish bulge.

"Yes." I realise I am staring.

"You all right?"

"I was trying to read."

"Oh right. Well I won't be a ticket." He looks away and smirks. "Your friend gone to work?"

I nod.

"Shame." He pauses for a moment. "You're new, aren't you?" He reaches a hand over the fence. "Name's Terry."

I reach up and touch his fingers and he grabs my hand. His skin is clammy and slack; losing its resistance, turning to fat. "Pretty intchya. Not like the others." He's pressing his thumb into my palm.

I snatch my hand back. "Thanks," I say, turning my back on him.

"Anytime," he says, ripping the cord on the mower, jerking it back to violent, juddering life.

Not like the others. I wonder what he means. Who else Carol has had to stay in this house. I look at the picture of Christine that she keeps on her cork pinboard. She has short dark hair and is standing with her hands in her pockets, her shoulders hunched like a boy. I feel a sudden stab of jealousy. All those other bodies, other people who have touched her.

I go upstairs and watch Terry through the bedroom window. He's pushing the mower over the same little patch. Like a maniac, up and down, his shoulders going red with sunburn. At one point he looks up at our house and I have to step back from the window. The air is thick with the oily reek of petrol and fresh-cut grass.

I lie on the bed waiting for the noise to stop like I used to when I was sixteen. If I close my eyes I am not in this house at all, but back in my bedroom at home. It's Sunday and Mum is still in bed, dozing. She doesn't hear the thud and then the terrible groan of the mower as it draws a berserk line across the nap of the grass and crashes into the hedge, blades still whirring.

He got mean after that. Spending too much time in bed, getting dizzy spells when he stood up. He crept up on you, wanted to know what you were doing. I know for a fact he went into my bedroom when there was no one else in the house. He watched daytime TV and got paranoid about every twinge. When they had a row, Mum accused him of turning into an old woman in front of her eyes. He had to take early retirement. He was only fifty-three.

The doorbell makes me jump. For a moment I think I should pretend to be out, but I'm curious. I've been here three weeks and no one has ever called.

It's Terry. He's leaning against the doorframe. He's put his shirt on, but the sweat is soaking through in big damp rings under his arms.

"Fancy a beer?"

"What?" I don't want to think about why he's here.

"A drink. I've got some in the fridge."

"Uh, no thanks." I try to close the door but he puts his foot in the way.

"Oh c'mon, aren't you thirsty? It's boiling out here."

"That's why I'm inside."

He shrugs. "Only being neighbourly. The one before you never used to mind."

"What one?"

"The other girl that lived here. Played pool, Scottish, dark hair."

"I don't know who you're on about." I push the door against his foot.

"Oh come on, love, I'm not gonna try anything funny, I just thought you might like a drink. No need to be like that."

"Another time," I say, pushing the door until he takes his foot away.

"I made a new friend today," I say.

"Oh?"

"He wanted to know where the Scottish girl had gone."

"Who was it?"

"Next door."

"The taxi driver? He's a slimy bastard. Keep away from him."

"Who is she? She rang for you yesterday."

"Christine."

"Why didn't you tell me before?"

"I don't tell you everything." She won't look me in the eye.

"I tell you everything."

"That's because you're young. Look, it was a fling that I'd rather forget about. It didn't mean anything. I'm with you now."

She says all these things with a sigh, as if they're a routine, as if there's a part of her that is disengaged and she's just telling me what I want to hear. She's not even looking at me.

"Fuck you."

"Where are you going?"

"Out."

I slam the door behind me, but it doesn't shut, it springs back on its hinges, sending something behind the door flying to the ground with a crash. She doesn't come after me.

I take my jacket off the minute I get round the corner. Even though the sun is sinking it's still boiling. It must be thirty degrees at least. Even the kids have gone in.

I walk to the main road and follow it towards the junction with the ring road. At the junction there is a choice between city or country. Go right, you'll be in town in twenty minutes, left, and it's farmland from here to the coast. I choose country, but after a few hundred metres the pavement starts to peter out and I have to walk along the verge. I think about going back, but I don't want to see her. I don't want anybody. I want to get out of this mess.

At the next junction I go left down a B-road that winds between a few damp-looking cottages before forking into two. I go right, down a dirt track, the hedge getting thick with brambles and overgrowth. It doesn't look like anyone comes down here much except to dump things: there's a rotting mattress slumped against a tree, a rusted shopping trolley being pulled into the ditch by bindweed. At the bottom of the lane is a path that seems to run along the edge of the field.

There isn't much of a view, because everything's so flat. The fields out here are tall and golden with crops, and beyond the tips of grain, I can see nothing but sky. I walk for miles, smashing at the brambles with a stick. All I can hear is the thud of my feet on the soft, peaty ground and the blood in my ears. It starts to get darker, but I don't want to stop, my legs feel like they've got springs in them, like I could walk for days. The sunset streaks the sky with broad strokes, majestic oranges and pinks.

Every now and then I turn round. Quickly, just in case she's following me, but there is never anyone there.

I get to a gate and a farm track and I stop for a few minutes to catch my breath. I can't really see the way ahead any more, the light has turned a smoky grey that makes it hard to distinguish between the path and the undergrowth. I can see the lights of cars filtering through the hedgerow further up the track. I'm getting cold now. I shouldn't have run off on her like that. It's miles to get home.

Something rustles in the hedgerow close by. It's something big and it's grunting. I grab my stick and hold onto the gate. My heart jumps in my chest.

I turn round to see a man carrying a sack over his shoulder, and what looks like a little girl, trotting along at his side. It occurs to me that they must have been following me.

"Rabbits," the man says as he gets close to me, "you want some rabbits?"

The girl is carrying three of them by the back legs. She holds them out to me and gurgles.

"Don't you mind her," he says. "Fresh today. I was going to take 'em up the pub and sell 'em but you can be my first customer." He's tall, with thick, beer-bottle glasses that make his eyes seem luminous, like moons. "Three for a fiver."

"For a fiver." The girl holds up the rabbits and swings them. Their necks are broken, their heads hang at odd angles. I try not to look.

"You're all right," I say, "I'm vegetarian."

"Vegetarian?" he booms. I take a step back from him.

"Me, meep," the girl squeaks, jumping up and down.

"What kind of rubbish is that? Real girls eat meat. Bit of rabbit stew. Lovely." He rubs his stomach.

This seems to excite the girl and she starts swinging the rabbits round in her hand. One of them catches on a tree branch, and its eye comes out with a *thuck*.

"Alice!" He grabs the rabbits off her. "You don't mind her." He puts his arm around her and she puts her thumb in her mouth and looks at her shoes.

"I've only got a tenner," I say.

"Even better," he says, "you can have seven for a tenner."

He drops his sack on the ground and opens it up. He counts out seven corpses. "There y'go," he says, pulling a carrier bag out of his pocket and shaking it open. "Even throw in a free bag." He stands up expectantly. When I hold out the note to him I realise I am trembling. "Thanking you," he says, folding the money into a small square and pushing it into the top of his pocket.

When I get back to Carol's it's nearly midnight. She's still up, watching TV. I'm disappointed, I half expected to see police cars blocking off the drive.

"You're back then," she says.

"I'm sorry," I say. "Look, I brought you a present." I open the bag.

"What the fuck?" She laughs and stands up. "A box of chocolates would have been enough." She takes them off me and looks at them, stroking the fur with her fingers. "I don't know how to skin them, do you?"

"No."

"Well, we'll have to do something with them. They'll start to go off in this heat. Where d'you get them?"

"I bought them."

She ruffles my hair. "Sweetheart. You shouldn't have." Then she looks at me properly. "Where have you been? You're filthy."

"Walking," I say, "I didn't notice the time, then I met this bloke with the rabbits."

"Poachers," she says. "Get a lot of them round here."

She puts the rabbits on the kitchen table. Seven of them laid out, stretching, like they're in full flight. I can't imagine skinning them. I wouldn't know where to start.

"Shame isn't it, really? Killing them like that," I say.

"Nah, they're a pest round here. All they do is fuck and have babies and eat all the crops. You're too sentimental. They'll make a nice stew."

Outskirts

"Isn't is against the law?"

"What?"

"Poaching?"

"No one's going to miss a few lousy rabbits."

I can't sleep. I have to get up and open the window and go downstairs for some water. The rabbits are still on the kitchen table, eyes glinting in the moonlight. I have to pretend they're not there so I can walk past them. I'll bury them in the garden in the morning.

I fall asleep about five and when I wake up Carol's gone to work. She's left a note on the table, propped up on one of the rabbits. *Rabbit stew for tea?! I hope so. C.* There are three kisses at the bottom, drawn really big like kids do.

I grab a knife from the kitchen drawer, turn the blade in my hands. I try to visualise how I can do it, but I'm too squeamish. What if there's blood? I don't know where to cut and then there's all the guts. I can't deal with that. Perhaps Terry can handle it.

When he answers the door, he looks like he's been asleep.

"Uh, sorry, love, I've been working nights this week," he says, rubbing a hand across his face. "Come in, come in."

His house has the same layout as Carol's. The only difference is the decoration. Instead of posters of Freddie Mercury and Queen and whales in a Canadian sunset, they've got blue flowery wallpaper and dado rails and lights above the reproduction paintings of Constable's 'Haywain' and Monet's 'Waterlilies'. It still smells of paint and wallpaper paste.

"D'you like it? The wife chose it, I put it up. Finished it last weekend."

The effect is to make the room feel even smaller, the pattern is too dense for such low ceilings. "S'nice, yeah."

"Wanna beer?"

"OK, yeah," I say.

We sit in the kitchen. "Here you go," he slides a bottle of Stella towards me. "Smoke?" He offers me the first of a new pack.

"No thanks."

"So what can I do for you?"

I shrug. I feel stupid asking him about the rabbits. "Fancied a drink," I say taking a big slug of beer. The bottle is slippery with condensation. Terry's on his second bottle already.

"You play pool?" He's talking really fast, I can hardly make out what he says. "The other girl, Scottish lass, they banned her from the Crown, she was too good for them. Couldn't have her embarrassing the lads."

"You what?"

"You play pool?"

"Never been much good at it."

I look at him properly for the first time. He's not so bad covered up, though his hair's disappearing at the front. Must be in his thirties at least.

"Nother beer?"

"Go on then."

He looks me in the eye as he pushes another bottle towards me. I give him a half smile. "Thanks."

"She didn't tell you about her, did she?"

The beer fizzes in my stomach. "No."

He tuts. "She was mad on her. They had big fights, out on the street, everybody watching through the curtains, you know, chasing each other round with knives. It would've been funny if it weren't for the fact that it was true. I had to go out and split them up. The wife thought I was going to get killed."

"When was this?"

"Bout two months ago. She must've left after that. Shame. I wanted her to do some work for me. Could've set her up with a few games. You tell her if you see her. I can sort her out with a few games. Hey, hey, don't cry."

I don't want to but I can't help it. "Sorry."

He puts his hand on my shoulder. "It'll be all right, you'll see."

He starts talking about his wife, about his job as a taxi driver. He's funny, he makes me laugh. He puts me at my ease. I watch him walk around the kitchen as he talks, his jeans slung low on his hips. I have never slept with a man before.

When Dad found out I was gay he went mental. He discovered

some magazines under my bed, said it was unnatural, that I would be the death of him. He went to lie down and didn't get up again for weeks. I left for university pretty soon after.

Mum took it better. She held my hand and told me all she wanted was for me to be happier than she had been. "If I had my time over again, there's no telling what I would have done," she said, eyes shining. "He'll get over it."

Terry sits next to me and puts his hand on my thigh.

"See? There's nothing to be scared of."

I want him to push me up against the wall and unzip my jeans, rub his hands roughly against my nipples, force himself into me. I try to stop the blush that creeps up my neck.

"I'm not... I don't..."

"It's all right, I know that you and Carol are – like that." He twitches his head to the left. "I don't mind."

"I do."

He doesn't take his hand away, instead it creeps further up my leg. "You just haven't had me yet, sweetheart," he says in my ear, so low and close it is almost a growl.

If it was anybody else, anywhere else, I would push them away for saying something like that. My thigh feels hot under his hand. Sweat gathers in my temples and runs down my cheeks.

"I've got to go."

When I try to stand up he stands up with me and kisses me. I don't struggle. He tastes yeasty, of beer and cigarettes. In seconds I am squashed up against the kitchen table. He rubs a hand between my legs, squeezes my nipples, bites my neck. He is fumbling with his flies. He pulls his penis out of his trousers and strokes it a little. It is purple and thick. I've never seen a real hard-on before. I think about condoms, but I don't say anything. I feel reckless, powerful.

"Fuck me," I say, pulling him close.

It hurts, but then I get used to it and then it seems to go on for ever. We get into a rhythm, like it's not us that's doing it any more. When he pulls out he comes all over my T-shirt in great white strings.

"There," he says, taking a breath, "there."

He washes himself in the sink, rubbing himself down with kitchen paper. "Want another beer?" he asks over his shoulder.

I study the mess on my T-shirt. I don't know what to say. The feeling is draining out of my legs. "It's all right," I say, "I've got stuff to do."

"You're not a proper lesbian are you?"

"I don't know what you mean."

"You like it too much." He smirks which makes me want to hit him. "Or maybe it's just me."

"Maybe," I mumble, making for the front door.

"See ya round then," he says, winking.

When I get in I can hear him through the wall. He's watching TV. I can still feel it, the shock in my muscles, as if he's still inside me. I have a bath and wash my hair, lie in the cold water listening to the mumble of his telly, the kids playing outside. When Carol comes home I wonder if she will smell it on me, if I will look any different to her, more experienced, older. "See," I will say to her, "see what you made me do."

I go into the kitchen and look at the rabbits. They're beginning to smell, a sweet, earthy smell. I grab one of them, roll its stiff body towards me. I pick up the knife and make a slit under the ears, and with one gentle downstroke, pull the blade across its back. The skin splits easily, revealing the pinkness underneath. There is no blood.

VG LEE
Still Precious

I was going blind. I knew it. It was progressive, persistent.

Insistent.

The same time of day – September last year – those same shadows falling across the far wall; I could see the hands of the clock. Not the individual numerals; even then they blurred when I tried to focus, but I could see it was half-past seven, or eight or six. What's an hour each way to the bed-ridden? Now all I saw was a white oval; like glimpsing a face on a moving train. No features, no numbers, nothing distinct anymore. Sometimes the relentless whispered 'tick-tock', seemed almost deafening, the sound echoing the sound of blood throbbing in my ears.

I told Jelly, "See, ha-ha, how my hearing improves as my sight worsens."

She said, "Maureen, your hearing was always acute. You need glasses. Half the world needs glasses over a certain age."

"I'm only forty."

"Forty's middle-aged." Subject closed as far as she's concerned.

'Jelly' is my pet name for her, from a time when we both only ever used pet names. I would be self-conscious now, using it aloud. I call her Angela, which is formal and suits our changed relationship. Would she be surprised if I used it – suddenly – out of the blue; awkward with its intimacy? I doubt it. Angela doesn't really engage any more, her responses are set on automatic pilot. Other things embarrass her – that she once found me sexually attractive, and how could she ever? All reason for my appeal has vanished from her memory. I think she wishes she could dislike me. I'd be so much easier to leave behind. Neither guilt nor pity would hold her, only this unfortunate fondness, our perverse meeting of minds when there is absolutely no other basis on which to meet.

I know there are women she desires – I see it in her eyes. Hardly anyone she actively likes. Is that unkind? I with all my vagaries am still precious – a sickly time-consuming plant valued for my rarity. Of course, I may be wrong. She may have her own secret agenda in which my removal is the pivotal factor.

Regarding myself, I choose to believe that for now my own sexual feelings lie dormant, share the same warm bed somewhere with my discarded good health. I look to be fed, watered and comforted. I can wash myself and attend to my personal needs – am still – no – am even more fastidious.

I took to my couch (*"For god's sake, Maureen, it's a sofa-bed"*) after my mother died. Over a year ago. It seemed the right thing to do. I considered myself inconsolable and intended to treat my 'inconsolation' (*"For god's sake, Maureen, there is no such word"*) with the respect and tenderness I felt it deserved. To paraphrase Wordsworth, I would become,

> *"...a fingering slave,*
> *One that would peep and botanise*
> *Upon her mother's grave."*

Here, I'm being playful – the actuality of dealing with death, however little I'd known of the woman behind the tight dissatisfied mask, proved anything but playful, of which more later – give me time to write through my protective layers.

Jelly. Even I'm becoming awkward about using this name. It doesn't fit anymore. Let me see. She appears to be a kinder woman now, in the manner of a slightly absent-minded warmth that ex-lovers acquire when they retain fond memories but life for them goes on elsewhere. Outwardly she's caring and reliable – no longer forces her opinions on me about the hundred-and-one professionals who could sort me out in a trice.

Physically, she's changed. She's become more womanly in an embarrassing old-fashioned fifties film-star style that surprises and confuses me. Her boyish hips that only suited jeans have rounded – it's been months since she's worn trousers. She tells me, they're all too tight. They constrict her and so she wears dresses and skirts.

Another thing – she used to stride. Fine legs – straight and strong; now her step has shortened as she bustles between the furniture and our small rooms and narrow passageway; tending my needs and her own, bolstering here, admonishing there, all with efficient good humour. Nurse Angela. I've flicked a lever and this,

this and this has happened.

"I don't fancy you at all, Angela," I say to the woman in the summer dress who is combing her hair in the mirror above the empty fireplace.

"Quite mutual, Maureen," her reflection replies. She pauses in her combing and smiles approvingly back at herself. She is going out with a friend to wine and dine at a restaurant that wasn't even open before my illness.

"Have you left me any supper?" I use a querulous, invalidish voice and 'hey presto', I've changed her channel again – off with smile, on with dark frown.

"I've made you sandwiches," she snaps, "Don't say 'supper', I can't stand that word."

Before going out, she puts a tray with a plate of sandwiches, a can of Guinness with a plastic straw (my own affectation) on the card table next to my couch; takes the clock from the mantelpiece and places it near me.

"There, watch the minutes drag or fly. Expect me when you see me."

She flounces out. Now where did she learn to flounce? This is more new behaviour and yet she manages it as if she'd spent a lifetime flouncing away from emotional scenes. I don't like it. It's not an attractive manoeuvre.

For all her bravado, she's never late home. Whoever this new friend is, she must be very understanding. I ask no questions; can't face the effort of putting names with faces and learning fresh potted histories. Enough to recognise her friend's car by the scrape of her reverse gears when she drops Jelly home. I could reach the window and take a surreptitious look but that, to me, would be a sign of weakness, or unwelcome proof of my returning physical strength.

I imaging the banality of their exchanges.

"I wish you'd let me come in for once, Angela darling."

"It won't always be like this. She'll get better – and if she doesn't – well, I'll just up and go. I'm not tied. I'm a free woman."

That's what she thinks. I'd nail her feet to these floorboards first... had I sufficient energy.

VG Lee

*

Alone at last, or alone again. Tonight I'll settle for 'at last', although this is the second evening in a week that she's been out with her mystery admirer.

Our friends, pre-Maureen-monopolising-the-living-room phase, have become her friends. Her sympathisers. Illness is a great embarrasser; a drier of mouths. Women I've known for over ten years wander tongue-tied around this room, searching for inspiration – a photograph or keepsake, anything to prompt something resembling a relaxed two-way dialogue. We have nothing left in common, they assume my interests wither at the door. Finally they break into hearty gasps, "Did you see... no, of course you didn't." (I refuse to succumb to television – have my illness re-assigned to 'couch-potato' syndrome). I counter with, "Did you hear... but of course not," knowing they have no time for radio, although my own intention to keep up with current affairs has flagged during the summer months.

I listen to music – am a voracious reader – fiction and poetry; although I accept that the poetry I choose makes me sentimental and dramatically desperate.

This evening, Jelly brought me in a microwaved chicken tikka. It was seven o'clock and I eat between eight and nine, otherwise an unbroken evening alone is interminable. I said nothing; followed the chicken tikka's progress from door to card table with assumed avid interest as if unaware that it might be for me to actually eat.

She said, "Don't eat it if you don't like it, but I haven't time to cook anything else."

I replied, "No, no – if you've cooked it especially, of course I'll eat it. It's a superb colour, although rather on the small side."

"It's a portion for one."

And invalids of course, have non-existent appetites.

I picked at it as she hurried back and forth between her bedroom and this room. She's established a habit of enacting much of her indoor life in front of me. Initially to prevent me feeling excluded, now she does it without thinking. There is something weak and placating and vulnerable in her doing this. Leaving herself open to be observed. She's so used to me sitting or lying here, three feet below her eye-level – I am literally part of the furniture. If the television was in here instead of in her bedroom, she would take more notice of that.

I said with a grin, "Was the rice supposed to be that chewy?"

"See you later." Shoulder bag in place, she made for the door. I called out, "Clock."

Back she came, grabbed the clock and tossed it down onto the duvet. Flouncing again. The front door closed firmly behind her. I heard the engine of a car start, perhaps ten yards away along our road, like a familiar greeting. Jelly's footsteps dissolved towards it and then the car door opened and closed; into reverse – must get those gears seen to – and smoothly past our house.

The chicken tikka wasn't really that bad.

When we first moved into this flat, several years ago, this was our living room – large and light – tall sash windows and a Victorian fireplace. We had the chimney swept and lit fires at the weekend. My job, to clean the grate and build another fire – a ritual of newspapers, wood, fire-lighters and coal – warming the room, welcoming the pair of us in, welcoming in our friends.

The room was never meant to be a bedroom, nor a sick-room. It needed people sprawled across two sofas with drinks in their hands and flushed noisy faces. Sunday mornings of feet up and newspapers strewn across the floor. And then my mother died.

When I first saw her dead, when I first felt her dead; well, she was not a person anymore; she became – like looking at a heap of fallen leaves. Not too cold, not too awful, still something of the picturesque, but very different from the live and kicking. Suddenly, almost overnight, I found I couldn't bear to be touched or to touch living flesh. Not saying I prefer to touch dead flesh, but there was something that sickened me, about the heat generated by another's live body. I expected this sensation to disappear, so I said nothing – you can get away with a lot when a relative or a loved one dies.

We came home after the funeral and the small party at my aunt's house – Jelly tried to embrace me. (I can't tolerate the closeness of some words. I search for chilly alternatives like 'embrace'; 'holding, cuddling, caressing' – such words still make me feel physically sick.) Anyway, she tried to take me in her arms and I was overwhelmed by her warmth, the closeness of her skin. I put up my hands to ward her off and the fingers of my right hand somehow became trapped under her arm and I could feel that her shirt was wet with perspiration. Not only that, it was as if my fingers had drilled through the cloth, her skin, and were stuck in a glutinous mess of blood and vein. I could feel the wet pumping of life in the creases of my fingers. I could smell blood. I blacked out.

When I woke up, I was in our bedroom, my face in pillows that smelt of her. The smell clung to the sheets, the curtains, the carpet; I couldn't stand it. I thought I would choke, began to choke. She crossed the room towards me, her face anxious, and a cloud of poisonous steam that only I could see, preceded her. The doctor came. I was given a tranquiliser. I managed to say before I fell asleep, "I can't bear her heat." Jelly was there in the room with me, but I was incapable of speaking directly to her; could not face the expression in her eyes of desperately wanting to do the right thing for me. The next day, *the friends* came round and moved me into here.

Remembering how she looked has made me very low. At that point I lost her, and where has she gone, and where did I go?

Of course, they could have put me into the spare room, and I may yet be tucked away out of sight, if my behaviour doesn't improve. It has a small window at the foot of the bed facing a row of garages. My day would be spent watching the comings and goings of the owners of the garages. Not all of them contain cars, some are used for workshops, Jelly tells me there is a thriving community out there. I suspect her intentions. Get me involved and interested – wake up the Sleeping Beauty.

She knows that curiosity would make me insist on having the muslin curtains removed. Let them see me, this 'thriving community', – a reproach to their rude health and their gleaming bodywork. Me, lying back white, against whiter pillows, raising one frail hand in salute to my especial favourites. Perhaps I'd fall in love with a mute face and familiar shoulder blades and my emotions would be uncannily reciprocated. A ringing of the front doorbell, tentative at first, then more impatient.

"Can I speak to her; the woman in the bed? Will she get well? I've brought her flowers. Whole seasons have passed and she seems no better." Such pity, such pathos.

Voices merging into earnest whispers, muffled footstep, Jelly tapping gently at my door, "Maureen, you have a visitor."

"Come in, come in," my voice painfully hearty, and there in my sick-room is my admirer; not mute, but rendered speechless by the presence of death and the dying. The dying (myself), fatally disappointed at the poor amalgamation of my waking dreams and failing eyesight. It's a boy, not a girl, or a girl, not a woman. Not good enough, not anyone who would ever do, who could make things better, whatever 'things', might be, not someone that just might have had me leaping from my bed.

Oh yes, the disappointment I'd endure in that small room would finish me off; alternatively I might be forced to get well.

At Jelly's suggestion, I'm writing a piece about my mother, although I know she'd prefer I choose a more cheerful topic. However, she has been consulting an enclave of Dulcie, J and her girlfriend P, who we have known for years. As I refuse to see 'anyone', as in the caring professionals, they have suggested I write 'Mother' out of my system. I was tempted to rebel at their cut and dried 'suggestion', but the promise of a laptop and several reams of white paper overcame my hostility. The laptop has not yet appeared. Dulcie is consulting her brother-in-law, who says major purchases can't be hurried and this is hardly a life and death scenario. I'd almost attempt suicide just to confound his complacency except I'm in a buoyant mood.

Jelly has at least bought me three good quality pens and several A4 notebooks, also a raffia waste-paper basket removed from her office in Holborn.

Although keen to start, I'm unsure quite how to. Suddenly, it appears that I have nothing to say about my mother.

*

Childhood: An arid subject. I am an only child. Mother's attitude to her only child: I had little visible use. Visibly, I was in all ways an encumbrance. I went unrated against any good household appliance, against bad household appliances – unfortunately I couldn't be taken back to the shop for a refund or thrown away.

NB: Dad left her for someone else. This defection appeared to surprise and annoy her. It happened when I was seven. I never witnessed any personal grief. I did not terribly miss him, his status was very similar to my own – even as a small child I must have realised this.

Did I always call her Mother? No. She was 'Mum', until she became seriously ill, then I used 'Mother'. It seems, after consideration, that I was abnormally obtuse. I called her 'Mum', when she was never anything as informal as that. I'm surprised she didn't insist on Mother, except had she, she might have asked to be known as Irene, or Mrs Turner, or even to revert to her maiden name of Shaw.

To sum up: I spent much of my life calling her 'Mum', which she never once really, deep down in whatever frozen mass she called a heart, answered to. Only when she was dying did I come near to giving her at least the verbal respect that she must have felt she deserved.

There we are. All sorted. Problem solved. Whence came my guilt? I have failed to honour my mother.

Jelly is reading a book and unaware that I am watching her. She is growing used to my scribbling. I heard her say to Dulcie today, "It's a good sign. She's much more 'up', lately," as if I was elevating myself ceilingwards. What she means in her modern, inarticulate way, is that I no longer bombard her each morning with a list of complaints. It astonishes me now that I ever did. How unsubtle I was. I'm easily astonished, when once astonishment, for me, was rare. I'm trying to recall my last instance of astonishment and there's nothing there. BI, Before Illness, I lived for forty years being only ever mildly surprised. I was indeed a cold fish. Am I any less of a cold fish now?

Regarding my ailments, I am certainly not well, but they have normalised, which is a word Jelly used several times this morning before rushing off to work.

She said, "I want to talk seriously at some point, about normalising our relationship, or at least normalising as much as possibly my life, spent as it is with you."

She was standing over me, a cup of tea in her hand which from my lowly position seemed threatening. I could see steam rising from the cup. Her legs were bare, and she wore grey leather sandals. I noticed how tanned she was. Had I been sedated while she went abroad for two weeks?

"You're extremely tanned," I said.

"I sit in the park every lunchtime, are you paying attention?"

"Normalise."

"Winter is coming."

"Yes..."

"But whatever time of year it is, I don't see why I should be forced out of my own home."

"Our home."

"In this instance, I'm talking about me for a change."

"In this instance?"

"If you're determined on the role of invalid I must have a life of my own as well."

"Which means?"

"I haven't decided, and now I'm late for work."

"Perhaps this evening?"

"No, I'm going out."

"So you're not going out, after all?"

She hadn't really been reading for several minutes.

"Actually I am going out," she looked at her watch, the clock, "a little later."

I squinted at the clock. She sighed.

"It's quarter past nine. Why don't you wear your watch? Why are you determined to be helpless?"

"Where are you going?"

"A party. It doesn't start till after ten."

"But where?"

She looked a little flustered; closed and opened and closed her book.

"Not far. Finsbury Park. I'm getting a lift."

"Naturally."

A stream of light sarcastic words fidgeted in my mouth but I held them back. I was beginning to depend on sarcasm, a futile defensive habit I didn't like. Did me no good.

"I won't stay long. A couple of hours. Don't wait up."

"Oh, I won't."

She crossed to the mirror and shook her hair out of its band.

"I'm going very grey," she said, pulling forward her one and only strand of grey hair and examining it. When I'd first met her, it had been no more than two or three long silver threads.

She watched me from the mirror, watching her.

What started me thinking about Mr Miller?

Sometimes I know how I look, what my features are doing from the way I'm feeling. Maybe not quite accurate, but I have a clear image. This evening, I saw my eyes. They were the eyes of a prisoner, screaming through reinforced glass and I remembered Mr Miller looking out of his car window, waiting for my mother.

Mr Miller: who waited for my mother, who liked to keep him waiting. Sitting in his car, fingers tapping the wheel, whistling silently and pretending nonchalance, pretending he wasn't looking, when he couldn't do anything else but look.

I only ever sensed his Christian name. It was something stolid like George or Harold; a third-league importance kind of name which went with a third-league importance kind of job. He wore a grey suit, carried a khaki raincoat – he was an unspectacular man – he was our man from the Prudential Insurance Company.

In those days, a man (Mr Miller) was sent around each week to collect the insurance money; had to sign my mother's payment off in a little creased book kept in a battered leather briefcase. When Mr Miller started taking her out for a drive, he stopped coming in. I assume the insurance transaction happened at some point during their evening.

He called their outings 'cheering your mother up', this with an apologetic smile to me, so I didn't feel excluded.

She loved the preparation, getting ready; the bath and her hair in rollers, set into tight crisp curls from the steam, loved building up her eyebrows with a stub of black eyebrow pencil, dusting loose pink powder over her face, neck and shoulders, perfume on her wrists and behind her ears. Always wore silk dresses; she liked the sound as well as the feel of silk. It was all about her feeling pampered even if she had to do it for herself. That swishing sound as the skirt moved against her legs, buoyed her up, sent her marching down the front path and out onto the pavement, swinging her white handbag and dazzling Mr Miller and the neighbours with her wide, red, promising smile.

But at the end of the day, Mr Miller was only Mr Miller. Just a man, neglected by his wife and children, a sad chap attracted like a shabby moth to her cold erratic flame. He wasn't nearly enough.

When she came home, she wasn't a femme fatale, not glamorous, not Mum nor Mother; just an angry murderous child, because no good time lasted forever and nothing and no one could live up to her expectations.

What could a Mr Miller do, but try harder and become more nervous and anxious? Eventually the affair petered out, mother cancelled the policy. No love was lost on her side, but I think it marked an end to hope.

Sorry.

I've had all night to think; to move on from Mother and Mr Miller, because I've hardly slept. Dozed – woke – checked the clock on the card table, wanting the endless night to be over and done with.

Just after midnight, the telephone rang in Jelly's bedroom. I have no truck with telephones. I've refused to become a cheerful gregarious invalid feigning interest in what goes on outside. The answerphone kicked in and I heard an unfamiliar man's voice, "Maureen, can you pick up the phone. It's about Angela."

I panicked. Few men ring us and I know the voices of the ones that do. Immediately I thought it was a policeman, some accident. I pushed myself to hurry, clumsy-bodied, knocking against chairs, catching my hip-bone on her bedroom door knob.

"Hello," I said breathlessly, "Is she all right?" I could hear music – not the Police Station, or party music – Brahms, Clarinet Sonata in F minor. I know my music as I know my poetry – recognised immediately that strange, hauntingly romantic mix of piano and clarinet, and then the sound became muffled as if someone had closed a door on it.

He said, "Ah Maureen," as if he knew me well, "I'm afraid Angela has a stomach upset."

"A stomach upset," I repeated.

"Yes, it's been coming on all day."

"She was fine when she went out."

"She didn't want to worry you." Such a reasonable man's reasoning voice.

"When is she coming home?"

"Not tonight. If she's better tomorrow, I'll run her back mid-morning."

"And if she isn't better?"

He laughed – not quite unpleasantly – as if his reply was so obvious to be not worth saying. "She'll stay put and I'll call a doctor."

"And you are?" I couldn't stop myself from trying to match his confident laugh with my own sarcastic snigger, which I knew wouldn't work, which would leave me vulnerable.

"We haven't met. I'm just a friend. Sorry, I've got to go – I think the patient calls..."

"Just hang on a minute," but he didn't. I was breathing hard into a dead telephone. I checked 1471 – nothing.

I made my way carefully back across the shadowy hall to my couch, my unwelcoming claustrophobic quilt, feeling that maudlin, gin-soaked depression creeping over me although I'd drunk nothing. I was frightened – seeing life as a gigantic globe rolling slowly past me, taking with it everyone I'd known and loved. Hard to believe in a world waiting for me outside. What if I tried to rejoin? Would I even be visible, or had I so diminished myself that all I'd represent would be a glimpsed flicker of light – flesh and blood Maureen gone.

I wasn't able to be angry. I'm not a complete fool. I'd heard my frail voice against his: sensible adult male, in control of the situation – car-driver, doctor-caller, decider of who goes where and when. I curled up in a corner of the couch and waited.

*

At nine a.m., she came home, not mid-morning. I'd tracked every sound in the street outside, yet when I heard her key in the lock it was a surprise. I hadn't expected her, had no forewarning; there'd been no sound of a car with dodgy gears to alert me. I was dry-eyed but like death. Past crying, past speaking. My white tragic face peering over the back of the couch; like a forgotten child waiting for her mother, so relieved but heart-broken.

There had been no stomach upset. I knew, and although she meant me to know, she was as distraught and frightened as I was. She comforted me; holding me tight and rocking us both, and I was glad, this time I didn't struggle to get away from her. We blubbed apologies and forgiveness and resolutions neither of us would keep.

In the afternoon when we were calmer, I went into her bedroom and we sat together on her bed, our backs against her pillows, watching television and holding hands, the way we hadn't done in over a year.

"So, it wasn't a party?" I said quietly.

"No Maureen."

"He is...?"

"He is."

"I see."

"No, you don't see," and she kissed the palm of my hand and pressed it against her cheek. Later, I came back into this room and tried to sleep.

I realise I have created an impossible situation. Even if I got well – and I intend to get well – we can never return to where we were before my mother died. Yet I do love her, in my own selfish way, and yes, I think she does love me. The parting when it comes will be like another death.

JACKIE KAY
Big Milk

The baby wasn't really a baby anymore except in the mind of the mother, my lover. She was two years old this wet summer and already she could talk buckets. She even had language for milk. Big Milk and Tiny Milk. One day I saw her pat my lover's breasts in a slightly patronising fashion and say, "Silly, gentle milk." Another day we passed a goat with big bells round its neck in a small village near the fens. The light was strange, mysterious. The goat looked like a dream in the dark light. The baby said, "Look, Big Milk, Look, there's a goat!" The baby only ever asked Big Milk to look at things. Tiny Milk never got a look in.

I never noticed that my lover's breasts were lopsided until the baby started naming them separately. The baby was no mug. The left breast was enormous. The right one small and slightly cowed in the presence of a great twin. Big Milk. I keep saying the words to myself. What I'd give for Big Milk now. One long suck. I was never that bothered about breasts before she had the baby. I wasn't interested in my own breasts or my lover's. I'd have the odd fondle, but that was it. Now, I could devour them. I could spend hours and hours worshipping and sucking and pinching. But I'm not allowed. My lover tells me her breasts are milk machines only for the baby. "No," she says firmly, "They are out of bounds." My lover tells me I should understand. "You are worse than a man," she tells me. A man would understand, she says. "A man would defer." I'm not convinced. A man would be more jealous than I am. Two years. Two years is a long time to go without a single stroke. I look over her shoulder at the baby pulling the long red nipple of Big Milk back and forth.

At night I lie in bed next to the pair of them sleeping like family. The mother's arms flailed out like a drowned bird. The baby suckling like a tiny pig. The baby isn't even aware that she drinks warm milk all night long. She is in the blissful world of oblivion. Limbs all soft and gone. I test the baby's hand, full of my own raging insomnia. The small fat hand lands back down on the duvet with a plump. She doesn't even stir. I try my lover's hand. She can tell things in her sleep. She knows the difference between the baby and me. In her sleep, she pulls away, irritated. I lie next to the sleeping mother and baby and feel totally irreligious. They are a painting. I could rip the canvas. I get up and open the curtains slightly. Nobody stirs. I take a peek at the moon. It looks big and vain, as if it's saying there is only one of me buster, there's plenty of you suckers out there staring at me. It is a canny moon tonight, secretive. I piss the loudest piss I can manage. I pour a glass of water. Then I return to bed next to the sleeping mother and daughter. The baby is still suckling away ferociously, her small lips going like the hammers. It is beyond belief. How many pints is that she's downed in the one night? No wonder the lover is drained. The baby is taking everything. Nutrients. Vitamins. The lot. She buys herself bottles and bottles of vitamins but she doesn't realise that it is all pointless; the baby has got her. The baby has moved in to occupy her, awake or asleep, night or day. My lover is a saint, pale, exhausted. She is drained dry. The hair is dry. Her hair used to gleam.

I'm not bothered about her hair. I am not bothered about not going out anymore, anywhere. The pictures, pubs, restaurants, the houses of friends. I don't care that I don't have friends anymore. Friends without babies are carrying on their ridiculous, meaningless lives, pretending their silly meetings, their silly movies, their uptight nouveau cuisine meals matter. Tottering about the place totally without roots. Getting a haircut at Vidal Sassoon to cheer themselves up. Or spending a whole sad summer slimming. Or living for the two therapy hours per week. Getting up at six to see a shrink at seven. That's what they are up to. A few of them still bang away at ideas that matter to them. But even they sound tired when they talk about politics. And they always say something shocking to surprise me, or themselves. I don't know which. I don't see any of them anymore.

What do I see? I see the baby mostly. I see her more than I see my lover. I stare into her small face and see her astonishing beauty the way my lover sees it. The big eyes that are a strange green colour. The lavish eyelashes. The tiny perfect nose. The cartoon eyebrows. The perfect baby-soft skin. The lush little lips. She's a picture. No doubt about it. My lover used to tell me that I had beautiful eyes. I'd vainly picture my own eyes when she paid me such compliments. I'd see the deep rich chocolate brown melt before me. The long black lashes. But my eyes are not the subject these days. Or the object, come to think of it. My eyes are just for myself. I watch mother and daughter sleeping peaceably in the dark. Dreaming of each other, probably. There are many nights I spend like this watching. I haven't made up my mind yet what to do with all my watching. I am sure it will come to some use. The baby dribbles and the lover dribbles. The light outside has begun. I've come round again. The birds are at it. The baby has the power. It is the plain stark truth of the matter. I can see it as I watch the two of them. Tiny puffs of power blow out of the baby's mouth.

She transforms the adults around her to suit herself. Many of the adults I know are now becoming babified. They talk a baby language to each other. They like the same food. They watch *Teletubbies*. They read Harry Potter. They even go to bed at the same time as the baby; and if they have a good relationship they might manage whispering in the dark. Very little fucking. Very little. I'm trying to console myself here. It's another day.

In the morning the baby always says "Hello" to me before my lover gets a word in. To be fair, the baby has the nicest "Hello" in the whole world. She says it like she is showering you with bluebells. You actually feel cared for when the baby talks to you. I can see the seduction. I know why my lover is seduced. That and having her very own likeness staring back at her with those strange green eyes. I can never imagine having such a likeness. I tell myself it must be quite creepy going about the place with a tiny double. A wee doppelganger. It's bound to unsettle you a bit, when you are washing your hair, to look into the mirror and for one moment see a tiny toddler staring back at you. It can't be pleasant.

The feeding itself isn't pleasant either. Not when the baby has teeth. I've heard my lover howl in agony on more than one occasion when the baby has sunk her sharp little milk teeth into Big Milk. A woman is not free till her breasts are her own again. Of this I am certain. I am more certain of this than a woman's right to vote or to choose. As long as her breasts are tied to her wean she might as well be in chains. She can't get out. Not for long. She rushes home with her breasts heavy and hurting. Once we went out for a two-hour-and-twenty-minute anniversary meal. When we got home my lover teemed up the stairs and hung over the bathroom sink. The milk spilled and spilled. She could have shot me with it there was so much. Big gun milk. It was shocking. She swung round and caught me staring, appalled. She looked proud of the quantities. Said she could have filled a lot of bottles, fed a lot of hungry babies with that.

I tried to imagine the state of my life with my lover feeding hundreds of tiny babies. I pictured it for a ghastly moment: our new super king-size bed (that we got so that all three of us could sleep comfortably and are still paying for in instalments) invaded by babies from all over the world. My lover lying in her white cotton nightie. The buttons open. Big Milk and Tiny Milk both being utilised for a change. Tiny Milk in her element – so full of self-importance that for a second Tiny Milk has bloated into the next cup size. The next time she mentioned having enough milk to feed an army, I told her she had quite enough on her hands. And she laughed sympathetically and said my name quite lovingly. I was appeased for a moment until the baby piped up with a new word. "Did you hear that?" she said, breathless. "That's the first time she's ever said that. Isn't that amazing?" "It is," I said, disgusted at myself, her and the baby all in one fell swoop. "It's totally amazing – especially for her age," I added slyly. "For her age, it is pure genius." She plucked the baby up and landed a smacker on her smug baby cheek. The baby patted Big Milk again and said, "Funny, funny, Milk. Oh look Mummy, Milk shy." I left the two of them to it on the landing outside the toilet.

Even when I go up to my attic I can still hear them down below. Giggling and laughing, singing and dancing together. "If you go down to the woods today, you're in for a big surprise." The rain chaps on my tiny attic windows. Big Milk is having a ball. I climb down the steep stairs to watch some more. Daytime watching is different from night-time. Tiny details light up. The baby's small hands are placed protectively on the soft full breasts. The mouth around the nipple. Sometimes she doesn't drink. She just lies half asleep, contemplating milk or dreaming milk. It makes me wonder how I survived. I was never breastfed myself. My mother spoonfed me for two weeks then left. I never saw her again. Perhaps I've been dreaming of her breasts all my life. Maybe that's what rankles with the baby taking Big Milk for granted. When her mouth expectantly opens there is no question that the nipple won't go in. No question. Every soft open request is answered. I try and imagine myself as a tiny baby, soft black curls on my head, big brown eyes. Skin a different colour from my mother's. I imagine myself lying across my mother's white breast, my small brown face suffocating in the pure joy of warm, sweet milk. The smell of it, recognising the tender smell of it. I imagine my life if she had kept me. I would have been a hairdresser if I hadn't been adopted. I'm quite sure. I would have washed the dandruff off many an old woman's head. I would have administered perms to give them the illusion of their hair forty years before. I would have specialised in tints and dyes, in conditioners that give full body to the hair. I would probably have never thought about milk. The lack of it. Or the need of it.

I lie in the dark with the rain playing soft jazz on the windowpane of our bedroom. I say our bedroom, but it is not our bedroom anymore. Now teddy bears and nappies and ointment and wooden toys and baby clothes can be found strewn all over the floor. I lie in the dark and remember what it was like when I had my lover all to myself. When she slept in my arms and not the baby's. When she woke up in the night to pull me closer. When she muttered things into my sleeping back. I lie awake and remember all the different places my lover and I had sex. All the different ways, when we had our own private language. The baby has monopolised language. Nothing I say can ever sound so interesting, so original. The baby has converted me into a bland, boring, possessive lover who doesn't know her arse from her elbow. There are bits of my body that I can only remember in the dark. They are not touched. The dawn is stark and obvious. I make my decision. I can't help it. It is the only possible thing I can do under the circumstances.

Don't doubt I love my lover and I love her baby. I love their likeness. Their cheeks and eyes. The way their hair moves from their crown to scatter over their whole head in exactly the same place. Their identical ears. I love both of them. I love the baby because she is kind. She would never hurt anybody. She is gentle, silly. But love is not enough for me this time. I get up, get dressed and go outside with my car keys in my hand. I close my front door quietly behind me. My breath in my mouth. I take the M61 towards Preston. I drive past four junction numbers in the bleached morning. There are few cars on the road. I stop at a service station and drink a black coffee with two sugars. I smoke two cigarettes that taste disgusting because it is too early. I don't smoke in the day usually. I smoke at night. Day and night have rolled into one. The baby's seat in the back is empty. The passenger seat has a map on it. There is no lover to read the map, to tell me where to go. There is no lover to pass me an apple. There is just me and the car and the big sky, flushed with the morning. I put on a tape and play some music. I am far north now. Going further. I am nearly at the Scottish border. I feel a strange exhilaration. I know my lover and her baby are still sleeping, totally unaware of my absence. As I drive on past the wet fields of morning, I feel certain that there is not a single person in the world who truly cares about me. Except perhaps my mother. I have been told where she lives up north. Right at the top of the country in a tiny village, in a rose cottage. She lives in the kind of village where people still notice a stranger's car.

If I arrive in the middle of the day, the villagers will all come out and stare at me and my car. They will walk right round my car in an admiring circle. Someone might offer to park it for me.

I will arrive in daytime. When I knock at the door of Rose Cottage, my mother will answer. She will know instantly from the colour of my skin that I am her lost daughter. Her abandoned daughter. I have no idea what she will say. It doesn't matter. It doesn't matter if she slams the door in my face, just as long as I can get one long look at her breasts. Just as long as I can imagine what my life would have been like if I had sucked on those breasts for two solid years. If she slams the door and tells me she doesn't want to know me, it will pierce me, it will hurt. But I will not create a scene in a Highland town. I will go to the village shop and buy something to eat. Then I will ask where the nearest hair salon is. I will drive there directly where a sign on the window will read, ASSISTANT WANTED. I will take up my old life as a hairdresser. When I say my old life, I mean the life I could have, perhaps even should have, led. When I take up my old life, old words will come out of my mouth. Words that local people will understand. Some of them might ask me how I came to know them. When they do, I will be ready with my answer. I will say I learned them with my mother's milk.

I am off the M6 now and on the A74. I read somewhere that the A74 is the most dangerous road in the country. Something new in me this morning welcomes the danger. Something in me wants to die before I meet my mother. When I think about it, I realise that I have always wanted to die. That all my life, I have dreamed longingly of death. Perhaps it was because she left. Perhaps losing a mother abruptly like that is too much for an unsuspecting baby to bear. I know now this minute, zooming up the A74 at 110 miles per hour, that I have wanted to die from the second she left me. I wonder what she did with the milk in her breasts, how long it took before it dried up, whether or not she had to wear breast pads to hide the leaking milk. I wonder if her secret has burned inside her Catholic heart for years.

I can only give her the one chance. Only the one. I will knock and I will ask her to let me in. But if she doesn't want me, I won't give her another chance. I won't give anyone another chance. It has been one long dance with death. I have my headlights on even though there is plenty of daylight. I have them on full beam to warn other cars that I am a fast bastard and they had better get out of my way. The blue light in my dashboard is lit up. It and the music keep strange company. Is there anyone out there behind or before me on the A74 who has ever felt like this? I realise that I am possibly quite mad. I realise that the baby has done it to me. It is not the baby's fault or her mother's. They can't help being ordinary. Being flesh and blood. The world is full of people who are separated from their families. They could all be on the A74 right now, speeding forwards to trace the old bloodline. It is like a song line. What is my mother's favourite song? 'Ae Fond Kiss'? "Ae fond kiss and then we sever." There is much to discover. I picture the faces of all the other manic adopted people, their anonymous hands clutched to the steering wheel in search of themselves. Their eyes are all intense. I have never met an adopted person who does not have intense eyes. But they offer no comfort. This is all mine.

Exhausted, I arrive in the village at three o'clock. My mouth is dry, furry. It is a very long time since I have slept. I spot a vacancy sign outside a place called the Tayvallich Inn. It has four rooms, three taken. The woman shows me the room and I tell her I'll take it. It is not a particularly pleasant room, but that doesn't matter. There is no view. All I can see from the window is other parts of the inn. I close the curtains. The room has little light anyway. I decide to go and visit my mother tomorrow after sleep. When I get into the small room with the hard bed and the nylon sheets, I weep for the unfairness of it all. A picture of the baby at home in our Egyptian cotton sheets suckling away and smiling in her sleep flashes before me. My lover's open nightie. It occurs to me that I haven't actually minded all my life. My mother shipping me out never bothered me. I was happy with the mother who raised me, who fed me milk from the dairy and Scots porridge oats and plumped my pillows at night. I was never bothered at all until the baby arrived. Until the baby came I never gave any of it a moment's thought. I realise now in room four of Tayvallich Inn under the pink nylon sheets that the baby has engineered this whole trip. The baby wanted me to go away. She wanted her mother all to herself in our big bed. Of late, she's even started saying "Go away!" It is perfectly obvious to me now. The one thing the baby doesn't lack is cunning. I turn the light on and stare at the silly brown and cream kettle, the tiny wicker basket containing two sachets of Nescafé, two tea bags, two bags of sugar and two plastic thimbles of milk. I open one thimble and then another with my thumbnail. They are the size of large nipples. I suck the milk out of the plastic thimbles. The false milk coats my tongue. I am not satisfied. Not at all. I crouch down to look into the mirror above the dressing table. I am very pale, very peelie-wally. Big dark circles under my eyes. I do not look my best for my mother. But why should that matter? A mother should love her child unconditionally. My hair needs combing. But I have brought nothing with me. I did not pack a change of clothes. None of it matters.

I pass the nosy Inn woman in the hall. She asks me if I need anything. I say, "Yes, actually, I need a mother." The woman laughs nervously, unpleasantly, and asks me if I'll be having the full Scottish breakfast in the morning. I tell her I'm just not sure what will be happening. She hesitates for a moment and I hesitate too. Before she scurries off to tell her husband, I notice her eyes are the colour of strong tea. I open the door that now says NO VACANCIES and head for Rose Cottage. I can't wait for tomorrow, I must go today. I must find her today. My heart is in my mouth. I could do it with my eyes shut. I feel my feet instinctively head in the right direction. It is teatime. My mother will be having her tea. Perhaps she will be watching the news. My feet barely touch the ground. The air is tart and fresh in my face. Perhaps some of my colour will return to my cheeks before my mother opens her front door. Will she tilt her head to the side gently when she looks at me? Following my nose miraculously works. There in front of me is a small stone cottage. Outside the roses are in bloom. There is a wonderful yellow tea rose bush. I bend to sniff one of the flowers. I feel the impossible softness of the rose petals against my nose. I sink towards the sweet, trusting scent. I always knew she would like yellow roses. I stare at the front door. It is painted plain white. Standing quietly next to the front door are two bottles of milk. I open the silver lid of one of them and drink, knocking it back on the doorstep. It is sour. It is lumpy. I test the other one. It is sour as well. A trickle of thin sour milk pours through the thick stuff. I look into my mother's house through the letterbox. It is dark in there. I can't see a single thing.

KATHLEEN KIIRIK BRYSON
The Day I Ate My Passport

I had a problem with passports.

Passport #3 had been misplaced in a sleazy Seattle tavern and never found again. Presumed stolen. Passport #2 had been thieved violently on a Milan-bound train while travelling. Unequivocally stolen. Passport #1 had 'fallen' out of my backpack at the Spanish–French border, but then had been returned in a package to my parents' home by a kind, anonymous Spanish person four months after the fact. Perhaps stolen. Who the hell knew? I had to turn it in to US Passport Services anyway when it showed up tardily, and I never saw it again.

After the loss of Passport #3, the United States Government got the notion that I was supplying a legion of wannabe Yanks all called Carrie Miller, and it was immediately required that I only be issued one-year passports for the foreseeable future, or at least until I proved a little more gratitude/responsibility regarding my luck at having been born in the Greatest Nation on Earth, Under God, Indivisible, With Liberty and Justice for All.

The fact was, I loved my passport. I had loved *all* my passports. I just couldn't stop losing them, or being relieved of them by passing pickpockets.

Now, I sat on the Hackney-bound 38 bus and stared at my fourth passport in eight years. It had, undoubtedly, the worst picture of the four: the year of issuance had been a bad hair year for me and I didn't even look alive (generally, a requirement for holding a passport) because my eyes were rolled all the way up in the back of my head. It really did look like a bad forensic photo of a dead, trailer-trash Barbie Doll. My mouth was even lolling open in the pic but, since I looked deceased, the lips had no blow-job sensuality – it just looked as if I had been drooling right before I'd been decapitated, or drowned, or whatever happened to the girlie in the photo to make her look so blondly stupid.

I know that *everyone* complains about passport photos but trust me, the picture on Passport #4 was so bad that even customs officials frequently burst out laughing, and then gestured their colleagues over to take a look as well. And I bet they see a few crap photos in their time, too. But maybe as a result of these reactions, I had grown strangely fond of this particular one-year passport, if only to reassure myself that I was still alive and not really as hideous as the picture – maybe it was a sort of people-who-gatecrash-funerals-to-affirm-their-own-vitality thing. I liked almost everything about the document: the horrible photo, the fact that it was a special-issue Benjamin Franklin commemorative passport, the blank pages waiting to be filled up with a rash of adventures, the eagle hologram on the inside.

Everything, in fact, except for the line struck through my old Student Visa with a special British Home Office designated number that, *should I leave the country and attempt to re-enter*, would let the UK customs officials know that a) I had an ongoing Immigration Appeal based on a relationship with a Member of the Same Sex and b) If I re-entered the United Kingdom once having left, for any reason, the aforementioned Appeal would be declared invalid and I'd be booted out of England as quickly as you could say Tolerate-The-Homegrown-Queers-But-For-God's-Sake-Don't-Let-Their-Filthy-Foreign-Partners-Stay-Here.

The bus was noisy; people were getting on my nerves and I felt hot, even though the weather outside was muggy-cool with pollution. I took another look at my goofy photo and then tucked the passport safely away inside my button-down front-jacket pocket. I wasn't taking any chances. I wasn't going to lose Passport #4. I thought of Sabine nervously waiting at home with the unopened letter from Immigration, and my stomach started to hurt. If it had been me, I would have already ripped the letter open; there was no way I would be able to stand the tension.

I looked down at my hands and tried to think of strategies, weighing things against each other on some sick moral scale: a good person would fly to California to see her grandfather. A good person would stay in the UK and fight for the chance to stay with her girlfriend. But if I took off for LA, chances were that I wouldn't be able to get back in the country, not with that fucking indicatory line in my passport. I'd have to kiss my relationship with Sabine goodbye, and even after four years I was crazy about Sabine, crazy in love. But if I stayed in Britain, chances were that I'd never see my grandpa again. And I loved my grandpa. I fell in a river when I was three and it was my grandpa who stepped right in and saved me from drowning. We even had the same birthday, Grandpa and me.

The ironic thing was, I wasn't too keen on London. I didn't want to move here permanently, or leech off the British Social Services system. I just wanted to be with Sabine until Sabine finished her degree and then we'd move back to the States, where no doubt the whole immigration nightmare would start all over again from scratch.

I looked out the scarred plastic window, as the bus passed by Angel Station, at the smugly heterosexual yuppies who walked by hand in hand. They never had to think about it – never felt self-conscious about holding hands, never had to consider they'd earn a bashing from it, never had to balance grandfather versus lover in terms of immigration as I now had to do. Even an unmarried het pair would have the choice of marriage in a situation like mine – though they might decline it – and this privilege of choice irked me. But the truth was, I didn't wish the choice on them, either. I wished them the bliss of ignorance.

In fact, I didn't wish how I felt on anybody: nervous, fearful, a right mess. I fingered Passport #4 through my jacket pocket. There was one other option that my friend Alice had mentioned. Alice was an American ex-pat who'd married a British gay man for money, and she was also a part-time crim. I'd given her a call, desperate to talk to anyone who'd gone throught the same immigration hell, and Alice had assured me she knew a perfect solution to my little quandary. To be honest, I didn't trust Alice as far as I could throw her, and she was a big butch girl far over eighteen stone. Still, I would be taking a day off work tomorrow and was meeting her for coffee, and we'd talk all about it.

I wasn't holding my breath.

The bus rumbled through Dalston, and I began to gather my things in preparation for disembarkment. Purse: check. Water bottle: check. Passport safe in jacket pocket: check. This is how I don't lose passports these days: by checking, and double-checking.

I started to feel motion-sick. I got off one stop early and began walking, dodging dog shit and McDonald's plastic hamburger containers. In five minutes I'd be home, and I'd see if the letter from Immigration stated whether I could go back home for a week or so and still retain my Appeal in process. Fuck, but my stomach hurt. For the last fortnight, I had felt dread every evening as I returned home: dread that the letter from Immigration had arrived; dread that it hadn't; dread of bad news from the States via the answering machine.

If Grandpa had died, I knew that Sabine would want to tell me face-to-face. So I was always gauging her voice when I called before leaving the office each evening, trying to tell if she knew something I didn't (she got home earlier than I did). I never asked, though. I would just board the homeward bus with a sense of sickening foreboding.

The last four or five days when I returned home from work, Sabine had greeted me with a kiss and a hug and then nodded towards the phone. There had been messages from my parents blinking, all along the same line: *We don't want to worry you, Carrie, but Grandpa's not doing too well.* Or: *You might want to give your grandfather a call, maybe.* That one had been from my father, and it was especially in his voice that I could detect what was wrong. Despite his slow, sweet, friendly words, I heard panic: he wanted to protect me; didn't want me to feel pain for staying. It was parental instinct. But I also heard his fear as a child: his father was dying. Then there had been a couple more messages from my mom, and even though she too was careful not to make me feel guilty, I could hear the worry in her casual words like subtitles in a foreign film elegantly translated to: *Your grandfather is dying, Carrie. He's not going to make it much longer.*

That's what she was *really* saying.

Tonight, though, Sabine was looking as nervous as me as I unlocked the door and walked into the living room. She was sitting on the couch, holding the letter. Her face was pale, and I realised she had a great stake in this too, aside from worrying about my feelings. She didn't want the responsibility of being the one I chose to stay for, the one I chose over my grandfather.

I grabbed the envelope and tore it open.

Dear Ms Miller,

Thank you for your letter requesting compassionate leave to go back to the US for one week. Some consideration was given to other countries' policies in relation to same-sex relationships. However, immigration policy is a matter for each country to decide. We have developed a policy which we consider to be appropriate to the United Kingdom for same-sex relationships, and have not based it on any other country's system.

I can confirm that it is not proposed to grant extensions of one year until a period of four years cohabitation is reached under this new concession. In this case you and your partner Sabine Mahl, a European National, have only lived together for three years and clearly fail to meet the requirements of that concession – even if, as you argue, you have been in a relationship for over four years.

As your solicitor knows, the decision to refuse your initial application was taken over two years ago, based on the fact that at that time the incumbent Government did not consider same-sex relationships as falling under Immigration Law, following which you submitted an appeal against that decision. Though the law has been altered slightly (see above paragraph), the hearing of the appeal is still awaited. It is of course tragic that you are unable to see your grandfather when he is seriously ill. The position is however that if you leave the United Kingdom your appeal will lapse. Since that is the only basis for your presence here, you would need to apply for entry clearance in the United States before attempting to return. I am afraid that I can give no guarantee that any such application would be successful. I hope this is of some assistance, and am sorry not to give a more welcome reply.

Yours sincerely,
Paul Jakeson
Immigration & Nationality Directorate
The Home Office, Croydon

Alice put the coffee cup down. "There is a way, you know," she said.

I stared at her. My throat was dry with nervousness. I had been in tears the entire night, after the shock of the letter's content. I had just assumed they would let me return to tell my grandfather goodbye – now I was aware that I wouldn't even be able to go back for a funeral. Suddenly, I grew conscious of the fact that I was still looking blankly at Alice. I felt like I was on the edge of something dangerous. Still – I wasn't a Catholic anymore; just thinking about an act didn't mean I was going to commit it. It would be safe to listen.

"It *is* illegal, however," Alice added.

I swallowed hard.

"That's why I'm going to tell you all about it hypothetically. For example, if you were to use your passport you have now to leave the country and go back to the States –"

"Passport number four," I interjected.

"Yeah, whatever. If you were to lose this passport accidentally while you were in the States – or even 'accidentally' wash it in the laundry – then of course your passport would have to be replaced and you would not have that little line and those little letters that are giving you such a headache at the moment."

My mind was whirling as I swiftly tried to calculate how many passports I'd have gone through if I did as she suggested. If I got a replacement passport, it would be Passport #5. Even though I'd been scrupulously honest about Passports 1-3, there would be no chance that US Passport Services would accept the loss of crazy-pictured Passport #4. Then something occurred to me. "Hold on. Don't they have to give me a stamp in hypothetical replacement Passport Number Five when I re-enter Great Britain?"

"That's right."

I set my coffee cup down so hard the table shook. I fixed my eyes on a bad watercolour of some obscure English Coast on the opposite wall. "It won't work. Next year we'll have been officially cohabiting for four years, and I'll have to turn my passport over to the British Home Office to get my 'leave to remain'. When they see that fucking entry stamp, they'll know that I've left and re-entered the country. My whole appeal will be declared invalid."

"Yeah well, that's the thing. You'd have to hypothetically lose *that* passport, too – what number did you call it? Four? Jesus."

"Five. Hypothetical Five."

"Anyway, you'd have to lose that fifth passport – or wash it – before you visit the Home Office, and get a new clean one."

Hypothetical Passport #6.

"No way." I pushed my almond croissant away, no longer hungry. "US Passport Services would never, ever believe me. I'm on their shit list already."

"You've done it before, haven't you? All those 'missing' passports?"

"I fucking haven't. Passports one to three were genuinely lost or stolen. Passport Number Four is safe at home in my dresser drawer and that's where it's staying."

Alice calmly took a sip of cappuccino. For a girl who prided herself on a rough-trade butch look, she was certainly mannered. "You asked me if I had any solutions. That's the only solution I know."

"A fucking lot of good it does me, too." I got up to go: trembling, pissed off.

"Go to hell," Alice said in a low tone so that only the adjacent tables could hear. Then, as I neared the door with my jacket in hand, she added more loudly, "It's not my fault you lost your first three passports. If you had been smart, you would have held onto them until a rainy day when you really *needed* them."

I walked through the door and out onto the pavement. I didn't slam the door, exactly, but there was an audible crash nevertheless. I stood outside the café and tried to catch my breath. What Alice was talking about was a crime.

When I got home, I confirmed this was the case: on the third page of my funny-face, Benjamin-Franklin commemorative passport, there it was – *deliberate mutilation of a US passport is a felony under US law.*

I lay back down on the bed, flat on my back, and thought about things, holding my beloved passport to my chest. Sabine wasn't home yet, so I had a little time for reflection, and slowly my anger at Alice turned to calm resignation. It wasn't Alice's fault the Immigration system was bigoted, or that my grandfather was ill. I'd have to give her a call tomorrow and apologise.

Later in the evening, I made a different kind of call.

Ring, ring.

"Hello? Who's that?"

"It's Carrie, Grandma. I was just calling to see – to see how things were going over there."

"Just fine, honey. Just fine."

"How's Grandpa doing?"

Pause. "Not so good at the moment, but he had a real good day yesterday. Would you like to talk to him?"

"Yes, please."

"Just a second... Bob! Carrie's on the phone."

Long pause. The telephone clattered.

"Hello? Who's that?"

"Hi, Grandpa. It's Carrie. In London. My mom and dad said you weren't doing so well at the moment."

"No, I'm not at my best, that's fair to say." *Pause.* "When are you coming back home?"

"It's not so easy at the moment, Grandpa. I can't leave work without losing my job." *I'm queer, Grandpa – bisexual. I have a girlfriend I'm really in love with, the real thing, a once-in-a-lifetime thing. If I leave, I'll never see her again.*

"I know you're a hard worker. I'm real proud of you. Well, you better hurry if you're going to get over here."

"I hear you, Grandpa. I'm trying to sort things out."

"I've got to go now – I'm getting kinda tired. You take care. You have a good time over there, but you hurry on over, you hear."

"Bye, Grandpa." *I know it's serious, Grandpa.* "I love you." *I know I should hurry.* "I'll call you tomorrow."

After I disconnected the transatlantic call, I stared at the receiver. Staying for love would be one thing, but my grandparents thought I was staying in England because I was having too much fun. Too much fun to go back and pay my next-to-last respects. I could call Grandpa back. I could tell him the truth. But then I remembered his remarks about the gay male couple that moved in next door to him and Grandma, and I knew I couldn't risk losing his love right before his life ended. I couldn't take that risk.

I couldn't take it. I couldn't take any of it.

The next day I carried my passport with me to work, in the zip-up pocket of my combat trousers, like some kind of protective amulet against my grandfather's death. It was the only way out that I could see that didn't involve losing either my grandfather or my girlfriend. All through the day at the publishing house where I did freelance editing, I found myself reaching down and patting the rectangle the passport made in the leg-pocket. I'd never really knowingly broken the law in my entire life, other than jaywalking and the odd joint. There was no way I could do it. But then I'd remember the sound of Grandpa's voice as he said, *Well, you better hurry*, and I found myself considering that I might be capable of a felony, after all. Why should I respect laws, anyway, when the same type of laws that kept me and Sabine from living together – either here or in the States – were in themselves immoral and wrong.

At my lunch break I went into the Ladies, locked the door of the cubicle behind me and sat down on the closed toilet seat. I wasn't there to take a piss. I took out the passport and had another look at the drowned Barbie doll. It still made me smile. My hand was shaking as I held the passport up and admired the singular way my head kind of flopped to one side. Felony aside, there was no way I could get rid of it. It was too beautifully awful; it had to be preserved for posterity. I sat there for a while, thinking about Grandpa, then I went through the pretence of flushing the toilet and washing my hands. When I exited the cubicle, there stood the Managing Director's PA – Karen – glaring at me.

"Problem?" she asked, in a rather icy, bitchy tone.

"Oh, yes." I gave her a really false smile. "Many problems. If you only knew, Kaz. If you only knew."

I felt my cheeks burning as I returned to my desk. Being arsey with the MD's personal assistant was a recipe for disaster – maybe even a recipe for a termination of contract – but at the moment, I didn't care. I felt really weird, like I was seeing everything through a kind of a glaze. I was damp underneath my armpits. The building was just too damn hot. I'd go down to the basement and photocopy a manuscript that had to be sent to the typesetters; it was cooler there.

It *was* better down in the basement. I found myself able to think with more clarity, though I still didn't know what I was going to do. I set the photocopier on automatic. It hummed its way through the folios and, a little bored, I glanced around the basement for something to look at, or do.

That's when I saw the colour copier.

I took out Passport #4 and looked at it. If I hypothetically lost or damaged it at some point, I'd still want to be able to look at the stupid photo whenever I needed a good laugh. I walked over to the colour copier. It didn't mean I was going to do what Alice had suggested. I took a furtive colour copy of the page that had my name and photo, then shoved the copy back into my pants pocket along with the passport, feeling suddenly guilty.

On the bus on the way home, I extracted the colour copy and examined it closely. It was colour-perfect. I could put it in my scrapbook in order to remember this whole great ordeal by.

Then, just like that, I knew I wasn't going to be able to go through with it. Not for Sabine. Not for Grandpa. Some weird patriotic residue prevented me from disposing with Passport #4. I couldn't do it, not after all the times I'd had to attest – truthfully – to my innocence regarding Passports 1 through 3. I didn't want to be a liar (or a felon!); it was the same instinct that made me apply for leave to remain on the basis of a same-sex relationship, rather than just marrying a nice gay guy, like everyone else did. I carefully folded the colour copy, stuffed it in the side pouch of my bookbag, looked out the window and sighed.

I had an argument with Sabine when I got home that night. Nothing too extreme – just some bitching on both parts that turned sour after a few minutes. I had knocked a bottle of wine over myself and the kitchen floor, then had blamed her for setting it precariously on the edge of the table. I was really moody, like I wanted to pick apart everything and test it, make sure the relationship was worth staying for. I could still go to California, I told myself, as I stripped off my T-shirt and combats and threw them into our old top-loader, turned it on and then mopped up the puddle on the kitchen floor in my underwear and bra. I could still go. Maybe Sabine wasn't all that.

Maybe she was.

She was in the living room, sulking in front of the flickering TV. I'd go join her once I'd changed into my pyjamas. Perhaps make things up to her. Perhaps explain that I wasn't thinking too straight at the moment. That I knew I was being a cranky bitch.

It was cool, later on. It was all right. As I lay my head in Sabine's lap and watched *NYPD Blue* and tried to think of nothing, of nothing at all, it was the first time I'd felt relaxed in weeks.

Then I sat up with a start.

Fucking, fuck!

"What is it?" Sabine looked alarmed.

But I was already running to the washing machine. Sabine was right on my heels. I wrenched off the spin cycle manually –

"Hey," interjected Sabine, "you can't do that –"

"Shut up." I reached my hand into the vat of cold soapy water and fished out my sodden combats, slopping water all over the freshly mopped kitchen floor. I didn't give a shit. There it was – a stiff rectangle in the leg-pocket. I unzipped the pouch and withdrew Passport #4. It was completely ruined. It was warped and ugly and useless.

I hadn't even been able to travel home on it, *first*. Inadvertently, I had just washed away an opportunity.

I sank to my knees on the kitchen floor, soaking my pyjamas, passport in hand. I was vaguely aware of Sabine there beside me, saying comforting things, but all I could think was: Fuck, Fuck and Fuck.

It was one thing being distracted because of stress. It was another thing being a bitch (I was probably going to lose my job, my friends *and* my girlfriend if I kept on like this). But see, I seemed to be fucking up my whole life in the process, too.

I tried calling my grandparents later that night, after Sabine had force-fed me chocolate Hob-Nobs and hot cocoa. It was my grandmother who answered the phone, again.

"Hi, Grandma."

"Hi, sweetheart. You doing OK?"

"Yeah. Can I talk to Grandpa?"

"Just a second, honey. Bob! Carrie's on the line!"

There was the same pause as last time. Only this time it lasted and lasted. My grandma came back on the phone.

"Carrie?"

"Yeah?"

"Grandpa's not feeling too well at the moment. He can't get up for the phone call."

"Oh." *Pause.* "Tell him I called. Tell him I said, 'I love you.'"

"I'll do that, honey. You take care."

"OK. You take care too, Grandma."

After I hung up the phone, I made up my mind to call in sick and go to the embassy the next day. I couldn't stand not having a whole passport. I was close to Grandpa, but what if someone I was even closer to died? What if my father or my mother died? Or my sister or one of my brothers? I'd have to wait for passport approval from the Department of State. Someone could die while that time expired. Right now, I felt country-less. I needed to have options.

I had been shaky when I started out on the 38 bus that would take me most of the way to Grosvenor Square, where the American Embassy was situated. Sabine had seen me off with a grin and a kiss, but I was starting to get paranoid, and I imagined that I saw something in her eyes that indicated that she wanted to wash herself of the whole thing, some sort of resigned exhaustion that might suddenly pop if I said the wrong thing. I had tried to be particularly nice in the morning, making the coffee, enquiring about her thoughts too, but underneath my smile my face had felt frozen. That's what happens when you just go through the motions.

I sat back on my seat and drummed my feet against the seat in front of me until some lady turned around and politely asked me to stop.

Fuck you, bitch, you don't know what's in my head, I thought, but I stopped anyway, and instead began to count the seconds before I reached Green Park Station. One-thousand-one, one-thousand-two, one-thousand-three.

I had reached one-thousand-one-thousand-and-four by the time the bus pulled into my stop.

As I walked through the tree-lined avenues of Grosvenor Square and approached the American Embassy, I had already started feeling a huge surge of guilt regarding my passport because, even though I hadn't washed it on purpose, I had certainly considered doing it. What if they made me take some sort of lie detector test, and my residual guilt spiked up on the polygraph like Mount Everest? Maybe they did things like that to test you after you had gone through Passport #4. I had no fucking clue.

Before I went inside, I looked up at the embassy. It was a huge concrete behemoth of a building, but to me its most frightening aspect was the forty-foot brass eagle atop the building. It was fierce. The whole structure, a big grey cinder block, made my heart beat faster: it reminded me of an Orwellian 1984 building; it reminded me of the Internal Revenue Service, unpaid Federal Student Loans, the Census, Oliver North, Republicans. I did not feel like I belonged here: this was not the same America as the green West Coast I was homesick for, or the America of dissidence and activism that Europeans tried smugly to ignore, then patronised in sneery newspaper articles about 'The New Yank Radicalism'.

I climbed the steps. My pulse was ticking away. I was going to be found out. I was a commie, a lezzie, an inadvertent destroyer of passports. Ignorance of the law was no excuse. Mistakes were no excuse. I went through the metal detector and past the armed guard in splotchy combat fatigues holding a sub-automatic. The military's presence here made me remember their personal brand of homophobia, now sold all over the world like other US multinational products: Don't-Ask-Don't-Tell™Spain. Don't-Ask-Don't-Tell™Israel. Don't-Even-Think-About-It™Singapore. I glared at him, but the beefy ex-frat boy in his buzz haircut and chiselled republicanite face didn't even glance at me.

I waited to sign the papers indicating my reasons for appearing at Passport Services. Ahead of me was a newly married straight couple complaining loudly about the 'hell' they had had to go through to get the proper passport stamp – three whole weeks, they had to wait.

Jesus. Imagine waiting three whole weeks. I wanted to scream down the entire room; let them all know the hellish wait I'd gone through for the past four years, but I knew if I did that the soldier would be on me in a moment for disorderly conduct, and they'd probably make some sort of weird mark in my 'file', and bar Sabine from ever entering the States with me, or something.

I handed over two new, identical photographs (quite a stylish image, this time) and signed a whole sheath of papers, detailing the history of every single passport I'd lost or had stolen or, now, accidentally washed in laundry. I underlined *accidentally* when I described the destruction of Passport #4, then worried that I was protesting too much. It didn't matter. It was the truth.

The air was suffocating in the room. I sat on one of the many seats away from the squalling babies and tried to read a pamphlet on absentee voter registration. A registrar called my name and I went up to the front of the counter.

"You've gone through four passports now," she said. She looked at me with cold eyes, and didn't blink once.

"One was actually returned," I pointed out. "Passport Number One. And I have Passport Number Four here with me. It was just damaged. I washed it in the laundry. Accidentally."

She stared at me; I couldn't read anything on her face. "OK, Ms Miller. Well, you'll have to swear a legal oath in front of a registrar attesting to these facts. We'll also have to contact the Department of State before we decide what to do regarding the mutilation of this passport."

"*Accidental* mutilation."

She didn't react at all, just kept her eyes on mine. "Are you prepared to wait?"

"Uh, yes."

"Have a seat." Her voice was chilly. "We'll call you up when it's time."

I took a seat, and that was when I saw the two British police officers come into the building. I watched as they went up and chatted to the same registrar I had just been speaking with. I watched as she glanced over towards me.

They couldn't prove anything, and it had been a fucking accident. *I really didn't mean to wash it!* I wanted to stand up and shout this, but instead I tried to avoid looking at them in case I looked guilty. There was a security camera mounted on the wall that was pointing straight at me. Maybe this was what happened when you went through a certain number of passports. Maybe US Law required that you were officially interrogated by the police.

I felt kind of weird. Really weird. Maybe the registrar hadn't been looking over at me after all; maybe it was just a coincidence. I'd find something to read. I'd try to relax. I had gotten bored with voting and tax advice pamphlets, so I dug into my bookbag to see if I had anything mildly diverting.

As my fingers touched a folded piece of paper, I felt heat rising up through me, like someone had poured boiling water in my guts and some sickening steam was rising, making me blush, making my throat go dry but my brow go sweaty. The colour copy. I had forgotten all about it. The British policemen were sure to search me. They would find the colour copy. They would interpret my possession of it as intent to destroy my own passport, and I had to admit there was no way it wouldn't look suspicious. Maybe it was even illegal to take a colour copy of a passport, like it was for money. Wasn't there something on top of the colour photocopier that stated that? Why hadn't I checked at the time? And, worse, this would mean that they would no longer believe me about Passports 1-3. Not with evidence like the colour copy. I would be put away for years. I would never see Sabine again. I would become someone's bitch in prison and eventually emerge, hardened and ruined, probably on smack and with a nervous twitch for the rest of my life.

I looked up at the counter. The two policemen were continuing to speak to the registrar. I looked up: the security camera was still trained on me; I wondered if it was picking up my physiological state. They probably had people monitoring my reactions even as I sat there: watching me shift, watching my eye movements, watching my face go red.

Past the security camera was the Ladies. Maybe I still had a shot. As casually as I could, I got up, bag slung over my shoulder, and made my way to the bathroom. My knees were trembling. I tried not to run.

Once inside the exceptionally sanitary facilities, I couldn't see any cameras, or bugs. That didn't mean a thing. This was the fucking American Embassy, after all – they probably even checked the contents of each flush. I entered one of the cubicles, locked it behind me and bent my head down, so that if there was some sort of camera in the ceiling then it would be difficult to see what I was doing. I removed the colour copy, still shadowing it with my head, and I tore it up in little balls and ate it, ate my goofy photo and my place of birth, the stiff paper rasping against my throat. I began to gag. The ink on the colour bit was probably poisonous or something.

Someone came in and entered the other cubicle, and I had to keep flushing the toilet so that they couldn't hear the sound of me tearing the paper. Maybe it was the fucking registrar. The two police officers had been male. Wouldn't they have to have sent a lady cop in after me?

I finished eating. Now there was no proof, unless they pumped my stomach. I left the cubicle and went to wash my hands. My whole body was shaking. I looked in the mirror. There was a rash from my neckline upwards. My face was actually purple.

"Are you OK?" A large, dishevelled blonde Midwest mother-type, late thirties, had asked the question. She sounded concerned. Maybe she was undercover. Get a grip, Carrie Miller, get a grip.

"I think so." The purpleness seemed to be going away, a little. I had never seen a blush like that in my life. "I'm just not feeling well."

"Oh, OK."

I exited, feeling slightly calmer now that the evidence had been disposed of. The two policemen were still up there at the counter, but they seemed to be smiling about something. Maybe it had all been in my head. I sat down.

That's when I started to feel like I was going to throw up.

I could *not* throw up. I could not throw up little pieces of a colour photocopy of my passport. I had a sudden flash of investigators piecing together the puke-stained passport copy bit by bit, until they had that crazy photo whole, once more.

People were looking at me strangely. I was bending over. I was going to throw up. It was all over now. Goodbye, Sabine. Goodbye, Grandpa. Goodbye, freedom. There was a security camera trained on me once more; even though I was bent over, I could sense it. What could I do? Nausea rose up in me. This was it, then.

Suddenly I got control of myself. I reached a hand out and fumbled in my bookbag for my inhaler. I pretended to take a big shot of it. It would be my excuse. Asthma would save my life.

"Asthma attack," I explained to everyone staring at me when I raised my head up. Already I could feel my heartbeat slowing, my gorge descending. I made sure the inhaler was in full view of the camera. People made sympathetic noises around me.

In the meantime, the two policemen had left.

"Carrie Miller," someone called out. I went up to the counter and attested to the affidavit in a daze, and was handed a new one-year passport, with the following phrase on the last page: *This passport is a replacement for a mutilated passport and an extension must be approved by the Department of State.*

'Mutilated' – yes, that was how I felt, too. I had my passport now, but nothing was certain. If I left the UK, I'd have to lose the passport – or wash it in the laundry once again – in order not to have visibly crushed the appeal. I would be breaking the law. I would be on Passport #6. I closed my eyes, but all I could see was that fucking brass eagle, and its claws were digging in me, just like the British Home Office, digging all the way into my heart with evil, bureaucratic talons. I had always assumed that bureaucracy was impersonal. I hated it, but it was like hating the tax service. Now I felt the fear that came with the insight that it wasn't impersonal – at all.

It *was* personal. After I ate my passport colour copy that day, I stood outside the embassy and I realised it was *very* personal indeed. My head was pounding, but I forced myself to look up at the eagle once more. It was huge. It was violent. It represented the country I missed despite myself, and the country in which my grandfather was dying. A country just as cruel as the UK when it came to queers and immigration. My grandfather was dying. I felt rootless, nationless, light with fury. I floated down the steps into Grosvenor Square. My grandfather was dying. I couldn't leave my lover.

The trees in the square seemed fluorescent and blurred, like their outlines had been smeared in bright green wax by a child's crayon. My ears were roaring as I crossed the road and walked towards them. I felt strangely tall, like a Colossus – like I would be able to stretch out a hand and stroke the top leaves, a green cloud under my palm. My eyes were stinging. My grandfather was dying. Like I could pluck the eagle off the top of the embassy and set it there, quietly in the branches of the weird, high, green trees.

JO SOMERSET
Passion Prioritised

When I met Sonia I thought my star was rising at last. It started off brilliantly. Having recently broken up from my lover of two years I thought it was a great idea to tag along to the jazz club with my friend Laura and meet up with her mates.

Sonia was stunning, in cool cream trousers, a sharp black T-shirt proclaiming "Fake it!" over her sharp breasts, setting off the glowing bare skin of her arms and neck. Her eyes glittered with sexuality, and strangely for me, I didn't feel shy or awkward: her magnetism was too powerful. Before long I was sitting next to her, buying her drinks, and drinking in the sax riffs and thrumming double bass solo in a haze of longing.

We talked between numbers. Nothing much, but enough to show that she was interested in me. In my new-found boldness I suggested we left the club together. I had stars in my eyes, and not an inkling of how things would turn out.

I should have recognised the warning signs on our first proper date. We went out after work, and while she was still stunning in a bottle green suit, without shoulder pads, that draped her body effortlessly, her eyes were different: distracted, darting about the restaurant. I know, because my eyes were glued to her the whole time. I was truly smitten.

"Take it easy, Maddy. We just need time to get to know each other," I told myself, as we ploughed somewhat silently through garlic mushrooms (me) and potato skins with sour cream (her). Trying to ply her with wine didn't work. She drank slowly, refusing my frequent offers of a refill with "I prefer to restrict my intake." I thought she was saving herself for later.

We gradually warmed up through the meal, and went on to *Much Ado About Nothing* at the Royal Exchange. The play's wit sparkled all over us in a delicious combination of raunchiness and slapstick. Long bouts of laughter chased away my tension, and as we walked through the streets back to her car I was carefree and frivolous.

"Let your hair down," I joked.

"That's not one of my priorities," was her strange reply.

*

In the weeks that followed, I discovered that her mental processes were oddly compartmentalised. Her life was dominated by a never-ending series of 'shoulds' and 'oughts' defined in official terms. I soon learned that meals out were governed by the 'allowable budget', and heaven help me if I suggested that she buy a shirt that exceeded her cash flow forecast for the month.

Yet with sex it was different. In bed, I had my lover to myself. She never failed to arouse me, nor I her, and time stood still through the early hours of many a morning, witnessed by the twinkling stars, yowling cats, and from time to time the milkman clinking down the street. We were utterly together, reaching the extremes of breathtaking excitement and ultra-calm. Nothing could come between us, we were on our way to forever.

We wanted to go on holiday.

"I'd prefer to plan this using SMART objectives," she said. I looked at her blankly.

"Specific, Measurable, Agreed, Realistic and Time-related. It's a winner every time."

"Are you having me on?"

"It's an absolute must if we're to avoid the failure of our action plan."

"Sonia, we're talking about a *holiday*, not building the Channel Tunnel," I spluttered.

"It makes no difference." She was adamant. "I don't court failure. In fact, I have never allowed a project to backfire. So let's be SMART."

"OK," I muttered, slouching in my chair. But I could not resist one last barb. "Are you sure you don't want me to get some training in SMART objectives before we go any further?"

"That won't be necessary at this stage. But there is actually an excellent personal effectiveness workshop run by the Chamber of Commerce that you might want to consider in the future."

We went walking in the Pyrenees (her idea), staying in down-to-earth *auberges* (my idea), and the weeks of freedom and mountain air simultaneously invigorated and exhausted us. Sonia's idea of having a daily planning meeting over breakfast meant that our days were packed and challenging, although I drew the line at another suggestion: abstaining from sex in order to conserve energy for our physical exertions up and down mountains was not my idea of fun. But going to bed early and getting up with the dawn opened my eyes – and lungs – to a new experience of light and air. We slept like logs, drank in the spectacular mountain panoramas, and came back relaxed, laughing and talking about living together. The idea was so easy, so natural, just what we needed to entwine our lives and spirits more closely.

So I was not prepared when I saw her after her first day back at the office. She was still beaming, but that alien gremlin was at work inside her again.

"Let's talk about our proposal for amalgamation," she started, the wine in her glass sparkling, while my heart missed a beat.

"That's not how I would put it," I said quietly.

"Oh. Well, let me put it another way. It fits in perfectly with my long-term goal to establish a secure base with a partner. We've considered the options, we're clearly committed to working closely with each other, and I think it's time to make a resolution."

Though my hand was shaking, I put my glass down deliberately, firmly, without spilling a drop.

"*Do* you mind?" I said. "This is not a company merger. It's not even a marriage. We're talking about living together because it makes sense – simply because we love each other. Full stop."

Her eyes were devoid of expression, but her mouth was sullen.

"That's what I meant," she said.

We sipped in silence, and I wondered if she was thinking what I was thinking. Perhaps we were incompatible. I was shocked when she broke the silence.

"Maybe I didn't express myself very well. I do want us to get a house together."

Her lips curved, a little wan smile which was so unlike her that my frustration dissolved and I smiled back encouragingly.

"Me too. When shall we start looking?"

She beamed. "Let's develop a strategy."

I let it pass, merely nodding as we started to discuss two or three bedrooms, garden or backyard, Withington, Chorlton or Old Trafford. We were surprisingly harmonious in what we wanted.

The next few Saturdays were taken up cheerfully trudging round estate agents: implementing our strategic plan.

My birthday was coming up. I did not want to do anything special, and anyway we were both saving seriously. We could muster the deposit between us, but reckoned we'd need a fair whack for carpets, curtains and furniture, as the contents of our respective flats would go nowhere near kitting out a whole house.

But I still woke up excited on the morning of my birthday. Light streamed into the bedroom and Sonia leapt out of bed, returning with a tray of tea and crumpets, while I lay luxuriating in being waited on. I was happy. It was going to be a good year, and I was sure she'd got me a maroon silk dressing gown I'd been enthusing over in Next a few weeks before.

Next to the tea on the tray was a small oblong package, and a card. My grin remained in place, but a tiny "oh!" escaped my lips, and I looked around for the bigger present.

"Open it, sweetie," she said.

I opened the card first. HAPPY BIRTHDAY! it proclaimed joyously, then underneath her signature, a little note: "Sorry I didn't get the present you wanted, but I had problems meeting the deadline."

I remembered the time we had arrived, breathless, at the parents' house for the first time. "I pride myself on never missing deadlines," she had said.

The package contained a dinky pair of earrings, and I felt like a shit as I unenthusiastically thanked her and gave her a kiss.

"You don't like them."

"I do. They're nice." They were.

"No you don't, you wanted something else."

"Well, yes, but these are nice."

"I thought you'd understand that it's not just a question of response times. We're currently experiencing a shortage of cash in hand, and have to prioritise accordingly."

I put the earrings on, and we ate cold crumpets and held hands.

I got over it, told myself I was being childish, and anyway it was true, we were putting aside as much as we could for the house. And she did have a very pressured job, and she *had* got me a present after all.

Actually, finding a house was proving to be a problem. I had to convince Sonia that we should each pay half for the house, despite the huge difference in our earnings. Anyway, her job in the high risk financial sector did not offer long-term security, and I relished the consequences of a stock market crash even less than financial dependence on my lover. The modest size of the mortgage we had applied for, plus the fact that we wanted somewhere that was in good nick so we could move straight in meant that some areas we were looking in were just too expensive.

Another Saturday arrived, and the houses we had seen were depressing: too poky, too dull, no garden or in a neighbourhood devoid of character. We sat in a steamy café supping nondescript coffee, riffling half-heartedly through the stack of estate agents' particulars we had collected that morning.

"What are we going to do?" I almost whined. She squared her shoulders. (This woman thrived on problems.)

"Let's list the barriers we're encountering.

"OK."

"One, the existing supply does not meet our original brief. Two, we're in danger of over-committing our financial resources. Three, a cost/benefit analysis I did on Thursday night showed that our assumptive predictions were seriously off-beam. Four, we're not meeting the agreed milestones for implementation of our strategy. And five, we won't get anywhere unless we revise our specification. We need a reorganisation plan."

"But that doesn't tell us what we should do."

"Yes it does. Draft a reorganisation plan, make target reductions, adopt a new strategy for achieving what is after all a complex and long-term objective." She drew breath. "Or set of objectives, actually. They break down into four main headings: Accommodation, Relationship, Security and Investment. Clearly each objective has a set of sub-objectives."

She saw my look.

"But we've discussed all this before. We don't need to go over old ground," she ended quickly.

"I don't want a two-up, two-down with backyard."

"Don't be so melodramatic, Maddy. You haven't even looked at the options, let alone re-aligned our strategy to adapt to the new information we now have about the circumstances."

I glared.

"It's called a situation analysis," she said patiently. "In fact, we should have had a contingency plan all along. We have not been monitoring our progress consistently."

"You should be employed by the Met Office," I said sourly. "The weather forecasts would be much better if they said 'Considering all the options, it could be sunny, overcast or rainy tomorrow. It would be beneficial to prepare for any contingency, as it is certain that at least some segments of the population will experience a significant percentage of one of the conditions forecast.'"

I scraped back my chair, got up, and stomped out of the café into the waiting drizzle. "I hope the bill for the coffee exceeds the demands on her current resources," I fumed, as I stood at the bus stop, missing the comfort of her Citroen.

"I mean," I said to Laura, who was mercifully in when I called round, "she's even got me thinking in bullet points. All I could think on the bus was: One, I don't want to spend my life governed by strategies and objectives; two, what am I doing with someone who never lets go?; and three, how did I get myself into this?"

"I thought you were mad about her."

"I am, was, am." Tears filled my eyes as I remembered the holiday, the deep gazes we gave each other in bed. "When it's good, it's very good." I wiped the tears away, but they were immediately replaced by more.

"But there's just too much of this... this regimented stuff."

"You've had arguments before."

"Yes. But this house-hunting business has brought it all to a head."

"Why don't you ring her when you've both calmed down?"

"I'm afraid I'll succumb again."

"Tell her what you want. You're a strong woman, for God's sake, not a pathetic creature."

"I feel pathetic."

"Well, you're not. Don't let her call all the shots."

I did try. Not straight away. I rang her at work on Monday. Not a good idea, on reflection, but my powers of judgement had been seriously eroded by the whole situation.

"Maddy, I've been reconsidering the whole thing." Sonia sounded uncharacteristically straightforward, if unwelcoming.

"What do you mean?" I wish I wasn't so ridiculously passive at times like this. Perhaps I should have done the Personal Effectiveness course after all.

"Well, we've talked before about the massive financial deficit we were getting ourselves into. We've discussed how to specify the standards for housework, and devised a system for self-monitoring."

She had such a lovely voice.

"I'm not sure our relationship is strong enough to cope with all those demands. We've only been together eight months, and although I want it – I do, Maddy – I don't think our relationship has reached the peak of sustainability which will allow us to subject it to so much pressure."

"What are you saying?"

"Let's take some time out. A cooling-off period."

I was devastated, went back to my office in the tiny box room next to my kitchen with my mind reeling. Why was she doing this to me? I sat down and tried to get back to what I'd been doing: dictating my report on the women's health forum. Halfway through, I gave up, buried my head in my hands, and surrendered to globs of grief.

Face red and puffy, I gave my nose five good blows, took a deep breath, and felt a different rumbling in my brain.

"One," I told the poster of Bob Marley on the wall, "she's a highly intelligent person. Two, she's reliable. Three, we have a wonderful time in bed. Four, she doesn't hide things from me. Five, we have the same tastes in food and music. Six, we both want a long-term relationship.

Seven, we've had arguments, but we've got through them."

Bob looked back at me enigmatically. I emitted a little "ha!" of satisfaction, and remembered Laura's words: "Don't let her call all the shots."

"Right, Bob, I'll do it," I said. I checked my watch. I would surprise her at lunch-time, lay out what I wanted, negotiate, talk about taking things more slowly. Yes, I would show her we had a future together.

With a smile I took up the dictaphone again. Shit, it was still running, must have left it on. I rewound, caught a load of blubbering. How embarrassing. Thank God I had not unwittingly given this tape to Andrea who does my typing. Fast forward. *"...intelligent person. Two, she's reliable. Three, we have a wonderful time in bed. Four, she doesn't hide things from me."* I snapped it off, aghast. That couldn't be me. Switched it on again. *"Five, we have the same tastes in food and music. Six, we both want a long-term relationship."* No!! *"Seven, we've had arguments, but we've got through them."*

I stood up, staring at the four walls around me. Small, it was too small, too tight, every surface smooth and straight. Bob's wild hair and face lined by experience mocked me. Through the tiny window I glimpsed a patch of sky and a magpie alighting on a tree-top. I rubbed my eyes and listened: the magpie's rough, guttural call; gusts of wind making the branches sway anarchically; children's high-pitched shouts and squeals; the distant hum of traffic sounding as always like the sea.

I ran out of the tiny, enclosed space, grabbed my coat and shoved my bike through the front door. The wind brushed my cheeks and made my hair stream behind me, while my legs rhythmically pumped frustration out of my constricted body.

I arrived out of breath, exhilarated, cool smile belying my thudding heart while I waited patiently for Security to issue me with a visitor's pass.

"Thanks, I know my way," I managed to say sweetly, and waited another aeon for the lift to arrive. The stomach-lifting *swoosh* up to the ninth floor suited me perfectly, and I emerged to stride triumphantly through the maze of symmetrically arranged work stations that made up the open plan office.

She was wearing her bottle green suit, somewhat incongruent with the white and pale pastels of her sterile surroundings. Perhaps that was the limit of human deviation that was permitted in here. I regretted my grey coat, but glanced with satisfaction at the bright yellow reflector strips still strapped round my ankles.

Sonia had not seen me yet, though several of her colleagues had. She was on the phone.

"Mmm, I suggest in the region of thirty per cent. No, our parameters are fixed." She tapped on her computer, and a pie chart was replaced by a grid of figures. "OK, well if you can't meet our requirements..." At the sight of me, her head jerked round and I could see she was thrown off balance. "Twenty eight? I'll look at it. I'll call you back in half an hour."

She turned slowly in her ergonomic executive swivel chair, the back of her head illuminated by the glow from her screen, cursor winking in vain to gain her attention.

"Hello," she said, in a plastic, non-committal way.

"I've got a few things to say to you, Sonia," I opened. I parried her dismissive gesture. "It won't take long."

"Not *here*, Maddy," she hissed.

"Why not here? This is your life, isn't it? This is what you live and breathe for. I've just been a pleasant adjunct haven't I, an inessential add-on?"

To be fair, her eyes looked pained. "That's not true."

"You've tried to mould me into a faceless zombie, just like all the others here." That was not part of my planned speech, but I liked it.

She stood up. "Let's talk about this over coffee," she pleaded.

"Why should we? I don't want to be shepherded into an 'appropriate environment'." My voice rose a few decibels. "You can keep your strategies and forecasts and implementation plans. I want a relationship. I want a *life*."

Almost imperceptible murmurs swept the room, and I nearly felt sorry for her.

"I want to wander in wide open spaces with you, wake up with no idea what I'm going to do, watch a bird building its nest. I want to do things for the hell of it – like going hang-gliding." She blanched.

"Where's the PASSION in our relationship? What are we doing

trogging round houses and calculating mortgage repayments as if that's all there is to life?"

"Yes, well, you know I think we made a mistake there; we hadn't thought through the implications of such a major commitment."

"I'm surprised you're not listing ten good reasons why we shouldn't proceed. You've even got me talking in business jargon, for fuck's sake."

"Maddy, don't swear."

"Why not? Will it wreck your precious career? I can't see it looking so rosy right now," I said, indicating with a sweeping gesture the dozen or so pairs of gleeful, popping eyes around us.

"Have you finished?" she asked icily.

"Yes," I said. "And we're finished."

I saw a tear glitter in her eye. Oh no, I thought, I really matter to her. Perhaps I had misjudged her. She walked beside me to the lift. I noticed the squaring of her shoulders, as if she was pulling herself together after a deal had fallen through.

"You know, Maddy, it wasn't all bad. On the physical side, it was very good."

Uh-oh, dangerous. Even now I wanted to nuzzle my lips into her gorgeous neck. The lift lobby was cool, grey, empty. The ascending numbers flashed dizzily as the lift made its way to the ninth floor.

"You always achieved my target number of orgasms."

"Aaaaargh." I screamed, propelled myself into the lift and punched the 'G' button. Outside, I drank the cool, clear air. "Never again," I told myself as I fiddled with the lock of my bike. "Rule Number One: no professional dykes."

MANDA SCOTT
Tuesday's Child

Monday's child is fair of face
Tuesday's child is full of grace
Wednesday's child is full of woe
Thursday's child has far to go
Friday's child works hard for a living
Saturday's child is loving and giving
But the child who is born on the Sabbath day
Is bonnie and blithe and good and gay.

The world stands still in the aftermath of the dawn. The woman lying in the heather, knowing better, nevertheless chooses to accept this as a gesture of appreciation for her artwork. She lies flat on her stomach with her chin resting on the bare skin of her forearms and stares out between the limbs of her tripod at the changing textures of the landscape she has just attempted to fix on film. It is good. As a culmination of three months' worth of early mornings, a frighteningly large proportion of her savings blown on a lens and an amateur's stab at astronomy, it is very good indeed. If it comes out. If the view on the film is anything at all like the reality and if she can do in the darkroom the things that she needs to do then it might, indeed, have been worth the time and the effort. And if not, then it is good to have had something to get up for in the mornings.

The dawn coughs and restarts. Larks and pippets cast up, singing to the vault of the sky. Crows add a counterpoint, a verse for the earth. A buzzard swings out over the sea, mewling like a gull. On the moor, rabbits tuck tight to the heather and keep eating. Nothing stops living for long, not even for art, still less for death, or the wish for death. There is something to be learned from that. The woman draws a wax-cloth pack from the front pocket of her camera bag, unrolls her gear and rolls up a joint; plenty of weed, not too much tobacco. She is going to give up the tobacco. Today. Now. This is the last one. Later this afternoon, when the negatives are drying, she will take her bike and go down to Murdo's place and buy a hash pipe like the one Grace had; a small one, hand carved, less than an inch long, with curving goddess figures in mother-of-pearl inlaid along the stem and a bowl you could fit on the end of your little finger. With that, she will smoke only weed. In time, she will give up even on that. She licks the paper and rolls it down, finds a book of matches in a pocket, lights up and lets the swirl of smoke mix with the mood of the morning. Life *is* good. She could throw the bag, the tripod, the camera and the film down the cliff and into the loch and still it would be good. This feeling is new. She will hoard and bring it out for inspection, later, when she has forgotten how she found it.

She rolls over onto one side, props herself up on an elbow and contemplates a different view. Away to the east, the ben rises up out of the dark night of the valleys. The new light of the sun catches the damp mass of the pines and the paler lie of the bracken above the tree line. Between them lies a flat sea of heather, like a blanket flipped in the wind, rolling gently as it falls. A single tree stands in the middle distance, long dead and petrified in the cold and wind and rain of a dozen winters. It reaches up in silhouette towards the lightening sky and, as she watches, a handful of jackdaws gathers to meet on the upper branches. The image is stark. It would look good in black and white. She fumbles in her bag and draws out another plate, slipping it into her pocket as she stands. The lens change is smooth, the new one comes to hand without thinking, the right length for the shot. She has spent years with this camera and she knows it as she knows nothing else in the impermanent blur of her life. She swivels the base plate on the tripod and dips in under the cloth to make the final adjustments that will frame the tree in the centre of the image. Viewed from here, the world is inverted, spun on its axis, upside down and left to right. A rootless tree grows down from a dark ridge of sky. To the right, the sky falls to the floor in an endless curtain. She comes out from under the hood and stands with her hands on her hips, head tilted, examining her composition. With the tree in the centre, the ben hogs the whole of the left-hand side of the picture; a rising wall of meaningless greys. She turns the camera five degrees to the south, angles the lens up and reframes. Now the tree is in the bottom right and the lightening streaks of the sky fill the rest. Tongues of orange flame seep out through long, thin knifings of red. Streaks of saffron bleed over both. This needs colour. The film plate in her pocket is changed for a new one, the lens stays the same. She slides under the cloth and tunes the focus to the bird on the topmost branch of the tree. She checks the light, sets the aperture and the estimates the time. In this light even with the lens wide open, the exposure will be long, close to half a second. There are possibilities in that. In the time it takes to slide the plate into the back of the camera, the idea takes hold. Smiling, she steps back to a place where she can't possibly rock the tripod and, with the trigger release grasped between finger and thumb of her left hand, she curves her right hand round the side of her mouth, takes in a breath and hurls it out with all the cathartic release of the morning:

"*Hey!*"

The back door to the cottage hangs open, the way she left it. She backs the Land Rover into the space at the end of the byre, unpacks her kit and lays it on the weed-crazed tarmac. The dog is there at her side before she pulls the keys from the ignition, all tousled hair and enthusiasm and questions. She hitches her bag on her shoulder and he lopes ahead of her down the path through the weeds and the remains of last year's garden. She talks to him as they go – "Yes, it was fine, thank you. It went well. I'm sorry I couldn't take you. Later maybe, when the sun's over the hill and it's not so hot" – and gives him a lens bag to carry, looping the cord over his head and through his collar in case the unthinkable happens and he drops it. He doesn't drop much, but a lens is a lens and they are not easy to replace even when the money is rolling in for each picture. Which it isn't, of course, or she wouldn't still be here.

He follows her up to the darkroom and waits outside the door as she unpacks the bag and puts everything where it belongs; the camera goes back in the box it arrived in, tucked into an alcove built out of pine and lined with raw silk that was a present from Murdo the last time he came back from abroad. The lenses go in the lens-drawer, one in each section, fitted to the millimetre, an artisan's dream. It took a weekend, just measuring and cutting the wood for that drawer and every time she buys a new lens she rebuilds the inner sections. There is pleasure in the making of things and it pays, in the long run, to take care of the kit. In the beginning they shared that, she and Grace, as if the building and making were part of the attempt to mould two into one, a blurring of the boundaries between life and creation and living. Later it became a joke, sharp-toothed and vicious, a needle to test out the weak spots. By the end it was simply yet one more point of friction.

The woman lays the new lens in its place and closes the drawer. Something hard presses against her thigh, a nudging insistence on the seam of her jeans. The dog has muscled in behind her. She turns and he grins up, daring her to tell him no. He is never allowed near the developing tanks – too many hairs in places that don't need hairs – but he can tell when she is in an indulgent mood and he will push as far as he thinks he can go. She takes the lens bag from him and makes him stay while she takes the films through into the processing room. She considers doing them here and now but these things are better not done in a hurry. Instead, she lays them on the side by the enlargers and shoos the dog out and closes the doors and leads him back down the stairs to the kitchen.

The kitchen is warm, warmer than it was in the pre-dawn grey of her leaving. Morning sunlight floods in through the window, picking out the ingrained honey of the woodwork, warming the sandstone flags of the floor, setting fire to the copper fittings on the range. It took weeks of work to get the colours and the spaces and the angles properly balanced and all of it was done on faith. Grace made her block the window against the morning sun so that they worked in darkness and by electric light all the way through until the last drawer handle was in place, then they got up early one morning and took the boards down and waited to see if the sun would do what they wanted it to do. It did and it was grand, but it was the full moon, later in the month, that made the real magic so that they undressed each other and stood by the window, letting the light of it weld them together in the places that touched. There were a great many places that touched that night, all of them changed by the moon. Even in all the known, long-travelled cycles of biology this night was different. It came in the taste of her, in the fresh, metallic edge of lunar madness; in the sound of her voice; deep and guttural, like a lioness calling her cubs; in the feel of the hands, tight in her hair, tightening, gripping again and again and then the final hard-held release. And then afterwards, standing again, kissing and between the breaths, her voice: "I'm sorry... your hair... I didn't mean to... did it hurt?" so that she could smile and shake her head and run a hand through the hair and say, "No. It didn't hurt. You never hurt me." And it was true, then.

Later, the moon moved round and the kitchen fell into darkness. They poured wine and drank it and climbed the stairs and then the ladder to the cramped crow's nest of the loft where there was barely room on the floor for the futon and no room at all to stand up but where the roof was one long window, pitched at thirty degrees and facing south so that it caught the full light of every star and planet that crossed the sky. They came together again with all the urgency of a first night but with five years of practice that knew the needs and the rhythms and the pressures of each so that two did, in the end, become one.

She lay awake at dawn the next morning, listening to the starlings fight for space on the roof-ridge and the kettle hiss on the hob down below as Grace moved round making tea. She sat up and turned round, fitting her back to the glass of the roof, leaning forward with the angle of it, revelling in the hard, cold pressure on the fine-tuned nerves of her skin. She tipped her chin on her shoulder and watched the leading edge of the sun carve its way out of the earth, far out on the shoulder of the ben. The colours of it hit her the way the wine had hit her blood; a light, effervescent sparkle of possibilities. She reached for her notebook and drew out the shapes of it, tried to think of names that would make sense of the colours, playing with titles for when the piece was done. Then, by chance, caught be a noise on the stairway, she turned to the west and what she saw there left her mute. Out on the far edge of the world, the moon kissed the sea; a swelling sphere, drinking her fill of misted grey water, crisped at the edges with silver. In all the years she had lived there, it was the first time she had seen the twin bodies so close, so big, so sharp, so perfectly balanced on the horizon. It was not an image to let go lightly. She bent her head to the paper, sketching, and she was still there, crouched forward, hugging her knees to her chest when Grace came up with the tea. It wasn't the same then, but there was enough left to show her what it had been and they drank the tea together in celebration of the miracle of light; the ultimate union of opposites, night brought into day, heat into cold, fire into water, Grace into Sarah and Sarah into Grace. All barriers gone. It was the best of all possible mornings and when they left the bed and retired downstairs for lunch, she had the title that she needed to complete the piece.

With time, she found that the magic didn't happen monthly, nor even necessarily annually. She read academic papers on the declension of the moon, on the changing clarity of the atmosphere and the optical illusions of space and light. She spoke to the older folk in the village, those who made a living in the days before meteorology progressed from art into science and learned from them how to predict the weather at dawn, how the rise of the sun brought with it the first layers of cloud and the phase of the moon made the sea give up more or less water so that those clouds were more or less full as they rose. The making of the piece became an obsession, a quiet one at first, shadowed in other work, immersed in other, better, reasons for living, but the seed was sown that morning, the wraith released and she can, when she tries, hold it responsible for everything that happened afterwards. She may have banished it now – the wraith and its aftermath – with the work of the morning. It is worth a try. And even if not, it is time she went back up to the loft again and spent her nights in a real bed. The sofa is not the same. Tonight she will go up. Or in a week or two, when the moon is old and no longer spends its nights staring in through her window.

The world is pitch black. Darkness enfolds her. This is what it is to be blind. Her fingers locate the things she needs without sight: the tanks, the tongs, the bottle of rinse. The timer sits to the left of the tanks, pre-set to the nearest tenth of a second. The tanks are warmed and the temperature of the solutions held steady to within a fraction of a degree. In this alchemy, precision matters and she finds peace in the discipline of it. She feels for the two plates, opening the second shot first because it is the least important and if she were to make a mistake, she would prefer it to be with this one. At her touch, the plate hinges open. The film slides into the placental depths of the developer. The timer ticks and she stands suspended in the no-time of waiting until the chime of its ending. All that moves is the tank, tilted and released, once every fifteen seconds, to keep the solutions moving. The vapours rise and mix and she changes solutions. The blackness begins to seep into her head and her eyes see colours in the swirl of smells. Developer is amber, the colour of honey. The stop-bath bites like lemon zest. She moves the film to the final tank to fix and, for this one, she counts the time in her head: *one thousand and one, one thousand and two...* She could reset the timer but by now the discipline is beginning to wear thin. The act of counting makes her wait when the dull monotony of the clockwork might give her an excuse to break the rules and look too soon... *One thousand and thirty.* She leans over and pulls at the cord beside the door. Smoked amber light pushes back the dark. The negative floats in the pale plastic of the tray. She takes the tongs and lifts it out, rinsing distilled water along the length and then holds it up to the light. Firecracker fragments of clear film explode out of the blurred haze of a sunrise. In all the chaos of crow-flight action, the tree is crisply, perfectly still. It is good. She has not made a mistake.

The remaining two films are more precious; the sun and the moon, the moor and the sea, waiting to be merged into one single piece. If she can do it. She locks the door, leaving the negatives on the side and goes down to stand outside the kitchen door and roll another joint. There is more tobacco in this one, perhaps half of the mix. She needs something to take the edge off the waiting and the weed makes the lightless space more interesting. The dog lies on the grass with his back to her. He is attacking a cow's femur that she brought back from the village three days ago. By now, this is nothing more than a displacement activity; there is no useful flesh left to be torn from the bone, no ligaments unchewed, no possible access to the marrow. She speaks his name, *"Finn"* and snaps her fingers. He looks up and away again, too quickly. He doesn't hold with weed. She nips out the joint, puts the roach in her pocket and turns in toward the kitchen.

Back in the darkroom, she drops the twin films into the tank. There is a challenge to holding the discipline against the expanding space of her head. Ego and alter ego fight for control. The temptation is always to rush it, to skip out a step, to open the door early, to let in the light and watch it fade to black in front of her eyes and know that the wraith is still loose and will be so for another year at least. She does none of these things and when the negatives come out of the final tank, they are perfect – as close as she can tell with the emulsion still wet. She clips them up to dry, switches on the top light and clears the surfaces ready for printing. She is light-headed and her body feels empty.

She works through the rest of the day. The magic of printing holds her to *now* in a way nothing else can do, possibly in a way nothing else has ever done. Torn fragments of images emerge from the dark. Test strips and partial prints litter the counters. After a while, she abandons the timer and counts everything in her head, no longer to keep the discipline but because she has become a part of the process, the breath of her count, the organic expansions and contractions of time are as necessary as the wavelength of light, the correct concentrations of developer, the fixer. Once, she finds she has forgotten to breathe for the length of an exposure and she stands still, drawing in chemical air, shuddering as the crowded oxygen struggles to fill the far corners of her lungs. The last lift of weed drains from her system and is barely missed.

Once again, she completes the tree first. It has grown since the moor, the reds are more violent, the yellows cut more deeply, the tree is burned to full black with the crow's flight ghosting above it. And yet there is more. Fresh colours seep in at the edges, new things that she didn't see in the original out on the moor. With experimentation, she makes a second print, bleeding away the fire and the sulphur and finding their opposites in a series of pale lilacs and pastel blues. When she is done, she has fire and no-fire; before and after; another merging of opposites. They need a better title than that. She passes both prints through the dryer and props them side by side on a ledge at eye height, away to the left where she can see but not look at them, where the feel of each can enter her head. Every picture needs a title as the final act of creation. Some arrive complete, with their names in place. Others take time and the grasp of the unconscious. She leaves them and makes an effort not to think.

The remaining print takes longer. Before starting, she goes down to the kitchen and makes a meal that could either be lunch or dinner. In the absence of smoke, Finn is amenable to bribery with the crust end of a loaf and a smear of butter. He sees the change in her and follows her up to the darkroom afterwards, lying across the doorway so that she can feel the presence of him as she works. She is pleased with that. It is good to have company on a long job and there is no question but that this one will take her through to the night. The birth started at dawn. It is fitting that its delivery should follow through to dusk and beyond. She is in a different space now, without the need for experimentation. Here, there are no unexpected colours, no hidden reality. There is instead, a precision, an *exactness* that drives her beyond the bounds of her customary standards. She seeks a printer's dream of colours to carry her one step beyond what the eye and light can achieve. The sun must be a certain luminous shade of gold, the moon a specific radiance in silver. The moor and the sea must merge in a ghost-light of greys and muted greens. Heather must sprinkle the land in just *this* ratio of lilac to white, waves carve *these* static monuments in steel and phosphorescence. She has carried the potential of this in her head for twenty-four months and nothing short of perfection will do.

The wraith is ravenous. For two years she has starved it, blocking out the yearning with sex or smoke or drink or a mix of all three. Later, with Grace gone, excesses of work and inadequacies of eating filled the obvious gap. In extremis there was always the promise of death to buy peace for a time. Now, as she works, she finds that it feeds on body fluids; on the sweat that pools beneath her arms and in the small of her back, on the tears that prick her eyelids and make tracks along the side of her nose. In the beginning, she can believe she has breathed too deeply of the stop-bath. Later as time flows back to the first morning and rewinds in a stuttering, jerky reprise of the discarded years, she gives up the lie. By evening, she feeds it with a wanton, wilful carelessness, building six-dimensional memories of taste and touch and smell, of the burr of a voice and the catch of light in an iris, the electric sweep of hair down the full length of her back, the sucking vacuum in her diaphragm that swells to bursting but never peaks and breaks. Tonight, if she works carefully, she can break it. By morning, she could be free.

She finishes after midnight. She could go to bed now, knowing that the final print is dry, that the benches are clear and clean, that there is nothing left but to mount and name the three prints that line her wall. She does not go to bed. The mounting takes no time. This, she could do in her sleep, were her sleep ever so ordered. Knife, straight edge and card combine to make a crisp, anally perfect set of lines at perpendicular angles. She keeps the mount edges narrow. None of these images needs the emphasis of width.

At the end, there is only the naming to bring everything together. The last piece has had its title since the first morning. *TUESDAY'S CHILD*; full of Grace, because they had been, on that first morning, both her and the picture. Now, though, there are three prints lined up on the bench before her. She moves them round, changing the order. The trees are in the way, a second reflection of fire and dark. In her planning, the sun and the moon balance perfectly on the horizon. She had never expected this piece to be part of a trio.

She switches off the safe-light and opens the door to let in fresh air. The world outside is as dark as the room around her. The house creaks with the changing touch of the night. The dog comes in to lie on the floor at her feet, twitching dreams of rabbits, whining questions and their answers, none of them for her. She has her pen and her white card, waiting to make the thing whole. If needs be, she can destroy the two unwanted children and keep only the perfection of the central print. Tomorrow, she can take it out into the world and it will be seen. This piece alone will remake her name. It will be photographed and displayed. Copies of it will circulate; maybe only a limited edition, maybe, if she is feeling profligate, an *un*limited edition sold on the mass market and hanging in half the homes of the land. Her one condition will be that the title remains with the picture. It doesn't need her signature, it is too obviously hers, but it needs the name so that somewhere, sometime, Grace will see it and know what it means. At that point, the wraith will leave her. This has been its promise from the beginning.

She sits until dawn. As the sun breaks afresh through the mountain, she takes all three prints and carries them up the ladder to the loft. It is a day past full moon and the symmetry is no longer perfect. The moon lags behind, not touching the sea, the colours are not as they were. She lays the prints out on the bed in the order they have held for the past three hours: sun-burst crow tree, sun-and-moon, pastel crow tree; fire fading to nothing. It has not been possible to separate them. She has the integrity left to see that and to know that the old plans must be discarded. She draws out her pouch. The wraith keens, sharply. She unrolls her gear and rolls up a joint; plenty of weed, not too much tobacco. She will give up the tobacco but not today, it is too soon. In time, when the keening is at its lowest ebb, she picks up her pen. The piece will be a single unit made of three prints in the order in which they are now lying. The new title belongs to all three. She leans over to keep her hand steady and presses the tip to the paper. The words flow as if they were there all along with a finality that makes them right. This is what creation is about. The wraith breaks through the weed as she writes but there is nothing she can do about this. At the end of it, she lays her pen on the bed and backs down the ladder to the bathroom to be sick. If she chooses, she can believe this is the weed. Upstairs, the white card lies under the central picture, the words balance in perfect measured copperplate: *YESTERDAY • TODAY • TOMORROW*; the story of her life.

EDANA MINGHELLA
Altitude Sickness

"I want you to know, I'll always want you. Love. xx"

I thought, two wants in the same sentence? Give me a break. Fine-tipped rollerball on tender crackly-thin parchment. I screwed it up.

The scent of daphne. A rain-soaked path through high forest. We walked in silence, breathing it in: the rain, the wood, the daphne. Only the second day and everything I had was sodden. I could feel a damp circle under my rucksack, around my waist. Wet patches were spreading across buttocks and thighs under guaranteed waterproof trousers. Even my notebook – at hand in anorak pocket in case of sudden inspiration – was soggy: the pages had crinkled, the black cover turned soft charcoal, the writing smudged.

Behind me, she said, "God. It smells absolutely beautiful, doesn't it?" Her voice was breathy and glad. I turned and smiled yes. I could hardly see her, my glasses were steamy.

The morning after we got back, she rang me. "I miss you already." She laughed, a high giggle. "How did this happen? Oh my god, how can it have happened?" Then, lower, glittering: "Tell me, doctor, is there a cure?"

I told her there was no cure for love, didn't she know? There were charities and trusts and research groups dedicated to finding a cure, rattling their tins outside tube stations, supermarkets, but as with cancer and the common cold, nothing definite had turned up.

"They make paper out of it," I said.

"Sorry?" She was panting slightly, hurrying to catch up with me.

"It's the daphne that smells so gorgeous." I held out my hand to help her up a short, slippery ridge. Fleeced glove touched fleeced glove. "They make paper out of it."

We climbed up and up, mostly not speaking. The rain was easing but the cloud had thickened, the air a tangible mist. Tiny microdots of water drizzled on my face. We were walking through cloud and I could taste it. The trees and rocks became indistinct blurs. The only sounds were from us: our laboured breathing and our boots dredging damp leaves, muted and eerie. I suddenly realised I hadn't seen or heard anyone else for at least half an hour, maybe longer. I looked at my watch: half past ten.

"We're not lost, are we?" She asked, her tone light.

"No, we can't be." I said. "We've followed the path. We'll be fine."

"Are you aching?" I asked.

"Not too bad, really, it's surprising. I must have been fitter than I thought. My calves are a bit sore, but that's it."

That's not what I meant.

We carried on walking through the white cloud. We saw nobody, none of the other trekkers, no Sherpas. Our pace picked up. I could smell my own sweat despite the chill air. I began to make an inventory in my head: enough clothes probably; Swiss army knife but no bloody torch and the matches will be wet; two Tracker bars, some pistachios and an orange left over from breakfast. We'd find shelter in the trees. Were there bears up here? Somebody would come and look for us. We would survive.

"I'm really glad you're with me," she said.

I wrote to her as soon as we got back. I found some postcards at the Cartier-Bresson exhibition, of India. Close enough. There was a beauty: women washing saris and laying them out to dry, swathes of silk in long shimmering lines. I wrote, *"Ring me Daphne."*

She didn't call home for the whole two weeks. Not even when we came across the improbable phone in a Tibetan tea house at 10,000 feet and everyone made calls for 200 rupees a minute, just because they could. We took our boots off before we went in: rows of expensive walking boots, clogged with mud, outside this shanty house. Inside, there was one room, a smoky parlour of red: brownish red floor, walls lined with red hangings and icons, sofa draped with fabrics of scarlet and vermillion, edged with gold. Two little brown girls watched wide eyed from the doorway. There was the phone on its table; beside it a stopwatch and logbook.

She said she couldn't speak to them. If she heard Alfie's voice she knew she would cry. She would wait until she could see him and cuddle him and smell his peanut-butter breath. She would bring him presents of gaudy puppets and silver prayer wheels and bejewelled boxes. But she couldn't speak to him yet.

We slept in a mountain lodge on the coldest night. A hard bench on a wooden floor, covered in blankets and our sleeping bags. We wore hats, socks, thermals: hers were black silk, mine Marks and Sparks once-white cotton. We kissed like new teenagers at their first party. Her mouth tasted of cheap sweet Nepali chocolate. It was too cold to explore skin or frozen nipples under the layers of clothes. We just kissed and held each other. She said, "I've never kissed a woman before." I said, "Practice makes perfect."

I checked my watch again. I had to bring my wrist close up to my eyes to see the delicate dial in the fog: nearly 11. I stopped walking and turned to her; she was a little way behind again. "Right," I said, "I think we should have a plan." I tried to sound calm but my heart was beating fast and I was beginning to feel really scared. No fucking compass, no fucking map, no fucking sense. "Yeah, OK, " she said, her voice muffled.

"It's 11.00 now. If we haven't seen anyone by 11.30 we should find shelter near the path, time out the rations and stay close together to keep warm. Someone will come eventually but I'm... uh, concerned that we might get really lost if we keep walking while we can't see anything."

She reached me, held on to my arm for support, catching her breath. She smiled and I noticed her mouth: full and wide, the lips pinkly sore. I offered her the special can't-get-it-at-home American lip salve that Jan had bought me as my going away present. She smiled wider. "Were you a Brown Owl or a girl guide or something?"

Jan and I sat over bottles of beer and Bombay mix, she patiently looking through my photos while I explained, telling my story. Jan licked her finger and thumb as she took each print. "Who's this?" she asked, throwing me a sharp look. The first shot of her: standing in the snow, legs apart, arms raised in triumph, against a panorama of the world's highest mountains. She's be-hatted, warm in her fleece and her cheeks are flushed red from exertion and excitement and sheer amazement.

"Ah. Well," I said, and reached for a swig of beer. "I was coming to that."

I concentrated on trying to see the outline of path. She said, "I don't know about you, but I'd love to find a nice old-fashioned English pub right now. With a roaring fire and a labrador stretched in front of it. On the blackboard: steak and kidney pudding as dish of the day."

"I'm a vegetarian," I said.

I thought, We're lost and we're going to die and it's going to be months before anyone finds our bodies.

"Well, OK, veggie lasagne or cauliflower cheese, then."

"Leek and mushroom bake with new potatoes and peas."

"Treacle tart for pudding."

"Apple pie and custard."

"No, crumble. Rhubarb. Hot, with melting vanilla ice cream"

"And one of those funny cups of coffee they only serve in pubs, you know, with their own plastic filters and a chocolate mint."

"Oh God," she said. "I hope we're not lost. I'm starving."

Coming home she kissed me in full view of everyone while we waited for our rucksacks on the conveyor belt. I was blushing, kissing her back, happy, ready to weep. Her luggage was amongst the first to come out. She said, "I'd better go." When I walked through Arrivals a few minutes later, she was there with the husband and little boy she'd left behind. I knew them from her photo. She picked up Alfie and squeezed him tight against her body. Her husband kissed her. I thought, "I know how her skin feels, how she smells." They were talking, but I wasn't close enough to hear, and they all seemed to be laughing or crying. Hubbie picked up her bags: tall man striding slightly ahead, small woman with a tired faint limp, the little boy skipping, dragging on her hand.

*

We trudged higher and higher. A new worry – altitude sickness. I struggled to remember the symptoms. Something about a persistent headache? Then I noticed the cloud was thinning. It felt warmer. The path became clearer. I could make out the bright red of rhododendron. And suddenly, we had climbed above the clouds. A view of layers of grey and white tufts and fluff, pierced with mountain peaks, lay before us like a grandiose painting of a still Arctic sea. Together we stared at this vision. I felt unexpected tears swelling inside.

A shuffle behind us, a giggle and a "Sssh". Three Nepali children huddled in holey jumpers, shoeless, grinning broadly. "Hello. Pen?" said one. Their upper lips were encrusted with snot. I took out my dwindling stash of rubber-tipped pencils. "Here you go, honeybunch," I said to the littlest. "Hello. Sweet? Chocolate?" he said, his eyes wide with hope.

We carried on walking, the kids running along beside us. In a few minutes we arrived in their village and saw the signs of our fellow trekkers: boots, waterproofs, rucksacks, stacked against a wall. We looked at each other. "Thank fuck for that," she said.

Days went by without a word. Finally I rang and left a message on her machine. "Mark, Helen and Alfie are not available at the moment." It was the husband's voice. "Please leave us a message and we will get back to you as soon as we can."

I said, "Helen. Can you give me a ring. I think you've got my number, haven't you? Um. It's Sarah by the way. Anyway, look... Hope to speak to you soon. Or even better, see you? Right, OK, bye then."

After I'd put the phone down I wished there was a way to erase messages but there isn't.

I went walking with the hiking dykes. Green hills in Surrey, part of the Pilgrim's Way. It was a light cool day, the clear sun of late English spring and a fresh breeze; my mother would have called it a good drying day. Strands of hair blew across my face and stung my eyes.

"Hi, I'm Mel." A younger woman, in black leggings and rolldown socks, was sauntering beside me. "I've seen you on one of these walks before haven't I? A woman of few words who gets impatient when we break for too long." She turned her face to me at a sparrow-angle, a half-smile on her lips. I laughed, and said, "That's me."

We talked about her work with homeless people. She told funny stories of mulligatawny soup-runs and having to respect peoples' pet rats or requests for odd clothing. One old man refused to talk to women, but he thought Mel was a boy in her white T-shirt and blue jeans and Doc Martens. So she played up to it, lowering her voice and trying to swagger when she walked. It turned out she was a stand-up comic in her spare time.

A kestrel hovered in front of us, and we stopped to watch it flutter its redbrown wings. I kept thinking it was about to dive but it just dipped and regained its height to hover again a few yards away. I wondered what it had spotted. Mel began to roll a joint. She licked along the top of the cigarette paper. I thought, you're very attractive and you're funny and you're interested. But you're not her.

I looked at the young woman through narrowed eyes for a couple of seconds, my lips pursed in a smile. She smiled back, squinting at the hit or against the sun, and offered me a puff. I shook my head. "We'd better catch up with the others," I said, "or we might get lost."

Her note came a week after my call.

Oh Sarah. I wish I could be different or that my life was different or that something was different. Or I'd met you before. You made me feel more like a woman than I've ever felt.

I want you to know, I'll always want you. Love. xx

We bought the paper in Thamel. A simple shop: three walls of shelves stacked with different grades and colours of paper and a large low table in the middle. On the table: notebooks, photo albums, fat diaries, decorated with tissue-fine pressed flowers; flimsy boxes fixed with brown leaves or bits of twig, writing sets scented with herbs and wildflowers. Hanging from the ceiling: paper lanterns in bright pinks and aquamarine. She bought me a new notebook to make up for the one ruined on the trek. "You can write about us in it," she said.

CLARE SUMMERSKILL
Single Again

I wouldn't say categorically that Susan was into S and M, but it's true that she tied me to the bedpost one night... and then she left me there while she went off to see her new girlfriend. Our relationship ended quite amicably, all things considered. I got custody of the laptop... She got the printer. Once again it was time to search for a significant other.

That's when I met Phil. Phil was stunning. The first dyke I'd ever been out with who could make other woman actually stop and stare. Phil was kind, generous, sweet, funny and sexy and she was also pathologically unfaithful... After the fourth affair that she'd had while she'd been with me – or at least the fourth one I knew about – I finally told her in no uncertain terms that since she had now gone so far as to move in with her latest floozy I had no alternative but to finish our relationship.

After that fateful conversation which I had hoped would bring her running back to me, I hadn't seen Phil again. The following weeks were absolute hell... Long drawn-out days of depression and loneliness with only the familiar casts of *Neighbours*, *Home and Away*, *Emmerdale*, *Coronation Street*, *EastEnders*, *Brookside* and *Prisoner Cell Block H* to keep me company.

On bad days I drank myself into a stupor at night, waking up sometime the following afternoon, and glancing pathetically over at the answerphone as I came to, to see if she might have left me a loving message while I'd been unconscious. I'd begun to hate the very sight of that bloody nought...

Phil had finally left me for a 'bisexual' woman who worked in a beauty salon in the day and took an evening class in business studies. How politically low can you stoop? And after ten weeks she finally called to tell me that Miss Best of Both Worlds had decided that she had been forcefully seduced and corrupted and had gone back to men.

I didn't think things could get much worse than they already were but then Phil informed me that even though she was now single and homeless she still didn't want to come and live with me.

I tried to look on the bright side. Maybe things weren't so bad as they seemed, if I could only just begin to think a little more positively...

I tried to remember something my therapist had once said about a glass of water and how you should look at it, but instead my mind started adding up how much someone could earn in a week if they charged £35 an hour...

I forced my attention back to the matter in hand. Right. So there I was, a Lesbian alone in London. Now, how should I begin to go about meeting other women? "I don't have to get off with someone, I just want to widen my circle of friends," I tried to convince myself, my cat, and a rather nice woman with a Scottish accent that I sometimes got through to at the Lesbian and Gay Switchboard.

For one scary moment I even considered putting a personal ad in the *Pink*, but the thought that someone might recognise it as me made me change my mind.

So instead I decided to dip my metaphorical toe in the pool of social frenzy that is The Brixton Hill Lesbian Social Group Gathering.

One Tuesday evening I spent over three-quarters of an hour sitting round a pub table with four other sad and desperate dykes. A woman called Charlotte ran these evenings. I'm not sure why, since she obviously was not by nature a very sociable type. She grunted a hello at me and said nothing more all evening. Two of the others were a couple, Sandra and Sue. Sandra was a little on the butch side and she told me straight away that they were interested in meeting new women with the intention of a threesome. They asked me things like "Have you been to the Candy Bar yet?" and "Do you like kd lang? We do."

The other woman there was German. She was called Ingrid and she wore a pair rather scary rectangular glasses. She talked to me about the strength of the Deutschmark against the pound, and told me that she spoke four other languages. I assumed that her conversation would be equally as dull in all of them...

After what I considered to be a polite amount of time I suddenly exclaimed that I'd left some stock boiling and had to tend to it immediately. Outside on the pavement an important truth hit me harder than the cold night air: that it isn't always better to have tried and failed than never to have tried at all.

I had nearly run out of ideas when I happened upon an 'alternative' way of meeting women. It came in the form of a leaflet that I picked up while visiting my homeopath. It was for a wild woman's weekend in Wales.

I read through it carefully.

"Are you at peace with yourself internally?

Do you feel in touch with the source of your creativity?

Do you yearn for a closer connection to the elements?"

The answers to these questions, I could not in truth tell you, but there was one more which was not to be found on the leaflet:

"Do you feel precariously close to running out of ideas of how to ever meet anyone ever again?" The answer came as a resounding "Yes!!!"

And so it was that I set off for a sacred site in the north of Wales to discover the mysteries of psychic and spiritual healing. To listen to the silence, to fly with the eagle, to learn about the wonders of starcraft, herbal lore and plant spirits and to try with all my shamanic body and soul to get just one single shag out of the next few days...

Predictably enough there was a torrential downpour as soon as I arrived. The organisers had thought it would create a magical feeling for the tents to nestle on the slopes of the mountain, but the rain produced a landslide of mud and stones and we all just stood and watched helplessly as the entire campsite slid down the hill towards a lake. We ran for safety towards the main house with plastic bags over our heads and spent the afternoon drying our clothes on radiators. On the Sunday the tents were for some inexplicable reason repitched even though there might well be more rain to come and I felt compelled to join in one of the activities so I plumped for drum-making, but by camomile tea-time I had decided that I was the only person there who might possibly escape being sectioned if anyone from social services had dropped by.

One more night to go and I would be free from this seriously disturbed group of women, most of whom were straight and thought it was really exciting to be free from their men for two days in the year. Asleep in my little tent, dreaming of meat and mattresses, I was suddenly awoken by a woman who introduced herself as Tanya and who without asking came in to join me.

My first impression was that she might have overdosed on the contents of her medicine wheel because her eyes were slightly crazed, but perhaps more significant was the fact that she was completely naked.

She leant right over me as she spoke, waving her huge pendulous bosoms in my face and it would have taken a far stronger woman than me not to have been somewhat distracted as she began to tell me that astrologically it was a very important date and would I come out and share the wonders and delights of the big dipper with her.

I told Tanya as politely as I could, "Thank you but no." I really had to get some sleep. But she burst into tears and between sobs informed me that since she had been adopted as a child she had taken rejection very badly and had an enormous need to be loved. She then took my hand in hers and placed it between her thighs, telling me that she had always wanted a Lesbian experience and could I satisfy her curiosity?

I was far too tired to deal with any conflict resolution at that point even though, coincidentally, there had been a workshop on that very subject earlier in the weekend, so I decided that the sooner I got on with it the sooner I might get some kip.

I performed the necessary act upon her, not completely unaware that the entire reputation of my Lesbian sisters was at stake. But the loud wailing noises that she emitted convinced me that I hadn't let down the side. She then fell soundly asleep on my lilo, pulled my sleeping bag over her, proceeded to snore rather loudly and forced me to spend the rest of the night on the groundsheet.

The next day I felt mortified. I had never had a one-night stand in my life and looking at Tanya over a bowl of muesli the following morning I realised that whether it was politically correct or not, in the clear light of day there was no way I would ever have touched this particular woman with a bargepole.

She said she'd send me a postcard from Canada where she was going next on a bear and whale watching trip and I wished her all the best. And as we parted I prayed that I would never ever hear from Tanya again.

I returned to my London flat exhausted. I checked the answerphone and saw that there was one message. I hadn't had a message in weeks! My heart leapt into my mouth.

Maybe Phil had changed her mind. Maybe she'd missed me while I'd been gone and my unannounced absence had driven her into a fit of possessive jealousy. Maybe I would consider taking her back and then one evening casually mention that she wasn't the only one who had been sowing their oats – that my life also had recently been altered by a brief but meaningful liaison with a wild wild woman up a mountain. I held my breath and pressed play.

"Hello. This is Sandra as in Sandra and Sue."

My heart sank. But then I told myself that if this was the only offer I was ever going to get from a real Lesbian – or in this case Lesbians – then perhaps I should stop being so fussy and just accept it. The message continued:

"We were just wondering if you might have Ingrid's number cos we thought we'd like to see a bit more of her, if you know what I mean! Call us when you get this message. Bye."

CONTRIBUTORS

Julia Bell is a freelance writer, editor and tutor based at the University of East Anglia, Norwich. Current publications include *Hard Shoulder* (Tindal Street Press, 1999) and the forthcoming *Devolutionaries: England's Writing* (Victor Gollancz, 2001) both co-edited with Jackie Gay. She is also editor of the literary magazine *Pretext* (Pen&Inc, UEA, 2000). 'Outskirts' is taken from her collection *Real Girls Eat Meat*. She is currently finishing her first novel, *Massive*.

Frances Bingham lives in London with her partner Liz Mathews; they work together at the Whitechapel Pottery, where Liz is the studio potter and Frances runs a ceramics gallery. A prize-winning poet, in 1999 her long poem *Mothertongue* was published in a limited edition handmade book. Her short story 'The Recognition Scene' is included in a forthcoming anthology of new lesbian writing from the Women's Press. A regular contributor to *Diva*, she writes articles on lesbian history and culture, concentrating on stories of women's lives and work. She has completed one novel, *Ikon*, and is currently working on another.

Cathy Bolton lives in Manchester and works as a Writing Development Worker for Commonword community publishers. She started writing as a teenager and her stories and poems have appeared in a wide range of magazines and anthologies, most recently *Rain Dog* and *Star Trek: The poems* (Iron Press). She shares a joint poetry collection, *Cheap Comfort* (Dagger Press) with her partner Jan Whalen. She also has a filing cabinet full of half-finished novels which she plans to complete when she retires to her dream cottage by the sea – generous patron willing!

Kathleen Kiirik Bryson was born on the northern Arctic coast of Alaska in December 1968 and grew up on the Kenai Peninsula. She left home at 18. Since then she has dug up Viking graves, been in a Riot Grrl band, exhibited her paintings in a brothel, trained as an actor and received her MA in Independent Film. She has lived many years in both Stockholm and Seattle, currently makes her home in London, and prefers overcast days to sunny ones. She works as a freelance editor and tries to divide any time left over between writing, acting and painting. Her first novel *Mush* will be published this autumn by Diva Books.

Julia Collar graduated in July 2000 with first-class honours in Religious Studies from the University of Wales, Lampeter. She was awarded a prize for her finalist's dissertation on 'Sexuality within New Religious Movements of Christian Origin', a success which has inspired her to return to university soon to start a postgraduate research degree. She lives with her beloved partner Anna and they are looking forward to celebrating three years together in April. Julia hopes to continue to carve out a career as a writer of academic material and lesbian fiction.

Emma Donoghue is an Irish novelist, playwright and literary historian, born in Dublin in 1969. She spent eight years in Cambridge doing a PhD before moving to Canada. Her fiction includes two contemporary Dublin novels, *Stir-fry* and *Hood* (winner of the American Library Association's Gay and Lesbian Award); a sequence of new fairytales, *Kissing the Witch*; and *Slammerkin*, which is based on an eighteenth-century murder. Her novels have been translated into Dutch, German, Swedish, Catalan and Hebrew. She has edited two anthologies, *What Sappho Would Have Said: Four Centuries of Love Poems Between Women* and *The Mammoth Book of Lesbian Short Stories*.

Stella Duffy has written three novels – *Singling Out The Couples, Eating Cake* and *Immaculate Conceit*, published by Sceptre – and four crime novels – *Calendar Girl, Wavewalker, Beneath The Blonde* and *Fresh Flesh*, published by Serpent's Tail. She has written twenty short stories, several articles, a short play for Steam Industry, a dance/theatre piece for Gay Sweatshop, comedy sketches for BBC Radio 4, and two one-woman shows. Stella is also an actor, comedy improviser and occasional radio presenter. Most recently she was in *Lifegame* with Improbable Theatre in San Diego and off-Broadway in New York. She lives in London with her girlfriend and a very hopeful future.

Frances Gapper (Gemini) lives in Southgate, a north London suburb, with Sue (Leo) and Clover, a black and white cat (Gemini). Fourteen more cats live next door. Her short stories have been published in various magazines and anthologies and include 'The Secret of Sorrerby Rise', 'The Bedwife and the Executioner' and 'The Great Tropical Hardwood Walkout'.

Linda Innes was born in Liverpool in 1961, and lives on the North East coast. She says: "My first writing accolade was winning a red and white plastic handbag for the best letter to Father Christmas (I was five, honest). Since then, I've had a poetry pamphlet published by Mudfog press, and some poems in magazines. I've also been a teacher (but I'm all right now), creative writing tutor, performance poet, stand-up comedian and arts administrator. Always slow on the uptake, after falling naturally into lesbianism at the age of 30, I can highly recommend it. Why didn't you tell me sooner?"

Jackie Kay was born and brought up in Scotland. Her first collection of poetry, *The Adoption Papers*, won the Forward Prize and the Saltire Award. Her first novel, *Trumpet*, won the Guardian Fiction Prize. She lives in Manchester with her son.

Ella Kaye was born in 1982 in Toronto, Canada, but moved to England when she was four and is now living in London with her parents, sister and dog. She is currently completing her A levels in Maths, Further Maths, History and Ancient Greek and plans to study Maths and Philosophy at university. Writing is one of her many pastimes, particularly scriptwriting, and she is in the process of directing a play she wrote. Ella loves theatre and is passionate about music, particularly jazz. This is her first time being published.

VG Lee is a novelist and poet. Her work has been widely published in anthologies and magazines. She is a founder member of All Mouth No Trousers, the literary cabaret group. Her novel *The Comedienne* was recently published by Diva Books. Born in Birmingham, she now lives and writes in Hackney, London.

Rosie Lugosi has lived all over the place but is now in Manchester and likes it there. She has an eclectic writing and performance history, ranging from singing loudly (yet in tune) in 80s Goth band The March Violets to her current incarnation as Rosie Lugosi the Lesbian Vampire Poet. She is co-organiser of Club Lash, the Erotic Oscar–nominated fetish night, and hosts the Creatures of the Night Poetry Slam at the Green Room, Manchester. As well as publishing two solo collections of poetry, her short stories, poems and essays have been widely anthologised.

Edana Minghella was born in 1959 into an Anglo-Italian family who ran a cafe and ice cream business on the Isle of Wight. She lives in London, has a day job in mental health research, and is passionate about writing. She writes fiction, poetry and drama. She has written a short film (commissioned by the BBC) and is currently writing a stage play based on one of her short stories. With her brother, Dominic, she is developing a film script. She also reviews film and theatre productions. Other passions include walking, cycling, the sea, Veuve Cliquot, singing, her lovely family, her lovely friends, her lovely lover.

Jeanie O'Hare was script associate at the Royal Court Theatre until last year. She is currently a freelance script editor working with emerging playwrights. In 1999 she was awarded a Jerwood Arvon bursary for short fiction. This is her first published story.

Hannah Richards is 25, and has somehow recently managed to complete a degree in English, while also juggling motherhood and spending time with her rather fabulous long-term partner, Jo. She loves living in Brighton, and draws inspiration from the seaside lesbian scene, which is bristling with beautiful women! To avoid getting a 'proper' job, she intends to continue writing lesbian fiction, and hopes to turn her ideas into a novel within the next year.

Jenny Roberts began life as someone else and spent nearly fifty years badgering the Human Genome Complaints Department to try and obtain a refund... After the gender operation, the reborn Jenny

Roberts paused for breath, identified as a lesbian, had a few flings, wrote her first novel *Needle Point*, founded the Libertas! Women's Bookshop in York, and fell in love with her partner, Ann. Somewhere in between she became friends with several horses, and one in particular – Shannon – to whom her short story is dedicated. She now splits her time between selling books and writing, and is working on her second Cameron McGill mystery, *Breaking Point*, to be published by Diva Books in Spring 2001.

Helen Sandler grew up in Manchester but has lived all her adult life in north London. After five years checking sums in the civil service, she broke out to join the ill-fated lesbian and gay magazine Phase in 1994. Since its demise she has worked freelance, including a stint as editor of *Diva* magazine. Her articles, short stories and poems have appeared in various magazines and anthologies. *The Sunday Times* claimed that her erotic novel *Big Deal* (Sapphire, 1999) was among the most explicit works of sexual fiction ever published and should be banned from Smith's. She is now the commissioning editor of Diva Books.

Manda Scott grew up in Scotland in the days before lesbian was chic. She trained in veterinary medicine at Glasgow Vet School and now lives in Suffolk, in horse country, with two working lurchers and a handful of cats. Her writing career has grown slowly in tandem with veterinary medicine. Her first three novels, all crime thrillers, feature a largely lesbian cast. The first, *Hen's Teeth*, was shortlisted for the 1997 Orange Prize, the third, *Stronger than Death*, was granted a 1999 Arts Council Award. Her fourth, *No Good Deed*, moves in a new direction with new characters. In between, she makes brief forays into the world of short stories, journalism, radio plays and television drama.

Shelley Silas was a winner in the ICA's 1996 New Blood fiction competition with her short story 'Via Calcutta'. She has been commissioned to write for two sketch shows for BBC Radio 4, *So What If I Am?* and *The A-Z Show*. Her first stage play, *Calcutta Kosher*, had a rehearsed reading with Tara Arts in 1998, and will be broadcast on Radio 4 in August 2000. It will be published in an anthology of plays in October. *Shrapnel*, her second play, was produced at the Battersea Arts Centre in 1999 by the Steam Industry. In 1998 she graduated from the University of East Anglia with an MA in creative writing.

Ali Smith was born in Inverness and lives in Cambridge. She has published *Free Love and other stories* (Virago, 1995), *Like* (Virago, 1997), and *Other Stories and other stories* (Granta, 1999). She co-edited *Brilliant Careers: The Virago Book of Twentieth Century Fiction* (Virago, 2000). Her new novel, *Hotel World*, is out in early 2001 from Hamish Hamilton.

Helen Smith lives in Manchester with her poet partner and their growing family. She is the author of *Burying Cloud* and co-founder of the batty smiths lesbian writers' group. Her short stories have been published by Onlywomen Press and *Metropolitan* magazine. At the time of writing 'Whatever You Want', she had not listened to the personal development tapes which feature in the story. Now she has, and she can recommend them.

Cherry Smyth is an Irish writer, living in London. She is the author of *Queer Notions* (Scarlet Press, 1992) and *Damn Fine Art by New Lesbian Artists* (Cassell, 1996). She wrote the screenplay for the short film *Salvage* (1999). Her work is included in *The Anchor Book of New Irish Writing* (2000). Her poetry collection *When the Lights Go Up* is due in 2000.

Jo Somerset lives in Manchester, where she divides her time between working for a large metropolitan local authority, tending her allotment, and numerous community and voluntary activities. Her writing found a voice through Commonword, Manchester's community writing and publishing organisation. She lives with her partner and their five children.

Susanna Steele was born and brought up in Northern Ireland, beside the sea. She says: "I live and work in London, which I love, but I miss the sound of seagulls in the morning. I work as a teacher, storyteller and writer – what I do depends on which day of the week it is. I write short stories and poetry and I've just finished a commission for a play for 7-11-year-olds called *Firebird*."

Clare Summerskill has been performing on the gay cabaret circuit for over ten years and in 1998 she took her one-woman show *What Lesbians Do... On Stage* to the Edinburgh Festival and London's Oval House. In 2000 she is touring with *Fantasy Heckler*. Clare wrote and performed in *An Evening with Katie's Gang*, a cult lesbian musical comedy shortlisted for The Drill Hall's New Playwriting Award. She has also written three plays for the reminiscence theatre company, Age Exchange. She wrote for and appeared in the pilot lesbian and gay sketch show for Radio 4, *So What If I Am?*, recorded in January 2000, and is currently writing for the station's new sketch show *A to Z*.

Sue Vickerman wrote a few articles on sexuality/education for national daily papers before turning to fiction. Her stories have appeared in *Wild Cards* (Virago, 1999) and *The Unexpected Pond* (Route, 2000), and poems have been included in *The Blue Room Anthology* (Diamond Twig, 1999). She performs at festivals with a group of poets called Shameless Heaney. She travelled to four continents, eventually falling in love in China and moving with her girlfriend to Berlin. Nowadays they reside in the shadow of the Brontë sisters in Haworth, Yorkshire, where Sue is working on a novel.

Robyn Vinten came to England in the mid-80s and forgot to leave. She lives in a rapidly becoming fashionable part of north London with her cat rather than her lover, because the cat is tidier. She plays football, tennis and softball despite her advancing years. She has had a few other short stories published in various anthologies.

More new writing from DIVA Books

girl2girl: the lives and loves of young lesbian and bisexual women
Edited by Norrina Rashid and Jane Hoy

The only book written by and for young women questioning their sexuality.

Girls from across the UK write from the heart about being gay or bi, coming out or falling in love. This lively and moving book, packed with true stories, advice and illustrations, is a must for schools and youth groups – and for any girl who fancies other girls.

"If this book had been slipped before my eyes when I was fifteen, maybe I wouldn't have wasted my time stumbling around in four-inch stilettos and pleated crepe dresses in some vain attempt to convince myself of my heterosexuality. I could have suffered these painful fashion excesses for the love of a girl instead – someone worth breaking my ankle for! girl2girl is life-saving and inspiring – and a great read, with or without crepe."
Skin, Skunk Anansie

RRP £8.95 ISBN 1-873741-45-6

Mush *Kathleen Kiirik Bryson*

If you often glance at your own breasts, other people will look at them, too. If they're not looking already. Touch is important. Try to touch the other person as much as you decently and within excuse can, but much more importantly: touch yourself. Touch yourself, in front of them: all the places they can't but would like to touch. Your breasts as if by accident, your lips, face, arms purposefully. Stroke your legs. Stretch your body out on the chair in front of them, imitate the habits of a cat. Tell me stories, Nicky will whisper in your ear in moments like these. You curl and fit your bodies closer together and tell her incidents that you remember. Your lips move against her throat, nuzzling a pulse. Perhaps she can cipher, without hearing, the words you speak from the movement and shapings of your lips against her throat...

Mush follows the progress of a sexual and emotional relationship between three Alaskan women. When Nicky and Carol meet Ellen in Seattle, the three women share an initially warm attachment. But the triad disintegrates as linked memories of the Alaskan wilderness turn simultaneously erotic and horrific...

A haunting and lyrical first novel, *Mush* examines childhood ties and the dynamics of a *ménage à trois*, skilfully weaving dreams and myths into a very modern setting. As sexy as it is disturbing.

On sale November 2000
RRP £8.95 ISBN 1-873741-46-4

Emerald Budgies *Lee Maxwell*

"Great flocks of emerald budgies are flying through your brain..."

What I had to do was make amends, not write stupid lists. Phone Martin and apologise, stop buying drugs, get a new flat, get out of the Tracey situation without damaging her psyche too much (stop thinking it would damage her psyche), concentrate on work, sort out my future. Fall in love (either sex). How hard could it be? I had a line of coke.

Ruth's got plenty to distract her from the grim secret that's worming its way back into her brain – but before long, it will be too late to make amends.

"Great energy – so much chaos – and I laughed out loud a lot too. This is a strange way to describe it, but Emerald Budgies is really charming."
Emily Perkins

Lee Maxwell's first novel is a darkly comic tale of disintegration, betrayal and revenge.

RRP £8.95 ISBN 1-873741-44-8

The Comedienne *VG Lee*

"There was nothing and no one left for me in Birmingham."

"I couldn't believe it at first – that Susan could switch from padded Valentines, eighteen inches high with 'Be mine forever', to not even stopping her car for me to cross on a zebra. If she hadn't recognised me with the added weight, she must have known it was my shopping trolley."

It's time for Joan to try her luck on the London comedy circuit. After all, everybody always said she was a funny woman...

"The Comedienne has an intrinsic truth that pulls you in before you know it. Although owing a certain something to early Jeanette Winterson, VG Lee is the first lesbian writer to specialise in that peculiarly Northern deadpan style that observes the humorous side of casual cruelty inherent in human behaviour." *Time Out* **(London)**

"What makes the book is its deftness of touch: Joan is so lovingly understated, her observations giving Victoria Wood a run for her cardy on many occasions... An easy, feelgood, summery read, and a joy to behold." *What's On* **(Birmingham)**

"A touching evocation of loneliness and the complex relationship between an ageing mother and daughter. A light touch, a wonderful laconic style and spot-on humour made it a joy to read." Andrea Levy

RRP £8.95 ISBN 1-873741-43-X

Needle Point *Jenny Roberts*

"The bruising and the torn skin were worse than I had ever seen before – even the most hardened users protect their veins."

Cameron McGill is on a mission: to find out why her sister, who never touched drugs, was fished from a canal with needle-marks all down her arm. Tearing through Amsterdam on her Harley-Davidson, Cam encounters radical squatters, evasive drug agencies and a particularly alluring policewoman. But it's hard to know who to trust in a quest that could claim her life as gruesomely as it took her sister's.

"Deserves to be read by more than a niche market... an excellently paced, well-plotted thriller." *Guardian*

"A fast-moving tale of revenge and retribution." *Time Out* (London)

RRP £8.95 ISBN 1-873741-42-1

And coming in Spring 2001:

Breaking Point *Jenny Roberts*

Cameron's back, and this time she's on the trail of animal rights activists and genetic scientists.